THE TAKING

THE TAKING

J. D. LANDIS

BALLANTINE BOOKS • NEW YORK

A Ballantine Book
Published by The Random House Publishing Group

Copyright © 2003 by J. D. Landis

www.ballantinebooks.com

Book design by Christine Weathersbee

The Cataloging-in-Publication Data for this title is available from the Library of Congress

ISBN 0-345-45006-X

Manufactured in the United States of America

First Edition: October 2003

10   9   8   7   6   5   4   3   2   1

For Denise

("the desire of my Eyes")

and for my sister, Susannah

and in memory of Edward, my father,
and of Uncle Raymond,
the first and last of the Amherst boys

God himself shall be the
principal agent of thy misery.
—Reverend Samuel Treat

Of God we ask one favor,
That we may be forgiven—
For what, He is presumed to know—
The Crime, from us, is hidden.
—Emily Dickinson

There are yet some homesick people in the town
and many who have a longing for the place where
they were born, which is now deep underwater.
—Walter E. Clark
Quabbin Reservoir, 1946

AUTHOR'S NOTE

This novel is set primarily in Greenwich, Massachusetts, a town that has been discontinued and sits today at the bottom of the Quabbin Reservoir. Greenwich, and three other towns as well as numerous villages, were taken, to use the word most often employed to indicate the confiscation of these towns by eminent domain, as a result of the Ware River Act of 1926 and the Swift River Act of 1927. These ordinances provided for the flooding of the Swift River Valley to create a large reservoir whose impounded water would be piped sixty-seven miles east to Boston.

The Quabbin Reservoir is 18 miles long, has a water surface of 39 square miles, and holds 412 billion gallons of water, which according to *The Boston Globe* is more than twice the capacity of Lake Erie. Its name comes from the Nipmuc Indian word *Qaben*, which has been translated variously as "land of many waters," "well-watered place," and "meeting of the waters."

Construction of this reservoir began in 1928 and was completed in 1939, at which time the few remaining inhabitants were ordered to leave the valley as the flooding began. In all, some 650 homes were leveled, 2,500 residents displaced, and 7,600 corpses removed and reburied outside the project taking line.

I have taken some minor liberties with geography and time, compressing each so the story told might flow more swiftly.

PROLOGUE

It was the first spring day of this new century. The graveyard ground was barely supple. There was rain, as if this were a movie.

I would allow no backhoe; the digging was to be done by men. The two of them struggled with the earth. It resisted their shovels. It broke like glass. I found this appropriate. The surface of our world is but a window that does not so much reveal as obscure its depths. So too the skin on our bodies.

The skin of the young gravediggers glowed in the newborn light. Rain and sweat swam into their eyes, oiled their long hair. Even in the cold air that clung to yesterday's dead winter, they removed, at the same time, the layers of their clothing: gloves, scarves, jackets, shirts of agitated plaid beneath which each wore an undergarment we used to call a Wallace Beery, with a placket at the neck and four buttons they stopped together to unbutton, one every few minutes, as men used to stop for cigarettes before we turned against the solace of tobacco.

They made fitful progress. This was to my liking. I was content to stand there in the soft rain with my boy and wait forever for the body of my one great love, Ethan Vear, to be given back to me.

We were in the Quabbin Park Cemetery, a repository in the

middle of Massachusetts created to receive remains from other, earlier graves. Before the Swift River Valley with its towns and homes and perfectly adequate cemeteries was flooded sixty years ago, an order went out to disinter some several thousand corpses from some thirty-five cemeteries and to bury those whose families didn't want them buried elsewhere, *here*. As Nathaniel Hawthorne said of death in New England, it possesses a good deal of real estate—the graveyard in every town. And so there was a taking from the Evergreen Cemetery and the Isaac Linzie Cemetery and the Packardsville Church Cemetery and the Dana Center Cemetery and the Cemetery Hill Cemetery and the Snow Cemetery and the Golden Lake Cemetery and, in the town I came for a time to call my own, the Greenwich Cemetery and from all the other named and unnamed cemeteries except the Indian cemeteries and the Vear family cemetery, which were left to drown. In the end, 6,551 bodies were replanted here in the Quabbin Park Cemetery. Or what was left of or from those bodies—sometimes merely a button and sometimes nothing more than a discoloration in the thirsty earth.

As the two of us had walked through the rain from my rented car, we stopped before a large tomb in which was buried, we read, one John Atkinson, who died in 1854, aged 89. He had lived, I was forced to admit to my boy, ten years longer than I. "So far," he said. Upon this John Atkinson's tomb was carved: I HEARD A VOICE SAYING DEPART AND JOIN YOUR FRIENDS IN A WORLD UNKNOWN TO LIVING MEN. I felt, as I often did when reading something ridiculous upon a headstone, like arguing with the person trapped within: *This* world is unknown to living men.

My gravediggers were, as is customary among those gathered in a cemetery, the most alive. They had first uprooted the headstone, which lay with its simple message directed, appropriately, at the heavens.

ETHAN VEAR

DIED SEPTEMBER 22, 1938

IN HIS 26TH YR.

"LOVE IS LIKE LIFE—MERELY LONGER"

ED/SRV

After penetrating the frost, they found the deeper soil more pliable. Or perhaps it never froze over Ethan's coffin. Steam rose from the skin of their handsome faces. The younger of them wore an earring. As they shoveled, they sank slowly into the grave. Mist rose from their hair, from their hands that were now beneath the coarse lip of dirt in which they were burying themselves. I watched so intently that I couldn't feel the passage of time. A rare privilege at the age I had attained.

Finally, I became aware the gravediggers had disappeared altogether. Only the blades of their shovels, cartoonlike, appeared, dancing in the air, dripping dirt.

Then he spoke to me. "Come here," he said.

I couldn't tell Ethan's voice from the boys', whichever one of them had called me. These were the same words Ethan had used to call me to his table for the first time. They were also the first words either of these boys had spoken to me. I knew myself well enough by now to know that I had deliberately confused these boys with Ethan. Or if not confused, replaced. I had watched them digging toward him, and the more they dug, the more I forced them to become him. So now, as I followed the order of that voice as I'd always, in my way, followed Ethan's, I looked deep down into the grave and saw my two young men standing like ghosts of Ethan upon his very coffin.

"You sure you want it up?" one asked.

I reached into my pocketbook and for a moment displayed the necessary papers. I knew I was not answering his question.

"Get the ropes." I thought he was talking to me until his partner reached up and took the edge of the earth in his fingers and hoisted himself in one swift movement that seemed a deliberate reminder of Ethan coming to me from a lower branch to my branch of some old maple. He even smiled at me, this gravedigger, self-consciously, not at his presence but at the ease with which he rose from below to be beside me.

"Pardon me," he said politely as he moved away toward their old red truck. Its bed was uncapped and receiving the rain and would in turn receive the casket and the rain would cleanse it. The two ropes he carried from the truck to the grave, each looped over a shoulder, dripped rainwater onto the toes of his dirty work boots.

He threw the ropes into the grave. Each boy jumped in after them. They straddled that wooden box at either end and lifted it and pushed beneath it an unfurled length of rope. Then, together, they threw the ends of each rope up out of the grave. When they emerged, they surrounded us with what I took to be their compassion until together they looked off over our heads and searched the distant trees. When they found what they'd been looking for they waved, or rather beckoned. And there, from behind a grand old oak that I was surprised didn't topple to the earth from his proximity, came a tall old man, erect, slow of foot but purposeful, dressed in black but for his white clerical collar. It required both his hands to grasp the huge black umbrella he held steadily above himself like someone pushing back the heavens.

What does one say to a ghost?

"I thought you were dead."

He was old enough to have lost, at least, some hearing. He quickened his step to come closer. His polished black shoes sucked at the wet, melting earth.

"I beg your pardon," he said.

"I thought you were dead."

"I am, Sarianna!" He laughed. "And you—I see you haven't gotten any taller." He laughed again. And more than anything else—his height, his gait, his clothes, his voice—it was that rare and unexpected sound of his laughter that brought Jeremy Treat back to me over the sixty years since last I'd seen him. With my strict New England unbringing and my ascetic, scholarly bent, I had found it strange that a minister, a man of the cloth and of God, an austere, moral, compassionate, suffering man, would ever laugh. I was as much surprised at the age of seventy-nine as I had been when he had used that laugh against me and my naïveté at seventeen.

"Don't worry—" I said to my boy. He didn't look worried at all. But his visible curiosity at having seen this grand, stark figure emerge from the veil and shadow of the trees was heightened by the man's preposterous and under the circumstances vainglorious claim to be dead. "—he's not dead. He's merely old enough to be dead."

"A hundred," said old Reverend Treat. To provide substantiation of his hardiness, he chose that moment to retract his umbrella. He was not wearing the black hat I only then recalled he'd been wearing the first time I saw him. The rain found him as it would not a ghost. It entered the close-cropped whiteness of his hair and rendered it radiant.

"A hundred years old," he elucidated, as if we were idiots. "And yet I've lived in three centuries. How are your mathematics, my boy? And exactly who *are* you?"

"This is my—" I began.

"My name is James Vear."

"My grandson," I said, and took back the hand he was either politely or roguishly holding out to Jeremy Treat.

"You were born in eighteen ninety-nine," my boy said to him.

"I hate to disillusion you," Jeremy Treat said to James, in the fetching way I remembered he had of speaking unpatronizingly to the young, "but you're *my* grandson as well. And you have the same name—"

"That's *enough!*" I said to him.

He shook his head indulgently and put his lips near my ear. As old as I was, I thought he'd smell older. But he smelled of the rain and of the oak tree's new buds and as clean as he had when he wore the shirts his wife and I washed for him and hung out in the summer sun.

"I had you once," he whispered, not so softly that I'd be the only one to hear.

"Nearly a century ago," I said to anyone who wanted to listen.

"By once I didn't mean how long ago, Sarianna, but how frequently—once. Once was enough."

"Once was all anyone had me, Jeremy," I confessed, no matter the comfort he would take in my innocence. "But tell me—did you mean once was enough for pleasure, or for procreation?"

"For pleasure," he lied.

"Bring up the casket!" I ordered the two young men.

They lost my affection immediately by looking to Jeremy Treat for what could only be permission.

He missed little. "My sons," he explained.

I found their ages in relation to him harder to accept than his in relation to time itself.

"Sons of my old age." He put a hand on the shoulder of each, his age-warped fingers bending familiarly around those knobs of bone and muscle in a young man's shoulder. "Their mother when I married her was no older than you when we met."

"Where is she now?"

"She left me," he said. "For someone younger." He found this unaccountably amusing.

"And Una?" I asked, saying her name aloud for the first time in years and grieving at the sound as I hoped he would as well.

"She's dead, I would imagine." His voice was as cold as he wished her to be. But I knew she was alive, or had been at the New Year, when she'd as much as summoned me here.

I remembered his wife, the one I'd known, and loved, too pretty to belong to a minister, I had thought, even one so handsome. I'd been unable to imagine that members of his Greenwich Congregational Church could keep themselves from envisioning the two of them entwined, as even I couldn't after seeing them together.

"Did you kill her?" I asked.

"I didn't need to."

"Then you drove her to her death?"

"There's a journey for which none of us needs a chauffeur." He took a moment to enjoy his little platitude. "Una was not, as you may recall, arrested, though of course it was she who killed him and, despite what I confessed to you, not I." He looked to see if I remembered; I did and couldn't help but show it. This gave him reason to continue. "Una was nevertheless confined to the asylum in Northampton—not long after you disappeared. She did the same from there as you did from the valley—disappeared. Who knows?—perhaps if you'd stayed you might have driven her sane. I had no choice but to have her declared dead after the requisite interval. Who knows this either?—maybe she's still alive . . . if you can imagine a woman who could possibly look older than you." He delivered this insult with the same self-satisfied charm that others would a compliment. Then his eyes went dark. "But enough about the absent dead. Shall we have a look at your *husband*?"

He spit this last word at me. It was the first sign of his jealousy. I found it immensely gratifying. But he was not so much addressing a question to me as ordering his sons to retrieve the casket.

Each of them took two ends of a rope in his hands. Together they leaned back against the foggy air and step by step moved away from the dark hole in the ground. It seemed but a moment or two until the casket reappeared in the world, balanced on the ropes but a few inches beneath the mud and curious gray light. They held it there now with just their feet upon the ropes. Such strong boys—I would have speculated aloud that perhaps he drank their blood to keep himself alive and strong, were I not convinced he would only be flattered by such contumely.

"Why are you doing this?" he asked.

"I want him buried near me."

"And where might that be?"

"By the ocean."

"Winter Island?" Was it possible he remembered I had mentioned, sixty years ago and more, that my parents had sent me as a child each summer to Salem Neck?

"The *other* ocean," I took pleasure in telling him.

"So you have abandoned New England for . . ."

"Cleone. The coast above Mendocino."

"Ah, yes. It is said to be most New England–like itself."

"I can look out at the ocean and imagine drowned cities."

"I don't think that's what is meant." He laughed again. "What's your rush to have him? You're only . . . what?—seventy-nine?"

"Have you memorized me, Jeremy?" I asked him as I had those many years before.

He took the question seriously and gave no indication of either contentment or consternation that I might have memorized *him*. "That implies a task. Let's just say that I remember you."

"I'm dying, Jeremy. There's my rush."

Whatever was left of the preacher in him caused him to look skyward. More even for God's ministers than for God's subjects, death is His unpardonable sin.

"Put the casket in your truck," I ordered his sons. "I'll follow you to Bradley." I had made arrangements to fly Ethan back with me from that old New England airport.

"But don't you want to see him? Don't you want to see what that bareheaded life under the grass has done to your husband?" Now like a schoolboy in love Jeremy was quoting my favorite poet as he had years ago first quoted her to me on the depleted marquee of his derelict church. Nonetheless, since these were not really questions, he felt no need to wait for my response. He said to his boys, "Open it!"

He thought to shock me. He thought to have me scream over this outrage. But he knew nothing of such loss. He wasn't a penitent like me. He didn't picture his late wife as I did Ethan, either in the beauty he wore in life or as bones in the earth. He hadn't remained true to her as I had to the one he called my husband. I had no fear of what time had done to Ethan. I had more fear of what it had done to me.

Still, I shielded James's eyes as the sons of Jeremy Treat opened Ethan's coffin.

And it was Jeremy Treat himself who screamed when he saw what was revealed.

BOOK ONE

THE REALM OF YOU

I came to the Swift River Valley as most everyone else was leaving. In this I was not at all like that favorite poet of mine, Emily Dickinson, who had written, "I do not cross my father's ground to any house or town." Indeed, though I was but seventeen years old in 1938, and liked nothing better than to be alone with a book of poems within the chaste clasp of my childhood bedroom, I had crossed my father's ground as often as necessary.

We lived on Dickinson Street in Springfield, Massachusetts. I discovered Emily while attending Forest Park Junior High School, where I was a most serious student and preferred to commune with the gifted dead than with my mundane and predictable contemporaries. I convinced myself, against such evidence as only mere truth could provide, that the street on which we lived had been named for Emily Dickinson. (And that I might gain entry to the house in downtown Springfield, on the corner of Water and Bliss, in which on two occasions she had as a young woman visited and slept—the present owners repeatedly closed the door against my entreaties.) This pretense alone made me happy to live on that wide, heavily trafficked, unattractive thoroughfare, pinioned mostly by two-family, double-decker homes, though ours was ours alone, detached and grimly middle-class and sniffish. I disregarded the fact that mine was a happiness obtained under the kind of self-delusion that all my life I have prided myself I have never practiced.

For example, I am willing to admit that I don't know whether I was attracted first to Emily's life or her poetry. I discovered some few but pertinent facts about the former from the essay Thomas Higginson had published in the *Atlantic Monthly* in 1891, five years after her death.

She and Higginson had exchanged correspondence for eight years before they finally met, on August 16, 1870. She told him about her domination by her father. Higginson characterized Edward Dickinson as "a man of the old type, *la vielle roche* of Puritanism." He was in fact an orthodox Calvinist. So frightened was she of his judgment that she didn't learn to tell time until she was nearly as old as I when I went off to college. When she was little, he had tried to teach her to tell time. She couldn't comprehend his explanation. She was afraid to tell him so and afraid to tell anyone else in case word got back to him. So she lived without knowledge of time. Outside of time. Or so deeply within it that she was blind to it the way those in love cannot see how love, like time, may waste us.

In my freshman literature class at Mount Holyoke, in which I was the youngest student, I offered up the preposterous theory that Emily's inability to tell time was a source of the fractured rhythms of her verse. That I was taken seriously was only one of the reasons I left college to live in the doomed Swift River Valley.

My father was also named Edward. He too read "lonely and rigorous books" and he too was a lawyer. He traced his ancestry back nearly three hundred years to a Chase who had landed a Pilgrim upon a shifting, granulated Massachusetts dune. That was on his father's side. Somewhere down that pedigreed line a Chase woman allowed herself to be not only ravished by but married to a French Canadian, who sought the greater heat of both a southern clime and a Protestant woman's blond and milky loin. Thus was my father born Renouer. Alas, he listened to the names people called him as well as to pronunciation of his actual name and had it legally changed to Renway. Thus did he name me Sarianna Chase Renway. But like Emily Dickinson, who sometimes spelled herself *Emilie*, as in "your bad, sad Emilie," I sometimes grasped the dying breath of *h* and called myself *Sariannah*.

(My mother was a Darling. In name only. So dominated was she by my father that I have almost no memory of her. Like many people lost to time, she loved antiques—I do remember that. She collected things wholly out of keeping with a newish house on Dickinson Street: bung starters and Silenius jugs supported by lascivious little cambered figures and salamander irons she would keep in the kitchen for decoration but never use to stimulate the browning of her pallid meats or her runny pies.)

My father was a man who imposed upon those around him both his pleasures and his disinclinations. You must love what he loved and hate what he hated. When I was six, he allowed me my first taste of soda pop to celebrate the execution of Nicola Sacco and Bartolomeo Vanzetti and later that year added a splash of rye whiskey to my pop on the night Ruth Snyder was electrocuted for the murder of her husband. When I was eleven, and unknown to my parents had begun to bleed, he attempted one last time to take his belt to my bottom (through my clothing—he had never shown interest in my nakedness) in the impotence of his rage over the discovery of the body of little Charles Lindbergh Jr.

That was the first time I crossed my father's ground. I lit out into the night and walked down Sumner Avenue to where it met Long Hill Street, at that very spot where local legend placed the village of the Agawam Indians, who attacked Springfield during King Philip's War 250 years earlier and over by Pecousic Brook in Forest Park killed their children hostages, a sacrifice to desperation and revenge our teachers loved to taunt us with but which thrilled us instead. I snuck behind the mansions there upon the palisades and slid on my backside to the bank of the Connecticut River. I found the usual hoboes curled up there under their Hoover blankets and on that chilly May night folded my arms over my girlish bosom and warmed myself at their fire until I realized that my bosom was of subordinate appeal and warmed myself even more by running back up the hill.

When I was fourteen, and was singing the words to "Blue Moon" while washing the dishes, my father walked over to the sink and lifted the drying tray above his head and released it to the mercy of the floor.

Having been forced by my father to skip a grade, either because he enjoyed the thought I was intelligent beyond my years or because he wanted me out of his life that much sooner, I started at Classical High School that same year. It was then I discovered another "sweet invisible," Elizabeth Barrett Browning, as well as the power I had over boys that grew, I discovered, in direct proportion to my denying them what they wanted. It didn't matter what I wanted, which was never one of them. So long as I withheld myself—smile, flattery, touch, or even hope of same—I was coveted. Like my father, I imposed myself upon the world to keep it from doing so to me.

As for desire, I felt none bodily. I felt none for anything but words and what I hadn't learned yet to call prosody and for flowers. Without an object, desire is not only aimless but incongruous. I felt myself privileged to have been freed of it before I was even lashed by it.

I went to Mount Holyoke College and not any of the other schools that solicited my attendance because Emily Dickinson had gone there. It had then, in 1847, been named Mount Holyoke Female Seminary but called simply South Hadley, after the small town in which it resided.

I lasted two semesters. So had Emily ninety years before me. "I am not happy," she wrote from college.

I was perfectly happy there, which was a better reason to leave than its opposite. Contentment is inappropriate for a seventeen-year-old woman.

Emily left not because she was unhappy studying Silliman's Chemistry and Cutler's Physiology, Smellie's Natural History and Mrs. Phelps's Botany. Poetry is grounded in the pith of things, hers especially. ("Bring me the sunset in a cup.") She left because it was the time of the Second Great Awakening. The girls were rounded up into conversion assemblies, where those who were "destitute of the Christian hope" were expected to de-clare for Christ.

So far as Emily was concerned, such a declaration could land her only in the "ark of safety." She preferred to "buffet the sea," as she put it. And added in that letter to the kind of friend I never had until I found her in the same condemned and fugitive valley where I also found my Ethan: "I love the danger."

In that we were alike, as I was to discover.

I did not go home to Springfield my entire freshman year. On holidays and some weekends, I hitchhiked out of South Hadley and took a room in a hotel or boardinghouse in close-by Amherst. It was more than Emily might have done—in her day the students were kept prisoner on weekends so they might, without distraction of family or friends or freedom, make Christ their portion. So I went to Amherst as her proxy and her stu-dent. There I traced her routes not so much upon the roads she'd rarely graced but in the woods that she was much in as a little girl and where she'd been told a snake would bite her and on the cemetery paths she walked and in the air both outside and inside the Homestead right on Main Street where she'd lived in her corner bedroom and thought and wrote and locked herself away with an imaginary key, saying to her niece, Martha, "Mattie, here's freedom," as I pretended I might do within the safe room of my own mind.

My parents had deposited me and my one book and few articles of girlish clothing on my first day at Mount Holyoke. After that, they never even threatened to visit. When my father wrote to ask if they should pick me up for the summer, I wrote back to say they should not. I didn't want to spend the summer in Springfield, I said. I planned to look, elsewhere, for work.

One midday I saw a typed solicitation tacked onto the bulletin board outside the dining hall:

FEMALE TUTOR SOUGHT FOR MINISTER'S SON

IN GREENWICH VILLAGE

ROOM AND BOARD PROVIDED

I tore the sheet from the board so no one else might see it. I thought at first it was the Greenwich Village in New York City and imagined myself running there as Edna St. Vincent Millay had from Camden, Maine. But then I noticed the post-office address and learned soon enough that Greenwich Village was smack in the middle of the Swift River Valley, which itself was smack in the middle of Massachusetts. As such it was scheduled within a year or two to be underwater. There were occasional articles in the *Springfield Union* about the impending death of the valley. But I'd paid little attention until now. It was even better than

New York City, which, one could imagine, would be there for-ever. This Greenwich Village was doomed.

My ride let me off where West Ware Road met State High-way 21. At that very corner was a sign that I took to be a good omen but my driver didn't: TRAVEL AT YOUR OWN RISK. Other-wise, I suspect, he might have taken me right to the parsonage door. I never had to wait long to hitch a ride. I never had to hold out one of those surefire old signs: IF YOU DON'T GIVE ME A RIDE, I'LL VOTE FOR HOOVER.

Before setting off north upon the state road, I transferred my small valise into my arms and climbed the nearby Great Quab-bin Hill. From its summit, as I first looked down upon the Swift River Valley, I saw it, I thought, "New Englandly," with Emily's own eyes: the forehead of a hill, the pattern of a chimney, a vane's forefinger, the steeple's very finger. But the nearest steeple was not, I was to learn, that of Reverend Jeremy Treat's church in Greenwich Village. It belonged to the town almost at my feet, Enfield. Prescott was to the west, Dana to the east, and, at the center of my gaze, appropriately enough, was Greenwich itself.

But I knew none of this then. I knew only that what I saw were four towns and pieces of other villages upon the floor of a valley as distinguished by its absences as by what remained. Its geometry was wanton. Farmhouses were missing from farms. What had been stands of trees were reduced to nubs, dark coins in the summer grass. Where fires burned to purge the land, they blackened it and sent up sobs of flame-chased smoke. Yet this entire world was girded by densely wooded hills perhaps half a thousand feet tall. They must have been thought of as protectors—from wind and wolves and human beasts. But they had turned into warders. They locked the valley before me into its destiny. What they and I now looked down upon would soon be drowned.

Only when I turned around and looked behind me, toward the south from where I'd come, did I see human beings. There seemed to be hundreds, if not thousands, tiny men dwarfed by the structures on which they were laboring. To the east and to the west, separated by several miles, lay two massive earthen walls. They rose from the surface of this world, thick curtains against the light and the air. They were like God's hands, I thought, held up at the bottom of the valley, as if at the gates of heaven, saying *No farther*. One day soon they would hold back the water. Everything and everyone before them would vanish.

The comfort I took in this extinction was not strange. If life is made more precious by its finitude, what of this little world before me whose end was predetermined and whose time was drawing near? It was the perfect place for a girl like me, as restless as water and as eager to flow into the ruts and narrows of existence.

So it was with gaiety in my heart that I crossed into Greenwich Village over a small mill-pond bridge (the mill itself had been demolished) and knocked on the door of a narrow white New Englander. I assumed it to be the parsonage because it was next to a small church which, though ramshackle, appeared more to hang from the low bright sky than to rise from the degraded earth.

A beautiful young woman answered. I had never seen such beauty as hers. Not in Greta Garbo's *Anna Karenina* or *Camille* or upon Falconetti in *The Passion of Joan of Arc*. And not upon the girls at college, even those who made claim, without their knowing it, to perfection: desire tight contained within their loose white frocks and faces framed by untended curls.

This woman stood in the doorway made up half of the sun behind me and half of the house's shadows behind her. She was vivid with welcome and pleasure. Above benevolent transparent eyes her fine hair was knotted loosely atop her head so that multi-shaded strands of it had escaped, several of them into the corner of her mouth. When she spoke—"You must be Sarianna"—that hair became darkened and moistened, and I thought it a most profligate gesture.

I was as taken aback by her precognition as by her beauty. "How could you know that?"

"Aside from the fact that we're expecting you—more than expecting, I should say . . . anticipating your arrival with great keenness—aside from that, who else would be knocking on our door these days? Or who like you?"

"Like me?" I wondered.

"They've all deserted us," she replied with what seemed an instant despair at the thought of having been forsaken.

"Who's deserted you?"

"The living." Now she smiled again. "The dead too."

"And which am I?" I tried to enter the bemazed spirit of her conversation.

"We know who *you* are. But you have no idea who *I* am. I might as easily be maid as mistress." She opened her arms. "Una Treat—maid *and* mistress."

I might as easily have gone into her arms as into her home. The moment I had crossed her threshold, she took the valise from my hand. Her palm was cool against my wrist, her fingers enviably long.

She took me immediately upstairs, for the main stairway lay

directly before the front hall in which we had been standing. I followed her three steps back to allow for the swing of my valise in her hand. She loomed above me, tall and slender. With every step she took I could see how eager her long skirt was to return its touch to the long smooth stretch of her leg.

The stairs bisected the house diagonally. At their top we were, then, obliged to turn around and walk down a brief hallway that passed the stairwell and then darkened into a narrower hallway on either side of which were doors.

"This," she said, touching a door on the right, "is where Jimmy sleeps. How lucky to have a house in which a child can have his own room. But listen to *me*—in the house I grew up in I got to carve my name in the wall of *my* room!" She touched another door, on the opposite side of the hallway. "And here is the bathroom. This is where you'll bathe. I'm sure you'd like to see it or even use it to wash off your travel, but I haven't cleaned it yet, or put your bath towels in. And here," she said, when we had run out of hallway and there was but one door left at the end, facing us, "is where the good reverend and I sleep."

This door she did not merely touch but opened. "Don't worry—the bed is made," was all she said by way of indicating what I should do. I entered. It was a graceful old bed, canopied for about half its length, without posts. Upon its sleeping surface was a worn, supple quilt. Blue calico snowflakes in the center panels and what looked like oak leaves and weeping willows along the borders lay upon a white background. "Isn't it beautiful," she said. "It's called a Willow Oak. I wish I could appliqué like that. The bed has a name too. Don't you love things with names? They seem to take on meaning. Imagine our children without names. Imagine our children with different names. The bed is called an angel bed. I suspect for the canopy and not for any sense of divinity. A marriage bed has little space for things celestial."

Their bedroom did not smell of sleep, as did those of some Mount Holyoke girls on Saturday mornings. Nor of mortal decay, as my parents' did. Rather of morning, though it was not morning now, when the air is innocent and the light is night's disguise.

I noticed upon the wall above that bed a sampler in which was stitched crudely a fond sentiment:

> "So I kisse my sweet wife
> and rest thy faithfull husband"

She caught me staring at those words. I took them in as evidence that marriage is not necessarily built upon the model of the one that produces its particular victim.

"My husband made that for me. Isn't it sweet? His fingers are too big so it's such a mess. But his heart is just the right size."

"Who's it from?" I asked.

"From him—Jeremy," she answered with a kind of puzzled enchantment that I might be just the proper numskull to whom to trust the tutoring of her child.

"I meant the quotation," I said like the little scholar I presumed to be. "See the marks around it."

"Oh." She leaned out over the bed and put a finger to each of the quotation marks. I wondered if she were a woman who made her way through the world by feeling it—I recalled how she had opened her arms to me in the downstairs hallway. I, in contrast, had made my way by thought. This was appropriate, I supposed, for a schoolgirl, but I was prepared to be shown another way and to experience what Emily called "Extasy," which for her was a matter of both life and death. "You know"—now Mrs. Treat rubbed those marks as if to erase them—"I never noticed these before. I guess I wanted Jeremy to have made it up."

"Maybe he did," I said, though I suspected from more than the antiquated spelling that these beguiling words had been another's before Jeremy Treat bestowed them upon his wife.

"Don't be silly," she said gaily, further confusing me concerning what she might believe or indeed whether it mattered if her husband were a thief of sentiment or the most courtly of lovers. "And here is *your* room," she went on with a kind of disconnection I was quickly coming to find more charming than disconcerting.

As we were still in her and her husband's room, I had a brief and perplexing yet not wholly unpleasant belief that I was meant to share their room with them. But immediately she opened a door in a corner of the room and beckoned for me to follow her.

"I so hope you like it."

There was a tiny bed in a tiny room open to the outside only through a curtained window in the wall at the head of the bed. At that moment this window delivered the rays of the declining sun into a patch on the floor upon which Mrs. Treat and I stood together. She held my hand and pressed it gently as we turned around to take in this engaging little world in which she planned to lodge me. There was a dresser for my underclothes and socks and those of my blouses that did not need ironing. A bookcase that held not even the usual single dark book but only a candle in its stand. Two lamps, one near the head of the bed for reading. A black flashlight on a nail in the wall because, she said, the electricity liked to hide from thunder. A hat stand with a wooden hanger on each of its hooks.

I pointed to a door. "Is that the closet?"

"There *is* no closet," she replied with encouragement. "Of course you may use the front-hall closet for any and all of your outer garments. But as for things like dresses . . ." She pointed at the hat stand.

It made no difference to me. "So where does that door lead? To yet another hidden room for yet another unsuspecting visitor?"

"The toilet!" she exclaimed. "Surely you didn't think you would have to make your way through our bedroom for *that*. I'm an *Orchids on Your Budget* kind of girl, as if you couldn't tell. Look!" She threw open the door. There sat a sink and toilet close enough to halve the little oval mirror on the wall. "Utter privacy," she added. "You're the only one in this household who need not share!"

Back in my bedroom, she moved aside a small rug on the floor and pointed to a register. "Heat will rise through there from the stove below. Otherwise, I fear, you'll have to huddle beneath this."

She unfolded a quilt from the foot of the bed and spread it out. "This one's called a Graveyard. You see it's bordered by a picket fence, just like a small cemetery, and here in the middle is the tiny coffin of the child and next to it is his mother's coffin— see how it's almost in the shape of a tear, like a mummy, or like a person lying down even, because people look like tears, don't they?—and here on the edge is the empty coffin of the husband, who's still alive. But of course he's still alive—he's the one who made the quilt! Not many men made quilts. He must have missed them terribly. And look! It's perfect for a bed—these headstones are called bedbacks, and these footstones are called . . . well, foot-stones! But see how when you put them together they look just like a bed. Perfect for sleeping. For*ever*!" She laughed for a moment but then became serious and put a hand on my arm. "I hope it doesn't give you the willies."

It was a dark piece, as rich and deep as chocolate. I was used to seeing in quilts such abstracted shapes as stars and diamonds, blue or pink or green, always against a white background. This quilt's background comprised within circles a doubled cross thus ⚛. It looked curiously like the symbol that I knew from my freshman botany text denoted a poisonous plant. But I had never seen anything in a quilt like the true shape and texture of the coffins. They seemed real objects planted in an imaginary garden.

"I'm sure I'll sleep like the dead beneath it," I quipped, thankfully to no effect. "But how cold might it get here anyway in the summer?"

"But we're hoping you'll stay on to the end, Sarianna." She said this with so sincere a longingness that I nearly said I would. And when I didn't, she said, "Come and meet Jimmy! Perhaps he'll convince you to if I can't."

"I have to use the toilet first." I opened the door to my little bathroom.

"How refreshing you didn't say you needed to powder your very pretty little nose."

I could hear her laughter, and her footsteps, as I closed the door between us.

When I emerged, she was nowhere to be seen. She had left me to find my way to her son. I was heartened by such immediate independence. The house was mine, she seemed to be saying, as much as it was hers.

I might have become momentarily lost were I not guided by a child's voice, singing. It was as high as a girl's voice. But there was a sweetness in it I'd never heard from a girl. Or perhaps it was a ripeness. It was a voice that sounded as an angel's would, were there angels, pristine and yet a little bit abandoned. I heard a piano, too, beneath the voice but resting on it, not the other way around.

Had I been more like Emily, I might have remained unseen in my room. She would listen to the piano played by those friends who'd come to visit her in the Homestead, hoping to lure her down the stairs, so they might see what pleasure they'd delivered with their music. She gave them no sign, and what music in its hymnal rhythms she made in her poetry she kept to herself. She was both solitary and solitude itself.

As for me, I preferred to be withdrawn and vulnerable at once. A girl may be most hidden who is most naked. Most impure who is most chaste. Emily was interesting not because she hid herself away—though that's what girls my age admired most in her, the romance of the outcast—but because she strode into the world on sonorous iambic feet.

I made my way down to a tiny first-floor parlor. Mrs. Treat was sitting at a small piano, playing from memory. Her head was turned toward her son and the open door behind him. As soon as she saw me, she beckoned with delighted eyes. I entered but stood by the door until the song was finished:

> . . . so happy you have come
> to help me spell and give the sum
> of numbers—what a mystery!
> until you teach—and history!—
> oh I can't wait
> until you've given me the date
> and told me how the world will end

and I shall call you, teacher, friend!

And I shall call you, teacher, friend!

"Is that for me?" I said. "No one's ever written a song for me before. Or sung one even."

"What about 'Happy Birthday'?" he asked.

"Not even that." My mother had occasionally attempted it before being shushed by my father. He did not disapprove of birthday celebrations; merely of what he called "that stupid song."

"How about I sing for you on your next birthday." It was less a question than a plan. "When is it?"

"When's yours?" I asked back; I didn't care for reminders of my birth, not because I didn't love life but because I loved it more than I loved those who had forced it upon me.

"October twenty-eighth," he answered with a polite impatience. "Now you."

"On the first day of summer," I conceded.

"Heck," he said.

"I know. We just missed it."

"Next year," he asserted.

"But your voice may change by then."

"To what?" he said, and could not keep from laughing even before I did.

I had anticipated a younger boy, who would need tending as much as teaching. But Jimmy, while not yet a young man and with the look of a boy still, was no longer a child. His hair was wild, folded over itself in some patches and sticking straight out in others, full of different colors, of leaves and honey and sunlight and that broom that Wordsworth said ran along the copses in veins of gold. His eyes were narrow and so purple as to be nearly black, beneath those girlish eyebrows young boys have, delicate, quizzical lunes that seem more pigment than hair. He was smooth-skinned and self-contained. But around him was an insinuation of shape, and of strength within that shape. An asylum in time that he would occupy. I could feel him grasping at the space in that room.

I looked at Mrs. Treat. How could he be hers? She was too young to be so on the verge of having a man as a son.

"I love how you're looking at me." She rose from the piano bench and came closer to me. "Most people can't believe he's mine but look at me as if they've been lied to. You look at me as if it's not I but nature that's played a trick. He's eleven years old. I was fifteen."

"Pretty soon he'll look like your brother."

"In the meantime, I have you to look like my sister."

"Do you have a sister?"

"No."

I was happy to hear that.

"You?" she asked me back.

"No one."

"Another only child, Jimmy." She put her arm around me and turned us to face him. "I know you've already had a meaningful conversation, but come and say hello."

He came forward and shook my hand. "How do you do, Miss Renway?"

"You must call me Sarianna." I sounded to myself like a teacher. "I don't mean you *must*. I mean, I would like it if you would call me Sarianna."

"It's always nice to have a choice." He took so quickly to my meaning that I was startled. I wondered if the children growing up in a time of Depression and under the vague suggestion of war were more likely to think about the freedom of their wills than children like me had been, growing up in a time of frivolous if wanton innocence. "Sarianna," he added, to show me he had made a choice.

"What would you like me to call you?"

"Often," he answered, and managed to say, "Call me often," before he laughed once more at his little joke.

"Jimmy," his mother scolded him, with as much amusement as reproof.

"So, are you going to take the job, Sarianna?" asked Jimmy.

"Do I have a choice?" I wanted to be chosen, not merely approved.

"No," he said.

"Then I bow to your will," I said, actually bowing. He and his mother imprisoned me in their arms.

Mrs. Treat asked me to fetch Reverend Treat from the church next door. She had to fix dinner, she said, or she would accompany me.

"Can you guess what we're having?"

She asked me this as we stood in her kitchen. It was the largest room in the small house, yet still compact. Hanging from hooks in the ceiling around a vast old stove were pots, seasoned black by fire and food. Pans hung from smaller hooks cemented into the brick of the kitchen chimney. There was an icebox, which I assumed they used in the winter, as well as an electric refrigerator that sat tiltingly upon the broad, disfigured planks of the floor. Knives were arranged by size in what looked like a handmade rack that leaned against a wall from one of the several wooden counters. These carried scars from knives and round black burn marks through which wood grain formed milky veins.

It was not like the kitchens on Dickinson Street in Springfield. There, linoleum had been discovered and was buckling the floors and countertops and spoiling the food with its odor and texture and unnatural colors. To say nothing of how its shine contrasted ludicrously with the muted brunette hickory of the aged and rickety Carver chairs for which my mother had paid a fortune and whose extreme uncomfortableness she excused by whispering whenever my father frowned upon sitting in one of them, "They are named for Governor John Carver of Massachusetts," as if my father might have been impressed by a politician who'd been dead for three hundred years and thus was of no more political use than his namesake chairs with their knob-ended armrests were an aid to digestion.

The Treats' kitchen seemed part of the earth itself, smoky and smelly and nourishing and comfortable. We were in the kitchen because, according to Mrs. Treat, the church was most easily reached through its back door. But I wondered if we were there also because she wanted me to understand this about her: she labored toward sustenance in a place that was to disappear.

I thought her question to me was perhaps her polite way of asking if there might be some food to which I was either particularly partial or averse. There was not. Besides, I had no idea what people here might eat for dinner. From what I had seen on my walk, there were no grocery stores, and the farms had been abandoned.

So I answered, "No."

"Neither can I!" she seemed most impatient to say, or to have said. It was a joke, much like the one her son had created not so much at my expense but with my naive collusion. Merry laughter burst from her, accompanied by the touch of her hand on my sleeve. "But go find my husband. By the time you return with him, I'll have something ready for the table."

I looked up at the kitchen clock. How early could they possibly eat in the country?

"Oh, don't worry," Mrs. Treat said. "You'll be a long time in the church with him. I forgot to ask—are you religious?"

"Oh, very."

"Liar!" She threw a dishcloth at me to chase me out the door.

The late-afternoon light in June remains bright but is softened by the moisture in the air and the insects that sometimes travel together in a fog of orthodoxy. In this light on this day the church looked less impressive even than the modest parsonage. White and wooden with crooked steps leading up to a small unpainted door, it stood against the haze and the vacant shadows of banished trees like a hand held up to stop the wind. Its windows were plain glass, rectangular, dead eyes staring out at a disintegrating world.

Hanging from its facade was one of those small marquees upon which there were usually posted hours of services and by some ministers a Biblical aphorism promising happiness and/or threatening damnation and by other, more inventive ministers such apothegms as THERE IS NO "I" IN "PRAYER" and the Unitarian GOD HAS NO RELIGION. But on Reverend Treat's there was nothing.

I wasn't sure whether to knock on the door of the church or enter unbidden. I had little experience of church during what might be called nonbusiness hours. I did, however, consider myself very religious. But my devotion took a form unsuited to the compression of compulsory piety. Like Emily, I found God's courtship arbitrary and despotic. If God made man, He was imperfect; if man made God, he was divine.

I pushed open the door. It was warmer inside than out, unlike a stone church like pretty Trinity in Springfield. The wood seemed to have gathered heat and would keep it until burned or ret. The church smelled, as many do, of books and feet.

I found him kneeling, but not in prayer. He had a pew turned upside down and was forcing a screwdriver into what must have been in the low church light a blind crevice. As he pressed down on the screwdriver, he turned it to gain purchase. He wore a black hat with a wide brim that rested on the pew like a level, as if to retard even the earth's turning until he completed his business. His sleeves were rolled up. His right forearm breathed with its efforts. His clerical collar, damp with sweat, strained against its button at the back.

It was from behind I approached him. He should hear me, for the floorboards sang and my heart beat with a captured rhythm of his own toil.

But I was almost upon him when he finally turned. He must have felt my shadow. It had crawled up his back from the sun coming through the small west windows until my head disappeared into his.

"Goodness," he said as he turned around and, still kneeling, looked up at me.

"Did I startle you?"

He rose to his feet. He was tall and not so much straight as rigid, though whether with muscle or conviction it was impossible to tell. He looked very much the sort of minister who existed more in tales than in tabernacles. His spirit appeared unassailable, from both without and within.

"Your approach startled me," he answered. "You do not."

He was older than his wife. What had I expected? A minister barely out of his teens? Una Treat gave the impression that each step she took, each of her many words, remained an adventure.

Her husband looked like someone who had found some truth and wrestled with it each day and each day emerged victorious in his faith. He was what the world would call a young man, but God would count him old. There was composure in his face, despite its angular beauty. Fulfillment occupied the lean of his body upon the framework of this world.

"Forgive me," I said.

He shook his head. "It's my own fault. I should fix this out in the light. Or not bother to fix it at all. We don't come near to filling the pews these days. Which I suppose is why I fix it. No sense praying for the saved, after all. But you're the first fresh face I've seen in here in months. Years, I suppose. You must be Miss Renway."

"Sarianna Renway."

"Reverend Treat."

If he had held out his hand, I would have taken it.

Neither did he remove his hat.

"You've met my son?"

"Jimmy," I said stupidly, as if his father might not know his name.

"He's not a normal child."

"He seemed perfectly normal to me." I defended that handsome and amusing young man.

"You misunderstand," he said impatiently. "I didn't mean there's anything wrong with him. I meant the opposite."

"That there's something wrong with everyone else?" I tried to amuse him as I imagined Jimmy might.

"Are you always this facetious, Miss Renway, or are you merely nervous at being interviewed for what I imagine is your first job?"

"I was under the impression I have the job, Reverend Treat. If this is an interview, then I'm interviewing you as much as you me."

"Impertinent too," he said.

"Which one of us are you describing?"

"That's enough," he said.

"Are you telling me not to talk?" I asked, because to me that was the rudest of actions and the most insulting.

"I'm telling you to listen," he said with enough apology in his voice to allow me to excuse the fact that he *was* telling me not to talk. "We were discussing my boy. You are to be his teacher. As such, you need to understand him. And I'm telling you about him."

"That he's not normal."

"Perhaps I should put it this way, Miss Renway. He's perfect. I don't mean in small things. He makes mistakes. He says things that aren't true and does things that aren't wise. He disobeys sometimes and at other times obeys too well. He takes pleasure in foolish things and fails to enjoy what would most profoundly please him. He speaks without knowledge and jumps without looking. He's a *boy*. He's young and brash and creaks with growth and lusts like any other boy too young for lust."

"So how is he not normal?" To me, who knew boys only from a distance and knew it was that distance that allowed me to know boys, he sounded normal. "How is he perfect?"

"He's the perfect representation of God on earth," said Reverend Treat with the utter conviction not of a priest but a father. "If God were an artist, my son is what He'd make. You'll see," he added, apparently able to read my mind.

"Then you must be the artist," I said.

"But I didn't make him," he responded quite definitively.

I changed the subject slightly. I said, "He sang for me. He has a voice like an angel."

"Ah, yes." He tilted his head to listen to his son. "Rather apocalyptic, don't you think?"

"What do you mean?"

"That business about your teaching him how the world will end. What's happening in this valley isn't the end of the world. Just the end of *this* world."

"If it's the end of this world," I inquired, "why are you still here?"

"Better yet, why have you *come* here? I've been here, after all, most of my life. *All* my life, aside from school in Boston. But you—whatever brings you here, it can't be the munificence of our room and board and pittance of a salary."

"I found it exciting," I confessed.

"Tutoring?"

"Coming to a place like this."

"Like what? A poor pretty valley in the middle of an economic depression in the middle of New England?"

He didn't give me time to answer before he said, "Don't be afraid to say it, Miss Renway."

There was nothing I was afraid to say. He should have realized that by now. "Because it's doomed."

"You're just another tourist."

I knew what he referred to. There were newspaper articles about people traveling here not only to watch the engineering of the giant dams but to witness extinction. I was no onlooker, however; why come to such a place if not to make a mark upon it?

"And you?" I challenged.

"As I said. Born here."

"And I was born *there*. It's not where you find me."

He looked at me for the first time. Which is to say, he looked into me, or tried to. I may have breached him with my shadow, but I hadn't touched him until now.

"Someone has to stay," he said. "Until everyone else has left.

It won't be long. I proclaim to empty broken pews." He put his hand upon the upturned bench.

"You're a shepherd," I ventured. I imagined it the language of a country church.

"We'll all be sheep when the waters come."

"And when will that be?"

"Would you like to run before the flood?" He didn't regard it as a question I might actually answer. He immediately explained. He even said, "Let me explain," in that didactic way the clergy had of preparing to deliver facts as if they were revelations. "The Metropolitan District Water Supply Commission, as it's grandly called, will cause us all to leave well before a trickle of the Swift River or the Ware River or even Fever Brook overflows a bank or, certainly, hits a dam. But you must understand—people were leaving here long before the decision to discontinue our towns. And there were never many here to begin with. It's one of the reasons we're being taken and why our taking caused so little stir in the Massachusetts legislature. We've never had a newspaper in this valley. Or a bank. Or even a secondary school. And what schools we had, like all churches but this one, have shut down. Which is what brings you. And as long as you're here, you might help me with this pew."

"Your wife told me I'd be a long time in church with you."

"Wait until you hear me preach."

I thought he was making fun of himself. I thought I might get to hear a preacher's laughter. But only mine insulted that little church.

We were to sit down to supper not in the kitchen but in a separate dining room, however small. Where I'd grown up, the dining room was used only for special occasions. Members of the

Renway and Darling families would gather in that cold room for Thanksgiving or Christmas or Easter dinner. My father would cut up a swollen, golden turkey, an exercise in geometry and power. He served each diner's plate separately, white or dark, according to the diner's preference, but never both. And no skin allowed to anyone. My father so imposed his will upon our guests in the matter of food (and table manners) that almost no one spoke unless called upon by him. He sought opinions on such matters as which presidents' likenesses Gutzon Borglum should carve into Mount Rushmore or whether you could call yourself a Massachusetts Democrat and still support Roosevelt's New Deal. He argued with himself, in the absence of opposition. We could hear one another chew.

Otherwise, I ate every evening meal while sitting between my father and my mother at the kitchen table. The conversation then was in my control, because each of them spoke to me, rarely to each other. I was the excuse for their marriage.

There was a large, square wooden table in the Treats' kitchen. But when Reverend Treat and I arrived from the church into the kitchen, I saw that table covered not with clean, empty dishes but with full, covered platters and pots of food.

He went immediately to his wife at the stove.

"Wash your hands first," said his son, who was carrying a pitcher of water toward the door to the dining room.

"Put that down!" His father's brusque order made my skin tighten and my eyes burn. I no more wanted to witness a father and child in conflict than I had wanted to suffer the same myself. My instinct was to flee. But Jimmy's was to obey. And smile.

He placed the pitcher on the table and went without hesitation into his father's arms. Reverend Treat closed his eyes against the pleasure of this liturgy. He held his son to him with a crushing tenderness. And when he released him, it was with reluctance: "Go along."

To me, he said, "You too," as he went to the sink, but he meant the opposite of what he'd said to his son. He wanted me to join him. He turned on the water and circulated a large cake of coarse Castile soap between his palms before handing it to me. The water remained cold, the soap unyielding. Together, we washed our hands in that movement that were there not soap on them would signal some great anxiety.

He then tilted back his hat and bent over the sink and cupped his hands beneath the water and put his face into his hands. The water ran down his arms along the striations of muscle and vein that appeared stamped upon him as emblems of strength. When he stood up, the water from his arms dripped down upon my ankles and my shoes.

"Towel," he said, and pointed toward one that hung upon a nail behind me. I held it out for him and he bowed and brought his face down into it before he took it from me and pressed it to him. Then he put it on my hands again, careful not to touch them, not even through the towel.

Finally, with his hands halfway clean but wholly dry, he went to his wife. He kissed her on the forehead, sniffed absentmindedly at her hair, and said, "What's for dinner?"

"Guess," she said.

"It's my turn." From the look on his face, he might have thought I meant it was my turn for such affection as he showed her.

Una knew what I meant. "I asked Sarianna to guess. Before. I'm sorry, darling. It is her turn."

I immediately confessed, "I have no idea what's for dinner— I just didn't want to miss my turn."

"Now you must take it." Reverend Treat seemed determined to hold me to my claim.

"All right, then," I said. "—chicken!"

This amused them both, as I'd hoped it would. Chicken had been a joke ever since President Hoover, stealing the idea from Henry the Fourth of France, had promised six years before, during the election of 1932, a chicken in every pot. As my father had said, "Who could be so hungry that he'd want what everyone else is eating?" Even the starving seemed to agree—they took the presidency from Hoover and gave it to Roosevelt.

"You're right," said Una. "It's—"

"I am?"

"Chicken!"

"Let us say grace," said Reverend Treat. Only then did he remove his hat. His hair, I saw, was nothing like his son's. Where Jimmy's was extravagant in length and as rich with indeterminate colors as his mother's, and soft, Reverend Treat's hair was coarse and curled and gripped his head as if in battle for his thoughts. Jimmy's hair held the light from the candles on the table. His father's cast it off.

"We thank you, Lord, for this food with which you've blessed our table. And for the arrival of Miss Renway, whom we also thank for this food, since You know as well as I that we don't eat like this every night. Nor should we in a world in which so many have so little. And I thank You personally for the blessing You have bestowed upon me in the person of she who prepared this food and set it out before us. As is said in the Book of Ecclesiasticus, 'As the sun when it riseth in the high heaven, so is the beauty of a good wife in the ordering of her house.' Amen."

Una addressed herself cheerfully to me. "What did I tell

you—maid and mistress, maid and mistress." And to her husband she said, "The Apocrypha, no less."

"Is there anything you don't know how to do?" he asked.

"That's a question you should never ask a woman," she responded. "Don't you agree, Sarianna?"

I was happy to be counted a woman by her, even if, but for her child and the husband who had fathered him upon her, she seemed almost a girl like me. Perhaps I'd had no real friends because I had been, like most schoolchildren, confined to those my own age. I had but only recently turned seventeen. Innocent and inexperienced, which I knew enough to know were not the same. Impressionable yet willful, or at least protective of my innocence and my ideas. Lonely. I was lonely, and had always been lonely, because the world had been, until this moment, empty. I had been like Emily on Judgment Day, alone, unknown by Jesus Christ, and waiting, like her, for what she called the "darker spirit" to take possession of my soul.

"That depends upon what one wants done," I answered. This caused Reverend Treat to appear shocked until he looked to his wife, who looked to me with absolute agreement as she repeated my very words—"That depends upon what one wants *done*."

Now that she had said it, her husband relented in his judgment of me as wanton or provocative. Clearly, here was a man who wore his armor in the world, without respite, and removed it only in the presence of his wife. Or did not so much remove it as have it taken from him, off him, by her presence alone.

Jimmy also brought him joy and in so doing relieved him of the weight of God, or the weight of representing God in a place that most, who were leaving, or all, who would eventually leave, must feel God had abandoned. His son was absorbed into our shared enjoyment. He was asked his opinion of the food. He was encouraged to speak of what reading he'd done that day and what he had planned for that evening. And he offered, without being asked and with what did not seem rehearsal, unless he was a better actor than I could judge, his pleasure in having me as his tutor.

I, in turn, praised him so far as I knew him: articulate, friendly, handsome, and disarming. Jimmy asked me what I meant by that last. "It means you've won me over," I said. To which he responded, "Yes, but how can you love me if you don't have arms?"

His mother found that hilarious, while his father displayed once again a preacher's didacticism: "Not that kind of arms, Jimmy. Weapons."

As Jimmy was clearing the table, and I'd been stopped by Una from joining him in that task, I expressed my surprise at how old he seemed. I'd expected a little boy. I'd known his age but not the independence of his mind.

"He does have a mind of his own," said Una.

"The less you knew of him, the better," said her husband. "After all, what do we know of you?"

"But you asked nothing *about* me," I said.

"Precisely."

"Were there others who applied for the job?"

"You were the only one."

"Can the only one be the chosen one?"

"The chosen one *is* the only one." He said this not to praise me but merely to define me. I didn't care to be defined.

"I don't believe in original sin," I said.

This, finally, caused him to laugh.

"What's so funny?" I asked.

How quickly he found me unamusing. "Who said anything about original sin? We have no one to blame but ourselves. Do you know Milton?"

"Lycidas." I answered what I took to be a challenge. That's
what we'd read in what I'd insisted on calling freshwoman English at Mount Holyoke—and how I'd taken to such muscular
sentiment for a beautiful drowned boy. "You, I suppose, love *Il
Penseroso.*"

"You tease me, Miss Renway."

"Characterize," I clarified.

He explained to Una. "She takes me for the ponderous *Il
Penseroso* and not the amiable *L'Allegro.*"

"Why shouldn't she?" Una touched her husband as she cen-
sured him. "Listen to yourself."

"Then I have even farther to fall." He returned her touch.
"Into gravity."

"I hope you don't mean the grave," she said.

"Paradise Lost," he intoned and took a deep breath as if to begin reciting. "You mustn't forget, Miss Renway: we Congrega-
tionalists have descended from the Puritans. Milton himself was
a Puritan. And Puritans were dissenters. They believed that
God controlled everything but at the same time that man determined his own destiny. There's a formula for confusion, if not
madness. What an awful paradox, yet what a beautiful ambiguity. They, and we, are followers of Calvin, who on occasion, at
least, saw evidence of God in our world. But we're the successors
of Luther, who refused to see God in a world so chaotic and ir-
rational and inequitable. It's Luther who taught us that having
faith is believing God is just despite all evidence that He's mon-
strously unjust. I suspect the world will test him soon. Prince
Konoye and Chancellor Hitler will see to that. The inheritance
of original sin is guilt, and the guilt is all ours, is it not?"

"The guilt is all *yours*, Jeremy. For bringing theology to the
dinner table," Una said with an amiable firmness. She turned to
me: "We have a rule here. No—"

"But there's something about Miss Renway that inspires me to theology," he explained.

"Well," she said, "perhaps if you'd call her by her Christian name, you'd be inspired to something less dreary."

He looked at me strangely. That is to say, he looked at me as if *I* should tell him what to call me. "Sarianna," I reminded him.

"Now there's a twice-good Biblical name," he replied but did not, I noted, use it.

I insisted on helping Una with the dishes. I found it necessary to explain that it had been my job at home to do the dishes, but that I had always done them alone, and it had been a dream of mine to have someone stand next to me, or me to her, while I was washing or drying or both.

"You wash, I'll dry," she consented.

"Fine. But let me dry next time so I'll know where things go."

"You'll have me wishing you would stay forever."

"You'll have me wishing I *could*."

There we stood, washing and drying together, having spoken of doing the same forever in a house that would be demolished in a place that would be lost for eternity to the sun and the air and to such voices as ours, speaking of forever in a world in which there was no such thing. I could not have been happier.

Reverend Treat came to get us so we might bid Jimmy good night. We followed him into the living room where there was a fire laid but not lit. The June night was warm. He had been reading to his son. And Jimmy had fallen asleep next to his father on a large green velvet sofa. Where Reverend Treat had been sitting lay the book, facedown. I recognized its dust jacket from the pile of books, all bestsellers by the likes of Trygve Gul-

branssen and Esther Forbes and Jolan Foldes, my mother bought
and kept and built and always meant to read and sometimes did
and then complained that the moment she finished she remembered nothing, not a name, not a story, not a word.

"Don't worry—it's not the Bible," said Reverend Treat. He
lifted his tall, thin son into his arms and raised him to such a
height that when he spoke he spoke through the boy's hair,
some strands of which moved with his father's breath. "It's *Lost
Horizon*," he said, pointing to the book with the hand that wasn't
holding Jimmy against his body.

Jimmy woke then. Surprised to find himself in his father's
arms but clearly accustomed to being there, he put his own arms
around his father's neck and pulled himself even higher.

"Good night, Mom," he said. "Good night, Sarianna. Can I
have my first lesson tomorrow?"

"Tomorrow is Miss Renway's lesson. You and I will show her
around. All right, Jimmy? We'll give her the tour."

"What if she hates it here and wants to leave?"

"She loves it here. Don't you, Miss Renway?"

"It's paradise, Reverend Treat."

Before long, I pleaded honestly to a weariness of travel and
said good night to Mrs. Treat and went to my room. I hadn't
been back since I'd left it, drawn to Jimmy by his singing. After
so many hours, I had a strong need to use the toilet. I did so
without thinking to close the door. I sat there and looked out
into my little moonlit bedroom, in which the moon, on what
Emily called its fluent route, had stopped for me as once it had
for her, amber, locked upon the windowpane and thus sustained
within the sky as if held in place by the absence of all natural
law. My window was the sky, and I was everywhere.

How strange that something so mundane and vulgar as an open bathroom door could give me so great an awareness of freedom. It joined with the sense I had that where I now resided, and where everyone around me resided, in these several towns, for miles in every direction, would shortly disappear from the surface of the earth. Whatever we did here would be buried forever. We were not confined by our fate but freed by it.

I had never felt as alone as I did in my bedroom here, not in any rooming house or hotel or trapped within the falsely gay, frightening pinwheels upon the wallpaper of my room on Dickinson Street. Yet it was a liberating aloneness. It was a kind of birthing of myself out of childhood, that I should have a job and be part of a household of strangers and belong to nothing more than those few possessions I now put away in my small room and that I should seek to sustain and understand myself in a place that was being torn apart even as I was coming together.

I turned my bed around so I could look out the window, and moved the lamps accordingly. I folded down my Graveyard quilt. Far from giving me willies, its sense of predestined death brought me reassurance. What do we have to lose, if we have to die? We can do anything.

I didn't take Emily's poems to bed. I even turned off the lamp against reading and captured the moonlight against my skin as I let my long, crisp nightgown fall over it upon me. But as I pulled the quilt up to my chin, against the sudden coolness even of this June night in the Swift River Valley, I pulled into my consciousness, as I often did, apt words of hers, *how midnight felt . . . how all the Clocks stopped in the world . . .* So it felt to me, going to sleep my first night there, as it did to her, imagining death.

*   *   *

I could not find sleep nor it me. I lit my candle. I lay there listening. Not for the hissing of stars or the grumbling approach of clouds or the pulsing of the moon or the insurrectionary chatter of passing insects. I sought a human sound and listened for the Treats.

The sounds of my own parents in our house in Springfield, particularly at night, had disturbed me. When they made a floorboard creak, or a pipe complain, or their voices couple in meager, distant good nights, I felt intruded upon. I would lie rigid in my bed at night praying for such silence as could be found only in an empty world.

But now I listened for the comfort of the Treats' presence, in the room next to mine. I wondered at their rituals: if they would talk, no matter that I wouldn't hear the words, and if the air in their room would be moved against the wall of mine when they threw back their quilt and sheets, and if the stiffness of his clerical collar might cause it to clatter like a coin when he tossed it onto his dresser, or I might hear the button of it pinch through the buttonhole behind his neck, and if she brushed her hair and kept a strand or two wet in the corner of her mouth when she first put her knee on the bed and stared down into his face. I wondered if they read at night, in silence, beside each other, their books a fence against the world, and I might hear their pages turn or even feel the movement of their eyes, looking at the words, at each other, at me through the wall, as invisible to them as they to me. And if they might, at this very moment, be listening for me as I was for them.

I heard nothing. Their light was visible beneath our shared door, where it met the weaker light of my one small candle and devoured it.

I waited until their light was out. I kept my candle burning until it was no more. I wanted them to know that I was there and safe and unafraid.

When it was dark on both sides of the wall, and the moon had been eaten by the clouds, I pulled my quilt up over my head and gave myself to morning.

I was awakened by the sound of a bell. I dressed quickly so I might go outdoors to hear it more clearly. Una still lay sleeping as I passed by. One arm crossed that part of the bed emptied, now, of her husband. Still sleepy, I was tempted to slip into that place and draw that arm over me. But I was also shy to be in their bedroom as one of them slept. I tiptoed out and then practically ran down the hallway and the stairs and out the front door.

The ringing of the bell was coming from the church out back. I found Reverend Treat pulling on the bell rope. His eyes were following the sway of the bell in the belfry above. He didn't see me until I was upon him.

"Did the bell awaken you, Miss Renway?"

"Isn't that why you're ringing it?"

He shook his head. "To call people to worship. Not that anyone comes—except a few on Sunday."

"It makes a pretty sound."

"Not as pretty as the bell in the old church. The bell was the only thing left of the old church when they tore it down two years ago. It was bought by the Poles down in Bondville for their church. Saint Adelbert's. Catholic—not that a bell cares. Or the ears that hear it."

"Why do you ring it if nobody comes?"

"To tell God it's morning where we are. In the last century they rang the bell at night too."

"God didn't know it was night either?"

He hesitated. I couldn't tell if I'd amused or riled him. I didn't care which. "For the curfew," he explained without conviction. "Now we don't have a curfew. But still we ring it when someone dies."

"What if they die in the morning?"

"We ring once for the death of a man. Twice for a woman. Three times for a child. It's stark. Not like this. This I ring to my heart's delight." The thought seemed to please him, to ring for the calling of the living, though no more rose from their sleep than, to that other, starker sound, rose from the dead. Only I this summer morning, come to him from my bed like one innocent of such languor as was induced by resignation.

"May I try?"

He put the rope into my hand. There was a pause in the ringing. I pulled the rope. The bell clanged once. But I pulled it again too quickly. The clapper hadn't moved far enough from the inside wall of the bell. There was no sound.

"It's harder than it looks," I said. "I hope this doesn't mean you have to preside at a funeral of some poor man."

He smiled at me for the first time. It was impossible to tell if it was me he took pleasure in or what he thought to be my callowness. "The bell announces a death. It doesn't cause it. Here—it should feel like this."

He put his hands above mine on the rope and nodded at me as he pulled down. Soon, the bell put out its tongue. We were together sending out that clean lambent sound across the valley.

After breakfast, he and I and Jimmy set out on what he'd called my "tour."

Greenwich Village itself lay on flatlands surrounded by green hills. In the distance, even, were what Reverend Treat said were here considered mountains, where there was a proportion to things and thus a harmony of form—Lizzie to the south, Mount Pomeroy to the west, and the most massive if not quite the highest, Mount Zion, to the north, a rueful green hand cupped over some precious trifle.

"Surely the water won't cover *that*," I said.

"What will the mountains be?" Reverend Treat asked Jimmy this question in a weary way that suggested it had been much discussed.

"Islands." Jimmy's hand swept excitedly against the horizon. He knew the answer but had trouble imagining it, as we do the mountains said to be under the sea.

"I'd like to climb it," I said. "While it's still there."

" 'Lo, a Lamb stood on Mount Zion. . . . ' " Reverend Treat was clearly quoting something. "Revelation," he allowed. "Most apt. Not to say you're a lamb, Miss Renway, or even the angel come down from heaven. But that many here believe that what's coming is indeed the Judgment Day."

"Do you?" I asked.

"This is all of our own making," he replied. "God doesn't take part in our politics—not in a little valley like this one, and not upon continents either where men are fighting over more than water. But I do believe we'll see in this place what's called in Revelation a new heaven and a new earth. Think of this covered with water, Miss Renway, as far as the eye can see and farther. Think of what the sea does to the sky. This will all be new."

"Even where we stand," I said.

We all looked toward our feet on the wide road that ran through the middle of this pretty town. Jimmy laughed, because he felt the same excitement I did at standing at a place that would disappear. He knew, with the freedom of his child's imagination, that for thousands of years after the flooding, for as long as men lived on earth and pondered the uncapturable past, people would try, and fail, to picture where we were at this very moment. And who we were, ancients to the future.

As happy as he was, Jimmy still took his father's hand. I held out my own to him. When he took that too, we continued on on our walk.

Reverend Treat dispensed information concerning what could only be called disappearances. The legal term, however, was *discontinuation*, particularly when applied to whole, incorporated towns like Greenwich (which I was embarrassed to learn I had been mispronouncing to myself and was said *Greenwitch*), Enfield, Dana, and Prescott. But unofficial towns and villages were also being taken, he said, reciting their names like some itinerant preacher scouring the land for lost souls: Millington, Cooleyville, Packardsville, Nichewaug, Bobbinville, Puppyville, Smith's Village, Pelham Hollow, West Rutland and North Rutland, Coldbrook Springs, White Valley. Good New England names, including the Indian, that one day would read like a Biblical list of lost cities.

But these were dismembered and deleted. The Greenwich Village School had finally closed and been immediately demolished to make room for the baffle dam, whose purpose was to deflect and circulate the water from the Ware River and thereby cleanse it. The Hillside School in Greenwich had closed a good ten years before but was moved intact to Marlboro. The Athol branch of the Boston and Albany Railroad had as long ago as 1931 reduced its Athol/Springfield run to one passenger and one freight/passenger trip a day, Sundays excluded. Now it had stopped running completely. The tracks were torn up, which he showed to me, overgrown little shadow boxes in the dirt moving off infinitely but uselessly to the north and south. We trod them for a bit, hand in hand in hand, each of us with our eyes up, as watchful for a phantom train as those who walk, fearful, in cemeteries after dark. With the gradual closing of the railroad, Reverend Treat said, so did the businesses in the valley that counted on it close.

He showed me where grist mills had been, a grain store, a meat market, a pool hall, the old Congregational church and the Independent Liberal church, sawmills, cider mills, a plating factory, a button factory, a match factory, a monument shop, a hotel, garages, grocery stores, henhouses, coal sheds, grain elevators, a wheelwright shop, a blacksmith shop, a barbershop, a box factory, a hat factory, an old powder-keg factory, barns, ice houses, a dry goods and notion store, and over by the east branch of the Swift River a little dam that furnished power for the saw-, grist, and planing mill that had been there for half a century and had supplied most of the lumber for the summer cottages built on the lakes and ponds by New Yorkers come north and for the two dozen summer camps on Quabbin Lake, all no more, including that mill, which itself was little more than clots of soiled sawdust among the anthills at our feet.

Some homes were now cellar holes beginning to fill with weeds and dirt and refuse. Others were empty but not yet torn down and were the true tombstones of this life, walls with windows into nothing. I thought of Emily's poetic houses that she, with her cruelest, happiest irony, called sweet and safe, glad and gay. They were *graves*, "sealed so stately tight," as these were open graves, looted by the vandals of thirst and cruel civic necessity.

Amid such inspiring ruins sat the occasional bulldozer, shards of wood or morsels of brick dripping from its moppish lower lip. Some were at work. Smoke and dust gasped and wed in their wake as they chortled on their way into someone's living room or scribbled in the dirt with trees they truncated. Jimmy was transfixed by them. And I by him, to see the boyish pleasure he took in depredation and to understand my own fascination with the subversive beauty in his happy dark eyes.

Homes that were occupied and thus far spared the trespass of the bulldozers were nonetheless run-down. Paint scabbed clapboard. Bricks were pitted. Shingles had eloped. Chimneys feared the wind. Fence posts were splinted. Flower beds were bruised. Even the clothes on clotheslines were drab and dirty, and the lines themselves crestfallen. Windows were missing screens and closed on this sun-soaked, buzzing, luminous day.

"Maintenance is hope," Reverend Treat pronounced. "The only ones who kept up their homes are those who bought a plot of land outside the watershed and moved their houses there or better get to it. The rest will be torn down. Soon. Including ours—the parsonage. Only the Vear place is doomed and preserved both. At least from the outside. It can't be moved in one piece—it's all rock. You can't even take it down and reassemble it elsewhere, the way they did one of the Baily barns on Turnpike Road and put it back together at the fairgrounds in West Springfield for everyone to see. It's like stuffing animals: you get to see everything but the life inside. You might as well take the paint off a painting and look at it. Old man Vear won't acknowledge the state's right of eminent domain. He refuses to settle with the commission. He won't sell them his house. He wants to leave it just as it is when the waters come. I hope he's in it when that happens. Reading his books and the last thing he'll see is the water turn the precious words back to a pool of ink."

I was surprised to hear a man of the cloth wish for the death of another man. It bestowed upon him a depth that only evil can provide. Or if not evil, that sharing with the rest of us of the desire for the annihilation of another, if only we're lucky enough to encounter that other.

"Take me there," I said.

"Not if it were the last place on earth," he replied.

There was too much to see in one day. Or too much I wanted to see. The more I walked over that condemned land, the more I came to love it. It was quite beautiful in itself, and not always despite the wreckage and dilapidation. What was ugly or empty or violently fractured put into fond relief what had so far endured. As Reverend Treat might have said, "Loss creates value."

I begged him to come out with me on subsequent days. There was little else for him to do. Alone, waiting futilely for his parishioners to arrive for prayer or for counsel, he worked on the church each morning, which is when I gave Jimmy his lesson and Una did her shopping. Sometimes, after we'd done the laundry together, she walked alone to King's, the general store and gas station on Main Street at the corner of Hardwick Road, and sometimes I went with her to walk a mile south to Greenwich Plains where the general store (and former post office) was run by the Dickinson family, who'd been postmasters going back to the middle of the nineteenth century and from whose name I took joy in that I found it no matter where I lived. But for stocking up Una drove the family Ford either north to Athol or south to Ware. It was she who begged me to accompany her on these trips. As much as I hated to disappoint her, and enjoyed her company, which I constantly sought out at home, I found I didn't want to leave the valley. Every moment spent here was a moment stolen from the inevitable end of things.

Soon I had Reverend Treat walking with me of an afternoon. Over time he told me a bit of his family background—descended from the Treats of Connecticut, which included a former governor of the state, though the family's most renowned member was that same governor's son, Samuel Treat. He left Connecticut for the Plymouth Colony in 1672 and became renowned as the fervid Calvinist minster to the storm-anguished pilgrims of Eastham, Massachusetts, as well as to those Nauset Indians he converted less with promises of Paradise than with portents of eternal "cineration" (one of his favorite words and plays on words) in the flames of hell. By the time of his death by stroke during the Great Snow of 1717, there were more than five hundred of his Praying Indians in the congregation; it was they who dug tunnels in the snow through which to take his body from his home to its eternal rest. At the same time, owing to the snow, Cotton Mather canceled Sabbath services for two weeks at his Boston church; even deer could not travel, though bears and wolves could, and they took 95 percent of all the deer in New England, immobilized for their satisfaction as if by God.

My own Reverend Treat and I went places in our valley even he had not gone to before. One was far enough away from home so that he drove us there and then we walked, up Soapstone Hill in North Dana, where we climbed into the abandoned quarry and emerged with pale yellow soapstone dust on our clothing.

Though he found it too warm for his black hat, each day he wore his black suit, or one of them, for I learned he had several. What he wore was always clean and so did he seem to be, shaven and bathed and smelling quite pure. On my way through the Treats' bedroom I sometimes stopped and looked among their things, clothing, books, hairbrushes and hand mirrors, touching them or just gazing at them, not in violation of their privacy but as a gesture of intimacy. I made no attempt to hide my explorations. Had I been interrupted at them, I would have gone right on with them.

I felt I was invited this way into their lives. They didn't make their bed until well into the morning, a task they often shared if both were home. She left many of her clothes about (though, aside from his rigid, polished black shoes, he did not), including her nightgowns. These were perfectly discreet, long and cottony, and yet they spoke much of her in how they were worn of their colors and soft and smelled of her soap and skin. My own nightgowns were made of stiffer stuff, as brittle as a surplice though starched only by restraint. I quite enjoyed these virginal garments, which I hugged to myself each night as I waited for their light beneath our common door to die so that nothing but my candle might illuminate whatever darkness lay between us.

I asked Reverend Treat if he would like me to brush the soapstone dust from his coat. He thanked me as he removed it for the first time on one of our walks and brushed it clean himself. He was sweating yet put it immediately back on. He told me then that he was lately getting more exercise than he'd gotten since graduating from New Salem Academy. And it was high time, because he'd be turning forty in less than two years. And his wife was much younger than he, he pointed out, as if I wouldn't have observed the same.

"I wouldn't want to marry as young as she," I said.

"Nor could you," he remarked.

I put a hurt look upon my face. This caused him to stop abruptly in our descent of Soapstone Hill. "I didn't mean you aren't attractive enough, Miss Renway. Merely that you're no longer young enough. But it did sound cruel to say. Forgive me."

"I knew what you meant," I said. "I was pretending."

"I thought so," he said.

But he hadn't.

Jimmy and I developed a special relationship from the beginning. We were closer in age to each other—he nearly twelve and I recently turned seventeen—than either of his parents was to me or even to each other. We were the two children in the household, yet neither of us was quite a child. I was a woman in form and temperament and independence, if not entirely in experience. And he was a boy at what I soon discovered was a distinctive age. His body hovered on the edge of change but had not yet changed at all; his voice, as well, remained that of an angel. And so the force of change, which would drive through his body with cruel disregard for patience or proportion, had so far left his mind intact.

He had no consciousness of his physical self, which he threw about with abandon and allowed great liberties of touch and unrehearsed affection. He nuzzled and bumped and caressed offhandedly. But he hadn't yet grown awkward or disproportioned. He was purity of form. He was invisible to himself.

This made him an ideal student. His body didn't intrude upon his mind. He neither fidgeted nor tried constantly to see himself in the mirror of the air. He wasn't testing his hair with his fingers, his skin with his nails. He concentrated wholly upon himself and me and what I taught him.

I taught him what his parents asked and what his school texts provided and as was fitting for a child who would be entering the seventh grade should any school remain standing in the autumn: arithmetic and spelling and geography and history.

But I also taught him what I saw he wanted to learn. We sat there in the parlor, he on the sofa, I in his father's chair, schoolbooks between us on a low table. He looked at me, his inky eyes dancing with mischief and zest. While his father's eyes were intense in their gaze, Jimmy's were playful and untroubled. And yet how dark they were compared to his father's gray, gray like the winter sky, ashen and foreboding, pale with the beauty of the conjectural sun.

I thought constantly of how his parents loved him. His father in particular, who loved him not merely because he was his son and a handsome, happy boy at that, but because he was the issue of Una, his wife. Jeremy Treat loved his wife with a passion that, more than God, saved his soul. Warmed his soul. This warmth spread to his son and came back to warm himself. And further heated his passion for his wife. And here was Jimmy, caught between them, within them, warm, loved, unafraid, charmed. He was, if not perfect (and who was I to say?), at perfection's moment, boy and man at once, each extinguishing the other's foibles and transgressions. His mother and his father tried to hold him with their eyes as they could not with their hands or with their words.

I taught him, because he wanted me to, what everyone must learn, though many never do: how to leave his parents.

I asked Jimmy to take me to a cemetery. Or what was left of one. His parents voiced no objection. They didn't want to go themselves. But on my first Saturday night in the valley, the warmest night of the young summer, they seemed willing for me to take their son, or him to take me, to the graveyard. Una even joked that it was what local folk did when they didn't want to drive to the Paramount movie theater in Springfield.

People not in mourning went to cemeteries to read headstones and compare themselves to the dead. I'd never enjoyed that. What was put upon headstones irked me: bad poetry, sentimental platitudes, magnified achievements, impertinent confidence in future congress. But the cemeteries in the Swift River Valley—there were no headstones, no coffins, no corpses. Only graves. Or, where the graves had been filled in, intimations of graves, which was even better. No matter what efforts had been made to eliminate the site of a burial, there was always a tracing in the earth, a give to the soil, an amputation of a tree root, or merely the felt presence of a departed spirit.

The Greenwich Cemetery was the closest and the largest. It had been built at a true crossroads, where the state highway and the Monson Turnpike and Greenwich Plains Road all met just east of where the railroad tracks had been. Jimmy and I strolled there after dinner. It was one of those "sweet summer evenings" that Emily described, when she too would walk into a cemetery—in Amherst, not far to our west—to read the names on the stones. Here were the visitors to her life with whom she was most comfortable and communicative, and who most inspired her images of fording the mystery across which they had leapt. I imagined her interrogating the daisies.

These were the longest days of the year. The sun was still above what would have been the nearby trees, if trees had been left by the commission. We let ourselves surrender to the artifice of solstice light. It shimmered with the threat of its own extinction, falling unnaturally upon the unsuspecting evening air, which begged for darkness and failed to understand this smug intrusion.

There was still a fence around the cemetery. In some places it lay down and in others leaned. Jimmy was just as Emily imagined God, wanting to climb over the fence, if only He could, if only He were a Boy. But I was God the scold. I insisted we find where the gate had been and enter properly and with respect.

"Who's going to notice?" he asked.

"No one. That's the best reason to do something the right way."

He said, "I see what you mean," and disobeyed me completely by leaping over a section of fallen fence.

"Come on." He held out his hand to help me over.

I shook my head and kept on walking around the perimeter of the cemetery until I came to the gate. It stood by itself, separated from the downed fence on either side of it, ornate when the fence had been plain.

Jimmy had followed me from inside the cemetery, step by step. We looked at each other through the gate.

"I wonder what's holding it up," he said.

"Nothing."

I walked through the gate, barely touching it. As soon as I was clear of it, and Jimmy with me, it collapsed behind me.

"Spooky," he said.

"Stop trying to scare yourself."

"I'm trying to scare *you*."

"Why would you do that?"

He hesitated before he responded. His dark eyes filled with blissful doubt. "So I could protect you?" It was a question asked not of me or of himself but of propriety.

"From what?"

"Everything," he said, and could not help but walk away from me for the first time.

I didn't try to catch up to him. I let him come back to me. By then I was sitting on the edge of a hole in the ground. My feet were inside, swinging like a child's against the forlorn wall of dirt.

"There you are," he said. "It's getting dark." The moon was emerging, a rounded blade that threw off sparks of sunlight from

its lean edge. It was trapped in a funnel of insect-vexed heat between earth and sky. It wasn't yet dark; the air was aglow.

"Sit down," I said.

"No."

I looked from the moon to him. He was trembling.

"What's the matter?"

"Nothing." He clasped his hands together to stop them from
shaking. He bit his lower lip. But he could not keep his eyes
on mine.

"Did you see a ghost?" I asked with too much condescension.

He took my hand. "There's a man at my grandma's hole."

"Which grandma?"

"Grandma Ryther. My mom's—"

"So I gathered. From her name," I explained, fighting trepi-
dation with logic.

"Why are you whispering all of a sudden?"

"Show me where."

Further in, at what must have been at its heart a small rise
in the ground, the cemetery looked bombarded, like the newspaper pictures from the war in Spain with trees gouged out
around Badajoz, earth spooned out around Almería. But the
many little craters were too symmetrical in arrangement to have
been caused through the disarray of artillery. They were evenly if
parsimoniously spaced and predominant on the south and west
sides of the hill, as if to lure the maximum of sun from the fune-
real New England sky. Thin new waxen roots had wormed
through some. In others, older, thicker roots had been disseyered.

The man saw us before we saw him. He stepped up out of a
grave just as Jimmy was pointing to it in the distance.

We stopped. He motioned us forward.

He was an old man, bent a bit with age, deeply wrinkled, but tall nonetheless and trim in the waist for someone so broad-shouldered. In one large hand he held a thick book. His other was huge around the weedy stalks of purple cow vetch, which made the blossoms all the more delicate an offering. The yellowed nails of his first two fingers softened the blue blaze of the lip-shaped flowers that even in twilight displayed the color of the midday sky. His dark suit was of thick flannel yet gave him an elegant look in this land of overalls and kerseys and loose summer shells on wiry, flat-chested women. The white shirt beneath it was buttoned to his Adam's apple. He wore a posh felt hat. Pulled down to rest on his eyebrows, it made of his huge black eyes two restless wheels upon the ruined landscape of his face.

"You're not from here," he pronounced in a voice surprisingly refined for one so staunch and wind-flawed.

"Which one of us are you talking to?" I asked.

"I know Jimmy Treat."

At the sound of his name from the old man's lips, Jimmy bumped helplessly against me.

"I didn't walk out of the earth, if that's what you mean," I answered the old man.

"Not *here*"—he aimed the flowers at the hill. "*Here*"—he twirled the flowers around his head, as if to paint the valley wide.

"I'm not from either. Are those flowers for me?"

"Not until you're dead and buried."

"What if I'm a ghost?"

He considered me carefully. His dark eyes brooded over what flesh of mine was visible, arms, calves, ankles, neck, and that narrow wedge of chest between the disengaged buttons and buttonholes of my summer blouse.

"A cemetery's the last place you'll find a ghost," he said with the kind of empty authority employed by theologians. "Ghosts haunt the living, not the dead. They take one look at a place like this, and off they go. Ghosts like houses. I've got a ghost at home myself. Like something out of Hawthorne." He waved his book at me and at the same time gave me that offensive little sideways toss of the head bestowed by those who leak references and can't decide if they'll be more pleased or less if the reference is taken. I looked back at him as if he were an idiot for assuming me an idiot. The wrinkles on his face squeezed into a satisfied, even flattering grin. He was now pleased, beyond what material warmth I brought to this graveyard, to have met me.

"A hundred years ago he put down an idea. He was always writing down ideas for what he wrote no more of. We all do that in our heads at least, don't we, young lady? We live to plan because we plan to live but no one yet's outlived his plans. He . . . meaning Hawthorne—" and the old man paused to ascertain my intelligence in following his way of thinking "—he saw in his mind an old house. In it a mysterious knocking might be heard on the wall, where once there had been a doorway but now was covered up." He shuddered in mock fright, to try to frighten me.

"If your ghost is at home," I said, "then who are the flowers for?"

"Paying my respects." He looked down into the empty hole and shook his head.

"Who to?"

"You know who, don't you, Jimmy?"

"This is my grandma's hole."

The old man reached out to the boy. I thought Jimmy would pull away, but the old man's large hand slowed down before it reached Jimmy's body, and then it stopped. It was up to Jimmy to deliver himself to the old man's touch. He leaned forward.

The old man clasped his shoulder. He smiled. His teeth were large and golden-black from the tobacco that had also glazed his fingertips and nails.

"Do you always bring flowers?" I asked.

"Not in the winter. In the winter there's no gush of violets along a woodpath, as he himself says." He held out the book as if it too were an offering. "In the winter, I can't find her hole. In the winter, I write in the snow."

"What do you say?"

"What else is there to say in a graveyard?—'I miss you.' "

"Who?" I asked.

"What I want to know is who are *you*." His voice was loud and ragged and smelled of tobacco.

"Sarianna Renway."

"What's your relation to this one?" He pointed at Jimmy.

"I'm his tutor."

"I approve of your classroom." Moonlight hung alone now in the moist evening air but darkness filled the holes around us. The dead had flown and left us three here talking.

"You didn't say who you are."

"Simeon Vear." As his name came out, off came his hat in his hand, and I saw that his hair was fine and white and so long it must have been coiled in the hat, for it fell down the back of his dark flannel suit and spread across his neck and shoulders like a light summer shawl or, better yet, a nun's guimpe, radiant with renunciation.

I went home eager to find out more about the Vears but not so eager to tell of our having met Simeon Vear. I made Jimmy promise not to. Since Reverend Treat had been the first to mention the Vear name to me, and because it seemed a name over

which he might lose some of the great hold he appeared to have
upon himself, I thought to ask him. But Una said he was, as
usual at night, in the church working on his sermon. Nor could
he be disturbed once he finished. She sent Jimmy up to bed and
urged me to get a good night's sleep. When I asked why I would
need it, she said so I would stay alert in church the next morning. I asked if Reverend Treat's sermons were that boring. She
put her hand against my hair, behind my ear, as if to capture
sound for me, and said his sermons were brilliant. She had married him for his sermons, she said. I thought that peculiar yet
immediately comprehensible. What more than a sermon might
combine passion with reason, faith with repudiation?

I bid her good night. As I headed for the stairs, I said, "Just
tell Reverend Treat that I wanted to ask him about Simeon Vear.
Maybe tomorrow, after church."

"The Vears!" She ran to me and pulled me around the corner
into the parlor and sat me down close to her on the green sofa.
There were tiny beads of sweat on her upper lip. Before she said
anything more, she turned off the NBC Symphony Orchestra
on the radio. She smiled as if to say that even Brahms was not
the equal of our conversation.

"Don't you dare ask Jeremy anything about the Vears, Sarianna. Ask *me* about the Vears. I know more about the Vears
than anyone. I was almost a Vear myself."

She sensed my confusion. "I almost *married* a Vear."

This didn't help. She'd had a child when she was fifteen. So
far as I knew she was married then, though she may not have
been when Jimmy was conceived.

"Simeon Vear?" I ventured uncertainly.

She swatted my arm and laughed. "I may have married an
older man, Sarianna, but not *that* much older. It was the son.

Ethan Vear. And when I say I almost married him, I don't mean we were close to marching down the aisle. I mean I couldn't get thoughts of marrying him out of my mind. Has that ever happened to you? I was fourteen. He was only a few weeks older."

Had that ever happened to me?

"When *I* was fourteen . . ." I began but could remember nothing of it. I liked to think that each moment erased, or at least consumed, the one before. It was better to contain the past than to be contained by it. Perhaps that's why I felt so immediately at home in this valley: it would soon have neither past nor future. Had there ever been a place where the present moment was at the same time as significant and as spectral?

"Ethan's father and my father were best friends," she went on, "even though they were very different kinds of people for both of them being in the wood business once Mr. Vear hired him. My father drank whiskey and liked to watch the trees come crashing down. Mr. Vear liked to cut them down himself, which I guess is natural because they were his trees, and he loved to read books at night instead of drink. Sometimes he would read them out loud to us—Ethan and I would sit there listening to how old Roger Chillingworth turned ugly right before the eyes of poor Hester Prynne and we'd look at each other hard to try to keep from changing, ever, and my father would sit there drinking and not hearing anything and we were supposed to feel sorry for him because she died. My mother, I mean. Not Hester Prynne. Ethan and I wanted to share the same tombstone just like at the end with Hester Prynne. My father couldn't even remember where my mother was buried, though he was the one who chose the spot, out where you and Jimmy went tonight. He didn't want her buried in the Vear plot, even when his best friend offered. *I* knew where she was buried. And I never knew her—my mother. Barely her name. Amelia Fitts. Then Amelia Fitts Ryther after she married my father. Everybody called her Millie. He was twenty years older. But she died in having me nonetheless. So Simeon Vear was like an uncle to me. Ethan and I grew up together. When I wasn't at the Vear place, Ethan was at mine. We were best friends, like our fathers. After Mr. Vear's wife died, he invited my father and me to move into their big stone house. So we did. And then Ethan and I fell in love. We didn't use that word for it—love. And we certainly didn't talk about getting married. But I couldn't stop imagining us being together forever. That's what marriage is, isn't it—being together forever?"

"I wouldn't know," I said as harshly as possible, to give some accurate idea that I'd neither been in love nor witnessed it in my parents.

Una put her hands on my shoulders and drew me against her. "Of course you wouldn't know. Even I don't know," she added gaily. Perspiration from her forehead dampened mine. I opened my eyes within her hair and watched it pare the frown of moon that misjudged our pleasure in one another.

"What do you mean you don't know?" I whispered. I felt my lips touch the lobe of her ear.

She moved me away but held my arms so that we might stare into each other's face. "Because I'm married now?"

"Yes. You and your husband seem . . . as if you will certainly be together forever." I didn't like using her words back to her. It was like repeating oneself—a sin against taste. But I didn't know how to describe aloud my impression of the passion they shared, the stability of their covenant. In addition, I was unused to discussing such matters.

"I love this so much!" She released my arms, but I could still feel her fingers upon them, keeping me where indeed I wanted to be.

"What?"

"Talking to you. There's been no one to talk to! Imagine what it's like being a minister's wife. You get to hear so much, but you get to tell so little. Lemonade?" she inquired and immediately explained: "There's so much more to tell you."

I followed her into the kitchen.

We took turns burking lemons. When we were finished, and there was lemon juice on our fingers, she ran hers through her long hair. "Look. I put this in my hair sometimes. It lightens it. And smell how good it smells."

She nodded toward me like a subject to a queen. "Smell it," she insisted.

I did, with an exaggerated sniff.

"Aren't I fresh," she said as she came up smiling and bringing her hair to her own nose with her fingers.

She sat me at the kitchen table and put cookies on a plate before me. Once she'd mixed our lemon juice with water, she poured the lemonade into thick ridged glasses that had become cloudy with use and showed me how I must hold a piece of cookie beneath my tongue.

The sour taste of the lemonade and the sugary taste of the cookies were broadcast on her expressive face as she told me how she had come to marry Jeremy Treat after having been in love with Ethan Vear.

"Jeremy Treat came back from divinity school in Boston. Well over ten years ago now. Everybody knew by then they were going to take our towns. They were going to flood us so Boston could have water to drink, and then here comes a man back from there who tells us he's going to look after us until they take our land and our homes and then will lead us out of here. He will never abandon us, he says. The big church was still standing then and we all went every Sunday and we saw a beautiful minister standing up there telling us he would never leave. Everybody loved him."

"You especially," I teased.

"No, not especially. But the same as everyone who saw him in his pulpit. He seemed unapproachable. He would appear and disappear. He didn't stand out on the steps gladhanding his parishioners after the service. He still doesn't. He's not a politician. But he did meet with people privately. It was Ethan's father who wanted us broken up. As if a Ryther girl wasn't good enough for a Vear boy because the Vears are English with just enough Nipmuc Indian to be able to say they've been here for centuries and mean centuries before the *Mayflower*. The Ryther men and the Vear men were certainly good enough for one another and were the ones who always went off hunting or fishing or chopping down trees together and left Ethan and me alone in the first place. Then when we fell in love, I got sent to the minister. There weren't too many Sigmund Freuds around here then. Only the minister. Little did anyone know what would come of that!"

Una looked gleefully into my face to be sure I understood what she meant. That the one to whom she'd been sent to suppress her love was the one who stole that love for himself.

"What about your own father?"

"My father didn't care about anything after my mother died. He disappeared into a bottle and eventually he just disappeared. I never saw him after Jimmy was born, and he never laid eyes on Jimmy. He abandoned me, Sarianna, right when I became a mother myself. I suppose he blamed me for killing my mother, but that's what men do to keep from blaming themselves. After all, if he hadn't fucked her, I wouldn't have been around to kill her by being born. Are you shocked?"

"My own father wouldn't have cared either."

"Not by *that*! By my *language*!"

"Nothing shocks me." This was neither boast nor confession. I knew that what I could imagine would surpass all that could happen. I was not yet a poet, like Emily, but we shared this strange comfort: neither the world nor God would ever surprise us, though both might disappoint or delight us.

Una put down her lemonade glass and took my hand. She leaned toward me over the kitchen table. "I could shock you," she whispered.

"How?"

"I have a secret." She put her lips to my ear. "Would you like to hear it?"

"No."

Abruptly she drew back. "You're a saint."

"Thank you."

"And a liar."

"You've called me that before."

"Is it true?"

"Yes."

"Liar!"

But it was true. I did want to hear Una's secret. But I didn't want her to tell me in order to fulfill my desire. I wanted her to tell me out of her own need to confess.

When I said nothing to defend myself, she went on with her story.

"What came of it, of course, as I was saying, was I ended up married to the minister. As soon it was clear that a baby was on the way. It was a terrible scandal in the valley. I was too young. He was too old. We were too happy. I think they would have ridden Jeremy Treat out of town on a rail if they weren't actually afraid he was going to leave town on his own the way people had begun to do by then. And that I'd hop up on that rail right behind him. They all thought he'd done it to me, of course. But it was the other way. He didn't seduce me, Sarianna. I seduced him. I didn't so much give up Ethan Vear as take Jeremy Treat. That isn't my terrible secret, by the way."

"What happened to Ethan Vear?" I asked.

"I don't *know* what happened to Ethan Vear!"

"You never saw him again?"

"Sarianna, no one has seen Ethan Vear since the day I married Jeremy Treat."

No, that's never happened to me.

I answered her question only when I was in bed that night, stretched out in the heat with my toes tangled in the sheets and the chin of moon alone providing light to cover and expose my body. I'd had no thoughts of marrying nor anyone I'd think of marrying should such thoughts occur to me. And when I'd thought of marriage itself, I'd thought with Emily that they'd have to dislocate my brain and amputate my bosom before I'd take a husband. The Treats' marriage was the first I'd seen that didn't make me feel that marriage was the punishment for sex and sex the punishment for marrying.

I might look like Una's sister, as she'd said. This was flattery to both of us, she to be as young as I and I to be as beautiful as she. But there was nothing between us; hence, room for everything. And everything was what she seemed determined we know of each other. Or I of her. Even her "terrible" secret, which I took to mean *redoubtable*, not *detestable*. She didn't pry into my life, my conventional past, but acted as if this life of mine had begun when I'd knocked on the parsonage door and been welcomed into hers. It was another way of giving birth.

As I lay there in the silence and the moonlight thinking of Una and the Vears and the arrival of Jeremy Treat into her life to take her away from Ethan Vear and apparently send him into exile or to the grave, I became aware for the first time since my arrival in the Treat home of sound from their room next to mine.

He was speaking. Not talking but speaking. His voice was muted yet compelling. It rose and fell in an oracular fashion, musically, but there was less melody than emotion. It was only when I stopped listening and was on that edge of sleep where every sound is magnified even as it seems to come from farther and farther away, that I heard a word, and then another, and then a few more before his voice failed or my ears failed or the night seized all the sounds between us. ". . . Pompeii . . . primeval . . . Esdras . . . castle of sunshine" (which I recognized as Emily's) . . . "innocent . . . daffodils . . . deluge . . ." I could make no sense of them in relation to one another. Their beauty lay in the impregnation of his voice within their sound. They were plain poetic words, rendered complex, single notes of music within a mass.

It was finished. I was forlorn. This silence was like none I'd heard before. There was no serenity in it. It produced no grace that comes from an awareness of solitude.

I felt a wind against the wall between us. The air grew cool against my skin. I heard outside my window the phantom sounds of nuzzling leaves from ancient and uprooted trees and then come through the wall the sounds of sheets and nightclothes.

The moon had disappeared. Not behind a cloud or wrenched into the turning of the earth. The sky was clear. The earth was idle. The moon had disappeared within my eyes. I lit my candle so I could see myself and they would see my light beneath the door.

They called to me. Not by my name but by their own, which each prayed over and over to the other. Or to me. Calling me to them. Not that I would come. That I would know.

Darkness and silence returned together. My candle went out by itself. I heard nothing but my own quick breathing.

I saw on my way into church the next morning for the Sunday service that Reverend Treat had put on the marquee a message addressed as much to me as to his congregation:

I TOOK MY POWER IN MY HAND
AND WENT AGAINST THE WORLD.
—EMILY DICKINSON

The few in attendance congregated in the center pews. I was accustomed to people taking seats as far as possible from those with whom they'd not arrived, the way two strangers sit like bookends when there's not a thought on the shelf between them. During assembly at Mount Holyoke, I'd always put myself in the back of the auditorium, at an end seat, where I could see and not be seen. Rather like God, now that I considered it within the context of this little church. Here everyone huddled the way I imagined they must have done in winters past when warming pans were used to cut the chill and human bodies sought to share the warmth that no religion brought to winter.

Perhaps we sat together because we were the choir. There was no organ. A small piano sat against the wall, to the left of the pulpit. Una, who had put me between herself and Jimmy in

a front pew, rose and walked to the piano. All talking ceased.
She began to play, and sing, and the others joined in the hymn:

> Mighty Jesus, by thy hand,
> Give us vict'ry in our land.
> Through you only are we found
> Even as our souls are drowned.
> Mighty is thy saving grace
> That takes all sinners from this place.
> As in'cent lambs are led to slaughter
> So our sins made pure by water.

Reverend Treat walked by Una on his way to the pulpit, as
she was making her way back to Jimmy and me. They stopped
for a moment and looked at one another. It seemed a ritualistic
gesture but no less fervent for that. In this house of God, and
before the likes of those who had condemned their love, they
made manifest that love.

Then he preached.

He took as his basis Emily's words on his marquee—"I took
my power in my hand / And went against the world." But for
his theological foundation, and in relation to this poetry, as well
as to our first dinner together, Reverend Treat put Calvin to battle with Luther. The former proclaimed, "The correction of
tyrannical domination is the vengeance of God," and those so
dominated on earth can do nothing but "obey and suffer." But
Martin Luther said that human beings must wrestle not only
with one another, flesh and blood, but also with principalities
and powers.

Reverend Treat let Luther's phrase—*principalities and powers*—
fall more than once upon our ears. So we created within ourselves,

without his ever having mentioned them by name, our puta-
tive adversaries, who were those very principalities and powers
themselves—Boston, the Massachusetts Legislature, the Metropolitan District Water Supply Commission, and the two engineers most responsible for the drowning of our valley, Mr. Frank
Winsor and Mr. Xanthus H. Goodnough, known throughout
the state of Massachusetts, in the words of one legislator, as a man
"so smooth he could sell Christmas trees in a synagogue."

Just when we might have marched off to war against them,
Reverend Treat returned to Emily and asked, "Which world is
it we must go against? I was led to this question by a young
woman who's appeared among us like a vision. While others
have departed at the approach of doom, she has arrived. Arrived
not like the tourists who come to gawk at us as if we were those
in Pompeii about to be preserved in ash. Not like the engineers
and laborers who come in vast hordes and live near us but not
among us in order to assure that no one will ever live here again.
Not like the lawyers and real estate agents and auctioneers and
antiques dealers and timber merchants and scrap merchants who
trade upon our misfortune and loss. No. She has arrived like an
innocent in that week of primeval silence described in the book
of Esdras. It is a week not in time as we measure it here but as
it's measured in eternity. It is a week that is precisely as long as
the week of Creation described in Genesis. A week of years, as
Ezra says.

"And at the end of that week of primeval silence, the dead
will be resurrected. God will judge all nations then. The righteous compared to the ungodly will be in direct proportion to
that same measurement taken of the hearts of human beings.
This will be the true Day of Judgment, which marks, in the
words of Ezra, 'the end of this age and the beginning of the

immortal age to come.' There will be neither sun nor moon nor stars nor noon nor night. And is this not an apt description of our valley, as it will be when the waters come? Or is it perhaps an even more appropriate description of the future of our entire world? The Japanese take Shanghai. The Spaniards destroy Guernica. The Russians try and execute their leaders. The Germans and Italians form an axis of destruction. And in our country we arm ourselves and starve to death and live on dust and drink the droplets of despair.

" 'I took my power in my hand and went against the world.' This innocent young woman, who has come to save us, recognizes the author of those words. Who else among you does? Emily Dickinson lived not many miles off to the west there and was more than anyone else *our* poet. *Our* prophet. The trees, the moss, the sand, the mud, the wounded deer, the red upon the hill, the daffodils, the bells in steeples, the breeze in her castle of sunshine—New England was our promised land, and hers. And how did she prophesy?—'And so there was a deluge, and swept the world away!'

"Which world is it we must go against? Not Boston. Not Berlin. Not Teruel. Not Tokyo. And not the kingdom of God either. Pastor Martin Niemöller stood in Jesus Christus Kirche in Dahlem, on the outskirts of Berlin where the Nazis eat and drink and plot the ruin of the world and yet themselves attend his church, and Martin Niemöller put his finger to his chest and he said, 'Here I am. Here is what I say: We must obey God rather than men.' And when the police came to arrest him, his entire congregation rose up and surrounded him at his pulpit and sang as if to hold back the heavens themselves that might have spit these armed barbarians down upon them, sang 'A Mighty Fortress Is Our God.' Were they able to protect him?

No. Could they keep him out of jail? No. Did God fail him? No. And I say: Here I am. And here is what I tell you: God must never be blamed for anything. Questioned for everything, but blamed for nothing. The world we must go against is the world we build within ourselves. It has no countries, no cities, no citadels. It is a world of disbelief. That this could be happening to us. That we should be at the mercy of principalities, and of powers too we cannot conceive exist and at the same time desire for ourselves. That we should even be alive for a brief time on earth and recognize it only at the moment of death: how precious was my life, we say for the first time ever, as we say good-bye to it.

"Take a lesson from her. There she is, between my wife and son. Venture into paradise on the eve of its destruction."

He kept his finger pointing at me even when he'd finished preaching. Despite the space between the pulpit and the pew, I could feel it touch me, pierce me.

He wasn't, as Una had said, a politician. He didn't stand outside the church to give his hand and voice to his parishioners. But Una did. It was she who was the diplomat, emissary not only from church to state but also from shame to approbation. Let her husband hide from sin, or from its presumption. She was impudent. Or innocent. Or both.

She stood with her legs apart and her arms open and her eyes inviting. There had been nearly five hundred people living in Greenwich ten years before. Now there were not a hundred and more left each week and few of those remaining came to church.

She introduced me to them. She held my arm as she did so. "This is the girl from the sermon," she told such people who would listen, the Hooks and the Blackmers and the Metcalfs and the Chickerings and the Ouellettes and the Pratts and the Uraciuses.

I might as well have stepped from the pages of the Bible. People stared at me, but they seemed unable to think of anything to say. They were a beaten lot, impoverished by the stripping of their land; they'd been left behind, either by fleeing relatives or their own departed vigor. They marched like ghosts out of the church, closed their eyes against the sun, and opened them only to look at me as if I'd risen from the dead.

I was finally spoken to when a large woman with a square head brought her tumid lips toward my ear and whispered conspiratorially yet with the clear intention she be overheard, "Be careful of the reverend. He likes them young—like you."

"Oh, Barna," Una rescued me, "he used to like them young. Now he likes them old. Like me."

"You're not old," said the woman. "Just used."

"*Well* used," replied Una with provocative satisfaction.

The woman clucked happily and walked off whispering, again to anyone willing to listen, "Shameful . . . shameless . . . shameful . . . shameless," happy not to have to decide. Her dress hung from her hips like a tablecloth.

Last out of the church was the old man from the cemetery. He had his hat in his hand and raised it, before he put it on, as a shade against the sun in his eyes. His long, loose white hair was almost invisible in the glare, against the white of the church behind him. Thus was his face isolated, a saint's floating free in a medieval painting, the brim of his hat a black halo set above his black eyes.

"Look," I said to Una. "There's Simeon Vear."

"How do you . . ." she began. Then she smiled. "He hasn't

been to church since he delivered me to Jeremy. Not that Jeremy would have him in his church. So what do you suppose he's doing here now?" She addressed me as if I might know him better than she. So quickly had she recovered from her surprise that I would know him at all.

"He's here because of me," I said.

This was beyond her. "Because of *you*?"

He added to my enjoyment of her consternation by walking directly to me and removing from the pocket of his flannel suit the remains of a flower that I guessed to be from among those he'd carried to Una's mother's grave.

"Thank you, Mr. Vear."

"My pleasure." He removed his hat. "Smoke?" He withdrew a pack of Viceroys from his breast pocket and knocked it against a large knuckle until several cigarettes emerged. He extracted one carefully with his golden-edged fingernails and then offered the pack around.

Una shook her head. Jimmy was clearly more interested in the old man's hair and face, seen now for the first time in daylight, than in his offering. Only I accepted, recalling that Jeremy Treat had told me of Samuel Treat's ban against smoking within two whole miles of his own more stately Eastham church.

"I didn't know you smoked," said Una.

"I don't." I'd never smoked. It had been too much the daring thing to do, particularly for girls at both high school and Mount Holyoke. Too much pride had been taken for so meager a transgression. It was treated like a loss of innocence among those who believed that innocence was somehow only of the body.

"No time like the present," said Simeon Vear.

"I'll have one too," said Una.

"I took this not to smoke it but to join you in the ritual," I said to Simeon Vear. "And to be polite. I was brought up not to refuse an offering." I displayed our sad flower as Simeon Vear passed a lit match between Una and me.

"I want to smoke mine," said Una, though she held her cigarette far from her mouth.

"It'll make you sick," I told her.

"I've smoked before," she said.

"I remember," said Simeon Vear.

"So do I," said Una. "Does Ethan still smoke?" she asked.

"I wouldn't know," said Ethan's father.

"Where is he?" she asked.

"I wouldn't know that either."

"Is he alive?"

He contemplated his cigarette. "Not to you."

Una wept. It was something I'd not expected to see, so cheerful had she always been. Yet now that tears had burst from her so briskly, I revised my expectation, though in retrospect and, for the moment, uselessly. What I had taken for good cheer was that indeed. But what I'd failed to understand was how her aggression on behalf of conviviality and adventure might so easily be diverted toward disquiet if not grief. I enjoyed her tears, not for her pain but for how they washed away simplicity. She was much more dangerous in her instability. And thus even more fetching.

Simeon Vear was also affected by her tears. But he didn't seem to think about their meaning, as I had, so much as to feel for their begetter. He threw his cigarette into the sandy grass and blew what smoke remained in his mouth out its corner as he put his arms around Una and said, "There, there."

Una hesitated for a moment before she rested her head on his shoulder. From that position, she was able to look right into my face. The tears were gone, but only, I discovered, from her eyes, which flashed a smile in my direction as she said to Simeon Vear in a lachrymal voice, "Tell Ethan I was asking after him."

"Ethan's dead, my little sad one," he said to her.

She pushed him far enough away to be able to look into his face while remaining within the grasp of his large hands. "Don't call me that," she said, though now her smile had moved from my face to his, and her command seemed its opposite.

He let go of her and kneeled before Jimmy, his hands now on Jimmy's shoulders.

"She used to love for me to call her that. Your mother grew up in my house when she was your age. Did you know that, Jimmy?"

Jimmy looked at Una. She let him answer for himself.

"Yes," he said.

"Would you like to come visit me?"

"I'm not allowed."

Simeon Vear pulled Jimmy closer. "Do you remember who I am?"

"Old man Vear." Jimmy answered with what his father called Simeon, as if to invoke Jeremy against a man he'd proclaimed his enemy.

"I wasn't always this old. I used to be as young as you are now. And then as young as this young lady here. And then as young as your mother here. And then as young as your father. That's how it goes if you can just stay alive. Look at me now—I'm old enough to be someone's grandfather. Do you know whose grandfather I am?"

Una slapped the old man hard across the face. What was left of her cigarette, which she had not yet sucked upon, flew from between her fingers and landed with a flash in the dirt between his knees and Jimmy's lusterless church shoes.

* * *

That evening, while Reverend Treat was reading to Jimmy in the parlor, Una called me out of my room into her bedroom.

"Sit." She pointed to the bed. I obeyed. It was the first time I'd sat on their bed with anyone present in the room.

"Are you angry with me?" I asked.

She stood over me. "You must have a lot of practice with it if you can tell so easily."

I knew what she suspected. "He followed me to you," I explained. "I didn't say he was there *for* me. *Because* of me. That's what I said. I met him by accident in the cemetery."

"Did you tell him my secret? How does he know my secret?"

"I don't *know* your secret."

"You said you didn't want to know it. You might as well have slapped *me*."

"I was lying. I told you I was lying."

"Then you *do* want to know it," she said gaily. "Sarianna, Jimmy is Ethan's child."

I said nothing.

She spoke to me then at length, as that twilight Sunday darkened and we alternately lay and sat and knelt and lay again beneath the angel canopy in deepening candlelight and were like two schoolgirls upon a bed in a dormitory baring our souls, as I had always imagined Emily and her great friend Jane Humphrey, "jumping into bed when you slept with me," as Emily wrote to her. How wonderful to picture girls together, and to be a girl together with another, rolling the world away as you gather each other up.

And while Una was the only one who spoke of matters rare and private, the listener's soul is bared as well, perhaps even more ruthlessly, just as a confessor is relieved while her confessor is oppressed. As shameful and shameless, which might be opposites, are not, so are confessor and confessor, which might be equivalent, opposite. Or so they may seem. When Una spoke of such matters as her betrayal of Ethan Vear and her seduction of Jeremy Treat, it was I who felt seduced and in that seduction itself, like Ethan, betrayed.

I saw her as a girl of fourteen walking this land on the eve of its official, legislated taking, before the houses were ousted and the trees excommunicated and the businesses humbled and the tracks of the railroad unscabbed from the land and the inhabitants both freed and disinherited. She was as beautiful as she is now, but lighter and sillier and, even when she discovered she was pregnant by her equally young lover, less burdened. It had been such a revelation, to join a household and live with a boy who from the first moment did not begrudge her presence but welcomed and enjoyed and finally seized upon it, and her. He took her for walks in the woods where he taught her to identify trees. He let her empty his traps and snares of animals they'd take home and his father and her father would skin and hang and cook and they would spend a whole evening eating, she the only female in the house, and she could not imagine herself happier, she said, except for the absence of someone like me, to stand by her doing dishes and to talk to about such love for this boy as she could barely contain. He led her to old Indian burial grounds with their shallow graves and what was left of great heaps of stones upon those graves to keep at bay such animals as he would capture for their food. He held her hand as they climbed the cliff to Bear's Den, where the Indians 250 years before gathered in their war councils over the roiling waters of the Swift River. Here, in one of the many caves, a kidnapped white child was hidden by the daughter of its Narraganset captor while she went in search of the child's mother because she believed that even a white child belonged with its mother. His room in the big stone house was like a cave. Up a long ladder down the hall from her own room was Ethan's wide dark corner attic room, with its one little window no bigger than her head and girlish shoulders and everywhere his clothes and books and furniture and leaves from trees and fishing poles and knives and a hatchet and the little soft stuffed animals he kept giving her for her room until he had none and she had them all, so much *stuff* around, she said, that he and she had found their way to his narrow bed as their refuge in this mess.

His father sent her to the Reverend Jeremy Treat for a talking to, not because Simeon Vear or even Ethan Vear knew she was pregnant but because he suspected she and his son might do what leads to pregnancy and he wanted his son free to pursue other more cosmopolitan women outside the doomed Swift River Valley. Ethan never spoke to her after her visit to Reverend Treat. She gave him no chance. She moved into the parsonage that very day. It was assumed the young reverend had taken her in as charity until she began to wear her apron high and her ring finger girded by the young reverend's late mother's gold wedding band. As for Ethan, he simply disappeared on the day of her wedding. Whether into the wide world or into a grave she had no idea.

This was a great disappointment to me. I knew he might be dead, or a ghost of himself inhabiting the vast Vear house. Yet she made me want to know him, not simply so I might know that part of her she'd left with him but for himself alone—he whom I knew only through her—so that my affection for him grew out of my affection for her while the mystery of his being was obscured by the very transparency of her own. I fell in love with him before I met him, in loving her and loving whom she loved and loving who was, at first, like God; a phantom, an imagined being, an image of perfection, forever adrift between desire and want.

Her Ethan had long hair like his father and black eyes and was as at home in the woods as by the hearth with a knife and whetstone in his hands and his boots and socks off and his bare feet maddeningly alluring. He knew nothing of love but what he discovered with her and he thus discovered himself in her. His body was boyish and manly and his voice cracked and he would laugh at these last remnants of childhood quavering up through him. He had nothing he didn't make hers. He put his food on her plate and shoved funnies under her door and gave her his Gunthermann racers and lined up his tin soldiers to protect her sleep. This was, she led me to understand, a benefaction that came only with love. A divesting of the self that led to an accumulation of the other. A disappearance into realization. He loved how they would stand together before the mirror in his room and simply stare, not at each other but at themselves together, a union of their images that was the only way they might see what they'd become in spirit. He loved when they'd been given baths together in a huge oval galvanized tub and even more when this privilege was abruptly withdrawn because they were too old for that, his father said, and Ethan told her privately and mournfully this prohibition came too late. Later, he loved for her to be naked and not to touch her and then to watch her dress, and she didn't know if the tears in his eyes came from joy at her beauty or despair at its concealment. He loved to wear the same thing every day—dark brown corduroy pants, a faded blue shirt with a black T-shirt underneath when the weather was cool, black boots—and his dress never varied once he reached the age to choose it for himself. He loved how they must sneak away or out of sight to see each other as they would see each other. He took her to a pond and scrubbed her clean with sand. He dried her when she was wet from swimming or from the cold pumped water at the kitchen sink. He read to her and acted out all the parts. He asked her riddles but couldn't wait for her to solve them and gave her answers with his hand over his mouth. He did her homework and gave her his to do and thus competed fiercely with her for the better grades. He took her up in trees and pointed to the world and told her we'll go there and there and there and there. He ate the oatmeal-raisin cookies she baked for him, one whole pan at a time, leaving only a single cookie for her which she always refused so he ate that one too with an appetite that signified a capacity for all things and with a selfishness that, because she had baked the cookies herself, she took to be the very essence of generosity. He planted black-cherry plants in the sandy valley soil and tended them until they bore fruit and watched her eat the cherries until her lips and tongue were the color of his eyes. He pitted the cherries and heated them and put them on vanilla ice cream and fed her with a giant spoon that made her laugh. In the winter, to keep her ice cream cold, he harvested blocks of ice from Greenwich Lake and brought them home to her on a sled they'd later ride down Russ Mountain almost all the way to the Stacy Cemetery. He took her to the same lake to watch the eagles feed upon the deer carcasses stiff and clean upon the ice. He played hide-and-go-seek with her from the time she first arrived at his home but never managed to hide without revealing himself and so finally became only the seeker and rarely managed to find her, he who was so good at tracking animals in the woods and up the hills that made their valley. He came into her room at night, from the time they were innocent children, and sat watching her as she sat watching him, silent, both of them, not out of fear of discovery but so as not to interrupt the converse of their eyes. They learned to speak while saying nothing.

"Would you want to see him again if you could?" I asked.

"Never."

"Never?"

"What if he's dead? What would he look like then?"

"What if he's alive?"

"I still wouldn't know him." She put her face into my shoulder and even then merely whispered. "Not a day goes by when I don't see him in my mind."

"I mean *now*. As he is *now*."

"There is no now," she said.

Una might be less a philosopher than a rhapsodist, but she was right. The past impaled the future and never stopped at now. Now was an illusion. Now was over before it began. Time disappeared. So would everything around us, here in Greenwich Village and out there beyond the hills too. Here was the world, shrinking down to what so many believed it had begun as, a garden soon to be destroyed by the works of man and the desecration of innocence. And here, before the fall, were Una and I, huddled together on a big bed, speaking to each other as I imagined women had spoken to each other eternally.

"There's a *now* in Emily Dickinson I love," I said. "She writes about leaving. Leaving everything. She says she's stopped being theirs. She says the name they dropped upon her face when they baptized her in the country church she's finished using. *Now*. And they can take that name and put it with her dolls. They can take that name and put it with her childhood. *Now*."

"There comes a time, Sarianna, when a girl stops quoting poetry and starts quoting things men have said to her."

I could not take offense at her. "So tell me what he said."

*   *   *

Una spoke of herself in such a way that she became as seductive to me in her caprice as she had been to Jeremy Treat in her cunning. She made of herself an orphan child, with a mother lost at birth and a father lost to the memory of the mother.

"I'd never been alone with him before. I'd never seen him when it wasn't a Sunday. Sometimes, in church, on Sunday, I'd look at him and wonder what he did when he wasn't up before us preaching and promising. I always sat next to Ethan in church. His father on one side of me. Ethan on the other. My father never sat next to me but next to Mr. Vear. My father avoided me. Constantly. I was my mother's ghost to him. He'd look at me as if he had no idea who I was or where I came from. He was sweet with whiskey and sour with life. The only one he ever talked to was Mr. Vear. That left Ethan and me alone. He'd hold my hand in church and we'd listen to the new minister tell us now that he'd found us, he would never leave us. Now that we were doomed, we were saved. Now that our world would shrink to nothing, it was infinite. Now that we'd been judged expendable, we were indispensable.

"You should have seen him then, Sarianna. He was not only beautiful but was filled with the beauty of God. He was our Jonathan Edwards. That's what he so much as told us. He'd become a Congregationalist preacher because that's what Jonathan Edwards had been just over west in Northampton. And he believed, as Jonathan Edwards had, that we participate in God because God puts his own beauty upon our souls. We are interchangeably beautiful with God. All of us. So all of us are saved, as long as we retain God's beauty. But if we sin, we become ugly. And God becomes angry with us. And punishes us forever. I'd hear Reverend Treat tell us this, and watch him tell us this, and

I'd hold Ethan's hand harder and harder. I'd dare him to take Ethan away from me. I'd dare him to deny the beauty of our love. Or that God was not within us both. So by the time I was sent to see him alone, he was already inside me. That man.

"I hated him. I went to him hating him. I knew why I'd been sent to him. Or I thought I did. It was still morning. Simeon Vear had taken me to the church. Not my own father, but Mr. Vear. 'The reverend wants to have a talk with you,' he told me. 'About what?' I said. 'About the age you're getting to be,' he said. I called him a liar. I said ministers were the last people to talk to girls about becoming women. Simeon Vear said that was true unless the girl didn't have a mother to tell her. 'I have a father,' I said. 'And do you love your father?' he asked. 'I don't even know my father,' I said. 'All the more reason for you to go in there and talk to Reverend Treat,' he said.

"So I went in there and talked to Reverend Treat. Or rather I listened to Reverend Treat talk to me. At least at the beginning. I was as much of a blabbermouth then as I am now, but he didn't give me a chance to talk before he began to talk to me. 'Una,' he said, and that was the first word he said to me, 'Una,' my name, and I'm not as strong as your Emily, Sarianna, I love to hear my name and I loved how he said it—no different from anyone else but so unexpected and so gentle. It was like God talking and knowing who you are before you tell Him. Not just my name. He said, 'Una.' Then he said it again, 'Una, I imagine you think you know why you're here. You think I'm going to lecture you. You think I'm going to quote the Bible at you and tell you things you ought not do and thoughts you ought not have and lives you ought not live. That's what Mr. Vear would have me do, I suppose. He tells me you've stolen the heart of his only son and that he fears for his son's life. Not that his son will die but that he'll cease to live. That he'll give himself to you before he's found himself. I know you're both very young, but youth has never been a means to measure love, has it? It's only old people whom love has disappointed who say there are some who are too young for love. Or so I'm told. About the young, that is. I was never so lucky as you. I fell in love with God before I met a girl who might have brought me to my senses. I tell you that not to convince you I have objectivity on my side but so I might announce my ignorance. I have no idea what it is you may be celebrating or suffering. Perhaps you'll tell me.'

"I couldn't tell him a thing. I couldn't believe what he was telling *me*. Not just that he was prepared to understand me and to accept me but that he would do it from a place of innocence or ignorance, which are usually the same thing anyway. He wasn't going to lord it over me. He wasn't going to try to teach me. He wanted me to teach *him*. He was going to seduce me with his virtue. Because he knew it was too late for me to seduce him with mine."

I was understanding her all the better as we lay next to one another on their bed in the candlelight that shivered in the dark June breeze as much as I did to be brought into such confidences as she revealed.

So I said to her, "But you *did* seduce him."

She gave me a playful slap. "But not with my virtue. I was sitting there before him fourteen years old and I was late and my breasts felt sensitive just from when I breathed and here was this handsome man, and tall—you've seen how *tall* he is, Sarianna—and all dressed up in his big black suit with that clean white collar . . . there he was proclaiming his innocence and telling me how lucky I was to have fallen in love. He was so *merciful*. It was like having an interview with Jesus Christ." She put her hand to her mouth. "I can't believe I just said that! But that wouldn't be much different than everybody thought when Jeremy and I got married. People don't want their religious marrying. Not the ones who know what goes on in the marriage bed."

"What does go on in the marriage bed?" I asked.

"Shall I tell you what the man does," she asked, "or the woman?"

"I don't care," I answered. "Just tell me how you seduced him."

I took my first bath that night. Until then, I'd washed in my own tiny bathroom, for its privacy and because I'd grown accustomed in my months at college to bathing at a sink and had found here in the Swift River Valley that even the dust from Soapstone Hill could be removed by hand or at least ground into my being with a washcloth. But now, on my first Sunday night in the valley, and in the aftermath of Una's confession, I wanted to submerge my body and to wash my hair in a torrent of water and to experience their lives in my mind by so familiar a physical act as giving myself up to the embrace of their common tub.

I carried my candle with me from my room, not because I feared waking Una in their bed where, exhausted from talk and girlish play, she'd fallen asleep virtually in my arms, but because I imagined its faint pale light would both conceal and soften me. The tub had a rounded edge so I placed the candle on a small stool that held bathroom reading—not a Bible but a copy of a recent and much celebrated book called *The Flowering of New England*—and slipped out of my summer dress. This caused the candle flame to shiver and send its lacerations of light halfway up my legs. I waited until all was still to remove my undergarments and stood for a few moments above the light, which produced a feeling of tangibility upon my skin. I looked at myself in the mirror above the pedestal sink and could see out from what I could not see, my eyes and face escaped the candlelight, the flesh below aglow in it yet shadowed.

The tub was deep but narrow, raised from the floor on feet rather devilish for a clergyman's basin but balanced in such diablerie by a purity of whiteness that could have been maintained only by Una's most rigorous scrubbing. I was surprised, then, upon first sinking into the steam that finally came when the recalcitrant hot water hit the theretofore rampant cold, to find that the inside walls of the tub were scratchy and rude and felt against my arms and shoulders the way I imagined a hair shirt would. And so, then, was the floor of the tub as well, against my thighs and backside and my spine and neck as I lowered myself wholly into the water.

The soap in the tub was not as harsh or unprolific as that in their kitchen sink. Indeed, it fairly frothed and gave forth a kind of gardeniac scent that at first almost overwhelmed me but soon replaced queasiness with tranquility. I remembered learning in my botany studies that the gardenia had been named after an American doctor with the felicitous name Alexander Garden. Emily herself had kept a greenhouse where she grew calla lilies and plumed cockscomb and pomegranates but probably not the jasmines of which she wrote the fainting bee might sip before, lost in balms, he consummates his life in dying for his love.

Una, I thought, had not died for her love but had sacrificed him. Ethan, in whose bed she had slept, seemed nonetheless a spirit to her, ethereal, distant, almost incorporeal in his youth and in the ebullience of his ardor. Jeremy Treat, on the other hand, professional man of the spirit, appeared to her an earthly

manifestation of redemption and thus of love. He filled the
room and he filled her eyes and he appeared before her like a
block of granite into which she might herself be carved.

She made him take her in. Not as an orphan but as a woman
who would return to her lover if he didn't. This was not, she admitted, seduction but manipulation. She didn't want to leave his
presence. In order not to, she must threaten to. "That's how it is
with us women," she told me: "we lay traps with ourselves as
bait."

As for seducing him, she had not so much desire as need to.
Her baby must appear not to be Ethan's, rather Jeremy's. But
her attraction to Jeremy, despite his physical impressiveness, was
pious: she wanted to sleep beneath his roof, not beneath him.
Of course in asking for a man's protection, a woman invited his
greater patronage. He came to her, as it were, because she was
there. He could not, he said, resist her. He couldn't bear her presence, but neither could he bear her absence. And thus, indeed,
she seduced him with her virtue. She was beyond desire, though
this meant something different for each of them.

He didn't force himself upon her. He fought with himself
over her. It was wrong, he told himself, to want her. He left it to
her to contradict him, which of course she did, for what woman,
she asked me in what was not a question, feels it is wrong for a
man to want her.

What she had not expected, in his taking her within the first
week of her residence within the old parsonage, was the depth
of his feeling for her that seemed to have been dug out of the act
itself, and how contagious this was, this love, this desire, which
claimed her own feelings and clamped her to him and rendered
Ethan truly a spirit then, in the form of memory, even as she
reached out her arms for him while she held Jeremy within

them. She could see Ethan over the shoulder of her new lover, a head above the bed, weeping like Jesus.

I tried to picture Ethan, to imagine his forlornness when his love did not return from the church to his father's home in which they lived together, not that night or any subsequent. He didn't see her again until the day, not long after, she married the minister. She saw Ethan enter the church at the back just before she and Jeremy, at the pulpit, were about to exchange vows. She heard him cry out for her, though no one else, she said, heard him. She saw him look at her with such bewilderment and anguish that she closed her eyes and kept them closed through the ceremony and opened them only when Jeremy kissed her for the first time as her husband and she looked over his shoulder this time at the very spot where Ethan had been, where he was no more.

That was almost twelve years ago. Ethan had disappeared and not been seen since, by her or anyone she knew. And that was why, I thought, I couldn't see him either. He was a body buried or drowned somewhere, or he was a man nearly the same age as Jeremy had been when Una had married him. The Ethan Una had confessed to seeing in her mind each day was still that boy in Bear's Den, that boy at the back of the church. In that sense, she'd been correct to say there was no now. Ethan had disappeared into time.

So does the bather on occasion. After going up on my knees to wash my hair under the faucet turned to its maximum output, I lay back and became lost to myself until I heard a faint knock on the door. Before I could answer or even decide how I might answer, the door opened. I looked up, and there I saw him, rising out of the candlelight and steam. He was still in his black shirt, but his jacket had been discarded, and his clerical collar had been unbuttoned in the back and waved about on either side of his neck like small white wings.

"I hope I didn't startle you," he said gently, nearly reproducing the first words I'd said to him. "What a wonderful idea," he went on as he tilted his head in the way of someone attempting to adjust his eyes to diminished light—"a candle. Very peaceful. I didn't know you were here. I did knock. Though I would have come in anyway. Or asked to. Do you mind if I close the door? I can barely see you as it is, but the candlelight is so much softer. I'd like to sit here for a bit. Have you a towel? I'll dry you when you're done."

I might have pretended he was talking to me and not to Una, in those uncharacteristically short sentences I imagined clipped by lust, or that he was pretending to talk to her when he knew it was I in the tub. I might also have clarified this issue immediately by speaking. But I preferred to hear him speak. And also to learn what he would say, first to her and only then to me.

But he said nothing. He took the candle in his hand and sat on the stool, so that his face was nearly as low as mine, as I lay back in the tub wholly submerged but for my head, the rest of me modestly veiled beneath the skim of soap and whatever corporal dross was being sacrificed to my cleanliness.

"What are you thinking?" I asked, because I was interested and because I thought it what a wife might say.

"Una," he said, questioningly but not doubtfully. From his tone, I couldn't tell if he wanted it—which is to say, the body in the tub—to be her or me.

At the same moment in which he moved the candle toward me, I rose toward him, halfway out of the water, which stopped at my waist and hid the lower half of me. The rest of me took upon itself the candlelight the way a canvas might take paint. I looked down to see myself exposed, golden-skinned and smooth. I might be seeing myself naked for the first time, as was a man. I wasn't shocked. It was only his eyes that had me, and all they had of me was only what I gave them.

"I didn't know," he said.

"That it was I?"

"That too."

"I hope I didn't startle *you*."

"You're in no position to mock me."

"Or at least not in so secure a position as you are to mock me."

"I can hardly see you," he explained.

"And if you could?"

"I wouldn't mock you."

"It wouldn't be Christian," I said.

"That too," he repeated.

"May I have my towel, please?"

"Of course."

As he turned with the candle to find it, I rose to my feet in what had become almost total darkness. He would have been alerted from the sound of the water falling from me that I would be standing. He rose now as well and turned back to me with my towel in one hand and the candle in the other. I wondered which of them he would first extend toward me.

"Are you always so nonchalant in your nakedness?" he inquired.

"And you in your observation of it?"

"When it's my wife's, yes."

"Am I hard to look at, then?"

"Only hard to see, Sarianna." But instead of coming closer with the candle, it was the towel he extended.

I held out my arms for him to wrap me in it. But he draped it over one of them and put the candle in my other hand.

"There," he said as he replaced the book on the stool and backed into darkness toward the door. "—a statue."

"Come to life," I replied.

By the time I was out of the tub and had wrung the water out of my hair and dried my body and made my way across the hall and into their bedroom, they were both asleep. Because the night was warm, they were covered with neither their quilt nor a blanket but only a white sheet. They were facing each other and thus he, on the far side of the bed, facing me. His left hand was curled where it rested lightly in the hollow of her waist. It opened and closed with her breathing, summoning me to approach. I shielded the light of the candle from their eyes and bent over them not so much to see them as to hear their breathing. I determined it was for both of them the authentic breath of sleep, heavy with patient innocence, and marveled at the unison of sound and rhythm they had attained in their unconscious coupling. I imagined they had gone to sleep in harmony. I wondered if such concord came from news of me he'd given her. That he had come upon me in the bath. That he had called me by my name.

Only the next morning did I learn he had indeed told her. Reverend Treat had gone early to the church. Una and I were left to our usual breakfast at the kitchen table, two young women with a coffee pot between us and our index fingers curled into the handles of our coffee mugs. I'd not drunk much coffee before, and never the mixture of coffee and chicory we drank now, because I'd never wanted to endure its rattling effects while alone and had never met anyone before Una I'd wanted to get rattled with. The girls at Mount Holyoke used to take coffee with their cigarettes, and gossip and undo the top button or two of their blouses. Only now had I come to enjoy the experience myself, from the smell that drifted up into my little room while I was still in bed to the chortling in the percolator on the stove and the sight of the coffee being spit against the glass crown and the way it combined with conversation to induce an excitement in the blood.

It was as she was pouring more coffee into my cup that Una said, "Jeremy confessed."

"What?"

She laughed and spilled coffee. "How he surprised you in the tub."

"I think it was himself he surprised more."

"He told me that too."

"That he thought it was you in the tub?"

"Not that." She rose to get a cloth. "Surprised at your—"

"Did he call me shameless"—I made reference to the large churchgoing woman's happy accusations that morning—"or shameful?"

"Surprised at your beauty, Sarianna."

"Then he must have thought it was you."

She came beside me and wiped up the coffee. "He remarked quite specifically." She dropped the cloth and put her hands on my shoulders and lowered them over my collarbone and down my chest, as if to feel where she believed her husband's eyes had been. "There," she said, with a physician's briskness as she removed her hands, "that proves it: we could not be mistaken for each other."

I laughed because she did. "That proves nothing. He even said I was hard to see."

"And you believed him?"

"It was very *dark*, Una."

"If it was so dark, Sarianna, then why did you ask him if you were hard to look at?"

"Because he didn't seem to care."

She took my hand and held it as she sat down again and leaned toward me with my hand her captive. "He cares for you a great deal." She was unable to contain her amusement. "A lot more now that he's seen you naked!"

"He couldn't even see me!" I protested.

"Then imagine what will happen when he can."

"I'm sure you'll learn of it long before I do. He seems to tell you everything."

"Of course he does." And here she raised her eyebrows in case I might miss the pleasure she took in being sarcastic at her own expense: "We have no secrets from one another. But of course," she went on as she let go of my hand and took a sip of coffee, "a man tells you everything to prepare you for the day when he neglects to tell you something of vastly more importance than anything he's told you previously."

"Did he tell you he called me Sarianna?"

"He did. Better late than never, I scolded him. He said it produced in him a feeling of intimacy he hadn't intended but welcomed once it passed."

"Passed! You mean it lasted only—"

"Passed *into* him is what he meant. Not passed out of him."

"What kind of intimacy?" I asked.

"What kind would you like it to be?"

"Not what you're thinking!" I proclaimed.

She shook her head. "When you tell someone what she's thinking, it's always what you're thinking yourself."

"Then you tell me: what am I thinking?"

"That Jeremy is irresistible."

"To *you*," I replied. "According to your formula, that's what *you're* thinking."

She sipped some coffee and narrowed her large and gentle eyes to ponder me. "He cannot be resisted," she said. "That's what I mean. His will is very strong. Otherwise why would we be here living in this place until the end of time? Don't try to resist him, Sarianna. Give him what he wants."

"He called me a statue!"

"I know!" she said with great delight. "But you mustn't take offense. It's not your body he wants. It's your—"

"He dried me with the towel."

"Liar!" She swatted me playfully with the dishcloth.

"It's my *what*?" I insisted.

"Your innocence."

I put my hands in my lap.

"Such as it is," she added.

We were interrupted at that moment by Jimmy, who had come looking for me as he did every morning. Had ever a boy been so eager for his lessons? "Come on," he said, and put his hand at my elbow. His hair was bed-pitched, his dark eyes (in which I now could not help but see the stain and cast of Simeon Vear) tapered still from dreams, and he smelled of whatever summer sunlight sought him in his bed at dawn.

"Eat something first," said his mother.

"What?" he said.

"You know what."

"Not the usual," he protested.

"I'll make you an egg," offered Una.

"Will you have one too?" he asked me.

"Since when do I have to eat what you do?"

"Since I want to eat what you do," he answered.

"Well, we do need a good breakfast," I said.

"Where are we going?" he asked.

"The last place on earth."

He smiled complicitly.

We left immediately after breakfast and walked north on the Monson Turnpike between Curtis Hill to the west and Parker Hill to the east. It was in Monson itself that Emily Dickinson's father courted Emily Dickinson's mother, also named Emily. I imagined him walking this far north with her. I looked down at the road for their shoe prints and put mine where theirs might have been and where within the year the road would be rinsed of centuries of footprints. Emily herself was walking with them, hidden within their future, as I was in hers.

Few others were about, whether walking or behind a horse or in an auto. Those few nodded or waved almost furtively, even when we smiled and helloed them loudly or raised our held hands in a gesture of solidarity. The land, as depleted as it was through the felling of trees and abolition of habitations and re-nunciation of human breath and footfall, seemed cheered by the relative absence of such fools as had believed in its constancy. It poked flowers out of road ruts carved in the spring mud by departing trucks burdened with the valley's salvageable detritus and sent forth rodents to follow the shadows of birds and ac-companied our lengthy walk with an encouraging south wind.

Eventually we forsook the road for the abandoned railroad tracks so we might be closer to Mount Zion. I had Jimmy listen for a train. I told him how a poet I loved had written that she liked to hear it lap the miles and lick the valley up, and the valley

she meant was just there over the hill to our west, "just there"—
I pointed—"there." "Listen," he said, entering into my game,
when there was no sound but our own breathing joined within
the wind, "here it comes," and he too pointed toward the west,
past Pelham and Mount Lincoln toward the valley she'd invoked
and toward the life I'd abandoned. We strained to hear destruction thunder in upon us and finally laughed together at our reprieve, imaginary as it was. As for Emily's valley and Mount
Holyoke College to its south, they too seemed fictitious, so isolated were we in our own lost world.

Mount Zion let the sunrise drip and gave us shade. Its fallen
trees, which lay across one another to form a carpet of wayward
filament, gestured pathetically in the breeze. North of Turtle
Pond, where the railroad tracks converged with the road, we
crossed the middle branch of the Swift River on the little bridge
that led to Soapstone Road and departed from that upon a tiny
dirt road into what in the Swift River Valley was rare standing
forest, until at a location between Woods Pond and Gibbs Pond
and the former Stacy Cemetery and the former Jason Powers
Cemetery we came upon our destination.

The Vear house sat at the edge of the forest huge upon a
hillock, looking down imperiously out of small windows placed
almost randomly among the rough cobbles and larger uncoursed
fieldstones that gave the impression the house might have fallen
rock by rock from the heavens. Its gable roof was slate and dulled
whatever sun the thick trees sanctioned. Rising from its center
was a great stone chimney, rudely pilastered from the round hems
of the rocks but holding a promise of warmth against the coldness of stone and winter. The only visible wood on the house
was its door, sheathed and worn and crooked from the battle of
the house with the earth of the hill beneath it.

As we walked through the remaining woods toward the house, Jimmy reached out and grasped my hand. He did it not with the usual tender and minutely hesitant slipping of his hand into mine.

"Watch out!" he said.

There before us on the forest floor was a long narrow wooden box. Suspended like the blade of a guillotine above its one open end was a door, held up on one end of a thin stick attached to another stick that disappeared through a hole halfway between the center and the other end of the box.

"It's a trap," said Jimmy.

"It's not very big," I said. "What's it for?"

"I don't know," he answered. "—squirrels, rabbits, things like that."

Still holding my hand, he knelt down and looked inside. "There's bait at the back. Look."

I went down beside him and put my face almost against the cool bed of leaves. I could smell dirt and the sweet vegetal decay that fed the living. I expected what Jimmy called bait to be meat, but it turned out to be green lettuce leaves mixed with chunks of carrot and strips of melon rind.

"See," he said, "the animal goes for the food in the back and hits that stick right in his way and the stick gets released and flies up and that makes the door come down. Boom. Just like that."

"And what happens to the animal?"

"Nothing."

"Nothing?"

"Well, it just sits there, I guess. Of course it gets to eat the bait."

"And then what?"

"And then it gets rescued by whoever set the trap!" he said gaily and pulled me to my feet.

"You've visited this house before?" I asked as we walked.

"You know I'm not allowed to."

"Then how did you know where it is?"

"I know where it *is*," he answered. "I just haven't visited it."

"Who showed it to you?"

"Mom."

"What did she say when she took you here?"

"She didn't say much. She just stood here crying."

"Do you know why she was crying?"

"I did ask her."

"I figured." He was that kind of boy, compassionate, curious, and so without guile that he would surely in his life suffer more from truth than most others do from fraud.

"Do you know what she said?" he asked me.

"How could I?"

"She tells you everything."

"How do you know that?"

"She's different since you got here, Sarianna."

"In what way?"

"Can't you tell?"

"Can't I tell! How could I tell? I didn't know her before I came here."

He laughed at himself. "I forgot about that. Besides, it feels like you've been here forever."

"How is she different?" I persisted.

"Less sad," he said. "That's all. Less sad."

"Is that the same as happier?"

He thought for a moment and said, "Not really."

"So what did she say?" I asked.

"About you?"

"Don't keep changing the subject—when you asked her why she was crying?"

He stopped walking and pointed at the house, to which we had come so close that I could feel its stones enclose us in their cooling of the air. "She said, 'My house. I'm crying for my house.' " He placed his hand flat upon it.

As if his touch had sent a vibration through the very stone, the front door opened, squealing on its iron strap hinges. It was a great slab of dark wood, covered with even darker scars and holes, violent black incisions in its adamant body.

Jimmy, startled, stepped back. I took his hand to pull him in with me, but he resisted.

"I'm not going in there," he said.

I let go of him. "Suit yourself." I took one step through the door.

"Wait!"

I looked back at him. "For what?"

He hesitated still. "I don't know for what. I just want you to wait. I don't want you to go in there."

"Are you afraid for me alone in there? Or for yourself alone out here?"

"I'm not afraid," he said without conviction.

"Then what is it, Jimmy—your parents' rules?"

I left him no time for consideration of this challenge. I turned my back to him and stepped wholly into the house.

"Wait!" This time he joined me. "Hold my hand."

As was to be expected in a house with few windows, there was much darkness. However, what windows there were on what I'd taken to be the two bottom stories let in shafts of silvery light that vibrated against the edges of the darkness and turned golden where it carpeted the thick pine planks of the floor. Old houses like this usually had low ceilings and tiny rooms to keep the heat in. This one had been opened up to what I guessed was a fourth story, and its interior walls removed or never raised, so it gave the impression of being one vast and open space, not unlike a church but for the absence of a steeple and thus a flatness when God presumably preferred something spired and thereby architecturally exalted. Such isolated fingers might point in adoration or in accusation, or both.

I knew the door had not opened by itself, or by the pressure of Jimmy's hand against the outer of the three or four layers of stone making up the thick walls of a house that gave a strange and immediate comfort by virtue of its very heft and fixity. So I was not startled when I saw on a fringe of windowlight a fall of white hair that were it not for the vague shadow of a craggy face might be taken for a spirit clothed in virgin white alight upon the household air.

"Look who's there," I said to Jimmy, not wanting to give our host the benefit of my attention.

I could feel Jimmy start against me as he saw the head of Simeon Vear turn in the flue of dusty gray light. But he contained his fear and surprise within our momentarily engaged bodies and was the first to address our host.

"That door didn't open by itself, did it?"

"Of course not," said the old man. "I saw you coming. I've been waiting for you. Not every minute since yesterday. But I've been waiting. Every once in a while I check. Lucky me. I looked out the window and there you were. I didn't expect you this soon. But I knew you'd come."

"Who?" I asked.

"You," he said. "But I hoped you'd bring him."

"Why?"

"For your protection." He laughed.

He came out of the light, but rather than disappearing into the darkness he was visible in it. He explained: "Your eyes get used to it. We don't have electricity over here. It's an old house. Been in the family since it was built—century before the Revolution. Around the time Massachusetts bought part of Maine and then lost all of New Hampshire. Not a bad deal, I'd say. Increase Mather came by here and gave my great-great-whatever-he-was-grandpa Vear a copy of *The Troubles Which Have Happened in New-England.* Old Increase himself wrote in his book about King Philip that the heathen people's land the Lord God of our Father hath given *us*, as he said, for a rightful possession. So it stands to reason that the troubles out here were mostly Indian. It was Increase also who told my great-great-whatever-he-was to build the house of stone. He told him about the one house left standing after the Algonquian burned down Warwick, Rhode Island—*stone.* So we end up with a minimum of windows and the maximum of stones. The only thing colder than the tip of an arrow in your heart is the pinch of winter on your balls. So it may be dark, but it's safe and warm. It's a peasant house built by what those meddling British called the squirearchy. Their lines of blood we Americans turned to stacks of money. Land we had lands of—you couldn't judge a man by his deer parks. But the Vears were peasants with some aristocracy of Indian blood loved in—one big room to keep warm in, dogs and all. I couldn't see snaking wires through it, any more than I'd want to get wired up myself. So we light it with kerosene and lamp oil and candles and heat it with wood. That's our stand of trees you walked through. We've been cutting them down and growing them back for centuries. That's what eternity is—a stone house and flowering earth."

"And when the waters come?" I asked, using Jeremy Treat's words against the man he could not abide.

Simeon Vear plucked a wooden match from a pocket of his

vest and drew it violently against a stone structure behind him, which I saw in the flare of the match was a fireplace so large that he might have stood in it and invited me and Jimmy in to do the same. From beside what looked like an old music box on the vast mantel he took a lamp and lit that and threw the dead match into the fireplace, where it bounced off a large black pot suspended from a chain. From another vest pocket he produced his Viceroys and shook one directly from the pack onto his lower lip and lit it with the lamp and held the pack in my direction. I shook my head. "Well?" I prodded.

"Take one of these first," he entreated. "Join me in the ritual."

I ignored his mockery. "Are you planning to be in it?"

He put the glass on the lamp and the cigarettes away. "They want to take it down. They threaten me with condemnation proceedings, which to me is just a fancy name for being born on this earth. They come and molest me with drawings of my butts and bounds." He laughed and slapped his backside. "They demand that I remise my home and land and with it all my history and family and crimes and the very breath of pleasures taken down the ages. Eminent domain. A fancy term for martyrdom. I'm sick of it all—the priest's cant, the statesman's rant. That's from the poetry of Ralph Waldo Emerson, young lady. No group's ever been worth an individual. And no individual who joined a group has ever kept his original worth." He paused to pick a spit-dark flake of tobacco from the tip of his tongue and to search my face for agreement with his sentiment, which I gave him with a nod of encouragement. "They want to buy it from me and take it down. Stone by stone. The thing about stones is, they're just stones until you put them together. Rubble. They don't want any structures up at the bottom of their ocean. Leaves the wrong impression. That someone once lived here. Or that there might be people in there still. Bodies. Or ghosts. Or memories so strong they live in empty rooms and get called up in dreams of strangers. It's bad enough they dug up the graves as where we met. They want this house to end up nothing more than rocks in water. The way they started when the seas withdrew and glaciers came and scratched the land and laid these rocks like eggs. They want them ground to sand that people drink. And what about you?" he said to Jimmy, putting the hand with the cigarette on Jimmy's shoulder. "Don't you think we should keep this in the family?"

"Why'd my mother hit you?" Jimmy parried the old man's aggressive familiarity.

"Don't tell him," I said, not so much to hide the truth from Jimmy as to keep it for myself so I might ease him at the proper time into knowledge and forbearance.

Simeon Vear stepped toward me with the lamp and brought it between our faces. He looked directly into my eyes for the answer to what he then said in such a way that it was both a question and a statement: "You know."

What I knew then, aside from what I'd known when I arrived within his house, was that he believed I was his accomplice. He might pretend to debauch me with a strange charm that languished, as he did himself, between gentility and vulgarity. But it was Jimmy he wanted. He believed I'd followed his mandate and delivered Jimmy to him. And so I had. But I wanted something even more precious from him in return.

"I know nothing," I answered.

He offered us something to eat. He said, "It's a long walk to get here. Feed with me."

He lit a candle on a large pine table in the kitchen, which occupied the west corner of the vast, opened house. Suspended above the table was a folding candelabra with six fresh candles in its spokes, but there was enough midday summer light from a window over the sink to let us see the food and one another. The sink itself contained a water pump that sat like a graceful bird, dipped for drinking as it raised its tail for admiration. A bucket overflowing with what looked like ashes was suspended from a nail beside the sink.

He took a plate of meat from the icebox.

"Sorry, no milk," he said to Jimmy. "Next time."

"What's that?" Jimmy asked.

"Hoover hog." Simeon Vear began to break it apart with his hands. "Otherwise known as rabbit. Never as much meat as it looks. It's all that jumping and copulating."

"You're pretty skinny yourself," said Jimmy.

Simeon Vear laughed and shoved a plate in front of the boy. "Eat up. Unless you don't like rabbit."

"I love it." Jimmy, who at home would have waited for me to be served, picked up a small leg bone and nipped at it with his front teeth.

"Did you catch this yourself?" I asked. "We saw a trap out there."

"Anyone in it?"

"I saw it first," said Jimmy. "It was empty."

"There goes supper." He tore a thin piece of gray meat off the ribs and and folded it behind his teeth.

"So it is your trap," I said.

"Who else's?"

"Una told me about how she used to help your son with his traps and you and her father would cook what they brought home."

"Well she told you wrong. Eat up." He put the rabbit carcass on my plate. "What I mean by wrong," he went on, "is we never ate anything before we hung it for a time."

"So why did you say, 'there goes supper'?"

"Larder's not as full these days."

"Ethan no longer traps for you?" I questioned.

"Oh, he traps, all right."

"So he is alive?"

"Now did I say he was alive?" he asked Jimmy, who was sucking on his rabbit bone.

"Who?"

"Your mom's old boyfriend."

"That's a good one." Jimmy raised his eyebrows at the preposterousness of the idea.

"Where is he?" I asked.

"Where do you think he is?"

" 'Ghosts like houses.' " I repeated the words he'd told me when we'd met.

"Mom's old boyfriend is a ghost?"

"Stay with me," said Simeon Vear to Jimmy, putting his huge hand on the boy's shoulder, "and let her look."

"Where?" I asked.

"Wherever I'm not," he replied. "Have some of mine," he then said to Jimmy and moved some rabbit meat from his plate to his grandson's.

I walked through the vast room from window to window, thus staying in the light. I noticed how the windows had been angled in the stone in some attempt to deflect an arrow's flight and been placed in their relation to one another not haphazardly, as they looked to be from the outside, but in such a way as to throw strong light across weak light, depending upon the time of day and, I assumed, the season. Thus did the windows with their age-rippled opalescent glass do battle with one another in daylight, while at night, I imagined, they relented under the influence of softer moonlight and the suasion of the stars and in the utter darkness under clouds gazed with blind longing across this unnavigable space.

The house was mostly empty, though here and there was an odd piece of furniture or two, none of it set up for socializing, and the occasional coarse small hooked or braided rug on the blond dark-scarred wood of the floor. Because the walls were uneven stone, nothing hung from them except some sharpened wooden clothespegs by the front door through which we had entered and by the back door across the house. These were unadorned but for the old man's black hat and an umbrella and a flashlight; in vain did I look for a young man's plaid or canvas shirt unmuscled and relaxed. There were several small bookcases shoved against the stones and in them books that from my brief perusal by the windowlight seemed to deal primarily with such practical matters as timber harvesting, fruit preserving, and the lives of birds and such impractical matters as the beauty, history, and theology of New England.

On the top of one bookcase I came upon a dog about to leap at me. I put one hand before my face and aimed the other at its teeth to tempt its bite before I might, if I were strong and fast enough, snap its neck. I kept from crying out through so strong a desire to preserve my solitude that I would rather be bit of than rescued. And by whom? Jimmy, my protector, was too distant now and in his grandpa's grasp, where he belonged, and was, besides, my ward. And Simeon Vear would love to watch me eaten, as I would him, a sign of what I took to be our mutual affection.

As I waited to be set upon by the snarling beast, I found it strange to be so peaceful and so thoughtful and so safe. He stood there quite the same, the sort of vengeful god who never states his purpose. My heart was quick but my hands were steady, and I put one in his mouth and felt his teeth all the way to the back and put the other on his forehead and down his neck and even after I realized he was mounted and quite as dead as he looked alive, I whispered, "Good dog, good dog," to what was clearly now a wolf.

He was so perfectly preserved, he made a case for beauty in death.

I felt he passed his bygone stealth to me as I walked on. But not his intelligence. I assumed all sleeping quarters must be on the upper floor, access to which I had not yet discovered, for there seemed to be no staircase. But there was, I found, in the northeast corner of the house, what would have been a bedroom had it walls but was certainly a sleeping quarters nonetheless. There was a small bed in the corner, pressed into the meeting of the two stone walls, which must give off a welcome coolness in summer nights but force the bed away in winter, if but an inch or two toward the fire in the middle of the house. Even now, in June, it kept a woolen blanket, red worn frail to russet, pulled up to two pillows. One was small and hard and decorative; on it had been embroidered a dictum and its source: SCHOLARS SHOULD NOT CARRY THEIR MEMORIES TO THEIR BALLS.—RALPH WALDO EMERSON. The other was thin and worn down from sleep. There was a head thereupon or, more accurately, therein—an indentation within the feathers and upon the ticking, and I thought it might be Ethan's and put my hand into that scoop of dream and time, first palm up and then palm down. Aside from what I might have felt of him upon the skin of Una, this would be my first touch of something I could be certain he had touched. I took delight that it should be his head, that most innocent and beautiful of parts, and so felt all the more foolish when I removed my hand and discovered wrapped around two of its fingers a long white hair. I was not at all repulsed, for I found Simeon Vear quite beautiful, in the way of an outcast patriarch, but I was certainly disappointed. Corroboration, such as it was, came in the form of a bedstand that held a gas reading lamp, a tin ashtray and butts of Viceroy cigarettes squashed until the paper split, a volume of Nathaniel Hawthorne's *American Notebooks* and R. W. Emerson's *Journals and Miscellaneous Notebooks*, and a double folding frame that held a photograph of a woman I didn't recognize and facing her a photograph of Una, a few years younger than she was now, or if not of Una—for except in indescribable beauty and transparent eyes it did not so much resemble her as embody her spirit—then Una's sister. I reacted jealously, not to Simeon Vear's possession by his bed of an image of his grandson's mother, but to Una's possession of a sister, whether she had one or not, for I was her sister now. Yet I didn't think to store this up and face her with it later. I enjoyed that spike of greed within my blood. I'd not been jealous before. It seemed a passion almost miraculous in its ambiguity. A thunderhead of love and hate exploded in the brain. I was, for a moment, almost dizzy with confusion. And what if this were Una herself and not her sister? Then I would be possessive of what I already had. And thus, I supposed, like everybody else—never a condition to which I had aspired.

In moving from the bed, I kicked the old man's bedpan, which told me what else, from the kitchen water pump, I might have guessed about the house's plumbing. It was empty, as was also to be expected: he lived not like someone who lived alone but with a consideration of the consequences of disorder. By his own admission, he shared his house with a ghost. There could be no more exacting companion. Even one who was invisible, or did not exist at all.

Nearly in despair of finding a way up into the top of the house and thus at least to the room that had held Una and Ethan so intimately if not to Ethan himself, alive or dead, I sat down on his old father's bed and thought of where Ethan might be in relation to where I was now. I realized he would want his father to be as far away from him as I wanted mine from me. I nearly ran, then, from one pool of windowlight to another, until I reached the opposite end of the house and saw, just as I recalled Una's mention of having climbed a long ladder to get to Ethan's attic room, the end of a thin, bristly rope. It was high enough off the floor to seem an invitation to a hanging, or to the ringing of a bell like that in Reverend Treat's Congregational church. Its other end was lost in space and darkness.

I had to find a chair to reach its ballish knot. I pictured Ethan stretching for it with his feet on the floor and gauged his height as that much greater than mine as I grasped the rope just above the knot and left the chair with both feet and hung for a happy moment gibbeted before I felt my hands burned by the rope and the rope itself moving with my body down to earth.

Out of the ceiling way above unfolded a ladder. Section by section it walked down toward me until its last piece settled just outside my feet and the rope lay coyly snaked upon the floor.

Without hesitation, but with a keen sense that I might be climbing into my own future, I grasped the sidepieces and put one foot upon a rung and the other upon the next and slowly made my way into the darkness above.

A faint light came through the rectangle in the ceiling into which the ladder would nestle when it was gathered back up. This light increased as I approached; it was sunlight, filtered to a weak silver by old window glass and by the distance this light had crawled along the attic floor and mostly by time itself, which, I sensed, had accumulated in that space for the decade and more since Una had abandoned Ethan.

When I finally reached that hole between thick beams in what was both ceiling and floor, I hesitated a moment in the hope that an arm, a hand, might come down through it to take my own arm, my own hand, and pull me up. But I was not disappointed at being left alone. To find my own way. Ethan was alive or he was dead. What I desired was to learn the difference between the two.

The trapdoor opened at the end of a narrow hallway, not unlike that on the second floor of the Treat house, but much longer. There was one small window not far from where I'd poked my head into the attic. The other was, as I'd suspected, at the other end of the house. There were half-burned unlit candles in simple sconces along the walls. I couldn't tell from the texture of the dribbled wax or the stiffness of the wick or any scent from either how recently they might have burned. But the floor was clean, and the walls and sconces dusted, and I could find no cobwebs. There are certain absences that spell a presence. As well, there was, besides an attic's warmth from gathered sun, some other heat. I could feel him, whether he was there or not. I could feel at least the memory of him.

"Ethan." I left my knees and walked enough to stand within a patch of sunlight, just as I had stood with Una in my little room.

He failed to answer. Yet I knew he'd heard me call his name, even as I failed to feel his eyes upon me.

I departed from the light and felt it slowly give me up to that other light a house away and to the almost-darkness in between. Far along the corridor, I opened a door. On the floor and on tables and stands and shelves and hung from the ceiling on wires or strings, was a vast and crowded collection of animals and birds and fish and turtles and snakes. They were exquisitely preserved. Many of them enemies in life, now they were placid and neighborly. Even the quiver of arrows and the sinuous bow hanging on the wall could not unsettle them.

There was a great stillness in this room. Here were death and beauty mingled into one.

Or so I thought, and so I reveled in the tranquilness, until the moment I saw, in the back of the room, a movement of a creature or its shadow, heard a faint scrape or scratch and the intake of a breath that I could not distinguish from my own.

The next room was the last along the corridor. Its door was at an angle to the others and to the corridor wall. Una had told me in her confession of a corner attic room, wide and dark, where Jimmy was conceived and Ethan lived and where, I knew, I'd find him now, as I might have found her years before, a child in the animal room, carving her name in the wall.

I knocked.

I knocked again.

I called his name.

I entered.

The room's little window was not much bigger than my head either. Though the window was covered with a piece of black cloth, I could see the shape of the light through it, an angled frame that held a portrait with no features but those to be imagined.

Upon a small table in the middle of the room I found a candle, half adjourned, a box of matches at its side. The candle and its drippings gave no sense of when last it had been lit. Nor did I believe it had been left for me. Nor did I want to. For I'd rather it were his, and recent, and necessary for his eyes to see as mine did when I Iighted it.

The room was very large, taking up the full corner of this vast stone building. Yet there was nothing in it but for a bed no bigger than old man Vear's at the bottom of the house and a tall, shallow wardrobe and a single upholstered chair and, at the table, a simple ladderback chair. The chaos of clutter described by Una had been swept away; he had emptied his life as she had his heart. Even the little bed, when I ran my hand along it, said nothing of their common presence in its grip.

Ethan was nowhere to be seen. I thought to lure him out by opening the wardrobe, where I found no such plaid shirts as I'd envisioned but a single faded blue cotton shirt. Beside it was a pair of brown corduroy pants, worn almost smooth at the knees and seat but reinforced at those same places by fabric sewn inside. I opened the wardrobe's inner drawers and touched black T-shirts Una had described and his underclothes and socks and knelt to see a pair of black boots upon the floor and slipped my hand within one and felt my fingers slide into the leather melted by his toes.

I sat down at the table. It was nearly as small as the table in Emily's Amherst bedroom where she wrote her poems, but it was of rougher wood and was endowed by me less with the mystery of art than the mystery of love. I found in its drawer, among more matches and a metal ashtray and loose shreds of tobacco and a cork-stoppered glass vial filled with dust, a single pencil and a pad of paper.

There were tooth marks on the pencil where the wood was shaved away to disclose the lead. I put my teeth where his had been and my fingers on the shadows of his own.

I wrote a note whose words would surely bring him forth and left it with the candle burning at its side.

Emily, as if she had imagined my own experience, wrote of nature as I myself had experienced Ethan, a stranger yet in his haunted house, "floorless," even, who did not seem to touch the floor, a ghost unsimplified, as ghosts must stay or lose their stature. So did I pass his haunted house in leaving it.

Simeon Vear walked us out the door. He seemed pleased that I'd failed in my quest. "Any knocking on the wall?" he asked, making what he must have thought sly reference to our first conversation by Jimmy's grandma's gravehole in Greenwich Cemetery. He smiled beneath his hat, and the lines on his face deepened into beamish scars.

"No," I answered, "but where once there'd been a doorway now was covered up."

"I can't find him either," he conceded to both my metaphor and my memory. He threw his cigarette into the dry grass.

"Aren't you afraid of a fire?"

"Stone doesn't burn."

He walked us to the edge of his forest. "Say good-bye," I said to Jimmy.

"Don't say good-bye," Simeon Vear ordered him. He then bent slowly toward the boy and kissed his hair.

"Come back," he said.

"Who?" I asked.

"You." He surprised me.

"Look!" Jimmy pointed at the ground. The trap we'd earlier

come upon was quivering. "It's sprung," he added, pleased to know and share the language.

"I'll say," said his grandfather.

"What do you think's in there?"

"Let's hope it's not a skunk." The old man held his nose and Jimmy laughed. "You check," he told the boy.

Jimmy knelt and opened the trap. "It's a Hoover hog!"

"Give it here," said Simeon Vear.

Jimmy started to pick up the entire trap.

"Just the animal."

Jimmy pushed his hand into the trap.

"Don't," I said.

"Let him," said Simeon Vear.

"Got him," said Jimmy.

He pulled the nervous rabbit out with one hand and immediately put his other hand around the rabbit's ribs. The rabbit moved its hind legs futilely against the afternoon air.

"I'm getting sick of rabbit." The old man touched his stomach through his suit coat. "Should we let it go?"

"No," said Jimmy.

Simeon Vear put his hands upon his grandson's and swung the boy around until the rabbit's head was dashed against the nearest tree.

"It's cleaner when you drown them," said the old man, whose hat had flown off in his twirl so his long white hair veiled his face.

Jimmy looked at the blood on his grandfather's large hands, a mere speck or two of which had found his own. "But slower, I bet."

"Crueler too." Simeon Vear smiled and tucked the rabbit under his arm, careful to let the head loll free to keep his coat dry. "Now say good-bye."

"Good-bye, Mr. Vear," said Jimmy. "Thanks for the rabbit. Food," he added and laughed.

"Don't forget," the old man said to me.

I watched him walk back toward the house. The dead rabbit swung nonchalantly from his hand, trailing cigarette smoke from its lolling head.

"Come on," said Jimmy, taking my hand to pull me toward home.

I waited until Simeon Vear closed the door. Only then did I let my eyes travel up the house. The black cloth was gone from the window at the top, in the corner. And now the window was a face, made faintly golden by candlelight. I thought for a moment it was Una's face, for it had her shape. But his hair was short now, and his eyes were dark enough for me to see them, even at that distance, dark, and they looked into mine with such hatred that I closed them so he would not see my delight.

Jimmy and I kept our secret, or so I thought, for the next week or more, as summer with its "torrid Noons" settled into the Swift River Valley and we as a family assumed a ritual of lessons and meals and books and walks and talks and silences and the music of the church bell, which rang more often now that I had asked for lessons in its ringing and Reverend Treat provided these with enthusiasm, as if he'd found an acolyte.

He was more relaxed and certainly more voluble since he'd interrupted my bath. We never spoke of this, but like all significant events between people, it had entered our mutual gaze. He possessed me now, as far as he was concerned. I, however, was the proprietor of this holding.

Yet I was unprepared for his summoning me as I was doing the supper dishes. We did not meet at night. His early evenings he spent with Jimmy, reading him a book or playing checkers or listening on the radio to news of wars or to *Dr. Christian* or *The Green Hornet* or even, in the long twilights, throwing a ball back and forth out behind the church. His moral steeliness dissolved when his boy approached, and whatever burden he'd assumed in remaining here to flock the others out he dropped for Jimmy and allowed himself the privilege of unconcealed devotion. And once he'd put Jimmy to bed, Reverend Treat withdrew into the night-locked church to work on his Sunday sermon. I was not allowed to see him in his attempts to reconcile not merely the ways of man to God and God to man but the far less scrutable ways of man to man. This meant that he bade me good night soon after he'd done so with Jimmy. I was usually with Una in the parlor, or still in the kitchen, the two of us, and he would come in and say, "Good night, Sarianna," and whatever flush he might have gained from playing with or merely being with Jimmy would already have begun to turn into a kind of ashen mask. Una called it his "wrestling with freedom" face, though never to it; what I believed she meant was not so much freedom as free will, that he might solve the paradox of his perplexingly beloved Luther whom he'd quote as having said that a Christian is a perfectly free lord, subject to none, as well as a perfectly dutiful servant, subject to all. Jeremy Treat wanted to believe in that very freedom of the will that Jonathan Edwards used as the title of his work in which he proclaimed that human beings are free. But where was freedom *here*, in the valley? Where was freedom in a land that would be wiped forever from the face of the earth? He felt the waters closing in upon him, and upon his ever-diminishing flock. To me the flood was its own brilliant paradox, which would both cover what we were and did and raise us high for all to see as it carried us away upon its meridian waters.

In summoning me from the kitchen he did not also beckon Una. Yet she came along without a word, which led me to suspect she knew of this and thus it was a plan between them. This furthered my satisfaction, that I should be both taken up by the two of them and plotted upon in what privacy they shared in my absence.

When we entered the parlor they waited for me to sit and then took seats on either side of me. I might have reached out my hands to each of them and formed a little chain of the sort Emily imagined wrapped around so dangerous a dissenter as herself behind herself, concealed. But we did not hold hands, and I, while I hoped to be growing into the kind of woman who would prove complex enough to replace transparency with ambiguity if not mystery, had nothing to conceal, or nothing that I would.

I looked at her, and then at him. "Have I done something wrong?"

"Jimmy tells us . . ." he began.

"That you took him to the Vear house." Una continued her husband's accusation, for that's what it was and that's what I wished it to be.

"Not so," I said.

"Jimmy's too young to make up such a thing."

"Lying is an art," I told him, "and you'd better hope your child has a talent for it."

"This from his tutor!" huffed the Reverend.

"I meant no criticism," I replied. "He *does* have a talent for it."

"That isn't what Jeremy meant, Sarianna," Una interceded.

"Really?" I was purposefully disingenuous.

But they were not eager to attend my sporting.

"It is you who is lying," he said.

"I don't yet have that art," I confessed. "But I do for the truth.

And it's this: it was Jimmy who took me to the Vear house, not I who took him. How could I? I didn't know the way."

"So you admit . . ." began the reverend.

"I admit I know the way now." I saw it in my mind, the way geography shrinks to a thought and landscape to a painting on the brain. I could even smell Mount Zion's sweet decay, feel the as yet unstrangulated Swift River running in my blood. I could see myself returning along those roads and paths and through that forest and fought even now, as I sat between these two whose unwitting help I would command to deliver me there, to restrain myself from immediate return.

"It doesn't matter who took who." Una calmed her husband by taking one of his hands in both of hers. "What matters is . . ." She knew what mattered. That's why she said no more. She too knew the way.

"Why did you go there?" he asked with a kind of wary sadness.

"Because you told me not to?" I asked playfully.

"I might, had I thought you might go, have told you not to take *him*. As for yourself, you're a free woman."

"Thank you," I said, doubly pleased to be so christened.

"Why, then?" he asked again.

"I wanted to meet Ethan Vear."

"How would Sarianna know of Ethan Vear if not through you?" he asked his wife, with none of the anger in his voice that the words themselves might be understood to contain.

"Perhaps from Simeon Vear." I came to the rescue of my friend.

"Stay away from the Vears!" he said with the constrained puissance I had come to recognize as his charming means of putting forth authority in an ungovernable world.

"You are full of proscriptions, Jeremy."

Una was so taken with my imitation of herself that she left him and leaned upon me, head on my shoulder, as she looked back at him. "You *are*," she said. "And it wasn't Simeon. It was me."

"You needn't," I told her.

She ignored my protection. "So did you?" she asked.

"No," I said. "But I did see him."

"*See* him!" She pushed away and looked into my face as if she might find him in my eyes.

Her husband took her back from me. He held her from behind with great care. He whispered so his words would not break her. "If she saw anything, it was his ghost."

"All the better."

"What do you mean?" He was surprised by her ease with this.

"He's there and not there."

One might have thought she had visited him herself. "Like God," I said to Reverend Treat.

"God is not a ghost," he said.

"Because all ghosts were once alive," I answered. "I *did* see him."

"God?" he provoked me in return.

"If God might be said to be a face in a window."

"Which window?" asked Una, who knew which window.

When Una and I were alone, and she was helping me finish the dishes I'd been forced to abandon for our little meeting, I asked her if he'd chewed his pencils.

"He did!" She put her finger near her mouth. "But not where most people do. He—"

"Right near the point," I said.

She put her fingertip in her mouth to demonstrate. Where I

might have found her jealous of my inquiry and quest, I discovered only rapt collaboration. So I told her what I'd written with his pencil and left, unsigned, on his table:

UNA SENT ME

She dropped the plate she was drying, fortunately with the dishcloth beneath it. When she raised the plate from the floor, shocked but unbroken, her hand was trembling, whether over the fallen dish or the revelation of my note could not be told.

"But I . . ." she began.

"But you *did*."

She had. And I convinced her.

"I'm your way back to him," I concluded. "You knew that. You enticed me with him for yourself."

She believed me because it was true or because I'd made it true by saying it. She confessed with her body, which leaned ever so slightly toward my own as we stood together at the sink, washing and drying, two women who by cleaning up remade the world, however minutely, one of them touching her arm to the other's.

"What would I do with him?" she asked.

"Nothing."

"Did you actually see him?"

"You told me his hair was long. He must have cut it."

"His hair?" She touched her own.

"Otherwise he looked like you."

"Then he must have grown less beautiful."

"Or you more."

" 'Nothing?' " she responded belatedly.

"What would *you* do?" I gave her question back.

"Give him to you," she replied, embracing me.

*   *   *

But if Una had been right in saying we women lay traps with ourselves as bait, and if she were my bait and I were hers, it was Ethan who set the trap for us.

Jimmy came in out of the afternoon heat with a piece of paper in his hand. He gave it to his mother. We were together drinking iced tea at the kitchen table.

She looked at the paper and pushed it toward me with an expression of amused expectation. "I think this is yours."

I read it:

UNA SENT ME

"Where did you get this?" I asked Jimmy.

"A man gave it to me."

"Did you recognize him?" asked Una, as if Jimmy might suddenly realize he'd met the man she claimed to be his true father and she might fly free of the burden of this secret.

"No," he answered, and I knew for myself it had been Ethan and not his father who'd insulted me with the return of my note. It had brought him forth, yes, but with a transfer of power I'd not anticipated from a creature so withdrawn that he would creep invisible from room to room in his perdu attic firmament and gaze out at the world.

"What did he look like?" Una asked her son.

Jimmy took off his baseball cap and ran his fingers through his sun-seethed hair. "How should I know?"

"Didn't you see him?"

"Yeah, but I didn't look at him."

"Why didn't you look at him?"

"It's not polite. Can I have a cookie?"

"That's not polite either."

"Please can I have a cookie?"

I handed him a cookie. "What did he say?"

"What, are you his mother now?" said Una.

"Then you ask him," I said.

"I meant about the cookie," she explained.

I grabbed the cookie out of Jimmy's hand.

"Hey!" He looked about to hit me with the other hand, but he would never.

"I didn't mean for you to take it back." Una took me by the wrist and pushed my hand back toward Jimmy's mouth.

He bit into the cookie while it was still in my hand.

"Take the rest," I said.

He shook his head triumphantly, and smiled, cookie dust and crumbs falling from his lower lip.

So I ate it myself and loved his little frown of disappointment.

"What *did* he say?" asked Una.

"He told me to give it to you."

"To *me*?"

"To *her*. That's what he said. 'Give this to her.'"

"So why did you give it to me?"

"Because your name is on it?"

"You read it?"

"Wouldn't you?"

She shook her head by way of agreeing she would. "What did he sound like?"

"What do you mean, what did he sound like? How do I know what he sounded like? What difference does it make?" Jimmy most disdained his mother's interest at the same moment he became interested himself, not in the man but in his mother's interest in the man. He looked at her as if she might have secrets from him, some hidden life of her own, and he was at once appalled and beguiled.

"What *did* he sound like?" I asked.

"Not you too!" Jimmy hit the table with his baseball cap. "Hey, maybe I should have given it to *you*."

"Why do you say that?"

"You think I don't know your handwriting by now? I knew it was you who wrote on that side of it. You said my mother sent you somewhere."

Una and I heard as one what he'd said. Our hands went together to the piece of paper and together turned it over.

i do not exist

"I told you he was weird," said Jimmy, taking a cookie on his way out.

I do not exist. How different this was from what was written by Mary Wollstonecraft, with whose life I'd once become schoolgirlishly intrigued perhaps because in the assertion of her passions her life was itself so different from Emily's even as she wrote a line that might have been Emily's: "Forget that I exist."

How much more profound, then, was Ethan Vear than Mary Wollstonecraft! He who by writing *I do not exist* establishes its very opposite, nonetheless proclaims the opposite of this very evidence of his existence. Have any four words ever better defined our condition? We do not exist for all eternity except for such moment in time as artists take to portray what Ethan puts in words: *I do not exist.*

So it was with this valley. It did not exist, even as we stood in its midst. So the earth itself. So the universe whose end was perhaps the only thing agreed on by scientists and theists. Everything, and everybody, was in the process of disappearing. This was the word used by Emily's sister, Vinnie Dickinson, when a fever ended their nephew, Gilbert's, "happy, brilliant life" in his eighth year and Vinnie informed some friends, "Little Gilbert has disappeared."

I pressed my hand against Ethan Vear's words. I tried to feel him upon the paper, some warmth or coldness, it didn't matter, life or death, there was no difference if no difference could be told. But I felt nothing, not him, not the words themselves.

"Did he write this?"

Una snatched the paper from my hand. "Not if he doesn't exist."

"I mean, is it his printing?"

She looked at mine on one side and his on the other. She knew enough to hand the paper back to me. "How did he know Jimmy to give it to him?"

"He must have seen him out the window."

"Do you think he recognized him?"

"As what?"

"Ours." She gave me a look of expectation that sometimes came upon her face, to signal such surprise as now she served: "Yours and mine."

I wondered if they'd had me here to take their son away. Not out of the valley, or even out of their home, but out of themselves, who loved him enough to know they must one day release him from that love. I may have made it my goal to teach him how to leave his parents, but perhaps this had been their goal in hiring me. Many a teacher is the blade that severs a child from his childhood.

Jimmy asked to see the dams go up. It was apparently not the first time. Jeremy Treat had little interest in these eternal monuments to temporality and resented, as I knew, those who came from the outer world to see these barriers rise to seal us upon the past. But now he had me to interpret the future. He said to Jimmy, "Let's take Sarianna."

Jeremy put me next to him in the car. Jimmy wanted to sit between us, where there was room if he would keep his long legs out of the paths of the gearshift, but his father told him to get in the back. He did without protest and leaned forward as we drove, one hand on my shoulder and one on his father's.

This was the first time we'd gone south from Greenwich. As if he could detect my anxiety, and could see my footsteps in the road on my way to him, though I'd never told him what road I'd taken, Jeremy followed another route back in the direction from which I'd come. So we went south on East Street instead of on the state road.

Along the shores of Quabbin Lake we saw the remains of summer camps. Some of these, Jeremy said, had been built as late as 1922, though as early as 1895 the *Ware River News* had reported that the Massachusetts Board of Health had suggested taking the Swift River Valley and in 1909 the Metropolitan Water Board had without the public's knowledge sent engineers and lawyers into the valley.

"I wasn't born yet," I professed my innocence and brandished my youth.

"Nor conceived," he added.

"Have you memorized me, Reverend Treat?"

He smiled much too privately and found safety in referring back to those summer camps built even as the discontinuation of the valley was being considered in Boston. "Maybe they thought if they stuck a bunch of kids here in the summer months telling ghost stories at night and diving off rafts in the sunny afternoons, the state would relent. It's like the Chinese holding up their babies in Hopeh and Chahar and Tientsin and Hangchow. Innocence doesn't deter; it incites."

"What babies?" I asked.

"The Japs stick them on their bayonets," Jimmy informed me.

"Japanese," his father instructed him.

"You should stop listening to the radio," I said.

"We can't keep the world out of here," his father defended both of them.

"Why not?" I answered. "The world's evicted us."

"It's our land the world's evicted. And it's our land that's evicted *us*. We'll be squeezed out into the world whether we like it or not."

"I don't like it," I said, "but you do, don't you?"

"I can't wait."

Was this why he suffered so, driven by desire to engage the very world his savior had died to save and failed in both?

All that was left of the camps were some resilient white buoys in the lake's waters. Paths still visible in the slash from the previous year's leveling of the woods led from one emptiness to another, ending abruptly where once there must have been tents and mess halls and crafts buildings and outhouses. The children who'd laid them and walked them had perished as surely as if they'd died. I listened for their cries in this same hot summer air as they had cried into. All I heard was the sun thrumming.

I thought of how Emily had written of doom as the house without the door, entered from that sun, and then of how Simeon Vear had told me of Hawthorne's covered doorway from behind which came mysterious knocking—and I saw the world as they did, as a vast tomb in which the living join the dead, at birth. And there's the sun, seared into the lid of our little world, illuminating all our limitations. Perhaps freedom grew with recognition of constraint. The more contained you are, the more powerfully you explode.

Jeremy put his hand on Jimmy's on my shoulder and kept it there as we rode down to the dams.

There were three miles between the dams. So great were the amounts of equipment and numbers of men required in their construction that men and machines spread nearly the whole distance from the one dam in the east to its big sister in the west, filling the air with dirt and dust and the grinding of gears and the gasps of hydraulics and the hollering of the voices of men over those of their dredges and compressors and impellers and windlasses. Trucks moved across the gutted land in disorderly convoys, carrying what amounted to the guts themselves, since the earth to be used for the dams' high embankments came from the earth around the dams, which was bitten off in ragged chunks by steam shovels and dumped into these trucks when the steam shovels' creaky jaws dropped in what each time looked like surprise. Railroad tracks ran raised above the ground to allow for the dumping of the muck brought up from the giant open trench dug out well below the level of the surrounding waters. Conveyor belts coiled the sides of the dams, their buckets grave on the way up and waggling almost idiotically on the way down, signaling that only the empty-headed might find life tolerable. Everywhere were ramshackle buildings, large and small, all without foundations, used to house the workers and feed them and harvest their waste and to provide power for the machines. There were blasting shacks for munitions and blacksmith shops specifically for sharpening the drills used to reach the bedrock to which concrete caissons had been sunk before they were filled so that upon them earth might finally be placed when the dams were completed. Already they were high, more than a hundred feet each, and growing as we watched. They were no longer God's hands. God is visible only at a distance. This close to anything, where the brush strokes show, the true maker is revealed. This, I think, is what Emily meant when she wrote that either Heaven was seeming greater or earth a great deal more small. Man, not God, is in the details. Men did this.

They were everywhere, spread over the land. We drove among them, if on the outskirts of the works, from the dam at Beaver Brook—though it was called a dike because it lacked a spillway—to the greater structure in the west with its forty caissons sunk into the bedrock that would be almost three hundred feet below the top when all was done.

There we walked among the engineers and workers whom Jeremy addressed with questions about the making of the dams and whose answers he intended for Jimmy's benefit though they were as much for mine, since I too was interested in the pith of things. I noticed how, when men saw Jeremy's collar and his dust-dappled black suit and hat and the way he carried himself obdurate and confident among those who were erecting these vast headstones upon his valley's grave, they became obedient and careful. They stopped in their labor and paid him respect with their answers to his questions and attention to his wiry, exuberant son and, he made sure, to me, whom he introduced only by name so that I might be anyone to him and thus a mystery to them, which Jeremy enjoyed, I could tell, from how he watched them try to look at me without betraying their curiosity.

It was while we were being told about the strange gray rain of concrete-wrung water that ran down the sides of the dam that Jimmy said, "There he is."

"Pay attention," ordered his father.

"Who?" I asked Jimmy, though I knew who.

"The man," he answered.

"What man? I don't see a man." Jeremy played the biblical rhythm of this line to try to bring Jimmy's attention back.

"The man who gave me the note."

"What note?"

"The note for Mom."

"Oh, that." Jeremy did not look away from the engineer who himself kept pointing at the conveyor belts carrying concrete up the dam even as he said, "I'd best leave you folks to your . . ." and hurried away.

Once again I'd underestimated their bond. Una seemed to share most everything with her husband.

Then he yielded: "Where is he?"

"There." Jimmy pointed into the crowd of men that stretched across the landscape like the figures in Pieter Bruegel's *Procession to Calvary*.

I didn't see him. I couldn't find him. "Where?"

"There." Jimmy enjoyed his sovereignty. His finger found no one, so I followed his eyes.

Ethan stood before me, for the first time. His face in the window might have been a painting, solemn and still with nothing moving upon his features but the panting light of the candle I'd lit. Now he was whole, if distant still, lost in the sun's luster and in the gray and brown dust of dried concrete and earth and among the men and trucks that slid by him like scrim on a stage so that he appeared and disappeared in light and darkness. Thus I saw him flickering in the air, tiny against the rising dam behind him but magnified for me, so distinct was he in those moments when he was visible. I imagined him reaching easily above me, as Jeremy did upon the bell rope, to grasp the knotted ball and pull the ladder down so we might climb into his old stone house. He was neither boy nor man but somewhere between, light on his feet even as he stood in one place, grave in the burden his body placed upon his surroundings. He seemed on the verge of disappearance or abduction, here and not here and in that way quite the ghost, not of someone dead but of someone much alive. So alive, in fact, that I felt him move, not that he did actually move, but I felt him move across this expunged ground and enter me. He claimed no possession, nor did I yield it, but I felt him join me and take root in me.

"It's Ethan Vear," I said.

"Impossible."

"He cut his hair," I said futilely.

"I would recognize him."

"So you don't?"

He looked up. I followed his gaze. He didn't see Ethan, but I did for one moment more. He was nearly hidden by the dust and the machinery and overalls and helmets and the grinding pounding gushing noise of this manufacture of these walls that I knew would become the exalted barriers of our world.

"He isn't dead," I said.

"Yes he is."

"How do you know?"

He put his lips to my ear, as I had to Una's and she to mine. "I killed him."

I did the impermissible. I interrupted Reverend Treat as he worked on his sermon.

That night was cloudy, starless, moonless. The humid air had drunk the darkness. It hung from hills to ground in blinding drops. I found my way only by following the shallow path worn by the reverend's fine black shoes from the back door of the parsonage to the front of the church. From the outside, the church was black within. But inside there was a glow of light from the pulpit. I followed it down the aisle, touching the rotting pews with the backs of my hands. Even before I reached him, and before he could have seen me in the darkness, he said, "It's about time."

I found him standing at his broken-down pulpit with a candle at its rim. His strong face floated, ashen, in the shaft of pallid light. None of that light had yet reached me.

"Do you know who I am this time?"

"I recognize your hand upon the door. I recognize your footsteps. I recognize your breathing."

"And you were waiting for me?"

"Not waiting. Anticipating."

"Am I that easy to understand?"

"You're not easy. Simple."

"I'm flattered."

I was simple the way it was said Emily's poetry was simple: short lines, brief verses, common words. But the poems, whole—great mysteries the way we all are mysteries, even to ourselves, and spend our lives looking for the one who can read us.

He laughed in church. Even when he'd show me how to ring the bell and I'd thunk the clapper hollowly and laugh with embarrassment, he wouldn't. Now he did. "I take it back," he said. "Anyone flattered at being called simple can't be all that simple. But of course the simplest things are often the most difficult to understand."

"Like God," I said.

"Like you. Come here."

I walked into the light and wished I were Una, to surprise him. He did flatter me with his boasts of recognition, not that he could know me but that he would so pretend. Yet I would prefer to show him wrong and to become the one I knew he would betray.

He had papers before him on the pulpit. He didn't bite his pencil like Ethan but nonetheless had a worrying habit taken out as writers do upon the instrument of their creation. He strangled his pencil beneath his middle finger and upon the tops of his other fingers, until it snapped in two. He then would write with the jagged half and save the other for sharpening. Thus were his pencils short, and even these he sometimes fractured. I had seen their remains along the walls and in the corners of the church, unworded and ashamed.

"Would you like to hear my sermon?"

"No."

He put his hand behind his ear. "You prefer to hear it through the wall of your room?"

If he thought to shame me, instead he pleased me. "Much," I answered. And added: "It appears there's even more about me you recognize."

"I see the light beneath your door," he explained.

"And I the light beneath yours."

"It's the same door, Sarianna."

"No it *isn't*," I insisted. He understood. Every door, like every person, opens into separate rooms. Every door protects the truth it violates.

"One might almost write a sermon about *that*," he conceded gracefully.

"Instead of?" I touched his papers.

"Sin." What is there about that word that makes men fleer?

"The woman who taught us poetry at college said we should write only about what we know."

"In that case, *you* should write my sermon."

I demurred. "You can't get someone to sin simply by calling

her a sinner. And she was wrong—the greatest writing is about what's unknown and discovered *through* the writing. So maybe I *should* write your sermon."

"You who know nothing about sin," he said sarcastically. "So tell me: do you think sin is what Jonathan Edwards called it—a property of the species?"

"No more than virtue," I answered.

He moved the candle closer to me. "You have a future."

"As what?"

"What would you like to be?" he asked.

"A poet," I said without hesitation. "Isn't that what everyone wants to be?"

He smiled over my naïveté. "I was thinking more along the lines of a cynic."

"But I'm a romantic!" I protested blithely.

"Una's a romantic," he said. "You're more the realist, for all your youth and poetry. Una's not well—romantics never are. Have you noticed? My wife is not well."

"Is she ill?" I knew nothing of illness. I was of an age of which it was said we think ourselves immortal, when childhood has met maturity and the two combine to heat the blood to the temperature of thoughtless, endless rapture.

"Haven't you noticed anything peculiar about Una?" He chose that moment to lift the candle from the pulpit with one hand and with the other to take my arm and walk me into the forlorn body of the church until we reached the front pew. It was the first I could remember his touching me directly and not through Jimmy or Una, both of whom until that moment had seemed to mediate his contact with any flesh but their own.

We sat. He placed the candle between us, so that the trembling barrier of its light might protect me from his scheming, or at least my notice of his scheming. He meant for me to think her mad, and wrong, when what drew me toward her, once her simple charm had satisfied my simple advent, was her fetching instability, her inviolable frailty.

"What do you mean by peculiar?" I answered finally. "I'm an innocent, Reverend Treat. I'm a girl. I have no experience of people. The people I know best are Emily Dickinson and Elizabeth Barrett Browning and Mary Wollstonecraft and . . . so . . . no. I don't find Una peculiar. No one's peculiar except to those who judge her so."

He had turned away to listen to my little speech, looking toward his pulpit as hidden in the dark as was his incomprehensible God. But when I finished, he turned back toward me.

"I had you brought here for her. Not for Jimmy. For her."

"So I might teach her *what*?"

"She's a child," he answered. "She can be taught anything. She has no control. Her affections are unruly. She loves too much and has too little to love. She loves without constraint. She loves eternally."

"How did you kill him?"

He was pleased I'd taken his reference. "I killed him by marrying her." He pronounced the sentence quietly, as if it had not been quite the manly way to do it.

"Ethan Vear died of love?"

He shook his head, which hovered deified above his invisible black coat in the shallow pool of candlelight. "He died of loss of love."

"She loves eternally," I reminded him.

"Exactly my point," he said. "Free her of him."

"I thought he was dead."

"Not to her."

"Poor man," I said. "He came to your wedding."

"Hovering like an angel at the back of the church—I know what she says. But he wasn't there. No one else saw him. He was dead by then."

"Dead to you, perhaps."

"And dead to you, Sarianna."

"I saw him at the dams."

"That wasn't Ethan."

"How do you know?"

"I've seen his grave."

Now he was triumphant. He rose from the pew. He extended his hand. He said, "Come ring the bell with me."

I gave him my hand. He led me like a child to the rope. He placed his hands upon mine on the rope.

"It's the middle of the night," I said. "Who do we ring for in the middle of the night?"

"At night we ring to wake the dead," he said.

And so we did.

We woke the dead. And Una too.

I found her in bed, having dozed off, apparently, in waiting for Jeremy to come to her from his nightly struggle in the church.

This night was so humid, the air so saturated with heat and darkness, that Una lay in a fog of candlelight, her nightgown above her knees and off her shoulders. Her hair floated wet and heavy. Her skin threw off her body's shape in light.

"The bell," she whispered.

"Are you awake?"

"Am I?"

"Can you get up?" I held out my hand.

"Jeremy?"

"Sarianna."

"You," which she might have said to either of us.

"Put on some clothes," I said.

"Where are we going?"

"Let's go see Ethan," I said as nonchalantly as if he were someone we met for a frappe every now and then.

"Really?"

She rose without my help. She removed her nightgown, slowly, because the moisture on her skin restrained it. Finally, both arms were raised above her head, tangled in the sleeves. She looked like one of the headless Fates, relieved of drapery.

"I can't get out." Her voice was cheerful about her predicament.

I reached up and pulled at the hem of nightgown and stepped back until it was off her all the way to her wrists, which she held out to me and we might have been dancing, one of us naked and the other not.

While she dressed, I got the flashlight from my room. It proved of little use outdoors, because the air refused the light, as it did the light from the headlights of her car, which reflected back at us and made it seem there was a car whose lights we followed when they were our own. We were our own protectors and our own deceivers both.

The fog was so thick on Kelly Hill Road that we went past the turnoff on Clifford Road and ended up on Doubleday Road and had to double back on Egypt Road.

"Where are we?" Una kept saying.

I knew the landscape better than she. I kept my head out the window and could sometimes see my face in the wet glass of the air.

We couldn't drive through the Vear woods and so parked at their outskirts and walked. We held hands in the forest. I told her what Ethan had looked like standing before the dam, in what I realized were exactly the clothes she'd described him as wearing when he was fourteen years old—brown corduroy pants, a blue shirt almost drenched of color, open at the neck, black boots, and his hair was so short she said, "No." I hadn't been able to see him until I described him to her.

The moon remained hidden. We tried to use the flashlight, but all it brought were moths that skirmished for its light. Despite the darkness, the big house was visible from a distance, not from any glow in its small windows but because it interrupted the invisible emptiness. It was a beast in this forest, breathing and smelling of pervious stone.

"This is your house," I told her.

"Stop. You'll make me cry."

I wondered if we should have carried Jimmy with us.

"Go in. Tell Ethan you're here."

"Not without you." She pulled me toward the wooden door.

"It's you he wants to see."

"Don't think I don't know that," she said to keep him for herself. "He spies on me."

I shined the flashlight toward his window at the top corner of the house. The light made a hose in the air that ended halfway up. "There he is," I said.

She squinted up the light. If she saw his window, it was only in her memory.

I put my hand against the huge wooden door and felt my fingers sink into the rents and notches scattered on its surface. But while I pictured such a siege as would have tried to chop and shoot through such a barricade as this, it yielded to my touch and creaked ajar and sang our entrance from its hinges.

Una chuckled. "I told them to oil it."

*   *   *

The old man was asleep in his bed in the back corner. The stone had kept the whole house cool, but the moisture in the air had come in, as water will and water would one day in torrents, through the smallest of pores and cracks and crevices, and down the wide, cold chimney, and so the house was damp and the beam of our light vaporous and the old man chilled enough to need his thin red blanket, which he held delicately in both huge hands beneath his chin as he faced the ceiling and his fine white hair fanned out over his pillow. I had never seen anyone this old asleep. I was relieved to see his nostrils bellow slightly and his eyelids quiver with such dreams as passed across their underside.

Una shook her head.

"What is it?" I whispered.

She didn't want to wake him. She merely pointed at him, in his bed in the corner, and shook her head again as she spread her arms wide to take the entire house in them. I knew what she signified: that he was exiled here where once he'd ruled the whole.

Which meant, to me, that someone, whether a ghost of his imagination or a living son, ruled him.

I let our light play on the table by his bed, dusting the books he seemed to love and settling on the double picture frame. I reached for it and picked it up and drew it toward us as I drew Una from the bed and let Simeon Vear sink back into darkness.

We looked at the photographs together. When she saw what might have been herself, she gasped.

"Who's that?" I asked, about the *other* woman.

"Elisha Vear," she whispered, distracted by what I would not yet let her discuss.

"His wife?"

She nodded.

"Dead?"

She nodded.

"Where . . . ?"

She looked confused.

". . . is she buried?"

She moved her eyes away, to the north.

"And this?" I finally asked.

"My mother," she said.

I raised the light so she would see my smile, and I smiled.

She didn't want to leave the house. There was her mother, long dead, whom she'd never seen alive, alive beside the bed of an old man sleeping. Una wondered, I thought, if he kept the picture there because it reminded him of her, whom it so resembled, or of her mother, whom he knew, Una realized, so much better than she herself could, though her mother's blood ran through her and her mother's face had been put upon her face.

"Come with me," I said, "and I'll tell you a secret."

"You don't have any secrets, Sarianna," she said with some satisfaction.

"Not my own," I answered, which caused her to relent, though she left the house reluctantly and looked to where we both knew the rope hung down.

"He isn't there," I said, to get her out the door.

It was the back door, smaller than the other but just as thick, locked from the inside by one of its several bolts, the only one that moved, the others having rusted.

"How do you know he isn't there?" she asked.

"I don't know," I said, because I didn't, and I was guessing, and I didn't want to take her back up to where she'd lived and to find him either sleeping or, worse, absent once again.

I hadn't seen this side of the house. She tried to point out for me, with the flashlight, a slightly larger window at the top, which would have been across from Ethan's room, and down from it, as she dragged the light that even in this mist could make out stone, a series of steps cut into the stones themselves.

"To escape from Indians," she said.

"What was to keep the Indians from climbing up then?"

"People with guns." She pointed an imaginary rifle at my knees. "We used to climb down here at night."

"And then what?"

"It didn't matter."

Only when we got to the little fence around the Vear family graveyard, deep in the forest beneath a canopy of leaves so thick that almost nothing grew upon the ground and thus few animals would visit and disturb the graves, did I tell her.

"Simeon Vear was in love with your mother."

"It runs in the family," she said, and walked into the graveyard.

There were Vears everywhere. They seemed to have been buried haphazardly, not in rows and not by time, not even by century, and not by age or even by love. Husbands and wives were widely separated, children were far from their parents, infants with their tiny horizontal markers lay alone. And yet, as Emily had put it, no moss had reached their lips and covered up their names, for all the stones were clean, of dirt and vegetation, and those so old that time would have rubbed out their marks and letters had been cut anew, their dates precise and visible, their angels and demons vivid, their stones erect.

"Here she is," said Una.

ELISHA VEAR
1884–1920
"The dead sleep in their moonless night—
my business is with the living."
—RALPH WALDO EMERSON

"Show me Ethan's," I said.
"Don't be ridiculous."
"Jeremy has seen it."
"There's nothing Jeremy would rather see."
"Why does he hate Ethan?"
"Why do you think?—because he loves me."
"And you love Ethan?"
"Wouldn't you?"

I found his marker. And with it, as I had hoped, him.

It was made of wood, not stone. It was rotting. It was the only marker in the cemetery untended. Dead autumn leaves had gathered at its base, where it strained out of the earth at an angle in what looked like an attempt to show its message to God:

ethan vear
died may 26, 1926
in his 15th yr.
by His own hand

When I looked up from the marker, there he was, standing behind it. I could see him even without the flashlight, and I didn't shine it on him because then he might be seen by Una as well. Una was elsewhere in the graveyard, waiting for me, refusing to search for what I'd found.

"Una." His voice was soft, pleading, supple. It was unlike any voice I'd ever heard. With that one sound, that one word, I felt him take hold of me.

"Una," he said again, not insistently, merely repetitively, as if it were the only word he knew and he used it as his language.

"Ethan," I begged.

"Where is she?"

"It's too late," I said.

"Who are you?"

"Sarianna."

"Leave me alone," he said. "Please leave me alone."

"I can't," I said.

"Then you know how it feels."

And I did, only at that moment did I. I felt tears come into me with the pain of their having been forced through my skin. I cried with none of the relief of crying. I cried without tears. I cried and the pain only grew.

He watched me. He was neither pleased nor distressed. I could feel his mistrust.

"I've never cried before," I sobbed stupidly.

"Neither had I," he said, and turned and walked away.

"Wait!"

I couldn't hear his footsteps. I couldn't find him with the flashlight even as the moonless night became extinct with a lifting of the fog.

"Una!" I called, not for me but to bring him back.

"Sarianna!" came her voice through the graveyard.

She had found her father.

His grave lay along an edge of the Vear family plot, as if he did not quite belong, even in death, to the family that had taken in him and his daughter.

His headstone had been incised by the same large hand that had etched Elisha Vear's:

MACKSWELL RYTHER
1870–10/28/1926
"The Unpardonable Sin"
—NATHANIEL HAWTHORNE

"My daddy's dead," she said, not unhappily. Perhaps death was to be preferred to abandonment. "I wonder what the unpardonable sin is."

"Leaving you," I comforted.

She put her arm around my shoulder and drew me to her. "Look—he died the very day Jimmy was born. I'm glad I didn't know."

She gazed into my face. "Your eyes are red. Are you crying?" She moved the side of her thumb first under one eye, then under my other. "No tears. You know what that's supposed to mean— the sadness you enclose exceeds the sadness you expose. But you didn't even know him. Look at me. I'm not crying. And he was my father."

"I saw *Ethan*," I explained.

She pushed me out to her arms' length. "Then you wouldn't be crying."

She refused to see his grave and wondered how I might have seen both it and him.

"Did he rise up out of it?" she asked.

"I couldn't tell."

"You should have asked him. He always told the truth."

"People don't rise up out of graves, if you want the truth."

"If I wanted the truth, I don't think I'd be talking to you, Sarianna."

"He thought I was you," I said to see what she might do with the truth.

"It must have been the fog." She laughed.

"He kept saying your name."

"It must have been the wind."

"There is no wind."

"My point exactly." She was quite pleased with herself.

"Come *with* me." I pulled at her.

"Do you think if he sees me with you he'll talk to you?"

"He did talk to me."

"I thought it was me he was talking to."

"I told him he was too late for you."

"Well, that's the first thing you've been right about."

"I thought you wanted to see him. Why did you come if you don't want to see him?"

"I don't want to see his grave, Sarianna—I don't want to know he's dead."

"But I *talked* to him."

Now she took my head in both her hands, her long fingers reaching down my neck, and pressed her thumbs gently upon my slightly swollen eyelids. "Don't you understand—I don't want to know that either. I don't want to know he's alive."

I thought he might follow us out. I thought he might spy on me too. But I could neither hear nor see him. The fog now was not so much lifting as being blown aside. The winds had come and took the forest in their paws but did not still the Universe; we were not raped by God as Emily had imagined being thus converted to His side. Indeed, the canopy above us shook, not in concert; a thousand separate arms slapped and scratched at one another. Cool air drove out the warm; sapless air replaced the moist and heavy. Our skirts were alternately lifted and blown between our legs. Our hair was danced. Our skin was swept. Our feet were roused.

"Isn't this glorious!" said Una in customary New England greeting of cool winds upon a smothering summer blanket. She shivered once and took my hand and pressed herself against my sleeve. I realized she chose me in my simple presence over the turmoil of a father dead and a lover in the elongating night shadows. She hadn't come with me to find Ethan. She'd come to find me.

The moon, revealed, was small in light, a peel of lemon floating in the sky. So it must have been the stars that lit the woods, almost to blazing, almost to blind, the stars so thick they took the night away.

The great stone house appeared before us flooded. The gathering of distant suns was called to serve this purpose: ignite the air around his home.

But inside it was dark. No light escaped a window. No face appeared to follow us out of the house's clearing and into the forest.

We drove back to Greenwich Village without the car's lights on. Starlight did not so much guide us as carry us upon it where it glazed the pitted roads.

I waited for another note from him. I made myself even more available to Jimmy, because I was certain Ethan would use him as his intermediary. But Jimmy brought nothing besides himself, and that was often, because he had no friends but me and wanted me to be his only friend. He clung to me, not as his mother did, leaning and holding on tight, but bouncing off me as we walked and stepping on my toes and hitting me constantly, gently, with the back of his hand, against my thigh or waist or the back of my own hand. I was never disappointed to see him, even though he brought no message. His was a refreshing love, as innocent as it was unconcealed, and I thought to learn from it as I felt that I was harboring a darker love, unspoken, unexpressed. Ethan had asked me to leave him alone, and that I was doing. But I'd made no such request of him and lit a candle in my window every night so he might find me.

Jimmy sat by me in church on Sunday and only there refrained from touching me. He was showing me how properly he could behave and God how well he could at least pretend to substitute rectitude for exuberance. His father called him up to sing and so he did, the solo in the hymn the rest of us were chorus to:

> God is my mountain, Him I climb
> To where the air is sweet.
> And if ascension is a crime
> No punishment He'll mete,
> For we are purified by death
> As cursed in our beginning
> Sure each of us with our first breath
> Begins a life of sinning.
> And when I reach the mountaintop
> Eternal life begins.
> For only God can make time stop
> And shrive my worldly sins.

Jimmy's voice had changed even in the weeks since I'd first heard it. It no longer resembled a girl's in its pitch nor an angel's in its purity. But it hadn't so much deepened as been closed in upon. It soared, still, particularly when the music called for it to ascend the mountain that was both God and death, but it did so with a rasp at its edges, an abrasion upon its innocence that made it all the more beautiful for being flawed. It was a voice in the process of destroying itself.

Una heard the difference too. As soon as Jimmy began to sing, her eyes quit the music propped up before her on the battered church piano and settled upon him as they might upon an intruder. She was frightened and curious. Her hands rushed the tempo, but Jimmy was stalwart and brought her back with the voice she watched as it fled his lips.

It was while the rest of us were singing the well-known chorus—"God is my mountain, God is my sea / God gave his only Son to purify me"—that Jimmy's right hand came up from his side and with a single finger pointed first at me, as if to get my attention, and then rose with my eyes upon it toward the back of the church.

There, in the shadows, stood Ethan.

He was framed by the door, seemed almost part of the door and to have come in through it, through it literally, because he was in near darkness back there, and I would have been aware of the light that limped down the center aisle of the church whenever the door was opened. He was barely visible. He was a shadow himself, cast by himself or by Jimmy, who stood directly between Ethan and Jeremy and absorbed the two of them within himself. Jeremy didn't see him. Ethan saw no one but me, if he saw me at all.

I wanted to get up and go to him, but not at the expense of privacy and of Una's feelings. I was equally driven to shield her from the sight of the boy whom she'd last seen at the back of another, dismantled church, on her wedding day.

I listened for his voice in the chorus. There were few enough of us in church for me to hear it, though I'd not heard him sing and his voice in the graveyard had been lost to me, no matter how I strained to hear it and could hear only my own voice in my head speaking as his, saying simple things, *Hello . . . I am Ethan. . . . I am alive. . . . Touch me. . . . I love you. . . .* and my name, *Sarianna, Sarianna, Sarianna,* over and over, not merely as I lay in bed at night but as I went about the day.

Jimmy, however, didn't hesitate to act upon his desires. His voice gave off his note of the last chord of the hymn while it still crumbled from the wiggly sustaining pedal of the church piano. Swiftly, he covered the space between the pulpit and the pews, and I smiled at him, as did a few of the others in admiration of his effort if not of his voice, and put my hand down on the bench next to me to mark his space.

He didn't stop. He walked up the aisle toward the back of the church. I turned my head to follow him. I was frozen with disbelief or would otherwise have joined him or restrained him. I felt he had overtaken me and that it was he, by his example, who was now cleaving me from my own childhood with its timidity and bookish languor.

Together, as we each looked at the back of the church—I from my pew at the front, he in rushing toward it—we realized that Ethan was gone.

And then, I saw, so was Jimmy, as if taken by the dusty light that held his shape, until the door of the church, in closing upon those of us left, feathered him away.

Una never saw him. Ethan, that is. Nor was she immediately concerned with Jimmy's swift departure. As she came from the piano to sit beside me, she whispered, as if I might not have noticed, "Jimmy left." She moved her face next to mine and giggled like a girl: "I think he was embarrassed—his voice is changing."

Then we sat together, the two of us, again proper ladies of the church, as Jeremy gave his sermon about sin. Once more, he invoked my presence and quoted admiringly what I'd said sarcastically about virtue as a property of the species. He argued against his own choice of hymn, "God Is My Mountain," in that he claimed we are no more born sinning than we are born righteous. It is for this reason, he said, that our sins are an affront to God. It is for this reason, he said, that God is abandoning the world—not our valley, which the world itself had abandoned and had thus preserved for God, but the world outside, the world of which each day we were less a part, where Austria had been conquered and annexed and now the synagogues of Munich and Dortmund and Nürnberg had been cast down, torn apart, flattened, bulldozed . . . and we were given an image of our own land, *our* towns, *our* houses, leveled, ravished. But God was taking refuge *here*—Jeremy raised his fist and brought it down upon the pulpit, in case any of us might doubt the place he meant—as Christ had always sought His place among the forsaken. As the world had worsened, our own little world had become the promised land. And the impending floodwaters, far from debasing our common home, would purify it. Those who remained—there were so few of us he seemed able to contain our presence within his hands now held above our heads in blessing—were the exalted, the sanctified. He begged us to stay and not forsake *him*. As long as we might stay, so would he.

I felt he was talking directly to me. Jeremy was engaged in a study of the world and had learned he must abandon it before he could inhabit it. I was engaged not in study but in experience, not of the world but of myself, and I had learned that I must inhabit myself before I might abandon myself. Each of us had come to understand that where we lived now was a sanctuary, the last place on earth in which sin might root. The war here was over. We had lost, and therefore we were free. We awaited the cleansing, and the closing over, of the flood.

It might as well have claimed Jimmy. He was nowhere to be found after the service, when first I stood with Una near the front steps of the church and later found Jeremy where each Sunday he wandered in the meadow out behind the church until everyone had gone and then he went back in the church to pray alone.

"Ethan was there," I told him.

"I know," he said in a concession to the boy's reality so surprising that I reached out for him as if he might *be* Ethan.

He gazed at my hand on his arm, the sun-brushed skin against the black of his sleeve. I wondered if he would put his hand over mine, to obliterate or protect it.

"You didn't see him." I didn't mind his knowing that I watched him closely enough to see with his eyes.

"I don't have to see him. He's always there."

"In the church?"

"Wherever Una is." Now he touched my hand, but only with a fingertip, tracing its fragile bones in such a way that I was chilled despite the heat of the swollen July sun.

"She didn't see him," I comforted him.

"She doesn't have to."

"I saw his grave." I realized I'd last given him my hand when he'd said the same thing to me in the church at night. I produced my own flesh when Ethan's came under threat.

" 'By His own hand,' " he quoted and only then released mine.

I returned with him to the church. Everyone was gone. I hoped to see Ethan and Jimmy together at the back, waiting for me. Or Jimmy alone, with a message from Ethan. Or Ethan alone. But only Jeremy and I stood by each other in that little church, which creaked when we knelt together, each on one knee, and Jeremy said, "Let me hear you pray, Sarianna," and I bowed my head and said, "God, forget that I exist."

It was when Jimmy failed to return home for lunch that they became frantic with worry. I'd not seen them like this. I observed how anxiety fed off partners in a marriage and drew them close even as it estranged them. Nothing they might say to each other brought reassurance.

Jeremy believed Jimmy had left to go back to the dams. Una believed Jimmy had left to go anywhere that was not the church, where he'd encountered his own voice announcing the death of his childhood.

His vacant place at the lunch table produced for them an image of him no less real than that of Ethan to me. He was present in his absence. There was scorn in his silence.

As for me, I ate my egg-salad sandwich and waited for them to realize, whether separately or as one, that I might have come to know him better than they and find him more quickly.

When they came to no such realization and I had finished my sandwich and was longing for a cookie and knew no polite way to secure one when they had barely touched their own sandwiches, I said, "I know where he is."

I didn't wait for an expression either of their consternation or their relief. I rose and took my plate from the table and brought it to the kitchen sink and took three cookies from the cookie jar on my way out.

*   *   *

I was within sight of the Vear house before I realized I'd never gone there alone. So often had I imagined returning that the journey had become in my mind a familiar one. I accomplished it without thought; the landscape was no longer a thing apart from me. In walking through it, I was walking through myself.

But now I was "standing alone in rebellion," as Emily had said of herself when she was but two years older than I. I had arrived without the protection of Jimmy or Una. I had emptied the world of influence and attachment. I was isolated in my freedom and my fear. Each step I took now was uncharted, each breath untried.

The house sat like a fist upon its hillock, grasping its secrets and inhibiting attack. As much for its perdurability as for its rigor, it was a frightening and unwelcoming structure. It stood in great contrast to the evanescence of all else in the valley; to imagine it demolished was to imagine the end of the earth. It might as well have been a tomb in which the living gather to hide from death.

I knocked on the front door. It seemed an absurd gesture, my small hand against so huge a plank. My knocking produced a sound no greater than a bird might make in landing on this wooden battlefield. I thought to call out, but I didn't know whose name to say: Jimmy's? Ethan's? My own, to announce a presence that I feared would be judged an intrusion?

The door didn't open this time as it had to Jimmy or to me and Una in the night. I pushed against it and felt it pushing back. I thought of ghosts inside and how they might resist my presence; they were for me not the spirits of the dead, in which I had no belief, but the minds of the living, made manifest in the things of this world over which they had influence, simple things like doors and light and graves and the flesh upon our bones.

I knew it was Ethan who was resisting me, but I wondered if it might be Jimmy too, come under the influence of the very man he'd left me for even as I'd marked his space at my side on the bench in the church. I saw now how absurd a gesture that had been. We might mark all the spaces we like but to do so doesn't fill them.

I went to a window. None from the outside could be reached from the sloping ground, as protection from attack. But I found in a pile of wood being seasoned an unsplit log and rolled it to the window and turned it on its end and stepped upon it and, as it wobbled against the uneven earth beneath it, gazed into the house.

I saw nothing. No one.

As I squinted against the greater darkness within, I felt two large hands come about my waist and lift me off the log, which toppled and rolled down the little hill while I remained in the air, as stiff and still as a tree that spends its life waiting for a wind.

Simeon Vear held me aloft even as he shifted me about so I might face him. I was a dancer in his hands, and he was an old man whose effort was congregated in his neck, its tendons sawing against a clean white shirt, this being Sunday still. He smelled of tobacco and his strange kind of learning, which extracted from his New England preachers and prophets a defense against expedient injustice and produced a scent of pussley, weedy but vaguely sweet. The brim of his hat touched my forehead; I pressed forward until the hat tilted on his head and finally fell off and rolled down the hill.

"You're very strong," I said.

This unexpected flattery caused him to assert his hold on me, which took an effort great enough to make speech difficult. His breath was audible but unworded.

"The door was locked," I explained my position at his window.

He shook his head and let me fall through his hands, which thus had, and took, an opportunity to violate me. His thumbs traveled over my ribs and breasts and neck and ended beneath my ears when my feet came to ground. He looked at me in a tender way, black eyes less lustful than wistful. His eyebrows were black too, not white, and had grown long with age and gave the impression of being tangled with unsummoned wisdom. He breathed deeply, a necessity caused less by his admiration of me than by his use of cigarettes.

"It's never locked." He looked suspiciously in the direction of the door. "There's no one I'm afraid of letting in."

"Or out?" I wondered, thinking of Ethan leaving by the window with Una, climbing down the stone steps at the back of the house, to do what, because she knew it mattered to me, she claimed didn't matter to her.

He wouldn't answer my question. "The commission sends its lawyers here and in they come sometimes when I'm out from home. All the better for me. They get to see I haven't packed." He laughed, so I did too. "They leave notes. They deposit ultimata like hard little mice turds. Each one more ultimate than the last. I'd guess they're afraid I'll actually sell them the house. Then they'd have to take it down. And they don't know how to take it down. Do you?"

"Do I?"

He was pleased to have surprised me. "Just take out one stone. Any stone. That's how to take it down. No different from a man."

I knew then how he'd suffered. The house was mortared and would withstand resection, but he'd been held together by the bonds of love and had his son excised, and what might have left a hole had crumbled him.

"He's inside," I said.

His face brightened. "Who?"

I had meant Ethan, but I said, "Jimmy."

"And he locked you out?"

"But not you," I further assured him. "Do you have a key?"

"A key!" He laughed. First he found his hat and then he went to the woodpile and picked up a log and strode to the door and screamed, "Open up, you son of a bitch!" and threw his hat, and then slammed the log, against the door.

It opened by itself.

Jimmy and Ethan were sitting together at the table in the kitchen. The two of them were neither looking at each other nor talking, but they possessed some understanding that was apparent in their very quiet, in the ease with which they leaned on the old wooden table and were at the same time indistinguishable and distinct. Ethan was real, and present, truly, for the first time, sitting mundanely at a table in a kitchen in contrast to appearing out of the fog in an old family graveyard. But it was not clear at first which one of them he was, not from the door where we stood, the old man and I, intruders, he in his own house, I upon this strange coupling of boy and man. Perhaps it was the dim light that sheltered their identities, or perhaps it was their resemblance: they were like two boys, brothers, not father and son, handsome, fine-featured, dark-eyed, and both had their long fingers atop their heads, settled upon or poking out of hair, so I was unable to tell Jimmy's long hair from Ethan's short. Jimmy must look now as Ethan had when Una had begun to fall in love with him, and this must both compound her love for her son and confuse her in that love, that he so resemble his father exiled from her arms and lodged forever in her heart.

It was Jimmy who made himself known. He turned toward us from the table. "I saw your face in the window, Sarianna. I unlocked the door for you. Hello, Mr. Vear." He was charming in his nonchalance. He smiled with genuine welcome. He was more host than guest.

Simeon Vear addressed his son. "Why was it locked? You know we never lock the door." He said this as he walked toward them. He stopped between them.

Ethan seemed not to hear. He didn't look at his father, and he didn't answer him.

"I locked it," said Jimmy.

The old man showed him none of the affection he had shown when last we were together here and he was the perfect grandfather, eating and slaughtering rabbit with him. Now he gazed at him with what I would have thought would be anger directed at his son and said, "Why?"

"He asked me to." Jimmy was uncertain of his confession until he saw Ethan nod. Jimmy nodded back, and smiled, and I realized he had become intermediary to himself. It had been for his own sake, and the satisfaction of his own curiosity, and not for mine, that he'd run after Ethan from the church.

Simeon looked from one to the other. A great sadness settled on his face, deepening its lines and weighing upon his eyes. "You can't have him too," he said, and I wondered if any of us knew to whom he was speaking, Ethan or Jimmy or me.

"Did he also ask you to open it?" I asked Jimmy.

"That was me," answered Jimmy.

"What about you?" I dared ask Ethan.

Immediately, Jimmy answered for him: "He told me not to."

"You can't lock me out of my own house!" Simeon Vear screamed at his son.

I turned to the old man, who was thudding a pack of cigarettes against his forefinger. "It has nothing to do with you."

"Who else is there?" he asked with patriarchal self-centeredness.

Ethan looked at me to see how I'd answer.

"Tell him," I said to Ethan, and this time locked my eyes upon him in case he might disappear in being spoken to by me like this.

"You," said Ethan, a word I found as satisfying as my own name, or Una's when he'd said it and *Una* was the first word I'd heard him say and I'd lost myself to his voice.

"Answer *me!*" Simeon Vear struck a match against the hearth of the huge fireplace.

"What is it you want from me?" asked Ethan in soft contrast to his father's outcry.

"I want you to talk to me." Simeon Vear approached his son with his pack of Viceroys held out before him.

"You," he said to me again.

"Nothing," I answered.

"Well, you've come to the right place," said the old man bitterly, his hand powdering the air with ash.

"Nothing," Ethan repeated.

"Unless . . ." I began, full of hope.

"Nothing."

I wanted to touch him, if only to establish some corporeality to one so evanescent and elusive. And I wanted to talk to him, or rather to hear him talk, if only to hear what had happened to him since the day Una had not returned. He seemed a perfect representation of this river valley: abandoned, mysterious, beautiful, doomed.

But if all I might have of him was nothing, and he were willing to grant me nothing, then nothing was what I would take. Nothing is always the beginning.

As for me, I gave him a cookie. And Jimmy too. The third I'd meant for myself, not having expected to encounter Simeon Vear. But I handed him that one, which left me with none. He held it in the palm of the hand in which a cigarette had burned down to his fingernails, its smoke making a heart-shaped wreath around the two fingers. He considered that cookie first with confusion, like some long-lost talisman of childhood, and then with gratitude. He stubbed out his smoke and went to the icebox and brought forth a bottle of milk. He poured some milk into a glass and placed the glass before Jimmy.

"I told you," Simeon said, and was the first to bite into his cookie.

Before he'd even swallowed, he stopped chewing and closed his eyes and appeared to be moving his tongue around in his mouth.

"Your mother made these?" he said to Jimmy.

Jimmy contemplated his cookie. It was oatmeal, with raisins. "Looks like it."

"Where's yours?" the old man asked me.

I shook my head.

Jimmy bit into his. "Definitely Mom's." He took another bite with a swallow of milk. "Go ahead," he told Ethan.

Ethan picked up his cookie from the table, looked at it for a moment, and extended it toward me.

"I'll share it with you," I said.

Ethan shook his head.

"Eat the damned cookie!" Jimmy was pretending to be outraged. "They're my mother's!" He took the cookie right out of Ethan's hand and broke it in half and gave a piece to me and a piece back to Ethan.

"He doesn't have to eat it if he doesn't want to," I said to Jimmy.

"You just want the whole thing for yourself!" he teased.

"If I did, I would have taken yours," I said back. "Thank you," I said to Ethan and put my half of the cookie to my lips.

"Eat the goddamned thing!" said Simeon, who had finished his and was lighting another cigarette.

I bit into mine.

Ethan bit into his.

Tears came to his eyes and remained in them as he and I and Jimmy ate our cookies in silence.

I was pleased to see Ethan's tears, even if they were for Una, and the memory of her, and not for me. I wanted, more than anything, to touch one of them, to feel whether it was cold or warm, to learn whether it would dissolve or stay forever upon my fingertip, to taste it in my throat and place it in my own eye and feel its sting.

But, as visible as Ethan remained in the fading afternoon light, and as still as he sat at the table, scarcely moving, scarcely breathing it seemed, he was unapproachable, almost intangible, no matter that I stared, committing him to memory: forearms set firmly upon the table, a muscle twitching but otherwise sedate, a stillness contradicted by the slants and curves of scars and cuts and scratches from his wrists to his elbows, new wounds and old that sang of strife and pain and quickness; his hands, delicate, long-fingered, veined, but careful, empty, nicked, scarred, not entirely clean, and as reticent as anything else upon him; moist black eyes that settled on nothing, inward-looking eyes I longed to see with for myself so I might see what he saw and penetrate his darkness; dark hair cropped close to his scalp so that the shapes of his head and face were unaffected by it and uninterrupted in their fair proportion, though his nose was not entirely straight and his ears were peculiarly elegant and his lips turned down in a melancholy curve that somehow added to his youthfulness. For he was neither boy nor man, perhaps because for all the plangent beauty of him, he seemed entirely spirit, on the verge of disappearance. Perhaps he had disappeared, forever, and left upon the mirror of the air only an image of himself, as he had seemed to be in the window of his room and at the dams and in the graveyard and at the back of the church, a specter brought to life by we who wished to see him, who saw him as we wished him to be, not only immortal but immutable as well.

And his voice, his voice, in the few words he'd said, was soft and gentle and intimate to those who'd hear it so, to me, who wondered, even as I tried to memorize him, whether I was imagining him.

He disappeared the moment I left him. Not from where he sat in the stone house or from the house itself but from *me*. I could neither remember him nor conjure him. As soon as Jimmy and I entered the Vear forest on the way back south, Ethan departed from me and I was left not with a vision of him but with a desire for that vision as much as for Ethan himself. It was a doubly tortured desire and unlike anything I'd ever felt: I was deprived even of remembering what I'd lost in leaving him.

* * *

I tried to get back to him through Jimmy.

"What did you talk about?" I asked.

"He doesn't like to talk."

"Why did you follow him?"

"To see if he had any more notes for you."

"For me?"

"Don't worry—he didn't."

"Were you surprised to see where he lived?"

"Were you?" he asked back.

"You remind me of him."

"Don't you mean he reminds you of me?"

Jimmy was keeping Ethan to himself and offering himself to me in Ethan's place. But he did so now without touching me as we walked home. He kept his distance. He made me come to him. I took his hand as we moved into the late-afternoon shadows that fell between Curtis Hill and the southern cutback of Mount Zion and didn't let go until we came to the front steps of the parsonage.

His parents were happy to see him and unhappy with him. They embraced him and at the same time chided him, which caused him to contest their embrace rather than yield to it. They should have known that it was time for him to cross his father's ground.

He didn't tell them where we'd been. I'd known he wouldn't. Love was a conspiracy, and he was part of it. When they asked him where, he said, "Nowhere special." When that vague truth failed to elicit his parents' further curiosity, Jimmy found himself unable to settle for either their trust or their indifference and for the first time lied to them: "Actually, I went to the cemetery." "A fitting alternative to church," his father conceded, not so much to truth, or even to his belief, as to the son he loved and to peace at the dinner table. "Did you meet anyone?" Una asked, and I wondered if she were thinking of Ethan again and that he might appear to Jimmy with another message for her and me. I wondered if both she and I saw Jimmy as our go-between. "A ghost," he said, and failed in nothing but the courtesy of a conspiratorial glance at me, who shared his lie and along with it the truth.

While his parents' relief at having him back exceeded their irritation at his elusion, we had from then on an uncommonly quiet dinner together. (I was reminded of dining with my parents, where I first learned how people express displeasure with silence and how that silence becomes a language of its own and its vocabulary squalid. It was not like Ethan's silence; it had no depth and its sadness was synthetic.)

After dinner, Jeremy did not take Jimmy off for himself. Instead, he took me.

I thought he might have wanted to probe me concerning Jimmy's actual whereabouts that afternoon—and in the process punish Jimmy by favoring me and punish me by turning Jimmy against me—but he simply sat me down in one of the two chairs before the radio and turned on the *Chase and Sanborn Hour* on the NBC-Red.

A man was arguing with a boy. The man's voice was spongy and vain. He threatened to sew a button on the boy's lip to shut him up. The boy called the man Mr. Fields and said he was determined to fight fire with fire. The man reminded the boy of what happened to little boys who played with fire. The boy's father interceded and said to the man, "Don't mind Charlie, Bill—his bark is really worse than his bite." And the man said, "I'll rip off his bark and bite off his limbs."

Laughter sputtered from the radio. Jeremy himself was amused.

"What's so funny?" I asked.

"He's a puppet, Sarianna—he's made of *wood*."

Indeed, the exchange ended when the man said he would sic a woodpecker on the boy.

Jeremy got up from his chair and turned off the radio in the midst of further laughter, though this time he didn't share in it. Neither did he sit down again. He stood over me and said, "That's the name we gave the men who were sent here two years ago to clear the brush and scrub."

"Charlie?" I inquired.

He laughed at me and in the midst of his amusement put his hand against my cheek, so his fingers nearly covered my ear beneath my hair.

I was tempted to lean my head against his hand, to rest there and take some comfort from his affection or support, whichever it might be, but I sat upright and rigid and did not allow my eyes to rise to his, which I knew were looking for mine.

"Can you be this inexperienced?" he asked.

I wouldn't let him trap me with my own words, as he had within the church at night.

"Of course not *Charlie*," I answered. "I knew it wasn't *Charlie*."

"I meant about the radio," he said. "That you're unfamiliar with—"

"You didn't mean about the radio at all," I told him.

He took his hand from me. What I missed in touch, I savored in sureness.

"Woodpeckers," he said.

"Yes," I agreed.

"There were thousands of them sent by the commission. They

didn't know what they were doing. They whored and drank and brawled in Ware and Palmer and here they killed one another felling trees and ripped their pants on slash. Pants with cuffs, the fools. Woodpeckers."

"How it must have bothered you," I said.

He moved his hand toward me once again, but thought better of it and turned away and knelt before the radio to tune it in. Men all over America were down on one knee before this machine, but few, I imagined, wore a clerical collar.

I anticipated the same terrifying voice that emerged from the portable wireless in poor Mrs. Wharton's story called "All Souls' " in the book *Ghosts*, poor Mrs. Wharton because she died, a year ago, before the book was published, something Emily magnified a thousand times. It was a voice that spoke in a foreign language and in the story terrorized the widow trapped within her own New England house. It was, I'd thought, though this was never stated, Chancellor Hitler's voice, obliterating all the poetry in the world.

Just then an announcer proclaimed that Armbruster's Orchestra was going to play something called "Flat Foot Floogie with a Floy Floy." How desperate and inane had the world become since "Blue Moon"; I felt old enough to feel how the past is stolen by itself.

Jeremy moved the dial and static came in through the trees left standing on the hills around us.

"Don't," I said.

"*News Testers* is coming on."

"I thought the gospel was the news."

"Only the good news, Sarianna. As for the rest, God and the world are at odds. The problem of evil is our greatest problem, not only with each other but with God."

"That God permits what He does?" I inquired.

"God doesn't permit; He conceives."

He turned off the radio and came and sat next to me again. We both stared straight ahead, listening to what silence might be rescued from the screaming of the crickets and the fiery birthing of the stars in the quick enclosure of this night.

After a time, without turning to me, seeming to address the radio before us, Jeremy spoke. "Sometimes late on Sunday I come in from the church where I can still hear the morning's sermon echoing not with what I said but with what I failed to say. I turn on the news at ten-thirty. I listen to Canham or Kaltenborn present what is not a sermon but a fact. The fact is always grievous, and out of this grievous fact I can sometimes feel a new sermon rising. I come in here empty and get filled with poison and have a week to find the mithridate—you don't know that word, do you, *mithridate*? It comes from the name of a king who ruled Pontus from the age of twelve for the next sixty years. But it sounds like the name of an Old Testament prophet. King Mithridates. He was so afraid of being poisoned that he began to drink poison himself, a little at a time, so that by the time he actually was poisoned, the poison had no effect. That's why I listen to the news, Sarianna. A little poison at a time so as not to perish of the great dose. Like this."

He turned to me now and took my jaw and chin firmly in his hand and forced open my mouth and touched his finger to my tongue as he said, "Gijón destroyed. Swallow." I looked into his eyes, which were as cold as Dr. Klein's had been within his tight and tiny wire glasses, who would come to see me in my childhood bed and made me hate him so much for his blank efficiency I burned my fevers off with icy will in order not to have this doctor sent to me ever again. And again Jeremy's finger to my tongue: "Tukhachevsky executed—swallow; Sidqi assassinated—swallow." With each little bit of poison—riots in the Sudeten, Nanking ravaged, the *Panay* sunk, Catalonia besieged—he touched me again and I swallowed again until finally even the touch of his finger to my tongue brought forth no moisture and my mouth was dry and I could swallow no more.

I was afraid that brushing my teeth would take the taste of him from my mouth but it didn't. The violation he had practiced upon me I took to be a liturgy, as he passed to me an understanding of his suffering over the world's sins, his flesh upon mine no different from a wafer of communion, symbolic while material. Besides, it was a good taste, for he was a clean man (all that austere Castile) and he yielded more to me than I to him.

He'd spoken no more after his sad recital of such infractions and barbarities as made him fear the world and distrust his Maker. He merely sat before the radio listening to Donnie's Orchestra on *Manhattan Merry-Go-Round*, unaware of the incongruity of his placing such pain in the path of such triviality. Only when I asked him if my presence there was his way of punishing Jimmy or rewarding me did he even look at me again, and that was to give me a bitter smile that was less an answer than a concession.

It was with that concession—far more valuable than an answer to a question I had asked mostly to make conversation—that I left him flat.

I always brushed my teeth before I put on my nightgown. My nightgown was softening now that I'd washed it so often, or Una had washed it for me, whichever one of us might be at the pail and washboard, scrubbing and wringing out, while the other rinsed in another pail and wrung out again and departed to the backyard to hang each garment separately as it came out of the wash, so that the clothesline filled up gradually with a family's clothes, its members jumbled by size and gender, age and experience. How we talked as we did the laundry, laughing from pail to pail, calling out to each other across the lawn from the wet and soapy back steps to the clothesline. How many black marks we might have received for Speaking Above a Whisper in the Wash Room in Emily's day at the Mount Holyoke Female Seminary. And how we ourselves whispered while Una stitched up any tears that might have been caused by the fervor of our laundering or our living and I watched her long fingers guide the needle and wondered at how quiet women became when they were sewing and how loud when laundering. These days there were so few clothes drying in the Swift River Valley, those that remained seemed less a hangman's leavings than the spirits of the flesh that filled and animated them. I had never before been so moved by garments on a line, swallowing the sun, frisking the wind, and on rare occasions that June and July gathering the rain. When it did rain, and my nightgown failed to dry, I slept naked, which I had never done before and found peculiar. I was warmer naked than clothed, so that naked I slept upon the top sheet and gowned beneath it.

That night, once I'd cleaned my hands and face and teeth and pulled the chain on the bathroom light, I ignored the nightgown that Una had folded and placed as usual upon the graveyard quilt folded at the foot of my bed. I lit Ethan's candle and put it before the screen in my open window. Then I lay down and in the darkness relieved only by that candle's strict light tried to bring back to myself the vision of Ethan I'd lost in leaving him that afternoon. But I could think nothing of flesh, only of words, and how they seemed eternal beyond the lives of those who'd uttered them or written them or inspired them. I was no doubt moved to this by Jeremy's tale of Mithridates and the notion of a poison becoming its own antidote and I wondered whether love might be the same, taken in tiny draughts against, for those so fortunate, its one huge onslaught. But I also thought of Emily, who had left only a single daguerreotype image of her physical self when she was exactly my age but otherwise nothing but words, and how my candle might compare to the "lamps eternal" she wrote of to Jane Humphrey and by which she claimed to read Jane's thoughts in her face as I could not read Ethan's upon his or upon the emptiness he left in every place he stood and in my mind as well. What a letter that had been, from Emily to Jane, and how little I had done compared to Emily, who was said to have done so little herself (by those who'd never read such a letter as that!).

I watched the candle disappear into itself as the night beyond it did the same and I myself ascended into darkness. I was no more able in sleep than in wakefulness to summon Ethan, of whom I could neither dream nor daydream. Thus was sleep a refuge from the absence he enforced. All I dreamed of was myself, alone, not so much abandoned as never taken up, undiscovered.

I dreamed I was exactly as I was, alone in my bed, seeing through sequestered eyes the candle gone and listening through the door for sounds of Jeremy and Una as they took to bed. But then I heard the door between us open and saw against the faint light coming from their room the tall figure of Jeremy. He stepped into my room and closed the door behind him. Thus was he too lost to darkness. But I could feel him over me and feel his breath upon my skin, so cool and comforting that I sank even further into sleep and lost my dream until I was awakened by the closing of the door between our rooms.

When I opened my eyes, my room was faintly lit, not by early-morning light, as I first imagined, but by a candle in my window, made whole and come to life. Its light was not sufficient to allow me to see what I did only come true dawn, a white clerical-collar button on the dark wood of the floor. Later that morning, I presented it to Una as we were boiling the sheets. She wondered where I'd found it, and I let her.

I was paid back, for my imposture, by Jimmy. That same morning, when I went to look for him for his lesson on Shays' Rebellion, he was gone. It was the first time he'd missed a lesson and the first time he'd abandoned me. I was initially annoyed, then angry, but soon I felt an admiration for his independence combine with an envy for his audacity. How he'd learned to fly away, that boy, and what confidence he had in the charm of his presence.

I knew where he'd gone. I was determined not to follow him there. As lunchtime approached, and to cover his absence, I told Una that Jimmy was off playing and the two of us were leaving soon to see the remains of the Shays house on Lighthouse Hill. She made me take peaches and plums and slices of bread and butter she wrapped in wax paper. I departed quickly, so as not to confront the reverend, who was not as credulous as his wife and more likely to want to embrace his son before allowing him to go off even to so admirable a destination as the Shays house. I was also not yet prepared to confront Jeremy with his presence in my dream the night before and to learn how kindly he might have looked upon me in the very moment I was imagining him there and feeling his breath wash over me.

It was the first afternoon I'd had completely to myself. That this liberty was obtained through the defection of Jimmy was not lost on me: freedom, I was learning, might well be a by-product of deprivation. I didn't merely enjoy Jimmy's company; I suffered in his absence.

Because the way to Lighthouse Hill out of Greenwich Village was for a time the way also to the Vear house, I walked west on Kelly Hill Road and left it only to go north on Clifford. I didn't stop until I came to the knoll that had incorporated the Jason Powers Cemetery, which I'd passed each time I'd gone to the Vear house but never visited. Once beyond Greenwich Village itself, I'd met no one. My presence in the cemetery was unnoticed, then, and I felt as the afternoon went on that I might as well be the only woman on earth, so empty was the world and quiet but for the singing of birds that made me feel like the sparrow in the psalm, alone upon the housetop, looking down upon the stones and dust of a destitute Zion. But like the river that went out of Eden to water the garden and split into four branches, here the Swift River divided into three and would join Fever Brook to drown my valley in order to water the city far away. This grave injustice seemed, as I lay in this cemetery emptied of its life, no more than the workings of the world and the accommodations of man. Everything in this valley was simple. There was no ambiguity in either the politics or the theology. We'd been left free to confine our confusions to matters ungoverned by laws secular or divine. Love was the anarchy of the heart. It obeyed no rule of man or God. Emily too knew this. In calling herself sane and the world "*in*sane," she wrote to the woman she called "Sister," Elizabeth Holland, to beg for her love and said she would rather be loved than called a king on earth or a lord in heaven.

Love, she said, was the fellow of the resurrection. I had for comfort molded a grave loosely to my body by moving dirt with my heels and hands. I lay in it with my head upon the lip of dirt

I'd made that formed a pillow for my neck and provided a contentment as to bamboozle death itself. Far from getting the willies, I exulted in such liberty as came from my attempt to experience oblivion, which itself was a paradox within my capacity both to understand and to endure. I tried to die and failed and in such failure was resurrected.

This coming to life was aided by the food that Una had packed for me and for her wayward son. The peaches sprayed across the back of my hand and the plums around my lips. I saved one of each for Jimmy and all the bread his mother had wrapped.

I saw him, finally, walking on the road toward home in time for him to get there, just, for dinner. The cemetery was, like most (for drainage, I assumed, and not as a head start toward heaven), on a hill. Low and gentle, it allowed me to observe Jimmy from a distance as he approached. Once again, he appeared to have been pressed out of Ethan's mold, lithe and light and dark-eyed, but he walked with a nonchalance I could not imagine guiding Ethan, purposeful only in his very discursiveness. Jimmy put curves in the road where there were none and kicked stones he didn't run to kick again and seemed to want to lay eyes on every bird that chirped at him or warned its brethren of his vague advance. And I, like someone just as young and just as heedless, couldn't help but want to stop him in his tracks and play with him a bit.

"Ooooooooooowwwwwwww," I sounded, and sank as deeply into my grave as I could and still see him.

He stopped. He squinted. He looked over at the erstwhile graves.

"Ooooooooooowwwwwwww." I could barely keep from laughing.

He turned to face the cemetery. His passion for danger made

him stand out in a luminous manly beauty against the shrubs and slash and pale dust hanging from the sun. He charged across the road and over the ditch and up the little hill. Only when he was upon me did I see he'd somewhere picked up a piece of tree and held it like a club against his thigh. I fought against my instinct to recoil and pushed myself up so I was almost sitting when he reached me.

His surprise was in his eyes alone. I saw him capture that surprise and bury it, to be able to affect the unflinching poise of a young valiant. Even his voice was newly bold. "Sarianna." Only my name. No "What are you doing here!" He tossed off his hunk of tree in deference to affection and ascendancy.

"James," I said in return, to deflate a presumption I nonetheless admired.

He looked around, or pretended to, to see whom I might be addressing. Then he laughed and jumped into the grave beside me. As he sat, his legs were long enough to surpass the phantom coffin's reach.

"Did you follow me?"

"I didn't have to."

"What's that supposed to mean?"

"I knew where you'd gone."

"Then why?"

"To bring you lunch?" I showed him the brown, stained bag in which I'd carried it.

"That's not why," he announced correctly even as he reached into my lap and opened the bag and grabbed the plum and bit into it with sufficient spirit to splash my cheeks and his own with its juices.

He raised his right shoulder and wiped his face against the short sleeve of his white T-shirt. The shredded skin of what was left of the plum was the same color as his eyes. "So how come you're here?"

"Because I didn't want to wait."

"For what?"

"You know what."

"Is there anything else in that bag?"

I moved it so he couldn't reach it.

"Tell me," I said.

"He wants to see you."

This was more than I'd expected. I didn't know what to do. I opened the bag and took out the bread and unwrapped it from the wax paper. "Here." One slice.

"Is that my reward?"

I passed him all the bread. He licked off some butter before he bit into it.

"When?" I asked.

"He didn't say."

"Do you know why?"

"He didn't say that either. I think it has something to do with Mom. He was Mom's boyfriend, you know." He seemed pleased to be telling me something he wanted me not to have known.

"Is that what he told you?"

He shook his head impatiently. "We don't talk about things like that."

"About what, then?"

"Not about you either." In such cruelty as this he took even more pleasure.

"I should hope not."

"He talks about himself," Jimmy whispered, as if this were a secret or what he'd heard was secret.

"What does he say?"

"Hunting. Trapping. Things like that. Indians. *He's* part Indian. He—"

He said this last with such enthusiasm that I couldn't help interrupting. "So are you."

He looked down at his slim, tanned arms and then back up at me convinced I'd merely flattered him. "I am *not*." He shook his head to get the pleasing notion out and then, unable to stop speaking of Ethan, went on with his story: "He showed me a *wolf* he stuffed. I thought it was alive! And cutting down trees. That kind of stuff. For boys."

"What else?"

He leaned against me and put his hand on my shoulder and his lips to my ear, just as his mother would. "Pain," he said softly, his breath against my skin bringing a pleasure that mixed strangely with that short word beginning hard and ending soft.

"You go home." I rose and brushed dirt back into the grave off my skirt.

"I knew it." He moved away from my feet next to him. "I should never have told you."

He was right. He should never have told me. I thought about this as I walked away from him toward the Vear house.

I thought I'd find Ethan at the kitchen table, where I'd last seen him, waiting for me. I pictured how I'd walk to him across the wide planks of the floor, so lightly they'd make no sound, and sit down opposite him, and only then would he glance up from the empty surface of the table and whatever he'd been thinking in the silence and emptiness would leave the blankness of his eyes and he would look at me and in that look would take me in. Capture me forever, so if he never saw me again, he would remember me. As he did Una, whom we both would share as she and I did him.

But long before I would come to the big stone house—yet having crossed Soapstone Road and thus having left behind the leveled woods and passed through the black-green curtain of the great Vear forest—I heard the sound of wings against the air and a bird sound that struck me as a parody of mine, except it was divided into threes and caught each time upon itself, *coo-coo-coo*. So Jimmy'd followed me, I figured, and thus he drove away my thoughts of Ethan. How, I wondered, had he raised his voice so high, and found so clean a melancholy call, when it was his very voice that led the quick attack upon the manhood convening in his limbs?

I expected the sound to follow me, but as I walked I followed it. And found its source, which wasn't Jimmy but a bird within a netted trap. The trap was divided in two, and this bird occupied the lower, shorter portion. It was a small bird, less than a foot long, and I took it for a pigeon. Its color was a soft brown, with white arrowy feathers bordering the tail. It was pecking along the bottom of the trap, trying to fit its small beak into slats along the metal bottom. I thought to free it—if for no other reason than to show Ethan that I myself was free—and had even kneeled to do this when I heard another bird. This one issued a deeper, harder sound, *cack cack cack*, from above. When I looked up, I saw it, a giant thing with its gray barred wings outstretched as it glided down in small semi-circles and then, as it noticed me, held its breath and made no sound until it dove and *cack-cackcack*ed in one long burst of irritated fiat. I didn't scream myself but jumped away and covered my head with my arms and watched the vexed thing look at me for a moment with golden eyes out of its black face, blood-white stripes above them arched like scars where eyebrows grow. The little bird in the trap must have heard the same mirthful cries, because it too looked at this beast and opened its beak to scream, its small stripped belly pumping air, but no sound came out. The larger bird landed atop the trap and stopped for a moment to smile down within before it drew its wings close and, nodding its head, entered. Both it and I—I imagined the small bird had its eyes shut awaiting death—noticed together that it was in the top half of the trap and that the door of this half closed right up. As it did, the entrance to the bottom half opened, and while the bird above tried to reach down through the mesh to grasp its prey, the little bird tried to take flight even before it had breached the door and fell into the air that bore it off without a backward glance at me or at its killer.

The big bird had been fooled. Rather than thrash about, it lowered its head and pecked at its breast. I approached it without fear and watched it shy from me, lean against the mesh until it lost its balance and toppled from the metal rim that separated the trap's two halves. Now it pressed against the mesh, its beak caught so that its throat was stretched and exposed and its claws held out horizontally to keep it in submissive pose.

I took the mesh in both my hands and found the place that had come shut from the weight of the bird and spread it open. The bird turned and shook its vicious head to tell me to let go. I did and it squeezed out and stood for a moment with its claws alternately tearing at the mesh before it called out *cack cack cack* and seized the air the moment I heard footsteps coming fast across the forest floor, cracking twigs and scuffling leaves.

"Ethan!" I cried.

He stopped away from me. He was winded and sweating and glowed in the dappled slanting sunlight. His eyes were huge, as black as the face of the bird that looked at me as Ethan looked at it and followed that bird up so I did too, my eyes locked within his sight, to see the bird rise slowly until suddenly it *cack*ed and *cack*ed and disappeared beyond the trees. Its cries hurt my ears. They were what Emily suffered from summer birds that woke her to the frightful, furtive obligations of her day, dirks of melody that stabbed her ravished spirit, daggers I felt I'd turned upon myself.

I looked down from the empty sky only to see Ethan pointing back up at it, a finger out, just as Jimmy had pointed at him at the back of the church. So I looked again and this time saw the bird again and in his talons the smaller bird, surely dead, though the air across its tail feathers moved them with a flashing white against the blue of heaven.

"I'm sorry!" I screamed, at what or whom I didn't stop to think.

Ethan shook his head disdainfully and at the same time smiled. It was a small smile, and it displayed more ridicule than sympathy, but it was at least, in its ambiguity, a human thing.

"What did I do?"

He knelt beside the trap and put his hand in where the larger bird had been. "Freed my hawk." I could hear his breathing in his voice, his running through the woods that brought him to me. He spoke softly enough for me to have to turn my ear to him and tilt my head. "Never touch another man's trap."

"I didn't know."

"What?"

"That . . ." I looked to the empty sky. I imagined now it was like the ocean and what Jeremy Treat imagined the world outside our valley was becoming—an orbit of unseen endless killing. "Why were you running?"

"The dove."

"That was a dove?"

"Mourning," he identified it. "Homing to its dovecote."

"I don't understand."

Now he put his hand where the dove had been. "I put it here. I leave. A goshawk wants its prey perched. It attacks. It enters up here. The trap closes on it. And opens below for the dove. When I see it flying home, I know." His voice was calm. He looked at me to see if now I understood. This was something he could talk about and did with pleasure in his eyes. He was teaching me.

"It was a decoy?"

"And a messenger."

"Were you going to hunt with the hawk?"

"Some do."

"And you?"

"Mount it."

He rose from his knees. "Listen." He pointed toward the sky. "Look."

I could see and hear nothing.

He reached for my face and nearly put his hand upon it. I closed my eyes and waited for his touch. Before it came, I heard what he had heard—*cack cack cack*. I opened my eyes to see what he had seen. But the sky remained empty for me, of everything but the sound of the bird.

"Where?" I asked.

He pointed into the distant sky, almost to the horizon. And there, finally, I saw the bird and with him watched it drift upon the unseen currents of the air, its short, bowed wings at rest, its long gray tail stiff in its coercion of the wind.

"It's laughing at us."

"At you," he said, and disappeared into the forest.

*   *   *

Did he expect me to follow? Jimmy said that Ethan wanted to see me. Was he somehow able to learn of Una by learning of me? Had this all been staged, and as the dove was the decoy for the hawk, was the hawk the decoy for me?

"Wait!" I cried.

I heard nothing, saw nothing. The forest he had disappeared into, he had disappeared from.

I didn't know which house to go to. Neither felt like home now, yet I was drawn to both. I knew I'd be missed in the one in town. In the one in the woods would I be remembered?

I ran toward him. Or where I thought he'd be. I couldn't find him, except in feeling he was watching me. I let him see me like this, as no one ever had, reckless, foolish, lost. I ran with my arms before me, to take the scratching of trees and prickers. I jumped what trees were down and rotting along this path that wasn't one except I tried to put my feet where his had been or might have been on this day or any other. I called for him in whispers that he wouldn't hear and with his name before my lips I traveled toward him.

I was aware of my humiliation. It didn't shame me. I reveled in it. Submission in the cause of love is an act of love.

When I came through the clearing to the great wooden door of the stone house, I barely slowed and pushed against it with both hands. It yielded immediately to my restlessness and swung open so fast it came back at me to throw me out. I caught it with one hand and held it at bay as I let in faded late-day light against the dimness of the vast ground floor. Still, all was shadowy, and one sense engulfed another as I smelled meat cooking and was overtaken by a hunger, not for food alone but for everything, for the satisfying of a desire I felt had replaced me with itself.

"Ethan," I called into the shadows.

"Look who's here." There, in the kitchen, the old man was standing before the stove with a glove on his hand and that hand around a split log half thrust into the open door of the stove. He completed the action and slammed shut the door and gave its metal handle a hard quarter-turn.

"Where's Ethan?"

"Who?" He laughed at the absurdity of his question and came toward me moving his fine white hair off his forehead as might a woman primping for her beau. He smiled. His bottom teeth were dark but not much darker than that part of his face the sun could find below the brim of his hat. He must roam the land all day, though whether to memorize it or to avoid the eerie quiet of this tomb of a house I couldn't guess. "Our boy was here."

"To see his father." I acknowledged our common secret.

"I'm his *grandfather*," he said.

"Of course."

"Not his *father*," he emphasized.

"Ethan . . ." I said and realized at that moment he didn't know.

"Not home!" he announced with the pleasure of having me to himself.

But announcement produced its opposite. Ethan came through the door.

"Look who's here," Simeon repeated, with a more ironic tone.

Ethan looked at me and then back at the door. He was unable to believe I was here, or at least that I'd arrived before him. I was as he had been to me, something of a phantom, appearing, disappearing, reappearing. I enjoyed his mystification. At the same time, I realized he'd not been watching me run through the woods. I wondered if Una suffered the same, in feeling that he spied on her. Perhaps he had the ability to resurrect himself in our imaginations.

He walked right past me and into the kitchen. I wondered if it was to tell me this was the price one paid for being ghostly—being *ignored*. I didn't care to be ignored. In that, submission bared its sensitivity as well as its antithesis: impudence.

I followed him. I nearly rode up on his heels. He looked into the oven, which gave off a puff of fragrant smoke that wreathed our heads. Within, there was in a blackened roasting pan a bird without a head that had been split down the middle and lay lewdly on its back, cooking.

"Your hawk?" I whispered, close enough to smell the smoke on his skin.

He rose and wouldn't look at me. He closed the oven door with the sand-rasped toe of his black boot and walked past the sink to a tall cupboard, which he reached to open. I stood away from him then and, giving him his distance, stared against his body. I saw his ribs through the thin black shirt he wore and the muscles in his shoulder breathe and his shirt ride off his neck when he stretched. His beard was barely visible and that only upon his upper lip and at the sides of his chin, which were darkened by small soft black hairs that lent a precious gravity to the peculiar innocence of his face, which was grim but kind. Though I'd not known him when he was young and Una had, I knew he hadn't aged as others would. He was in all but years barely older than Jimmy and shared with him a restless passion for stable pandemonium. It was clear he'd never shaved. His skin was unlined, except where thorns had nuzzled it. Time had not touched him, because love had; or as I better understood it, time, and love, had abandoned him together. He wasn't living in the past, but he was waiting there for life to change. Until it did, neither would he. He not only contained his past; he embodied it.

So intently did I study him—no doubt so I might finally have an image of him when apart—that I failed to understand what he was doing. I watched him walk from the cupboard to the table, from the oven to the table, from the icebox to the table, from the bread box to the table, and all I saw was a body moving back and forth against the gray stones of the walls. It was only when he stopped moving and stood at the table with his back to me that I looked beyond him and saw he'd set three places.

The old man, who was not tall enough to reach the candelabra, lit the thick, round, blackened candle in the middle of the table. Then he stood behind a chair as Ethan was standing behind another. I thought they might be in prayer until Ethan looked over his shoulder and said, "Come here."

I approached, and he indicated a chair between himself and his father. I sat down, and only then did they.

No one spoke. Ethan had placed the bird on a plank of wood and now carved, its limbs and meat falling away with what seemed the most economical of strokes of the long blackened blade of the knife. For a moment I imagined him at my parents' home on Dickinson Street, for Thanksgiving, showing my father how it was done.

He put the meat on a platter and served me and then himself but not his father, who had to stand to reach for his food. I waited for Simeon before I tasted it. Ethan waited for neither of us.

"Chicken?" I asked, though I had never eaten a chicken like this, with meat so rich and brown and chewy.

"Merganser," he replied.

"I don't know what that is," I said.

"Duck."

"Merganser," I pronounced it.

"Hooded merganser," he specified.

"Ask him how he caught it," the old man said to me.

"You ask him."

Simeon gave me a look of stymied futility but nonetheless said, "How did you catch it?"

Ethan didn't look at him or answer him. He dunked some bread in gravy from the duck and shoved it between his lips with one finger and looked down at my bread and said, "Go ahead."

"Your father asked you a question," I said.

"What was the question?" he asked.

"How did you catch the merganser?"

"Like this." He brought his hands together abruptly.

"With his hands," I said to Simeon.

"Please don't talk to him," said Ethan.

"That's all right." Simeon addressed himself to me.

"He doesn't talk to you?" I asked him.

Simeon shook his head, meaning Yes, he doesn't talk to me.

"Why not?" I asked Ethan.

"You better be careful," said Simeon, "or he won't talk to you either. He can go days without talking. Months. Years."

"When was the last time he talked to you?"

Simeon knocked a cigarette out of his pack and lit it with a match struck against the side of the table. "It was a long time ago," he said to me but for the first time looked at his son.

"Don't!" Ethan rose and took a step or two away and then turned back as he realized what he'd done.

"Look at that." Simeon addressed me. "You got him to talk to me. That's the first thing he's said to me in twelve years."

"I was talking to *you*." Ethan pointed at me.

"You son of a bitch," said his father, more in triumph than in contempt.

"Don't what then?" I asked Ethan.

"Don't try to know me."

"I couldn't anyway," I answered. "You don't exist."

"Who does?" he said, and turned around and walked out the door into what I realized only then had become night.

This time I found him in the woods. Only because he wanted me to. I was making my way south by aiming for what flakes of moonlight had drifted to the forest floor through the dense crowns of trees. I could see nothing but this light that lay before me and when I reached it disappeared within me.

He was waiting for me in the darkness. He was visible in the darkness, even his black eyes against the blackness all around us. He didn't radiate light so much as contain it. I saw him and nothing else. We might have been in a world empty but for us.

I was the same for him, or how else would he have held out his hands to stop me without touching me and traced me with his eyes and seen the tiny scratches on my arms?

"You're bleeding," he said.

I held both arms out toward him. I felt he could heal me if only he would touch me.

He pointed. "You're a map of your travels."

I knew what he meant. The cuts I'd made on my way to him at home had dried; my new cuts shone with slender streaks of wet scarlet.

"They're nothing," I said, meaning the opposite.

He looked away. I thought he might be sickened by my blood. He turned around and gazed into the forest and found among some old black quaking aspens a young tree whose trunk was marked by dark scars in the otherwise almost white bark. He tore some off. It almost turned to powder in his hand. As he returned to me, he spit in the other hand and then put the aspen bark into his mouth and chewed it vigorously as he wiped his spit into my cuts and I saw my blood turn pale within my wounds. He held both my arms while he chewed and then let go of each in turn as he took the mush from his mouth onto his fingertips and spit directly on my wounds and rubbed the sodden bark upon them.

"I feel better already," I said, which was true, though I could not have explained which part of me had most benefited from his care.

He stopped touching me. "Long sleeves," he instructed, though I preferred his medicine to timorous prevention.

"And you?" His arms were bare. I took hold of one and turned it over. What should have been its sensitive underside was hard with muscle and with veins that felt musical beneath my fingers. What scars he had were old and painless, what scrapes and scratches new and raw and prurient. I'd never dreamed, I realized, of touching him. To do so now was therefore like anything undreamed of. The phantom boy had turned to flesh. It was almost more than I could bear, this reality. I didn't know what to do with it. I dug into his body to try to unearth mine.

"You can't hurt me," he said. "Thorns don't. Prickers. Nettles. Brambles. Briers. Fish hooks. Ax handles. Snake bites. See those?" He put his finger down near mine and pointed to four faint stafflike lines that ran straight from his elbow almost to his wrist: "Bobcat. And that's"—a ring of scar tissue around the bottom of the thumb of his other hand—"from a snapping turtle."

I pushed into his skin with my nails. "What about *pain*?"

"What *about* it?"

"Jimmy said—"

"Not this kind." He tried to pull his arm away. "Now you're hurting me," he said.

I knew he didn't mean in his arm, which I held on to.

"His mother," he began. Or so I thought. Except that was all he said. He turned his eyes from mine and in so doing caused me through no physical force to let go of him. It was a loss I felt in such a way that I wouldn't have been surprised if he'd left the ground and flown away.

But he merely retreated in the direction from which I'd come and was about to pass wholly into the dark tangle of the trees when at the same moment he stopped and I said, "What about her?"

"Una." He said her name not to inform me of it but to call me by it. He addressed me as her.

This time I didn't whisper back my own name.

"I want you . . ." he began.

"Who?"

"You. What's your name?—Sarianna. I want you to get her back."

"Una!" I cried, not knowing whether I was calling her to him or warning her away. Or whether it was her he wanted or revenge upon her. "Una."

He disappeared within her name.

By the time I arrived home, Jimmy was in bed and Jeremy was in church and Una was lost without me.

"Where *were* you?" She was sitting at the kitchen table, her hand around a glass in which there was but sewage of tea leaves.

"Didn't Jimmy tell you?"

"Jimmy tells me what you want me to hear."

"We were at the Jason Powers Cemetery."

"I know!" She was delighted now. "You were hiding in a grave. How do you dream up these things? You're like a child yourself."

"And Jimmy less."

As if offering Jimmy's own proof of this, she said, "He told us you'd gotten separated on the way home. That's why he was here for dinner and you weren't. Are you hungry? I saved you meat loaf."

"I ate."

"What?" she asked, not where.

"Merganser."

"That's a dirty old thing. It eats frogs."

"Hooded."

She didn't know what I meant. He hadn't cooked one for her. "Did you catch it with your bare hands—that smelly old thing?"

She grasped both my hands and put my palms to her face. She breathed deeply. Her eyes closed.

"I'm so tired," she whispered. "When Jimmy came home I thought he was bleeding. There was blood all over his shoulder, I thought. It exhausted me. I stayed up to wait for you. Now . . ."

She kept hold of my hand on the narrow stairway. She didn't bother to pull back the covers of her bed but lay down atop the quilt.

"Take off your shoes first," she said.

She made room for me. I lay down next to her. She put one of my hands to her face again. She moved the other around her waist and her head to my shoulder, where she fell asleep.

Jeremy found us like that. He disentangled us. I became aware of him not when he moved my hand off Una—for my hand had no feeling and so he might have been tearing away the very swell and dimple of his wife's buttocks, where my fingers and the heel of my palm had settled as she moved in her sleep—but when he took her breath from me and my lips cooled and I opened my eyes.

I saw her face and his hand beneath her head, quite as if he'd severed it and held it forth for my apprehension.

"Quiet."

I said nothing and waited while he pulled down a pillow from the headboard and gently placed Una upon it, where she smiled a sleep smile, or what I imagined was one, since I'd never seen this before on anyone, a tiny but sincere sign of comfort or pleasure appearing only upon the lips and only for a moment.

Finally I turned and saw him above me. The remnants of his church time still clouded his face, though there was some color driven back by the sight of his wife upon the bed. I wondered if I should go and he would take my place. I took a breath to ask and felt his finger touch my lips.

He shook his head and gestured for me to rise.

Though I'd discarded nothing but my shoes, I felt peculiar coming off the bed with my clothes disheveled and my hair stuck to my face. My dream the night before in which he'd seen me sleeping unclothed had left me less discomfited than this. I was not, I supposed, prudish, but I was scrupulous. No man had seen me rise from bed; I would have preferred to have done so unsummoned.

When he turned his back I straightened my skirt and rubbed my eyes. I thought he would lead me out to the hallway, but he turned toward the door between our rooms and walked to it and opened it and waited there for me. I walked by him and waited for the door to close or for his steps behind and then for the door to close. In fact, he chose a third: to follow me in but not to close the door.

I sat down on the bed. That left him no other place to sit. He stood apart from me, across the room, which meant he was barely farther away than the length of his own long arm. I might have asked him what he wanted, or he might have said what he wanted, but I realized what he wanted was what he had. I realized this from how he stood in the dark against the wall and didn't move at all except for a kind of shudder that produced an outline of his dark-clad body against the indiscernible whiteness of the wall. He fairly shimmered, not with light but with a lightness of feeling. He was trembling with uncertainty and anticipation.

"I dreamed of you last night."

I said this so softly I wasn't sure he'd heard, for he made no response and my words therefore remained conspicuous in the darkness that separated us. I could hear them, but no longer in my own voice: "I dreamed of you last night."

What he finally answered were these phantom words, long fled from me: "Then I must have dreamed of you." His voice came out of the wall. There was nothing visible now but the faint rectangle of light that had become the door between our rooms, hiding away his wife.

"You were here," I said. "But in my dream you closed the door."

"Yes, I was here."

"What did you see in your dream?" I asked, knowing full well.

"You."

"And I saw you in mine."

"I was here," he repeated.

"And now?"

It was a long while before he replied: "And now I'm not."

He closed the door. The room was black.

"This is more than I can bear," he whispered.

I removed my clothes and fell asleep before his eyes.

All that was left of the Shays house on Lighthouse Hill was the cellar hole. It was bounded, however, on all sides by its walls, flat stones so flushly placed that they appeared grown out of the earth, in contrast to the rounder, larger stones of the Vear house that might have rained down from above.

We had approached the house on Turnpike Six, a rolling old stagecoach road that headed directly west to Amherst; indeed, where it intersected Prescott Road there was a sign for Amherst, a sign that would one day have pointed across the waters, were it to be allowed to stand on Prescott Peninsula, which, it was intended, would soon be a dry green tongue thrust down out of northern Massachusetts between the west and middle branches of the Swift River, forbidden ever after to human settlement. But at this time, when our world was not, as Emily called the world entire, conclusion, we might have walked straight to Amherst, as much a sequel to me as was heaven to her. But Jimmy wouldn't have loved her own stately, scrupulous home as he loved this deserted, depredated place, where a "little rebellion," as Thomas Jefferson slighted it, was plotted by the local farmers against the very principalities and powers of the state of Massachusetts that was taxing them beyond survival and foreclosing against them beyond pity.

I had taught Jimmy, because his father had wanted him to know the history of his dematerializing birthplace, the facts and meaning of this rebellion, from the return of these same farmers from the Revolutionary War to the salutary effect of Shays' Rebellion upon the framing of the Constitution of the United States. But what Jimmy loved most were the battles of men with pitchforks and walking sticks against the guns of the federal arsenal in Springfield (busy these days, noted Jeremy, when an entire Austria might simply disappear in less time and for less reason than would Greenwich Village) and tales of rebels on the gallows. He especially liked the story of Henry Gale of Princeton not far to our east, who had the rope around his neck on the Worcester Common when news of his pardon arrived. What Jimmy didn't like was the name given the new road built within the past three years just to the west of the project taking line and running the entire length of the impending reservoir: Daniel Shays Highway. Jimmy recognized what hypocrisy there was in the recognition of that very sort of rebel who, were he to arise today, would be more likely led down such a road in chains than have it named for him.

As for Daniel Shays, he was forced back this way from the Springfield armory, took one last look at his home, was nearly apprehended in nearby Petersham by the government troops that did manage to capture the rest of his army, and disappeared into history. He was never seen again, at least not as Daniel Shays; it was rumored he settled in the northern reaches of New York State and died there some years later.

And so on this cloudy August day, Jimmy Treat stood in the cellar hole of Daniel Shays's last known habitation and closed his eyes and tried to will himself back to the days when there were people here and history was made. But he could no more complete this journey than would those who would someday gaze upon the waters that would cover this valley and look for me and Jimmy among its departed souls.

What he found frustrating about this, I found inspiring. No

matter what records we might leave, we would always take ourselves away and remain forever indecipherable. Few of us would
cover our tracks as well as Emily Dickinson, who had remained
sweetly invisible despite such revelation in her verse as should
carve her into the minds of all who read her. Yet how much better to know her lost. How much better to know that I'd be lost
and Jimmy lost and Ethan lost. How much sweeter then such
moments as this, a boy playing in the ruins and a girl sitting
watching him. The clouds scouring all blue from the sky as
the wind picks up. The boy's hair disordered by that wind
and its colors softened by those clouds so that now, I realized,
it was like that jasper Elizabeth Browning named her son's
hair, the fair Penini's, gold and brown and rust, which Jimmy
brushed back against the wind's insinuation, the first sign of
vanity I'd seen in him. But he was heroic now himself, assuming
what he imagined was a pose of the men who gathered in this
very space a hundred and fifty years before and plotted treason
in the name of justice.

Jimmy aimed an imaginary rifle, sighting down his long arms
with one eye closed and the other opaque and obstinate, a black
stone set in the resolute beauty of his face. For a moment, with
the shifting of the sky and the arrangement of the wind, I
couldn't tell Una and Ethan from each other as I looked at
Jimmy. When that moment passed, so they had passed into him
and his face was different then, combining and obliterating his
parents at once.

He aimed the rifle at me and smiled. "C'mon, Sarianna!" He
motioned me with his head into the cellar hole.

I got up and brushed the dirt from my summer frock and
was climbing over the stone foundation when he extended a
hand to me. As I raised my rear foot to bring it down to the cellar floor, Jimmy stepped back gracefully and raised our held

hands so that we might have been dancing the Yam. It was a
new grace in him, this care he took and his balance and the
distance he put between us even as our hands were joined for
what was, once I was settled standing next to him, no apparent
purpose.

"I'm so glad you took me here," he said.

"Why?"

"It makes my mind go wild. How you have to concentrate."

"I'm glad we're here too."

He turned to face me, still holding my hand, turned fast with
his eyes wide, sweeping toward me, and I thought he was taking
me by surprise, shrugging off his boyhood and hoping for my
arms to catch him.

But it was his hand that let go of mine and his eyes that
looked beyond mine.

"There he is!" he whispered.

Now he was playing again, he was boy again, afraid of what
he'd felt compelled to do and taking refuge in a game.

"Is it Daniel Shays himself?" I teased, "or Henry Gale with
no one else to save him?"

"Please let me go," he said, and though I wasn't holding him,
I put my arms about him then and tried to keep him. But he
turned away and wouldn't look at me but only beyond me up the
hill where he ran. I couldn't see what he was running to until another boy, an older boy, stepped out from the shadows and
waved, at me or at Jimmy I couldn't tell, until Jimmy waved back
at him and the older boy motioned, faster, faster. As soon as
Jimmy reached him, Ethan turned away as if I didn't exist.

I barged into the Vear house. As I'd made my way up Pelham
Road and then, impatient, left the road to wade through Dicky
Brook, in which I'd slipped and fallen, and finally entered the

Vear forest to the west of Woods Pond, I was sure they'd have bolted the door again.

But first I tried my shoulder, to which the huge door yielded so easily that I came farther into the house than I'd intended, with more emotion than I'd want to display to those who'd hurt me.

When I saw they weren't at the kitchen table, I pictured Ethan taking Jimmy up the ladder and to his room. It was no place for a boy like Jimmy, of an age when the physical impression of a place so empty and lonely might settle within him and become the canon for habitation. So I dragged one of the kitchen chairs to the rope and stood on the chair and found I had to swivel slightly to grasp the rope and only then, having turned toward the back of the house, did I see a faint glow of light coming from the nearly perpetual darkness of Simeon's tiny corner of his ancestral home.

"Hello," I called.

There was no answer, but within the distant lamplight I could see the dilating red eye of his cigarette and how its smoke usurped the nearest window's soft late-morning light.

"Simeon?"

"Who is it?"

I jumped off the chair and felt in landing that there was still some of Dicky Brook's water in my shoes. As I hurried toward the old man, I could see he had so little interest in me, whoever I might be, that he was looking into the book he had open on his lap as he sat up in his bed with the gas lamp lit next to him and his ashtray on the bed against his leg. He wore glasses, in which I'd never seen him, and no hat. The glasses' frames were as black as his eyes and were large and gave him a studious look that somehow justified his pretense at scholarship. The distortions and rage that age and loss and obstinacy had brought to his face were, if not erased by his spectacles, softened.

"Who did you think it was?" He had yet to look at me.

Still he went on reading, or pretending to.

"Millie?" I ventured.

Now he looked over the top rim of his glasses, but at the photograph next to his bed, not at me.

"Tell me about her."

"Elisha was a good wife," he muttered into the book.

"Not her." I pointed. *"Her."*

"The Marble Faun," he said.

"Is that what you called her?"

He raised the book slightly from his lap as if to allow me to read its spine.

"I didn't ask what you're reading."

"You should have." He went on reading, even as he added, "It would have been more polite."

I watched him read and smoke and tried to will him with my eyes to look at me.

"I know everything," I said finally.

"You're wet," he said tenderly.

He had me undress. Against my modesty, he claimed he couldn't see me through his spectacles, which were made for reading and rendered everything beyond his book a blur. When I asked how he'd known my clothes were wet, he replied he could feel them on the backs of his hands.

It was a cool day for August, grainy and gray, without a breeze to move the moisture in the air, which swaddled the stones of the house and those of us in it, whoever we might be. I was chilled even without my dress and slip. The old man slid from beneath him the thin red blanket and presented it as he looked at me in my underclothes. I was surprised to feel how warm the blanket was and wondered how much passion he must have stored within.

I spread my damp clothes out on the seat and back of a small wooden chair and, wrapped in Simeon's blanket, sat down beside him on the bed.

"Who else is here?" I asked.

"Ever gone to a dance, young lady?"

"No."

"Well if you ever do, don't look over the shoulder of the one you're dancing with."

He was quite pleased with his little analogy and stuck a fresh cigarette into his smile.

"If you know everything," he said, "why harrow me over her?"

He picked up the photograph of Millie Ryther and with it, necessarily, the picture of his wife, Elisha. The two of them, together in the double frame, he looked at through his glasses, from one to the next, back and forth, and then he lay them both down across his chest and crossed his arms over them and reached up with one hand to remove the glasses. Now there was no pretense that he couldn't see me. "Well?" He stared in such a way that I felt it must have been how he'd looked at these women, one his wife, one his best friend's wife.

"She was your lover," I proclaimed.

He spread a large hand over the photograph of his wife and looked down at Millie Ryther. "But I was never hers."

"Is that a riddle?" I asked.

He shook his head. "The girl who knows everything knows nothing." He patted the bed. "Lie down here."

"Why?' " Men liked us supine. We liked them standing. How much stronger we were.

"Why!"

I did anyway. He was charming but restrained. His white shirt buttoned up to his neck looked like a nightshirt, his white hair like a nightcap whose tassel's fallen back. He was an old man with a young woman on his bed, and this might have been all he wanted from the world now that he'd lost all else.

"Una is yours," I said.

He didn't care I knew. "Let's hope so."

"Did you kill her father?"

"*I'm* her father."

"You know who I mean."

"A tree fell on him."

"Who chopped it down?"

"Nobody."

"It fell all by itself?"

"Trees don't do that. We *sawed* it down. Used a two-man crosscut, as I recall. Still do."

"You and he?"

"Me and *him*." I knew whom he meant. He needn't have raised his eyes toward the top of the house.

"Why did you tell me he was a ghost?"

"Because I stopped existing for him."

"You for him?"

"He was never real for me. That's how it is with your own children. He was real for her."

"His mother?"

"His *sister*."

"Una."

He gave me a vacant look. "If he has another, isn't mine."

"Is he up there?" I couldn't help asking.

"Whether he is or isn't."

I brought my attention back. "Ethan killed Mackswell Ryther?"

"Was a tree."

"And who killed Ethan?"

He didn't hesitate. For him, as for everyone but me and Jimmy, Ethan was gone. "He thinks it was I. I suspect it was his sister."

"Jeremy says he's the one who killed Ethan."

"And the boy thinks it's me. What's the difference."

"Because you're the one who brought her to Jeremy," I said accusatorily.

He would have none of it. "I thought it would do them good to be put away from each other."

"Is that the unpardonable sin?"

He laughed and caught some smoke in his throat and coughed and then laughed within his cough. He was still breathing smoke when he went up on an elbow and looked down into my face. "The evil go to heaven. And if there isn't a heaven, they believe there is and they believe they do. The unpardonable sin is that no sin's unpardonable."

"Murder, for example," I prodded him.

He lay back on his pillow, abandoning me to my twin follies of innocence and ingenuousness. "Murder's the sin most often pardoned, I'd venture. Call it war and all's forgiven."

"But you didn't approve of a brother and a sister's . . ." With a cynic like Simeon Vear, I had no need to complete a phrase I might have been too decorous to utter in the first place.

Now he actually sat up in bed and squashed out his cigarette as a substitute for me. "Don't tell me what I approve or disapprove. Or what I should. That's the government's job." He paused to enjoy his rhetoric and lit a fresh cigarette. "They're half, to start with—different mothers. Born within a few weeks of each other, to protect my good reputation, you might almost say. And I had no objection to the principle—how could I, given my cahoots in their progenation. But as for those *two*—they weren't right for each other."

"How?"

"They were too alike. More than any brother and sister. They were getting lost inside each other. I didn't care for that. They were taking each other's soul away."

"Is that what you told Jeremy?"

He turned to me on his side. "I told him I was Una's pa. I told him the truth. And what does he do?—he goes and makes me his father-in-law!"

"He detests you."

"He thinks *I'm* the sinner." He turned me to face him. We lay together on the bed like a couple separated only by time.

"She doesn't know," I whispered.

"Doesn't know what?" he said with the imperious mistrust of someone who himself knows too much.

"That you're her father."

"Of course she does," he said patiently. "That's why she hit me. The boy's my grandson. She knows that."

"True," I said.

He nodded and closed his eyes. He put his hand on my shoulder, not to pull me toward him but to anchor me there. I waited until he was almost asleep: "Ethan is Jimmy's father."

He opened one eye at a time. "Say again."

"Ethan is Jimmy's father," I whispered even more conspiratorially.

The old man gave me the smile of someone dying happy and

whispered back at me, in covetous triumph, as he closed his
eyes, "Ha! That makes me both his grandpas!"

As eager as I was to leave him for more remote parts of his
house, I was compelled, for the moment at least, to remain by
his side and thus to form, as a man fell asleep beside me for the
first time, a couple strange by virtue only of time, not of sympathy or circumstance.

I bent over him. I brushed some white hair from over his
closed eyes. I imagined him young and doomed to love.

My clothes remained damp, despite the late emergence of
the sun, which slowly combed the floor in dewy beams. I kept
Simeon's red blanket around me as I left him and wandered
through the house, trying to impress myself upon it and at the
same time to absorb it the way one does a poem, not by memorizing but by submersion. It was more a cathedral than a home,
infinite and yet unlike the heavens comforting, God's safe room
within the boundless dread unknown. With the old man asleep
and Ethan and Jimmy, whether they were present or not, shadows of my imagination in the upper reaches of the house, I felt
at home for the first time in my life, free of parents in their
heartless tangle, free of desire in the parish house. I needn't tip-
toe. I needn't hold my breath. I was at once invisible and plain.

Hungry, I went in my bare feet over the centuries-smoothed
floorboards to the icebox and removed a plate of leftovers from
its cool, tremorless darkness. Whatever it was, some small-boned
forest animal whose meat was sweetest at its fragile ribs, I ate it
clean and slowly, sitting in my blanket at the kitchen table, feeling the sunlight leave me quite as if I were myself the sun, red
then pink then rusty with the wasting of the day.

Finally, I made my way to the rope from the ladder and reached it from a chair. The ladder was a hand unfolding toward me joint by joint, and without hesitation I yielded to its guidance and when I was atop it pulled it up behind me as I might were this my home and this my ritual at the close of day.

I went down the long corridor directly to his room. I would have knocked but wanted to find them pure at what they might be doing, if they were doing anything at all, or midword if they were talking, so I might be trapped within that word and delivered into their conversation.

The room was empty, of them and, as before, of nearly everything else. It felt familiar to me, but I couldn't recall having visited it in memory. I wondered if perhaps I'd appropriated Una's memory and was seeing the world as she had, though for her this room was full of toys and books and tossed-off clothes and Ethan as young as Jimmy, whereas for me it was exactly as remembered, empty but for the shadow of a man and a chewed-up pencil and the clothing that this time I couldn't bear to touch. But I wasn't so much she as he, sitting at the desk, standing at the window from the other side of which I'd first laid eyes on him, and, later, when darkness had picked its careful way through the forest and I'd watched it snag upon the tops of trees and let in momentary drops of starlight, lying on his bed.

I didn't fall immediately to sleep but lay there in the dark, without even the mercy of a candle, trying to fit my body into his upon the thin mattress, where it seemed a genuine ghost, the very shape and stamp of him, invisible. Because he was bigger than I, he swallowed me, and so I sank within him and beneath him into sleep.

*   *   *

I awakened not to daylight but to candlelight, behind which dawn was soldered in the August fog. The window near the bed was open, its black cloth pulled aside, letting in the wet thick air that placed a halo around the candle's flame and softened the black eyes staring at me. I pulled his father's blanket around me, not out of modesty but to restrain my shivering from the damp breeze and from his presence.

"Where were you?" I asked.

Ethan looked surprised that I offered a question and not an explanation.

"Hunting."

I went up on my elbows and saw the bow propped against the foot of the bed, the quiver slung across his shoulder.

"Any luck?" What I imagined hunters asked each other.

He reached to the floor and raised a cloth bag by its strings.

"A bear?"

He failed to be amused. "One squirrel. One skunk."

I sniffed the air.

"If you don't use dogs, and you drown them, they don't discharge."

"You eat skunk?"

"Squirrel," he answered, and I guessed that's what I'd had for lunch.

"And the skunk?"

He turned and picked up the candle from his desk and walked toward the door. I could see the darkness fold in upon me even as the first light of day struggled through the window. Why was he always leaving me?

"I thought you were curious." Even as I wondered whether he meant by *curious* that I was interested or I was peculiar, I nearly leaped from the bed and followed him into the room next door, where he lit a gas lamp with the candle flame and all the animals jumped into perished life.

In a corner of the room there was a huge work area free of animals except for those he emptied from his bag onto a large tabletop, around the perimeter of which were neatly arranged such implements as hammers, saws, shears, scissors, tweezers, pliers, needles, thread, surgical knives, and bone-snips as well as rolls of cotton, tubes of glue, jars of beeswax, a bag overflowing with excelsior, spools of wire, balls of twine, linseed oil and turpentine in cans, and a small bag of glass eyes that shuddered and changed shape each time it was touched. On the floor nearby were large cloth sacks of tow and borax and cornmeal.

Ethan reached into his cloth sack for the skunk. Back in Springfield, skunks used to come out of Forest Park at night and challenge neighborhood dogs for garbage and I'd awaken to their scent as if my mother were poaching poisoned eggs. I'd never been so close to a skunk as to this one and was surprised at the inviting plush of its fur and the sad impishness of its face. Ethan turned the backside toward us. He held it with one hand and with the other parted the hair around its anus, on either side of which were two small ducts to which he pointed with his first and fourth fingers.

"Is that where it sprays from?"

He nodded.

Putting the animal on its back, he reached for a knife and in one movement cut from its breastbone to its tail. He peeled back the skin around its rectum and pointed with his bloody fingers into the shiny gore. "Scent glands." As soon as he said the words I could see them, swelled with frustration, safely lurid now.

"Are you hungry?"

I didn't know if he thought to disgust me or feed me.

"Very."

He thrust a cup into the bag of cornmeal and powdered the animal's flesh with it. Then he made incisions from its palms to its wrists and from its soles to its hocks and all down the tail, from which he peeled back the skin and took the tail butt in one hand and with the other stripped the tail out of its skin before he peeled the body skin over the hips and the chest. He sliced the ear linings and loosened the eyelids and the lips and severed the nose and split the lips and split the eyelids and cleaned out of the nostrils what gristle was left and only then did he pick out and scrape out all the meat.

The scent glands, I saw, had remained intact. He had cut around them and left them sitting by themselves in their little pouch of fat.

He rubbed borax into the skin and scraped it clean and rinsed his hands in a bucket of water and poured borax into another bucket and added water to that and then the skin to that.

"I didn't see where the arrow went in," I said.

"I trapped it. The arrows were for deer."

"I'd rather eat skunk."

Which is what he cooked for me for breakfast. And for himself. Simeon was gone from his bed and from the house by the time I went to return his blanket and retrieve my clothes.

"Where is your father?"

"Out."

"So early?" It was barely dawn. Light stopped at the windows. The house was black inside except where two gas lamps grieved.

"Every day."

"Where does he go?"

"Away from me."

"I asked you where, not why."

He was startled by what he took to be my effrontery, when I was merely impatient in my curiosity. Yet it drew him a step closer, curious. "He wanders."

"Where?"

"Wherever the water's coming."

"What about you?"

"I can't wait for the water." In his black eyes I could see the water, approaching in waves like this light of day.

He cooked the skunk in a skillet. Its sweet smell drew me to it. I watched how he moved the spatula, beneath and around the meat, gently, ceaselessly, the muscles in his forearms fretting his skin.

"I love the way it smells," I said.

"Skunk," he answered, and laughed at me. I'd be a willing victim of his laughter. I'd let him find me foolish and himself alive at my expense.

He pointed at the cupboard. I set out plates for us and forks and knives and my own contentment at this servitude along with them.

When we sat, he waited for me to begin. I worked at the meat and felt his eyes on my hands.

"Tough," I said.

"Skunk," was his droll reply once more.

I bit into the meat. It was unyielding, yet its juices sweet and earthy.

"This is delicious!"

Like any cook so praised, he lowered his eyes so to gaze privately upon his pleasure.

*   *   *

Breakfast settled in me like an opiate. So content was I to sit across from him in solitude and silence, and so unwilling to abort what was a dream undreamed until it had been gained, that I forgot my charge and was reminded only when Ethan asked, "What do you teach him?"

"Where is he?" I looked off into the great expanse of the house. It was Jimmy now a spirit and the one I longed to see, if only so I might remain and not be forced to find him elsewhere.

"He went home at dinner hour. I wanted him to hunt with me at night."

"You took him from me," I remembered.

"He took himself."

"You signaled him."

"How?"

I stood and looked at Ethan and motioned him to come to me, faster, faster, faster.

He didn't stir. "Maybe I thought he was you."

"Or his mother?"

"You're more like her than he is."

"Why did you both leave me then?"

"He wanted to be free of you."

"That isn't what I teach him," I said and now held up my hands to keep them both away.

Nonetheless, I left reluctantly. "Come back with me," I said.
"No."

"Are you tired?" I asked, to provide him with a reason to refuse me so forthrightly. He looked not at all tired. He looked like someone who doesn't so much yield to darkness as absorb it. His eyes were austere.

"Yes."

"Are you going to sleep?"

"I don't sleep."

"Ever?"

He nodded sheepishly, as if sleep were a virtue for which he did not qualify.

"What do you do, then?"

"I wait."

"For what?"

"To wake up."

He was a haunter of graveyards and a hunter in the night forest and a wanderer of the land. He never slept, the way Emily said the dead never sleep, waiting for love to scoop up the Dust and chant "Live!" His was the "Extasy" of death—he had died of love and love was yet what kept him alive and all he lived for.

"Of course," I said, because I understood this about him. He was the least sophistical of men. He *was* alive and dead, awake and asleep; he had taken on not the sins but the properties of man.

He offered no acknowledgment of my belief in him. He rose from his chair and I leaned forward into the air his body stirred.

I followed him to the door. "What are you going to do when I leave?"

"Mount the skunk."

"And then?"

"By then it will be night."

"She says you spy on her."

"I don't need to spy on her."

"Why isn't there anything of hers in your room?"

"But there is," he said, and made me feel the interloper.

"Then you certainly don't need me to get her back for you."

"I don't," he said in such a way I couldn't tell if it was statement or question.

He made me leave alone. He wouldn't come with me. He

wouldn't speak to me. He disappeared from me even as he stood before me. Had I not been afraid to touch him, I might have hammered on his chest and felt my hands dissolve.

I found them huddled in welcome. They were together at the kitchen table, silent as I walked in, with a deeper silence enclosing them to tell me they had left off speaking for some time. Even the valley sounds of birds and breeze and mourning breaths of fallen trees couldn't penetrate the disquiet of this unnerved serenity.

They looked at me as one, though each had a different reason to resent and fear my absence.

"Hello," I said, and went to the cookie jar.

"Where were you?" asked Jeremy.

"At the Vear house," I said in a forthright way that averted confession. "Doing your bidding."

"Where did you sleep?" asked Una.

"Upstairs. In the corner room. Beneath the window. In the small bed."

"Why did you run away from me?" asked Jimmy.

"You little liar!" I laughed and went at him so that he jumped out of his seat and ran from the kitchen out the back door and I followed him, just as if we had rehearsed this escape, all the way into the church.

There I cornered him to the side of the pulpit where he stood among a few of his father's discarded pencil pieces, crushing what shards of sermon might have emerged from them or have been tossed aside as if to blame the vessel for the venom.

"I'm sorry." Jimmy's apology embraced no penance. It was neither meek nor supplicating. It was a demand. The boy stood tall and vital against the raw wood of the church wall, his long fingers thrust deep into the pockets of his dungarees, his long hair disheveled into an immutable beauty.

"He said you wanted to be free of me."

"I didn't put it like that." He enjoyed feeling no need to deny whatever he'd said.

"How did you put it?"

"I told him I wanted to get away from you."

"Why?"

He almost came to me then. But he hesitated and fastened himself to the church. "So he could get away from you."

"Are you trying to keep us apart?"

"I just wanted to go where you wouldn't find us. I'll bet you did go to the house, didn't you?" He waited for my reply with his delicate eyebrows raised and his lips pursed sardonically. When I finally nodded but once, he went on: "We didn't go anywhere *near* the house. We walked through the woods all day and he checked his traps and he showed me where he put a pitfall trap and how to build a deadfall trap and he promised he's going to take me to Rattlesnake Hill to show me the rattlesnake caves."

"You love to be with him, don't you?"

"Don't *you*?" he snapped.

"What if he were your father?" I snapped back.

"Then I wouldn't be who I am," he answered without thinking, for that was how the truth was found.

I found Una in my room. She was sitting on the side of my bed, her head turned so she might stare out the window. I saw she had made the bed, for I remembered having left it quickly the morning before so I might take Jimmy to the Shays house. Her fingers rested fitfully in the graveyard embroidered in the old cloth, digging for repose.

"I slept here last night," she said. "So I changed the sheets. Look." Now she pulled back the quilt and the top sheet from under my thin pillow. "I swear—they're clean."

"You didn't have to change them."

"Oh, but I *did*." She finally looked up at me, full of mischief.

"You weren't alone?" I asked.

"Why? Are you ever alone in this bed?"

"Who do you think . . . ?" I began and realized that in my regard at least she was referring to the presence of a creature of the imagination.

"Jimmy was late for dinner." She looked at her watch. "But still we waited for you. He told us you'd become separated over at the Shays place. He said we shouldn't wait for you. So we didn't. You missed one of your favorite dinners. We even had corn on the cob. I ended up eating your ear when you still didn't come. Jeremy went out to the church to work. He's having a terrible time with Sunday's sermon. I waited for him in bed until I couldn't stand it anymore. I thought of him out there in the church with nothing to say and nothing to say it about. I thought of you not coming home to us and where were you and what were you doing. I wanted to talk to you. *Then!* So I came in here to find you. I knew you weren't here. But being here myself brought you back. I got under the covers. It's true. And when I fell asleep, I dreamed your dreams."

"How do you know they were mine?"

"Because I was in them. And I'm never in my own dreams. In my own dreams, I'm the dreamer."

"And in mine?"

She leaned over onto the bed so that her head lay on my pillow. She put one arm under the pillow and the other on top to form a shelter for her head. "In your dreams," she answered softly, "I'm you."

*   *   *

What I saw that night was not a dream. But if I had been dreaming, I would have seen myself, for it's possible to be dreamer and dreamed of, to hold the camera and to turn it on yourself. In fact, such images of me were the only that existed, to the extent that dreams might be said to survive. My father had been opposed to photographs, which he said were useful only as evidence in court and even then were subject to manipulation and misinterpretation. My mother had bought a photo album whose cover was plush and pink and lettered BABY'S FIRST YEAR, though by the time I came upon it while going through my mother's bedroom bureau I was in my eleventh year and was both relieved and gratified to find it empty of anything but protective photo corners she'd pasted hopefully onto every barren page. In the yearbook of my high school graduation class there was a blank for my face, and of my achievements there were merely the scholastic honors I'd achieved and someone's facetious but percipient version of the requisite prediction of each student's future: "She'll go far . . . away!"

There was no farther away I could have gone than this, for the twenty-odd miles between Dickinson Street and this parish house in Greenwich Village were the equivalent of not merely a world but an existence. We were cut off here not by communications—we were still vulnerable to the inanities and intrusive sadnesses delivered by NBC, local station WARE, and the *Springfield Union*—but consciousness. Our lives were afterlives and benefited from the vision thus afforded as well as from such disappointments as must afflict those who die and expect to travel.

What I saw was this: his face at my window.

I had gone to bed, earlier than usual after a mostly silent dinner that suffered from the absence of Jeremy, who had remained

in the church into the evening looking for something to say
about a world in which language was each day being further reduced to the rhetoric of persuasion and accusation.

I read for a long while and found myself as confused with
Emily as Una was with me. Like her, I knew I had no life but
this, to lead it here, no death beyond the dying of the world itself, no tie to the world to come except the realm of . . .

I lit the candle for him to find me and placed it before the
window screen and blew out the one by which I'd I read. I lay in
this altered darkness for a time, held within the cone of light
that spread from my windowsill to my pillow, exposing me in
the faintest terms, nightgown tangled at my knees, hands behind my head, head cocked, hair halfway across my face, smelling of soap and the vapor of the dying trees that formed the
parchment of this flayed land.

I knew when Una had entered their bedroom, because the
light came through the bottom of our common door. But she was
as quiet as I, perhaps lying in the same position as I, picturing
the same man. But the man who came to her was her husband,
and I could not so much hear as feel his arrival, from a pressure
on the wall between us to the rippling of the boards of the floor
beneath my bed.

I strained to hear him speak. He would give his sermon in
the morning, and now was when he read it to her and tested it
upon her, and she, who claimed to have married him for his sermons, would lose herself in his language and his name and his
calling to her out of the darkness that was his subject no less
than it was what we all were subject to.

But he said nothing. I could hear his breath catch at the edge
of words, catch and falter at the barrier meaning raised to stifle
sound. His breathing came more quickly, and I thought he might

scream. But Una soothed him, soothed him with his name and her own breath caught within it and then a cry from her quite unlike anything I'd heard before, a supplication and a celebration in one.

I turned from such intimacy. I put my hands over my ears and let my gaze leave the wall and float over to the window, where it joined the fan of candlelight and sought with it to brush away the moonless bleak hollow at the heart of night.

There was his face.

There was nothing in the empty night but Ethan. He might have been hung from a limb of some great tree that had grown out of and been nourished by darkness and reprisal. He wasn't pressed against the window but held steady at a small remove and leaned against the backward wall of light. He was at once both barely visible and wholly revealed.

I couldn't move. I lay in bed beyond his vision. He stared at me and saw nothing.

"Una!" I cried. "Una! Come quick!"

It was Jeremy who burst through the door. He had a candle in one hand and was unclothed except for drawers and the promise of a bathrobe whose collar he had hooked in a finger on his other hand.

He put his candle next to my extinguished one on the small table by my bed and let his robe fall to the floor and reached for me and raised me half off the bed and took me in his arms.

"It was only a dream," he said, in a muted version of the voice he used to preach. He didn't mean it was only a dream. He meant that in a just and righteous world it would have been a dream. Jeremy knew that redemption and reprieve were guesswork.

"I wasn't sleeping," I said.

"I didn't think you were. I was protecting you."

"From the truth?"

"You shouldn't listen to us. I wasn't hurting her."

"Look." I pointed to the window.

The candle had burned out. Ethan's face was still there, but Ethan was gone.

"I don't see anything."

Jeremy had kept hold and turned me with him. So it was out of the corner of an eye and over Jeremy's shoulder that I saw Una come to the doorway and stop there.

"Come back to bed." Her voice was throaty and her skin incandescent even in the soft light from her husband's candle. She was smiling, beaming, she couldn't stop smiling as she looked at him and seemed as unable to see me as Jeremy had been to see Ethan.

He released me gently and stood up and turned to his wife and picked up the candle and raised it so that for a moment, or perhaps two, his arousal was evident and if anything made Una even cheerier.

When they closed the door behind them I was left in utter darkness. In darkness I went to the window and closed it down before the screen and pressed myself against it until even the pure white of my careworn gown disappeared into the night and I into "the realm of you."

I was up before the Sunday church bell rang, though Jeremy too was gone from bed and Una lay there sleeping with the remnant on her lips of whatever smile had replaced the one I'd seen.

Before going to the church I went around to the side of the house out of which my window looked. I thought I might find a ladder leaning there against the wall or propped up on the pitched berm that ran along the house foundation to draw off rain and melted snow. But there was none, nor any lying in what grass remained among the stumps of trees that once provided shade. And so I pictured him climbing up the house, which lacked the stone holds of his own but nonetheless displayed a sill cock on which he might have taken his first step and adequate casing around the first-floor window and drip cap above that and weepholes into which he might have placed his fingers and beneath the eaves fascia from which I imagined him suspended as he looked out of the night into my window and could see his own reflection and, far back in the room, my body huddled on the bed until I disappeared deep within this image of himself as my shadow had within Jeremy the first time I walked into his church.

I let the final bell take me into church on this Sunday. It awakened me from the reverie in which I looked up toward my own small window in this simple house and saw a phantom flying in and another flying out, him and me, meeting in the virtue of air, above this shorn, depopulated land, above the coming flood. I thought, as Jeremy had told me to when first we walked this land, of what the sea does to the sky. I saw the sky transformed and filled with people in their exodus, not just Ethan and me but everyone who sought refuge in the wind from that new earth about to be born in flood and fire and gas and blood.

So vivid was this image of our drifting off among the very humanity from which I'd always felt an outcast that I came to wonder if its very clarity signaled its unreality and if Ethan therefore had not appeared at my window in the night. Reality itself was not so clear. It was ambiguous and indistinct, "that phraseless melody" Emily sang and in the singing only became harmonious, just as the world was rendered true by art and dream alone. Did it matter then if he had come to me? Or even if he existed? What was a reverie except a poem being painted by the pliant brush of thought?

So it was that in this haze of peculiarly contented uncertainty I approached the little church. Whoever was to enter had entered. There were no stragglers but me. And though the church door remained open, only silence and darkness issued forth. Jeremy had sometime that early morning finally placed a message upon the marquee: "A CITY THAT IS SET ON A HILL CANNOT BE HID"—MATTHEW, 5:14.

Inside the church, Una was already at the piano against the wall and Jimmy was standing silent before the pulpit. He refused to look at me as I took my seat at our usual pew, between his mother's purse and his own Boston Red Sox cap. Around me and behind me there were fewer parishioners than ever, even with the addition of several dusty, mistrustful folk from Dana Center, whose own Congregational church had been given back to God and to the bulldozers on the last day of July and who sat together at the back as if they belonged to another religion. So it had been every Sunday, as one family after another abandoned their homes to implosion and fire and their lands to the impending waters as they escaped a dying world for what Jeremy knew was a world of the advancing dead.

As we waited for the hymn, our hymnals closed because there was no reference on the hymn board, Jeremy walked in from the back of the church and stepped up to the pulpit. "My friends," he said, "every Sunday you come in here and my wife and son lead you in a hymn that most of you seem never to have heard before in your lives. But here's a song I think you know."

He nodded at Una, who smiled delightedly and began to play a catchy melody that everyone must have known because it came from a movie of just a year before and had become a kind of silly anthem of Depression perseverance. Indeed, a few people in church began singing the song, though Jimmy stood quietly in his place, looking toward his mother for his cue. She provided it by lifting her hands from the piano to stop the singing and beginning again for Jimmy, who snapped his fingers as he began to sing and when he sang shrank his body into dwarf-like stature:

> Hiho, hiho, hiho!
> Don't join the CIO
> And pay your dues to a bunch of Jews
> Hiho! Hiho!

As some people laughed and others looked around to see if the church might have been turned without warning into a theater, Reverend Treat motioned for his wife and son to take their seats and even before they were in them said to us, "We here are the Jews hoping to enter America. We too are having our lands taken and our homes burned and our history erased. The president of the United States convened a conference at which twenty-eight countries discussed what would be done with the Jews. And the United States said it would meet its usual quota for Jewish immigration but would not raise that quota. Nor would any other country raise its quota. And do you know what will happen to the Jews left behind? Think then of what will happen to any of us left behind.

"I'm in despair. I'm in despair of the world and I'm in despair of myself. I can no more take the world out of myself than I can take myself out of the world. I know we've all thought, and I have myself preached, that we've been abandoned by the world. But I now realize it's the world that's been abandoned. Not merely by God. And that it's we, in the Swift River Valley, on the verge of our exile, who have, like the Jews, nowhere to go. We, deep within our valley in which all must die, are the city set on the hill. We are the light of the world. And our light is dimming. In Proverbs it is the virtuous woman whose candle goeth not out by night. But that light is dimming too, and the virtuous woman can no longer be distinguished from the adulterous woman, who says, 'I've done nothing wrong.' There are four things never satisfied, the Bible says: the grave; the childless womb; the earth in its hunger for water; the fire. To which I add, yea, a fifth: woman. The way of a man with a maid is said to be a wonderful thing. But so, it is said in the same breath, is the way of a serpent on a rock. Maid and man and serpent are on the rock together, as they have been since the birth of time. And we are that rock. We are the city on the hill."

I wondered if only I knew what he meant and why he might have made the leap from war to woman. Una seemed not at all concerned with his confusion and his confessed anguish. She was relieved he'd found anything to talk about this morning and laid it perhaps to their passion, which remained upon her in a way I'd not observed before in my cloistered life: she was dreamy and self-contained and the bearer of secret pleasures buried in her blush. She stared at Jeremy as if his hand could stretch from pulpit to pew and were at this very moment open upon her skin beneath her clothing. She had forgotten the button he'd left in my room. She knew nothing of the candle in my window that he lit when it went out. She would give him to me if she could have Ethan in return. But the only way she could permit herself to have Ethan was through me. I was caught between husband and wife; and they were trapped within me.

Jeremy was exhausted and seemed to have nothing more to say. He stared straight ahead down the narrow center aisle of the church, his eyes widening, his mouth closing so tightly that the bones in his face came into sharp relief and he might have been grinding the world itself to dust between his teeth.

It was Ethan he saw, Ethan who proved himself no ghost, no image only, but a handsome tall thin black-eyed short-haired quiet modest young man who walked softly toe to heel down the narrow center aisle of the church to claim his bride.

He whispered, "Pardon," as he turned left into our pew and brushed past a couple sitting at its end and when he reached us went right by Jimmy and then by me so I could smell on him wood smoke and trees and the night air and the morning damp. He parted Una and me without gesture and sat down between us on the hard bench.

How I longed to touch him. How I longed to take his hand and claim him. But I sat like a good little churchgoing girl with my hands folded in my lap.

Una moved away from him. I could hear her skirt irritate the old wood of the bench that had not been worn smooth but the opposite, had been abraded and coarsened by the telling of the truth. But she wanted the distance only to look at him. And he looked straight ahead, at Jeremy, awaiting word.

Only Jimmy tried to touch him. Only Jimmy reached out, his arm across my lap, pushing across my thighs one and then the next, his hand finding Ethan's arm, grasping it, tugging at it for attention.

Ethan put his hand over Jimmy's to stop him and gave Jimmy's hand back to him, all the while looking at Jeremy for some word. Jimmy blamed me for this rejection and made a fist and hit my leg with it, once, hard, before he took his hand back and hit his own leg with it.

Now Jeremy spoke: "In that same book of Proverbs God looks through the window of His house and He sees a young man void of understanding. This young man is flattered by a woman who perfumes her bed with myrrh and cinnamon and invites him into it to take their fill of love until the morning. He goes to her like a bird to the snare, unaware that many strong men before him have been destroyed by her. 'Her house is the way to hell,' says the Bible, 'going down to the chambers of death.' "

Now it was Ethan who reached for me. I put out my hand to him. He took it. We stood and, with Jimmy unable to force himself between us, walked to the end of the pew and out of the church and off in the direction of the old stone house.

BOOK TWO

THE PRIVILEGE OF ONE ANOTHER'S EYES

"This is your room." He pushed the animals aside. He made space for me. He found, beneath the stuffed bodies of so many owls and ducks and what I took to be otters or weasels or beavers that I would not have known it was there, a narrow bed. It was, as Emily characterized a coffin, a small domain. It was exactly like his own in the next room.

"Is this my bed?"

He wouldn't answer. How could he? How could it be her bed and mine at once?

I sat down on its edge. He stood over me but off, away, taking a step or two back but never his eyes from me.

"Sarianna."

"I know," he acknowledged.

He left me alone. I had nothing to unpack. I'd brought nothing with me from the church but my surprise and pleasure.

I lay down on the bed. The feathers in its pillow gave way and not only yielded to my head but embraced it. I wondered if the linens had been changed since Una slept here as a girl. I held the ends of the pillow over my face and breathed. It didn't smell of her or of time passed. It smelled instead of stone and wood, beeswax and the cleansed hides and furs and feathers of the birds and animals who appeared surprised to find me there.

How empty the room must have seemed to Una when there was nothing in it but her dolls and budding dresses and Ethan's tin soldiers watching over her. I wondered where she'd carved her name and guessed it would have been in the wall between their rooms. I searched that wall and found nothing but the dark grain of the wood that spelled such words as seemed left by the fingertips of the wind as it had barked through the forest, a puzzling language of long lines and gentle curves that Ethan alone, I suspected, could read.

Then I found it, in the dark bottom corner of that wall, not far from the foot of the bed and near what I discovered to be a small opening cut in the wall where it touched the wooden floor and the stone of the exterior. The wood had been fitted back to form an unhinged door, just large enough for a body to fit through, a young body, like his or mine or hers as it must have been. It now occurred to me that the first time I had entered this room, and sensed the movement of a creature, Ethan had been here, and he had used this little door either to escape from me or to abide with me. What I might have taken for a ghost was more a shadow.

Her name was here, right beside that door. I had to feel for it. It was too dark for me to make it out with my eyes until my skin had first. I placed my finger upon, and then within, each crudely carved letter and number and slash:

UNA RYTHER
7/20/1922

I placed my palm upon her name without knowing if I intended to erase it or absorb it. Only then did I feel at the base of my hand a name I recognized instantly and even the fragile, fervent printing from the note he had written for me and her:

beloved of ethan vear
2/3/1923

I imagined her carving her name in the heat of summer, a ten-year-old girl on her knees before the small, hidden door that led to and from the room of the boy she loved, or would come to love, so much more than she would a brother because she didn't know he was her brother.

I pictured him in the chill of the following winter, eleven years old, who must by then have seen her name carved here but was reluctant to join it with his own until he knew his heart, whose blood he spilled as surely as he might have literally by taking from this wood such particles as made up the word *beloved*.

I walked to him next door and asked: "Did you save the little shavings of wood from when you carved your name into the wall of my room?"

He wondered how I knew him so well. He needn't answer. His eyes took mine and held them.

"Where are they?"

He had been standing at the small window. Now he went to the table and opened the drawer and withdrew the small vial filled with dust. He handed it to me. I removed the tiny cork and sniffed at the contents.

"Wood," I guessed, and wondered if he might be tricking me. He nodded.

"And you know just which grains came from which words?"

"I do." He seemed forced to step toward me, that I would know so well the capacity of his love to grant him extraordinary powers.

He took the vial from my hand.

"Spell out your name for me," I said.

Slowly and rhythmically he tapped the dust from the vial onto the tabletop and studied it and with a fingertip separated individual grains until he had two piles, from the smaller of which he arranged the dust until it formed the name *UNA*.

Some of it became lodged under his fingernail, where it resembled dirt.

I took a deep breath and puffed my cheeks as if to blow away her name and the very idea that he might have collected some six months after it had fallen to the floor the dust of that name too.

In merely watching me, Ethan provoked my righteousness.

"I love her too," I said, and held my breath as he carefully brushed her back into the vial with the aid of a matchstick.

"I have to go."

"Away?" he said with neither pleasure nor regret.

"I have to *go*," I emphasized.

He laughed, quite like a boy at bathroom humor.

"I'll get you a pan."

"Fine," I said. "I'll use it at night if I have to."

"Come on then," he said.

I'd hoped he would take me down the stone steps built into the exterior of the house. But he went down the hallway to the ladder and lowered it and led me out the back door and across the clearing there, in the opposite direction from the family graveyard, to a small, weathered shack that sat so closely pressed between two trees it appeared to have grown out of them.

He opened the door for me. Its springs whined. I tightened my nostrils instinctively and stepped in. "Thanks," I said, and waited for him to let the door swing shut.

"You don't have to hold your nose," he said with his own held closed from within so that he imitated my nasal sound.

"Very funny." But I was less annoyed than self-conscious.

He took it as a compliment, smiling as he let go the door.

As I sat down, I listened for his footsteps, wanting him to walk away but not leave. "Are you there?" I called out.

I could hear nothing but the uncertain cries of birds. I looked up for flies but there were none. There were cobwebs, empty of prey. Spiders were known to be fastidious, as well as ravenous from the endless effort of their fabrication. I closed my eyes and breathed deeply.

The odor was clean, almost sweet.

"You're right," I announced.

When I was done and pushed open the door, he was standing exactly where he'd been when he'd closed it.

"Ashes," he said.

"What?"

He had a bucket at his feet. He picked it up and let me pass and walked right in and took a scoop from the bucket. "Ashes," he repeated as he let them float into the deep hole. He then sprinkled some around the periphery of the hole, on the rough wood on which I'd sat. He rubbed with his fingertips until these ashes vanished. Now all the fingernails of that hand were dirty, and at the same time purified.

"You'll get a splinter," I said.

"Did you?"

"You make me blush."

He looked into my face. "No I don't."

I followed him to an ash bin at the side of the house. He opened it and placed the bucket inside.

"I didn't even hear you leave," I said.

"Or come back," he replied.

*   *   *

His father returned at dinnertime. They were, I realized, like an old couple who no longer see each other and yet are compelled by circumstance if not by desire to bear tacit witness to each other's existence.

Ethan cooked, the meat of some kind of animal he'd no doubt killed. Once again he set a place for his father but otherwise ignored him. And me.

"What did you do today?" I asked Simeon hopefully.

"Got one day older." He smoked while he ate and thus kept his mouth too busy for further grousing.

It was easy to be silent. I rather liked it. No one asked me what I was doing there. So I needn't answer. I hadn't decided what I was doing there, only that the purpose must be mine, even were I to lose my heart or life in the process.

I cleared the table without being asked and enjoyed how my industriousness fixed the two of them at the table. No one had waited on them for years. They were mesmerized. They sat like gluttons glued to their chairs by the cumbersome aftermath of their indulgence.

I walked into the huge fireplace to build under the black pot a small fire to heat water I'd pumped noisily into the pot at the sink. I stood by the fire as I waited for steam to rise from the water. It was August and customarily warm, but the air was damp and the stones of the house cool, so as the fire wrung moisture from the air there was comfort within the small orbit of my exile. Finally, I removed the pot using a large thick leather glove that hung outside the fireplace just over the stack of summer kindling. I carried it to the sink and washed our dishes and had begun to scour the pan in which Ethan had roasted the meat when he appeared next to me.

He put a hand into the bucket that hung on the wall by the sink and came forth with a palm's worth of silvery gray dust, which he dumped into the pan I was washing. He took the steel wool from my hand and pushed it around inside the pan until he'd made a frothy paste that purged the animal grease and left the pan almost polished.

"Ashes," he said, and left me to dry.

I waited for him the whole evening to come to me. I lay on my bed in my clothes and watched the room turn dark and the animals recede into its shadows and finally disappear. I felt they were neither protecting nor threatening me. They were dead, for all the verisimilitude of life with which they'd been bestowed by Ethan's artistry. They were what he was himself: as beautiful as nature might make, and as real, but gutted.

The bed shrank around me. It forced me into a tight curl of my own being. The darkness without and the darkness within were of equal pressure, so I was paralyzed, rigid with a desire to stretch, to float off into sleep or into his presence. But the bed became no bigger than I was, crushed, constricted not by sleep but by its opposite. I began to recite in my mind Emily's poem as if it were a prayer, *ample make this bed*, remembering even as I spoke the words to myself and to whatever god is that most fickle of gods who bequeaths sleep, that Emily's bed, with its *mattress straight* and *pillow round*, was yet another coffin, never to be invaded by the yellow noise of sunrise.

So it was dreams of death that got me up, though I was not asleep, just as dreams of death will waken anyone who isn't dead, startled into life by images of life's demise. I walked in my bare feet to the wall between our rooms and felt the wall and waited for my eyes to steal what light from darkness it possessed before I went through the little door he'd made and came out in his room.

"Ethan," I whispered, even as I looked for him and felt for him and knew he wasn't there.

I was on his bed asleep when he returned in the morning. I had no memory of having fallen asleep. Though our beds were identical, in his I'd found oblivion and in mine misgiving.

When I opened my eyes, he was there. His arms were full: my other dress, my skirt, my blouses, my pair of shorts, my dungarees, my socks, my two nightgowns, my underthings.

"Where did you get them?"

He looked at me blankly.

"*How* did you get them?"

He raised his eyes that I might follow them from the ground up to my window.

"You went into my *room*?"

"Yes."

If my clothes weren't proof enough, he brought my book out from beneath the clothes.

"It was the only one," he explained.

He must have thought I was like someone who owns no book but the Bible and cannot live without it.

He put the book into my hands and the clothes at the end of the bed.

"That one isn't mine." It was a dress. I'd never seen it. It wouldn't fit her now. She would have kept it safe in her closet from those years ago when she'd worn it here.

"Put it on," he said.

If he thought to have me protest or even fly off back to the Treats—if this were a challenge to my love for him or his for Una—I would disappoint and please him at once.

I sat up and reached behind with one hand and unbuttoned my wrinkled, slept-in dress and with the other hand, as I raised my body from the bed, pulled the dress off over my head.

He took a step backward even as I rose to stand before him. My skin was wrapped about in the morning light from the window behind me. I could feel it over my ribs and in the shallow breathing of my stomach and in the pulse that moved above my heart and sounded in my ear. He stared at me. I was the very sun and blinded him.

"Look," it was now my turn to say.

He closed his eyes.

I put on Una's dress. It fit me perfectly. It was a girl's dress, pink, flowery, puffed at the shoulders, the skirt pleated, fagoting above the breasts that would display nothing more than promise.

"How do I look?"

"It isn't you." He stared. No matter who he was talking to, I took pleasure from it.

He fed me berries for breakfast. He took me to the woods—or at least I followed him into the woods—and when he stopped to pick some huckleberries, he gathered them in his palm and turned back toward me and held them out to me. I took some with my fingers and put them in my own palm. Before I could eat even one, a bird came down out of the trees crying, *pai pai*, and flew by my open hand close enough for me to see spots on its breast and its large, dark eyes challenging me for the food. I brought my hand to my mouth and shoved all the berries in at once.

"Delicious," I lisped through the fruit and its tiny seeds.

"Hermit thrush," he said, moving his finger along the invisible trail of the bird's departure.

"Just like you," I answered.

He shook his head. "I don't care to fly."

"I meant the hermit part."

"I'm the opposite of a hermit," he said, and started quickly away from me.

I didn't catch up to him until I found him picking berries off a strange tree that seemed to have birds' nests settled upon the ends of most of its branches.

Once again he offered me berries from his hand. I took some. But before I'd eat any, I looked for more birds in the tree.

"Are those nests?" I asked.

"Witches'-brooms."

"Real witches?"

"Real brooms?"

"They look like brooms."

"Then they must belong to witches."

"Tell me the truth."

"They're caused by mistletoe."

"That's nice," I said.

He shook his head. "Mistletoe is a parasite."

"It is?"

"Try a berry," he said.

"What kind?"

"This is a hagberry tree."

"No wonder they call it witches'-broom," I said, and put several of its berries in my mouth.

Which I immediately spit out, making whatever sounds a girl makes when she's tasted something awful.

He enjoyed my distress. "By next month they'll taste like cherries."

"Thanks a lot," I said.

He said, "I'm sorry," and reached out and picked some of the fruit's skin from beneath my lower lip.

I would have eaten handfuls more to have him keep touching me like that.

He led me through the forest. There were no paths. Moss robed the earth. It rose in wrinkled folds to swathe the rotting logs I quickly learned to jump or vault instead of step upon. Amid such wreckage stood tree after giant tree, great arms rising from the shoulders of the earth, some of them consumed by mosses growing up their trunks so high I couldn't see where the green cloak ended and the bark emerged. Everywhere, down here, were shrubs, which no sun reached and for their efforts to stay alive had become crabbed and hostile. Yet here and there within the underbrush were seedlings and saplings that stood around like little deer, too naive to hide, their heads turned toward whatever sky drifted visible through the distant, placable canopy.

And now we roam in sovereign woods, I thought of Emily writing and wondered if she had roamed like this, on the heels of a boy, breathless from a forest's passion for itself.

Ethan finally stopped at a stream dammed by beavers, whose ragged homes clustered along a bank of the pond they'd caused; the interlace of their kidding had produced a solid revetment against collapse but not, I knew, against the drowning yet to come. I found him kneeling, staring at the surface of the water, on which insects skidded and from which the black limbs of fallen trees reached in awful prayer.

I stared with him. "See any?"

He shook his head. "Long gone." He pointed to the dead

trees' visible parts. "The beavers drowned those trees. Then the bugs come and live in them. And the birds come for the bugs. Woodpeckers. That's what I'm looking for. They make their holes going after bugs in the snags. And the ducks nest in the holes. Mergansers. You remember. And—"

It wasn't whether I remembered. It was that he had. And that I'd entered his memory, eating merganser at his table, which he'd caught like this: I moved my hands as he had when he'd demonstrated how he'd trapped the duck we'd had for dinner.

"No," he said. "Like *this*." He put his hands over mine and brought them fiercely together. "And then you break its neck." He twisted my hands in opposite directions and let them go so suddenly I could feel a duck fall from them.

So could he. He looked at me as if I'd killed our supper. His black eyes softened and he nearly took my hand again.

Just as he had shown me how in the pond all life emerged from the building of a dam and how even man was fed through the dying of the trees, so he taught me how the forest itself was born and died and constantly renewed as much through death as birth. He was my Preceptor, as a boy named Ben Newton had been for Emily Dickinson, teaching me too what was most grand or beautiful in nature, a faith in things unseen, and in life.

We climbed a small hill and he took me into the sun as it moved from the east toward the south and brought out the hard dark garish glossy green of the spheral lobes of the leaves of the great white oaks. With hickories, they thrived here in the sun, while on the other side of the hill, where it was cooler and darker and breezes flourished, red maples and hemlocks sat among the oaks and softened their aggressive coloring even as they shrank from the massive crowns of the oak that governed the forest in a godly selfish way.

He put an acorn in my palm. I'd never really studied one, though they used to blanket the sidewalks of Fountain Street and I'd crush them without thought or hope on my way to the Washington Street elementary school each autumn morning— the ridges in the nut, the tiny swellings of the sweet meat against the tough skin, the knobby cup that grasped the nut about its shoulders and at the same time offered it like a small brown teat. Indeed, these acorns nourished so many of the woods' animals—"deer," he said, "the turkeys," which amused me, "squirrels, coyotes, blue jays, *mice*"—that they failed in their primary purpose, which was to spread and propagate the tree.

Fires also kept the oaks from so dominating that they might destroy the forest by overspreading it. The Nipmuc had used fire to clear the land. Oaks couldn't sprout after fire. Hurricanes, too, provided balance through destruction, and so did disease. There were galls that came from nematodes, roundworms that in another variation invaded the intestines of humans. There was a fungus, the name of which Ethan didn't know, though he did know the sad name of the disease with which it infected the oak: heart rot.

When too many trees were purged, those that remained lacked the very protection provided by their former competitors and might die of sun scald or, in the absence of a wind break, be thrashed to death.

In the quiet of the breathing forest, with a boy's soft voice in my ear and the world empty, I felt I was in the midst of human history. Trees warred. Nature schemed. Death endured. There could be no hermits here.

We sat on a coppice oak. Its various trunks rose from a single set of roots and in their middle provided what was almost a sofa, on which we could sit and lean back and look up through the hard dark green of the leaves to the silver streaks of grazing sky.

The pale gnarled bark was harsh against my skin, and I kept fidgeting until Ethan moved a bit and showed me a smooth area and I asked as I slid into it how it had gotten that way and he said, "Me," which, if was true or not, caused me to imagine him coming alone to this tree and sitting here waiting years for her to come back to him.

He called all this their wood lot, all this, forest stretching out in a wheel from where we sat in this coppice oak. He told me how the Vear family, tributaried from the blood of the Nipmuc Indians and the Pilgrim settlers, had harvested and sold timber but had always grown it back, here in this place, whereas the other English homesteaders had stripped all of arable New England of everything but rogues and some pasture oaks they left for the mercy of their cows. It was these trees that seeded those fields as were given up to time and overfarming and the movement of the populations into cities. Nurse trees would thrive, sumacs and alders and aspen, quick studies that would against their knowledge or at least better judgment provide shade for their successors, hardwood maples and oaks. And these, along with fragrant applewood, which burned the best of all, heated men.

All life, all heat, was from the sun. I knew that. I'd studied carbon and hydrogen and oxygen in freshman botany, I even knew, because I'd memorized it, $6(H_2O) + 6(CO_2) + Energy = C_6H_{12}O_6 + 6(O_2)$, which Mrs. Holdfast claimed was the basis of all life, though even as I embraced the formula for the sake of learning, I resisted it for the sake of poetry. And here was Ethan, retaining energy the way the clouds and tides and winds and trees and plants did, embodying such power as to destroy himself or ignite himself, and me.

"Look at this," he said as we walked off the hill. From a large tree stump, gray and pale and creased with death, sprouted a young tree, whose smooth bark shone with a purply sap. "Chestnut. And those." Dead chestnut trees littered the floor. They seemed to have fallen, one upon another, at every angle, evidence of their lapsed predominance.

"He told me they were everywhere once. When he was a boy. Nothing could destroy them. The railroad bought them for ties. Telephone poles. The farmers made fence from them. Chestnut lasted longer than stone, he said they said. Than stone. And then."

"What killed them?" I asked.

"The thing they never got."

"Is that a riddle?"

He must have thought of Una then, for he smiled and put his hand over his mouth. "The blight," he answered through his fingers. "Look." From another stump grew another sprout, but this one's bark was furrowed, and what had been purple beneath the skin was orange now upon the slender, adolescent trunk, the color of the blight fungus.

"They live for a year. When they die their spores are carried by the wind. To trees like that one"—he pointed to the healthy chestnut growing from the torso of its dead father—"and sicken them."

"Who is 'he'?" I asked.

Ethan pointed to the great dead trunk.

I sat at his feet like the student he'd once been to his father. His blue canvas shirt was open more fully against the heat than it had been at the dam, and I saw when he breathed or raised his arm to point, his chest, as smooth as a boy's, as hard as his heart had been made by the dying of his love. He was not so much muscular as compressed, worn down to what appeared an essence of flesh and bone. He was beautiful beyond belief.

He had been for me as much idea as materiality, more perhaps. But now, as we sat in or walked through these woods he so loved, and about which he knew so much, and from which his family had prospered for several centuries, he became specific, tangible. As Emily had seen *Nature in her beryl apron*, so I saw Ethan. But as it was unclear whether Emily intended *beryl* as a color that adorned Nature or a mineral that shielded her, so did the Ethan I saw remain unknown, unreal, as I felt myself become. This, I realized, was what love did: it brought forth the flesh but rendered it spirit.

He surprised me then by saying, "You want to walk back down on the road?"

"Road? What road?"

He showed me roads, such as they were. Barely cleared paths, with ruts made by and for wheels, of horse-drawn carts or gasoline tractors, as well as, he explained, the runners of sleds that horses pulled in winter. These roads were invisible within the undergrowth and the thick convening of the trees until you were upon them. They branched off from one another into all corners of the Vear woods, though some had been reclaimed and would have to be cut again when there were trees again on those wood lots to which they traveled, were there ever to be trees here again.

"You can't harvest if you can't haul," he said. "You can fell and buck and you can split, but if you leave them they rot."

"Where have you been?" I thought to ask.

"Everywhere."

"Beyond the valley?"

"Never." He delivered this nonchalantly, as if I shouldn't be surprised, but he did add more dramatically, like a prophecy, "Ever."

As we made our way out of the woods he identified for me the hardwoods—white oak, white ash, black cherry, sugar maple, yellow birch—and the softwoods—pines and red spruce and Douglas fir—that were sold for lumber. And the Vears always cut their own. They never sold timber on the stump.

"Are you rich?" I asked.

"Enough not to answer," he said, and led me almost out of the forest where a marsh stood and he named the plants and herbs and weeds and shrubs as he showed me each: sweet fern, buttonbush, blue vervain, which I knew from my reading came from the verbena, a holy bough borne by priests, joe-pye weed, groundnut, jewelweed. As he cradled them in his palm, he recited their names like poetry, poetry of a plain sort, of the earth, of Nature in an apron though without the adornment of image, and this, I knew then, was his display of riches.

"Here." He put into my hand some jewelweed. It was one of the *Impatiens*, I guessed from the way its corolla couldn't be distinguished from its calyx, its heart from its flesh. But I took it as a jewel, an offering of what was impermanent and named, as if this were a riddle, after what was eternal. I wondered if for him it symbolized this valley he had never left, soon to be drowned and thus, in a way, and by virtue of its destruction, preserved forever.

"It has another name," he said.

"Impatiens," I hastened to say.

"Touch-me-not. Watch."

He put a thumb and finger around one of the plant's ripe pods. He brought them together toward the pod. The moment they touched it, if they touched it at all, the pod exploded and its seeds flew all over his hand and mine and his pants and the skirt of Una's dress.

"Touch-me-not," he said again, unnecessarily.

"I won't," I said, and reached for him and found him with my hand, only his shirt, I suppose, and only for a moment because I let go and laughed and so he nearly did too. Yes, now we'd roamed in sovereign woods, *now*, and I realized that when Una had said there is no now, she'd either forgotten or never known that there is this, when time stops and the heart does too.

Jimmy'd come to rescue me. Or Ethan from me.

"I've been waiting for you all day!"

It wasn't clear to which of us he spoke. He was sitting with his grandfather in the aftermath of dinner. Simeon smoked and watched Jimmy as Jimmy watched us; his dark eyes were narrowed, mistrustful. There was a new gravity upon him, a hurt that both aged and beautified him. Just as I'd run off, so had he.

"Who sent you?" I provoked him.

"Where were you?" he asked Ethan.

"I took her to the coppice tree."

Whatever betrayal this was, Jimmy showed none of it. "Did you have fun?" he asked me.

"Fun?" I asked back, and this disturbed him.

"How come you two don't talk?" he asked.

"We do." I looked to Ethan for evidence.

"I didn't mean *you*," Jimmy said cruelly.

"He hates me." Simeon spoke without looking at the boy. He'd looked at none of us.

"Why?" Jimmy's hand went out and grasped the sleeve of the old man's clean white shirt.

Simeon shook his head. "You're asking the wrong person."

Jimmy turned his eyes to Ethan, but Ethan said nothing.

From the way Ethan looked back at Jimmy, I realized then that what he sought in the boy was not that part of himself he recognized but whatever there was of Una that lived in her son, separate from himself.

Jimmy knew that look. He brightened up and smiled at Ethan and said, "Can I stay here tonight?"

"I'll walk you back home," Ethan answered.

I stepped away, into the shadows, only slightly out of the reach of what twilight left us each distinct. I unbuttoned Una's dress and pulled it off over my head. I held it out. "Give this back to your mother."

Jimmy took it from me without question and without seeing me. Ethan saw me, but only until the dress left my hand.

He was out all night again. I slept in his bed, but only until dawn. At first light, I claimed my bed and waited for him to come to *me*.

I heard him before I saw him. I was lying, I realized, awake, when I'd thought I'd been asleep. I'd so concentrated upon him that I'd lost consciousness of all else. I heard him and thought it was a dream until I opened my eyes to see him and he wasn't there.

I begged him to come to me and was talking only to myself.

There was no more sound of him. I got up and went to him, tiptoed in my nightgown and bare feet to his door and through it. My nightgown was soft now, from being washed or from my acquiescence I didn't know, only that it embraced me with each step and cupped my skin quite sensitively.

He had his back to me. "Did you see her?" I asked.

He was startled. "What are you doing here?"

"Thank you for my nightgown," I said.

He turned around. He looked at me in it. "Not her—I saw *him*."

"Jeremy?"

"He was waiting for the boy."

"Where?"

"In the church," he answered, and I knew he had.

"What did he say?"

"He said, 'Thank God.' "

"What did he say to *you*?"

"Nothing."

"Did he even see you?"

"He saw the boy. He was very happy to see the boy."

"What did he say to *him*?"

"He said, 'Did you find her?' "

"Me?" I said, and regretted I'd made it a question.

"Who else." It wasn't a question at all. Who else.

I closed my arms around myself, pulling my nightgown tight with both hands, and left him as he wanted to be, alone.

So was I the next day. He simply wasn't there. Nor was Simeon. The house was mine.

At first I felt peculiar, alone here for the first time, concealed from the world like Eve among the trees yet not called forth by God as Adam was. "Where art thou?" God asked Adam. This had caused me, on my very first day in Sunday school when those of us little girls able to read read together from Genesis, to interrupt: "But can't God *see* Adam?" I knew the answer and was pleased to have it confirmed so early in the Bible: we are hidden from God, and none so much as women. This is what made us divine, this obscurity, this sovereignty.

Thus was I. I went to the outhouse in my nightgown, made coffee for myself for the first time in my life, took the cooling grounds out to the compost, picked vegetables from the garden, dressed, read poetry, borrowed Simeon's edition of Hawthorne's *American Notebooks*, which I was surprised to see had been published for the first time only six years before, in 1932, and in which I discovered that Hawthorne himself had had a most remarkable idea for a book, never written: "the race of mankind to be swept away, leaving all their cities and works. Then another human pair to be placed in the world, with native intelligence, like Adam and Eve, but knowing nothing of their predecessors or of their own nature and destiny." Was this not Ethan and I, I thought, leaving this world behind, making our way toward an inscrutable future?

Late in the day I hid myself in my room before the others returned and that night stayed awake and listened for Ethan's departure. I followed him into the night, which was black from the sheet of cloud that tucked the rest of the world into sleep. I had the flashlight from the peg by the front door and shined it on the ground before me. Ethan had no light yet made his way through utter darkness as if the sun were out. I could hear him only, not see him, until the light from my flashlight flickered and faded and the batteries ran out and I was enclosed in that utter darkness and only then could see him, I didn't know how, for he wasn't wrapped in light, there was no light, but there was Ethan, visible in the darkness though as dark himself as were his eyes.

He stopped. I did too. I could hear his breathing move toward me, until it joined with my own and I couldn't tell the two apart. There was something alit before him, two small white flames that suddenly leaped into the air and then erupted in the same moment they disappeared and a high quick shriek rose from Ethan's hands.

I must have made a sound myself, crying out in fear and pleasure.

"That's enough," he said.

I didn't know if he was talking to himself or to me.

"Here," he said.

He held the animal he'd caught, a white rabbit, with both hands under its front legs, squeezed, and then moved one hand down the rabbit's body, which emptied into itself so that it grew larger and larger in its hind parts, and then the other hand, and just when the rabbit looked as if it might explode, Ethan raised it above his head and like someone trying to ring the strongman bell at a carnival came down with it between his legs. The insides of the rabbit flew out and splashed behind Ethan into the leaves on the forest floor.

When he straightened up, he gave one shake to what was left of the animal and hung it on his belt.

I finally stepped toward him. "Are you angry?"

"Surprised."

"At me?"

"At me," he said. "I didn't know you were following."

"How can you see when it's so dark?"

He moved his hand toward me. I thought he would take my face in it. But he used it merely to point into the woods. "Look."

I looked away from him for the first time. There in the darkness I could see the shapes of trees, small black spaces within the thickness of their leaves, the thick black paint of sky above us, the rabbit's entrails shining at our feet and the spattering of blood across the leaves that was darker even than the darkness of the night.

"How?" I asked.

"They say our eyes get accustomed to the dark. But I think it's darkness lets us see."

I reached toward him and touched the rabbit at his belt. "What do you call it what you did?"

"Dressing. Skinning it—that's dressing also."

I could feel the rabbit cool even in the short time I held my hand to it.

"Now what?"

"More hunting."

"I want to come," I said. "I want to do this with you."

"They circle," he said. "We'll have to run."

"Back to where they started?" I asked. "That's what circling is."

"We still have to chase them."

"What about your traps?"

"We'll see," he said.

"I'd rather run after them."

He touched my hand to hold me back. "First we walk."

I waited until he had four or five rabbits cooling on his belt. Then I asked, "What are they for?"

"Your breakfast."

The first light rose from behind the trees and nearly blinded us so used were we to seeing in the dark.

He'd left the tailbones on the rabbits and when I asked why he said so I'd know they weren't cats. He salted the rabbits and rolled them in flour and fried them in oil and onions while I made coffee.

"How is it?" I asked.

"Chewy."

"I meant the coffee."

"I know."

"Aren't you going to smile?"

"At what?"

"At your little joke."

"What joke?"

Now he smiled.

"It's wonderful," he said.

"The rabbit?"

"The coffee."

He grew even younger when he was happy. It wasn't merely that his eyes softened from their hard, sad glare or his mouth relaxed or his shoulders lost their grip upon him. He became a boy almost, or what I understood a boy to be, which comprised what Jimmy'd shown me and what I imagined a boy might be, as young as I or younger still, the age he'd been when Una left him and he disappeared into sorrow.

I loved to look at him. It seemed, sometimes, the only way to capture him: with my eyes. It was as if his existence depended solely upon my seeing him. When I failed to see him, he failed to exist.

"Are you letting your hair grow?" I asked.

"My hair?" He put his hand upon his head.

"Yes, grow. It looks longer."

"Than what?" Now he ran his hand over his hair.

"Than how you cut it."

"I don't cut it."

"Or *have* it cut."

"I don't have it cut."

"Then how . . . ?" I began but stopped, because I knew he wouldn't know. "It's short," I said. "Would you like to see?"

But there were, I realized, no mirrors in this house. I remem-

bered Una's describing how they stared at each other in a mirror
in his room, as if they were one being, not two. The mirror was
gone, along with everything else. Only the image remained, carried by his memory everywhere.

"You have no idea what you look like, do you?"

"Nobody does," he answered.

"You're very beautiful," I ventured.

He concentrated. "You have no idea what *you* look like."

"None at all." I waited. "Tell me."

He looked at me. "I can't see you yet."

What comfort I took from *yet.* He might as well have told
me I would live forever.

As I had my first day in the Swift River Valley, two months
later on a hot August morning I found Jeremy Treat in the church
on his knees. This time he wasn't working on the pews, though
they had further disintegrated, less from use, since there were
ever fewer people remaining in the valley, than from negligence.
The whole little building was coming down around him, and all
Jeremy could do was kneel—not in prayer, but in surrender.

The sun now seeped into the church through cracks in its
walls. It daubed the rough floor in narrow lines of light that
formed a trap in which the pastor clustered, his long limbs tight
against his forsaken soul.

That same light bent around me as I came upon him. What
for him was strict was for me pliant. The sun sang on my skin,
while on his black coat it died away.

But I was in him now. I didn't startle him this time. He felt
me there before I was and rose, quite as if I had redeemed or at
the very least aroused him.

"Sarianna," he said.

"You were looking for me?"

Now that he'd found me, he felt no need to confess. He came up to me, quite close, and grasped my arm.

"She wants you back. She so misses you she's taken to her bed."

"And you?" I ventured.

"I'm not the one who's left."

"But you are," I said, thinking how leaving and staying could both be meant by *left*. And I meant to both bless and irritate him by reciting, "At least to pray is left, is left, oh, Jesus in the air, I know not which thy chamber is, I'm knocking everywhere."

He was shocked by those lines. Who wouldn't be, by her repetition of that word and the perverse courtesy of simple rhyme for once and the inexorable rhythm and the terrible sense of loss and being lost. It was a prayer to end all prayers; it put the lost *I* back into *prayer*. I granted him the clemency of my not saying the next four lines in which the sinner herself is abandoned by Jesus Christ of Nazareth.

"There's more to life than poetry, Sarianna," he said preachily.

"More to life, certainly," I concurred, "but less to life without it."

"And you think it's life you've run off to find?"

"I think it's life that's running after me."

"And so you hide among the dead?"

I wouldn't let him rile me. "Where else does life chase us but the grave?"

"Very good," he said.

"You agree?"

"Not at all," he replied. "But it's a good line. Is it yours?"

I answered him with the silly silence of the flattered.

Pleased at having pleased me, he released my arm now, even as he confessed, "I want you back as well."

"Be that as it may," I said more stiffly than I might have wanted, "it was the two of you who sent me to him."

"Don't be ridiculous!"

I couldn't be intimidated. "You to take him away from her," I reminded him, "and Una to keep him away."

Perhaps, then, it was the truth that caused him to confess further: "Actually, I *was* looking for you. You've had a letter from your father. He's quite impatient with you. He's received several notices from your college. He wants to know if you're returning to South Hadley before he pays your tuition."

"You opened my mail!" I merely pretended indignation. The image itself I enjoyed—his illicit slitting of the envelope, shame and pleasure so fused he couldn't tell one from the other.

"When you weren't here to do the same—of course I did. It's your first piece of mail since you arrived," he added, creating an excuse by way of novelty and in the process ridiculing an isolation from the world, in which I took only pleasure.

"I have nothing to hide from you," I said to Jeremy, and hid it all by turning on my heel and leaving him alone to the exhausted succor of his church.

Una had taken to bed, all right, but she scarcely seemed distraught. I ventured into their room on the pretext of looking for the letter from my father. There was Una, lying languorously on the snarled bottom sheet, uncovered in the heat, immodest in the riding up and down of her pale nightgown, waiting, it seemed, for someone to appear, anyone to whom she might talk.

"Poor Jeremy," she said the moment she saw me—I might never have been away. "He's heard on his radio that the Japanese have melted down their Temple of Humanity to make weapons. He's trying to write a sermon about this. You'd think he didn't know that the cross and the sword are the same. I feel so sorry for him. He can't sleep. He hasn't been to bed since you left. And I haven't been out of bed!"

She giggled as she grasped my wrist and pulled me down to sit by her.

"Tell me everything," she said.

"Jeremy said I'd received a letter from my father."

She waved a hand. "Oh, that. I don't know where it is. It had something to do with school. You don't want to go back to school. Or even if you do, I don't want you to."

"What do you want?" I asked, and moved my hand across her forehead, where the warmth of her skin had attracted and held some wisps of hair that I pushed back into place.

"That feels so good," she said.

Was it no longer their bed? Jeremy had said she'd taken to *her* bed. Had Ethan or I come between them so far that he would no longer kisse his sweet wife and rest her faithfull husband?

"Have you seen Ethan?" I asked.

"Have *you*?" she asked back as if this were a game.

"I'm sorry," I said.

"For what?"

"Do you know where I've gone?"

"No."

"Did Jimmy bring you back a dress?"

"There it is." It had been thrown across the back of a small chair.

"Did you see him?"

"Jimmy?"

"No—Ethan."

"How could I see him?" She looked away from me as she spoke.

"He was here. He was here at night. He came to my room to get my things. He found this dress in your closet."

"He's always here," she said.

"Did you see him?"

"I never see him."

"But you looked right at him in the church."

"Jeremy claims he wasn't there."

"But he took me away. Why did you think I'd left?"

"You were there too?" she asked. "At my wedding?"

She claimed not to see him because the last time she remembered seeing him she was giving herself to another man. He was locked there in her memory, gazing at her from the back of the church as she married Jeremy. Whether Ethan had been there or not, she'd seen him there. She couldn't allow herself to see him again, even when he appeared before her, next to her, as he had in the church on Sunday. I was the one, she was telling me, who must see him for both of us. He had reappeared in the world just as I had entered this world. I didn't claim to have drawn him out of his dark asylum. He had come out for Una and had found me.

"I didn't mean your wedding day," I explained.

"May twenty-sixth," she said dreamily.

"Nineteen twenty-six," I quoted from the marker on his grave and escaped from this terrible truth through the door into what had until lately been my little bedroom.

"He's not there either!" Una called out merrily.

Only the Graveyard quilt was left. I sat down upon it on the bed. Oh, I noticed, and the candle was still there, halfway gone and gripped about in its own wax fingers, Ethan's candle in my window, summoning him, showing him where I'd slept beyond his eyes but not his reach.

"I washed your sheets."

Una stood before me in the doorway, as Jeremy had done in the darkness of night.

"Alone," she added. "I missed you. No one wrings like you, Sarianna."

We lay there on my small deserted bed all afternoon. I didn't know who I was for her, myself or Ethan, or who she was for me, herself or Ethan. Yet so long as we kept nothing between us, we were one and could distinguish of the other only the scent of hair and the peaceful draw of breath. This might have been nothing more than practice for me, holding someone else, studying the loss of my body in another's. But for Una it must have been familiar, nostalgic in a bitter way, holding Ethan in holding me.

It was the darkness that awakened me. The summer air washed in the open window and covered us with the fragrance of the malva in her garden and of the fireweed that colonized those home sites burned and pinked the blackened earth and of the purple loosestrife drifting from the marshes by Walker's Mill Pond and heated just enough by the curving red rays of the drowned sun to keep the insects from our flesh. Nature, like Emily, preferred pestilence.

I left her sleeping in my bed and found the letter from my father on the small table on her side of their marriage bed.

Dear Sarianna:

Mt. Holyoke has sent their third and final request for tuition. They have given me your address only out of threat of not being paid. I am surprised to say the least to find you hiding in that condemned wasteland. What can you be doing there that you cannot do in civilization.

Since you can't stay there and not be drowned, you might as well go back to school. I've received your grades and as usual don't comprehend how someone so aloof and so obstinate can perform so superiorly. But then I've never pretended to understand you. Only to pay your way. If you wish me to continue, let me know immediately. Otherwise, go your own way on your own.

The world will be at war soon. Where better hide from reality than in a cloister of higher learning.

Your mother would, I am sure, send whatever greeting she could muster in her concern for your well-being.

Your loving father,
Edward Chase Renway, Esq.

He had put his seal upon his signature. It was the only thing I liked about his law office in Springfield, with its manure-scented leather chairs and its pictures on the walls of fat-faced Governor Curley and of President Roosevelt who looked so like my father with his wire glasses and parted white hair and stern little mouth that the only thing on which my father and I agreed was our dislike of him, his political, mine personal. I loved how the silver handle of the seal stood in the air at such an angle that it invited pressure and how, when pressure was applied, the paper being sealed yielded with an exquisite and almost fleshly surrender. I also loved how the word *seal* referred both to the implement and to its product, one so sturdy and the other—mere colorless impressions pushed into a piece of paper—so spectral. On those rare occasions when I was deposited with my father in his Elm Street office on Court Square, while my mother shopped nearby on Main Street at Steiger's and Forbes & Wallace for linens and girdles and scarves to hide her neck, I would sit at a table in his anteroom scarring sheets of paper with his seal, hoping I might eventually wear it down and smooth his name to nothing.

I tore up his letter and left the pieces for Una to find, so she would know I'd never leave her behind.

Jimmy was waiting for me on the dark lawn beneath the window of my room, where he used to play ball with his father and would now, I imagined, prefer to be alone, contemplating the stars and whatever emptiness the sky provided as an emblem of my defection.

"Hello," he said cheerily, as if he'd come upon me by accident and we hadn't been apart for longer than we'd ever been apart.

He must have been at an age when a boy can change in days. His hair had settled in a bit. There were lines in his face as he smiled at me, beside his eyes and lips, lines that glowed for but a moment before darkness filled them. They weren't the lines of time; they came from gaiety and knowledge. And he stood still now, heavier not on the earth but in its grip, peculiarly confident of his place in a world that was disappearing and must have seemed to have taken me with it.

"Aren't you going to say anything?" He leaned into me as he spoke, up against me almost, his shoulder well above mine now, his cheek floating on my hair.

"I was looking at you," I answered truthfully.

"So I leave you speechless?" he joked, and was familiar again.

"What do you want?" I asked.

"I think you know," he said.

"Then we both want the same thing."

"I wouldn't know about that." He paused. He put his hand on my arm. "I mean, *I* don't know what I want. I thought maybe *you* do."

"What *you* want?" I asked.

"How does a person know? Everything runs together inside. First it's this and then it's that and then it's both of them and something else besides. I don't *know* what I want."

"Or are you just afraid to say it?"

"Hell," he answered, "I'm afraid enough to think it!"

He laughed and took my hand and pulled me on our way.

"Where do you think you're going?" I planted my feet.

"With you," he said.

"You can't."

"Why"—he tried to yank me forward—"*not?*"

"Because he's mine!" If I'd thought this would cause him to release me, I was wrong. He clung to me with both hands.

"And whose are you?" he asked, and with his question answered what he wanted.

He took his hands from me but wouldn't leave until I walked away.

Una was still on me, or in me, or both, when I returned to the big stone house. Ethan wasn't waiting for me—he didn't yet anticipate me as I did him—but was drawn to me as he hadn't been before. He followed me about. He watched me change my clothes as I imagined he used to watch her, still and staring but protecting our modesty through a distance provided by his own preoccupation. Back down the ladder, he stood behind me in the kitchen as I pumped water into a can for the endlessly thirsty fleshy roots of the clivia I'd potted and the aspidistra I knew could survive in the cool darkness of our home and the vallota I knew couldn't but that took just enough of the dying summer's light to send forth its incandescent clusters of scarlet flowers. "Look at them!" I marveled, and he did, nearly pressing against me from behind, breathing on my neck and taking in whatever there was of Una in my hair and on my skin.

"I went back," I said. "I saw them all. It turns out it *was* me he was looking for. Jimmy. For Jeremy, I mean. And Jeremy said it was for Una. She and I . . ."

He either didn't want to know or didn't need me to tell him. If he saw in my eyes what I saw in my head, he wouldn't be able to tell us one from the other. I gave him what he wanted. I gave him Una.

He took me to Rattlesnake Hill. I didn't remind him that he'd promised Jimmy. He wouldn't remember. He had little memory of anything he'd done or said since Una left him. Perhaps that's what he'd meant when he'd written that he didn't exist. And when he'd carved on his grave's marker that he'd died in his fifteenth year. I'd realized in this valley that we're constructed of the past. Thus it was that I was no longer a child, for children believe they are made of the future.

Take the past away and we're ghosts. So it was to be with these little towns, emptied of their folk this pious morn, as John Keats wrote of a little Greek town on a little Greek urn, their streets forever more to be silent, not a soul but us perhaps to tell why they're so desolate. We who remained here were ghosts in the making. Liberated from time. And memory would be what Emily called a withdrawn delight whose contemplation she compared to a "bliss like murder"—a bliss like murder, almost as dangerous to say as to think. Ethan might be a murderer, of himself, of Mackswell Ryther. Emily said we love the wound because it reminds us that we died. Ethan loved the wound because he loved his death more than his life. I loved Ethan, and I loved his woundedness, but I hated his death.

We headed north at the point Soapstone Road joined the old railroad bed. As was usual, we said little to each other but communicated in what we shared: the smell of burned homesteads, the missing railroad ties that had left an image of a fallen ladder on the land, the tree stumps everywhere and everywhere around them little bypassed pieces of the trees they'd been, the junk-filled hole in the ground where the North Dana piano-leg factory had been, which was the shape of a piano, I observed, just the way Pottapaug Pond was shaped like a piano, and Ethan said, "You're right."

We stopped at the Old North Dana Cemetery and sat down in what was left of the graves and listened to the slow summer purl of Fever Brook just off to the east. It carried water the way it would once the valley was sealed up by the dams in the south. Then the water would back up and both branches of Fever Brook and all three branches of the Swift River and the diverted water of the Ware River would coalesce and rise until only the very top of Rattlesnake Hill, which we could see just beyond Fever Brook's west branch, would be visible. By then, all the people would be gone and all these graves would be indistinguishable tiny pools of unrecollected grief.

"Where will you go?" I asked Ethan.

"Nowhere," he said, when what I wished for him to say was he would go where I went or at the least take me where he went.

He had told me he couldn't wait for the water. Perhaps he thought he would rise up on it and float away to where he'd never been or remain at the bottom on the submerged land he so loved that had yet been the province of his pain. Here he was, exulting in a place he wished to disappear. It wasn't much different, I realized, from the joy that's suffered generally by those who love what cannot stay, their life on earth.

Or the heat of the sun. It was a dry, hot day, that strange imagined taste of the desert that can infiltrate New England air, when the north wind blows the moisture out to sea and the sun meets no impediment and is a single unrelenting breath.

I thought it was a paradox that we'd climb toward the sun in order to be cooler. But we did, we climbed up the east side of the hill through thick shrubs and around the trunks of fallen trees until we reached the top and the thin air dried us and cooled us even as it let the sun burn more strongly off our skin. From the summit we looked down at the completely abandoned Doubleday Village with what was left of its demolished sawmill lying still beside the stream that once had powered it and now merely scoffed as it sauntered by.

Finally, going down the western side of Rattlesnake Hill, we came to the small caves and deep-cut ledges where Ethan said rattlesnakes had lived.

"What about now?" I asked.

He shook his head. Even the serpents were wise enough to leave.

"Have you ever seen one?" I asked.

He put his arms out before me. I imagined them cradling a huge snake draped over both.

"Here," he said. "Here. Here. Here." He pushed his fingernails into places on his arms. At each place he left two small marks, which, as I watched them, slowly faded, revealing smaller, darker marks I hadn't been able to see. Now I took his arms and brought them toward my eyes and found even more old puncture marks among the scars from animals and the little cuts he'd gotten from thorns and briers and blackberry shrubs and trees that scraped him as they fell beneath his ax or saw and seasoned logs he carried to the fire in the winter in the big stone house.

"How much is in you?" I asked.

"Enough."

Enough not to kill him, I knew, but to make him immune, if not to love then at least to venom.

I bent and pressed his arms to my face and as I did saw a flower growing alone out of a leafless plant.

I put Ethan aside for the flower. I caressed it gently. "Do you see how it resembles a pipe?" I asked. "It's even called Indian pipe."

He was amazed, though whether by me or by the flower I couldn't tell and couldn't tell either whether it would have made any difference.

I'd never seen this flower living, only a drawing of it on the title page of the very first edition of Emily Dickinson's poems. There had been a place in Amherst called Rattlesnake Gutter; it was said to have been the only place this strange flowering plant might be found. I thought that a wonderful coincidence, here on Rattlesnake Hill. Perhaps it grew where poison was the currency, for it was a saprophyte, nourished not by the sun but by dead organic matter, a ghostly flower rarely seen.

We sat with our backs to the rock and looked down again into Doubleday Village and beyond that toward Nichewaug, named, said Ethan, for the Indians who with the Nipmuc had first settled this valley and had lived here in peace until some Boston people decided around 1700 that they wanted more woods to harvest and came here to kill the Indians and ended up creating a town called Volunteersville.

"What kind of Indian are you?" I asked.

"Look over there—" Ethan pointed high toward the southeast. "That's where we Nipmuc first settled." He paused and then very gravely said, "Lake Chargoggagoggmanchauggagogg-chaubunagungamaugg."

When I'd stopped laughing, I made him say it again.

When I woke the next morning, there was beside me on my bed a huge stuffed rattlesnake, copper brown with black rings so evenly slipped upon its skin it looked divinely, coldly proportioned. Its eyes were peculiarly expressive beneath locked lids, projecting through their hard little windows a wonder and anger and ecstasy and malice. Open mouthed, fangs extended, it smelled of glycerine and alcohol and skin paste and lacquer, its body stiff with plaster and burlap but the skin of textured diamonds its own, black-banded, alive beneath my fingers. Hanging from the fangs was a note in Ethan's hand:

PROOF

Ethan and I left one morning long before dawn to walk past Hardwick and then along the Ware River to Winimisset. I had been reading aloud to Ethan and Simeon from Simeon's copy of *The Narrative of the Captivity and Restoration of Mrs. Mary Rowlandson*. After dinner we would sit together on an extremely uncomfortable, straight-backed deacon's bench which in the winter Simeon said he put out in front of the enormous fireplace in case anyone might want to sit on it, though no one ever did. In these wasting days of summer, the bench remained against the stone wall beside the fireplace, and there the three of us would lodge while I read by gaslight, between two men who didn't speak except through me, and the only words I could get them to share were Mary Rowlandson's.

Her diary had first been published in 1682, in Cambridge, Massachusetts, to which nearly two hundred years later Emily Dickinson would travel—the farthest she would ever go from home—to see a doctor about her failing eyesight. Those eyes, which needn't see to see, were said to have been dark, "set in a small, pale, delicately chiseled face." Emily herself offered to someone who asked for a picture that her eyes were the color of sherry left in the bottom of a glass, as she said her hair was chestnut and her body small, like a wren's. She sent no picture. There was none except what had been taken at Mount Holyoke Female Seminary when she was my age and thus gave the world one more photograph than there'd been of me.

Mary Rowlandson was more like Una than Emily, a traveler *out*, peculiar, yes, but only in endurance. Ethan sensed this similarity to his lost love. He would close his eyes and listen to my every word, which were Mary Rowlandson's words and began with the Indian attack on her town of Lancaster, Massachusetts, in the winter of 1676 and in the first paragraph described the tomahawking of a baby at its mother's breast and the disemboweling of a settler as he begged for mercy. Mary Rowlandson was wounded and, with her youngest daughter, also wounded, taken captive by the Indians. She told the story of Goodwife Joslin, who was pregnant and whined so much to the Indians about the hardships of captivity and being homesick that the Indians tomahawked her and her two-year-old and threw the corpses into the fire for all to see them burn and be warned not to grumble. Ethan especially enjoyed that story. Mary Rowlandson wasn't like Goodwife Joslin. Mary Rowlandson didn't complain. She became one with her captors the way Una had become one with hers, Jeremy. Even when her daughter died of her wounds in the Nipmuc village at Winimisset, Mary Rowlandson didn't give in to despair but cured her own wounds with a compress of oak leaves, learned from the Indians, and watched as these same Indians buried her child on a hill in Winimisset.

It was that hill Ethan wanted to see. For it had been a Nipmuc burial, and Ethan was a student of Indian obsequies. Indeed, on our way out of the valley, as darkness first struggled from the trees and we were by then well beyond the taking line and thus beyond the emptying of all graves not Indian or Vear, he stopped by piles of stones here and there and said, "There's one. . . . There's one. . . ." He knew the Pegan from the Norwottock; the Quinsigamond from the greatly feared Mohawk, who affronted superstition by covering themselves in rocks and thus appeared to rise in attack from the land of the dead; the Massachuset out of the east from the Sokoki out of the west, whose burial stones had sometimes been carried with them from the Connecticut River and were thus distinctive, at least to Ethan, who could read a tree's biography in the veins of a leaf and the future of a day in how it bent to the wind.

"The rocks were meant to keep animals away," I said.

"Yes." He was impressed with me.

"Una told me," I confessed. "And you told her."

He was unwilling to talk about her. So I was not.

When we departed the Ware River and rejoined Hardwick Road in Winimisset itself, we came upon a small hill to the west of the road. It was not like most of the hills back in our valley. There, the trees were downed and had been strewn in their fractures with scrub and brush and sometimes remnants of bulldozed homes in preparation for the final burning said to be coming in the new year; the hills themselves were ghastly swells of whiskered silt, pocked with trenches from which the roots of trees begged for light and reason. Here, this hill was thick with green and moist with life.

"She's here," said Ethan, and led the way, while I followed and tried to find in Mary Rowlandson's book that February day in 1676 when her daughter died and was laid to rest somewhere on a hill in Winimisset.

Toward the top of the hill, heaps of stones began to appear with some regularity. Ethan stopped at each one and poked about in some, always careful to replace the stones when he moved on. In a few the bones had been pulled up and picked clean by animals; he showed me bite marks, which looked more ragged and ravaging than the neat incisions made in his arms by fangs of toxic snakes. In some there were no bones but only shreds of cloth or buttons or dried up locks of hair that seemed the grass that grew from death.

Finally, he found where she was and he knew it. The stones were undisturbed. He showed me where animals had dug around the grave, their footprints long since gone to time and weather but their efforts visible in the holes they'd made and some scorings on the rocks. But the rocks were piled high and neatly, and they extended well beyond the confines of a body of a girl.

"This is Nipmuc—" He showed me how any flaw in a rock was positioned toward the inside, resulting in the grave, as viewed by anyone who didn't dwell within it, appearing much like rocks in a formal-garden wall, precise and rounded and climbing like a pyramid in steps and to an apex. "*This* is Nipmuc—" He brought forth from among the rocks tiny pieces of what by now was thin, nearly friable leather on which had been scratched drawings of the lady's slipper, whose root the Indians had used to fight internal parasites, and blue devil, which was a newly introduced plant here at the time of the Indian wars and whose flowers Ethan said he used to eat whenever he was bitten by a snake.

"She died in winter," he said, which I confirmed from the book. Otherwise there would be dried flowers here and not their representations. That was Nipmuc also.

Ethan removed the rocks one by one from the center, giving them to me to pile around the grave so he need not toss them. I took pleasure in my bit of physical labor, minor compared to his and light enough to allow me to watch him bend farther into the grave with each rock given and admire how he concentrated upon nothing else but this material rooting out of death's canopy and still included me, so potent was his energy, and how the faded blue of his shirt clung darkeningly to his wet skin in the heat of the day and made him too look scratched upon the shaded air, God's best flower toiling toward redemption.

Finally he was done, or appeared near to be, throwing out rocks in the rhythm of his quick breath until he gasped and before he breathed again removed from the grave a tiny, shrunken body. He threw it toward me. It landed at my feet. I took it first to be the remnants of the girl, perfectly preserved yet cured by death into a miniature. But when I picked it up, I found it was a doll, made of corn husks that were no longer green but had been dry-bleached to the beige of flesh, tied with threads that held their colors, and tacked down here and there with bead-headed pins. While it looked like an Indian, whatever Indian had made it had given it hair not of braided yarn but of corn silk, the hair of a white girl.

Ethan stood over that girl as she lay deep in the grave. She was all a skeleton now, every visible bone in place, staring up at us with empty eyes so dark from our shadows upon her they looked like Vear eyes, black with loss and mutiny. She wore a dress, a pretty dress, the dress of a girl who had been Sarah Rowlandson, dead in her seventh year, run away to God.

Ethan cried upon her silently, honoring her grave with his few slow tears even as he stared at her in her pretty dress. Then he took my hand, which he held so lightly that it must have been for its own sake and not to keep from falling into the grave beside her.

We returned only so far as the Vear forest. By then it was deep into night and we were tired from having covered so many miles. Ethan, as well, was able to relax only when he was back in our valley. He'd never been beyond it before. I knew he held me responsible, though I had merely read from the book and he had been the one to want to follow it. I was happy to bear that burden. I must, for I was planning yet another journey, also, in a sense, from a book. He must learn to leave, as he must learn to have been left. Or I would stay and drown here with him.

He took me to a large windowless shed. It was filled with traps and saws and sawbucks and axes and knives and razor blades and candles and cloth rags and tin cans in order of size on a workbench, each containing some different necessity for taking down forest trees or animals. On the walls were trophies of the hunt, the beard and long pointed spurs of a turkey, a flying squirrel tacked-up still, a couple of stiff fish on which he showed me the telltale three incisions made by the leister he'd carved from a deer clavical, and the head of a deer staring off to the side and over my shoulder.

"This is cozy," I said, and looked around for a chair, a bed. I did see a blanket in a corner, multicolored stripes against a rough gray background. I realized how tired I was when all I wanted was to lie down on the raised wood floor with that blanket over me.

"Come on." He lowered a quiver over his head and slanted it across his back, hung a bow from his shoulder, and handed me a small leather pouch as he turned away from me.

"Gunpowder?" I asked as I dropped the pouch in his rucksack.

"Tobacco."

He led me through the forest until we came to a huge Norway maple. Without a word he went behind me and put his hands around my waist and pushed them toward each other as he lifted and I felt I was being thrown into the air, a backwoods ballerina flying into the arms of a tree. The maple was like a hand itself, its low, strong side branches fingers I gripped and then stepped upon as I made my way up with Ethan right behind, beneath, every so often taking the sole of my shoe in his palm and pushing it up and placing it carefully on the next branch, until he said, "There, here," and he scrambled up beside me and passed me and suddenly there he was, sitting not in a crotch of the tree but upon a floor of boards built into several crotches. He reached down for my hand and hoisted me up beside him.

"What's this?" I asked.

"Our blind," he answered.

"But I can see everything."

"And nothing can see us."

It was a platform in the sky, walled in by leaves and roofed by stars so thick they held some heat of day and at the same time gave forth a chill of color, their white light cold with the mystery of distance.

I shivered.

Ethan lit a candle and moved it toward me.

I put my hands above it. But he'd intended it for light, not heat. From the rucksack he took his father's book and the pouch of tobacco. "Read." He handed me the book. I knew what passage he wanted, which he loved to hear me read as much as he loved, though he would never say it, to hear his father tell the story of the great King Philip, from whom Simeon claimed they were in part descended.

Mary Rowlandson went to see Philip. He had formerly been Metacomet, as his brother, Alexander, had been named Wamsutta. The year before he took Mary Rowlandson, 1675, Philip had gone to war to oppose the English trespass upon, and seizure of, his native land. After many great and brutal victories, Philip was betrayed by a Pocasset named Alderman. Philip was shot dead and then beheaded and quartered. His head resided for many years upon a pike on the main road into Plymouth Plantation. One day Increase Mather came upon Philip's skull and stared at it for a long time before he removed the jawbone as a souvenir of the man he called a "blasphemous leviathan." Alderman, his killer, had long since claimed one of Philip's hands, which he preserved in a pail of rum and displayed at taverns for the price of a drink.

Mary Rowlandson may have been the only white person not to have feared Philip. She made a shirt for his son, for which she was paid in horse meat. Then she made his son a hat, for which Philip invited her to dinner and fed her a pancake fried in bear's grease, proclaimed by her one of the pleasanter meals of her life. But what Ethan most enjoyed was the story of how Philip offered Mary a smoke, which she refused. "Refused!" said Ethan, entering again into the story. I read on: " 'For though I had formerly used tobacco, yet I had left it ever since I was first taken. It seems to be a bait the devil lays to make men lose their precious time. I remember with shame how formerly when I had taken two or three pipes I was presently ready for another, such a bewitching thing it is. But I thank God He has now given me power over it; surely there are many who may be better employed than to lie sucking a stinking tobacco pipe.' "

While I read, Ethan removed a small white piece of paper from the pouch and sprinkled tobacco onto it. As he chuckled at how Mary Rowlandson had so deftly put *sucking* and *stinking* so near one another to create her effect, he rolled this cigarette and licked it and lit it and handed it to me.

I might not have taken it to my mouth had it not been to his, had he and Una not smoked together.

"Like this?" I asked, and blew smoke into the air where his had been and disappeared.

He shook his head and took a deep breath.

"I'll cough if I inhale it," I said.

"Yes."

I inhaled it and I coughed.

He reached around me and put his hand against my back. So startled was I that I stopped coughing and breathed deeply of the night air just to force my back against his hand. The air was sweet with the smell of our tobacco. Such a bewitching thing it was indeed. "Here," I said, and reached out to put the cigarette into his other hand. He took it and drew smoke from it and passed it back to me. I smoked it and heard its paper crackle and leaned against his hand, leaned so completely that I would surely have fallen over had he not held me up so strongly.

"It can make you dizzy," he said.

I let him think that and put the cigarette once more to my mouth before guiding it to his lips and placing it between them.

Gently he lowered me to the floor of the blind and lay down beside me and fell asleep so quickly that the last of the smoke was still leaving his mouth. I leaned close and breathed it in and took the cigarette and let it burn down in my fingers until I could feel its heat and then carefully I put it out.

I stared at him asleep for what felt like hours, as the night grew darker and the wind picked up. Thick dark maple leaves that were loosening for the coming autumn blew down onto the floor of the blind. Hidden within them were a few dry clusters of immature yellow flowers from which leaves had failed to unfold and within these clusters some aberrant flowers both staminate and pistillate that seemed the very image of the two of us huddled here, man and woman indistinguishable in the closeness of night, boy and girl stopped by time in candlelight. I found the biggest leaf and fanned his face with it, until its leaf stem severed and out from it a milky juice ran down my thumb and wrist and onto his bottom lip, where it turned the color of night and evaporated. With the leaves came the fruit of the tree, pairs of winged seeds that danced in the wind in spirals and landed on our clothes and in my hair, their pale green beginning slightly to brown, their nutlets joined between wings so straight that some looked wed in a whimsical geometry of desire.

The wind became, in time, fierce. It appeared as much a product of the forest as the forest's assailant, thrown off by wricking, twisting trees and their heaving limbs. It was an ocean of trees, and we rode on the top of a wave, seeing nothing but the water that the wind was, seeing everything.

Trailing the wind to the west was the wind's endowment, announced at first by a rumble in the sky so faint it seemed a quiet throbbing of the earth below. Yet I was drawn to look up and out and saw a film of blackness spread across the stars and into the very darkness separating them; there were degrees of lightlessness and what had been obscure was now opaque. Yet just as everything was dark and shadows fled and trees recoiled, a flash of light peeled back the sky. In that moment heaven was revealed, suffused with light and beauty and consisting of absolutely nothing but distance.

As the wind passed through us, taking with it the flame of our candle, the thunder came closer and grew louder and appeared to generate the lightning, spitting most of it out across the sky but the rest of it down until it struck hills and mountains, each of which appeared for a moment to be white with snowlike light. I listened for the rain I was sure was pouring down from the swollen clouds the lightning ravaged. I listened for it to come creeping through the woods, a wall of water heralded by drops the size of grapes.

"Wake up," I whispered, and heard my words harvested by thunder before they reached his ear.

"What's that?" he said, in answer to the thunder, not to me.

"Quick!" I said. "—we're going to get drenched."

He sat up, not quickly at all. He sat up sleepily.

"I can't believe it," he said.

"It's only a thunderstorm," I assured him. "It'll pass."

"That I was asleep." He rubbed his night black eyes like a child. Then he looked out into the storm, which brought its darkness now so close that while I could feel his breath on my face I couldn't see his face except when lightning flashed. Emily had called lightning "the fire"—the first words she's known to have said.

"I'm afraid," I said.

"Of what?"

"Sitting high up in a tree in a lightning storm." As soon as I said it, I laughed. "You won't let me die, will you?"

"How could I," he answered with such perfect ambiguity that I reached out for him if only to assure myself he was really there.

Before I touched him, the sky exploded. Now its lightning dropped straight down, glowing beams of an enormous house that was at once both rising above us and settling around us; thunder shook our blind to the rhythm of its flashes. With the hand that might have touched him, I pointed out into the night at supple strands of liquid light that hung from the tumid clouds and wound around and through the lightning but never reached the earth. I jumped to my feet and grasped with one hand and then another at the dissolving, threaded remnants of these watery ropes that swung toward us.

"Come on!" I screamed to Ethan, as though we might climb them to the sky.

He rose and stood next to me, so close that even flashes of light couldn't come between us.

"What are they?" I asked.

"Rain."

I brought my hands down and held them palm-up before me. Nothing.

"The rain stops," he said. "In the air. They're virga."

"They're the most beautiful things I've ever seen."

So they were, in the midst of this most violent of storms, cords of water that hung above the valley in imitation of the rivers teasing us with immortality.

Now the lightning spread across the forest in a calligraphy of fire, writing poems in a language that was God's alone, their lines uneven and their words obscure as they were savage. Distant trees died as they were cleaved with great cracks of sound. Then they fell, snapping limbs until they settled with a hush on the forest floor. Moss hummed with flame. Birds fled into the lightning and were never seen again.

All the while, Ethan and I huddled together without touching, the better to look at each other. He stared at me with a strange passion in his eyes, a hunger and a sadness mixed while we went from dark to light and back again as Nature imitated Life.

"Don't move," he whispered, as if I might or could, so locked was I into his gaze.

He reached behind himself and took an arrow from the quiver and the bow from where he'd laid it on the floor. On his haunches, he silently moved back from me as he fit the bow-string into the nock of the arrow.

His arrow points he'd made himself, from agate, clouded, not striped, yet still translucent. The string was from the sinew of a deer. The bow itself he'd scraped and shaved from a horn-beam whose short and crooked bole protected it from lumber merchants, dense and heavy so it took great strength to bend yet gave in its release a great velocity; from the heartwood came the gentle brown and from the sapwood the pale white, colors snaking up and down the bow in comely, deadly fusion.

He wet his fingers and with them brushed the arrow's fletching smooth. Only then did he lay the arrow on his bow hand and draw the bowstring back, sighting down the arrow not at me but by my side. I felt relieved and at the same time forsaken.

He held his breath and waited. He was completely still yet flickered from the lightning. I disobeyed and turned around and saw what he was aiming at, a doe that was as still as Ethan yet with the lightning also came and went.

It was not strange at all that I wanted to put myself in the way of that arrow. Not to die but to be made alive. When the arrow's loosed, and it's in flight, in those moments before it strikes is one not most alive?

The arrow tore my dress and grazed my skin as it flew out of the blind and into the side of the deer, just over her front legs. She shuddered in the lightning and fell between its strokes.

Ethan moved toward me and I feared he was on his way

down the tree when he stopped and put two fingers against my side, against my skin where my dress had been torn by his arrow.

"It's nothing," I said.

He showed me my blood on his fingers. "Without you I would have missed," he said. "Come on."

We made our way down so fast we might have been swung from those cords of rain that only when we hit the ground evaporated and left us standing in the descending sun.

The doe stared at me.

"They die with their eyes open," Ethan said. "And their ears like this." He took my hand and put it beneath the doe's loose ear. "If it's up like this"—he had me pull the ear erect—"it's alive."

"Poor thing," I said. Its blood emptied from its wound in a steady stream as if its heart were pumping fast and joyfully.

"Who?" he asked as he removed the arrow. "Look." He put his fingers into grooves cut into the shaft of the arrow. "An old Indian trick. For the blood to flow through. To bleed to death."

He turned the doe onto its back and placed it so its head was uphill and began to gut it from its anus on up. He practically had to saw through the tissue around the vent, which he took great care not to perforate. He lifted the vent entire from the carcass and held it out and had me tie a string around it to keep the excretion discrete. While I did that, he put the same two fingers he'd pressed to my side into the hole he'd made in the doe's lower abdomen and used them to lift the skin while he cut straight up to the breastbone and then sawed with his knife until the diaphragm separated from the rib cage. When he turned the deer on its side, its insides practically fell out at our feet. He moved his knife point in among them and came out with the liver and the heart. "Dinner," he said as he removed the gall sac from the liver and the membrane sac from around the heart.

I held those organs in my hand while Ethan slit the doe's throat so he could cut out the windpipe, which he said would spoil. He sprinkled black pepper over the remaining flesh to keep insects away. Then he found a patch of moss, which he raked of dirt with his fingers, and turned the deer over on what had been its stomach and splayed its legs. The last of its blood thus drained away.

Ethan had me collect kindling while he kneeled by an old fire pit and arranged what charcoal remained, to which he added the dry small pieces of wood I carried to him in my arms and placed by his feet while he crouched by the fire. I put one hand on his shoulder for balance each time I came with ever-larger pieces of wood, until finally he took my hand before I could lean on him and said, "That's enough," meaning, I hoped, *enough wood*, and pulled me down to my knees next to him so that just as night fell the fire came up and spread its light and warmth over us as we stared silently into its burning heart.

Once he'd returned from the shed with various supplies, wrapped and tied in the blanket I'd seen there, by which time the fire had coaled, he cooked the liver for us, and the brains, which I'd never had before from any animal and ate sparingly until I allowed myself to taste before swallowing and then I positively begged Ethan for some of his portion, which he neither ate nor shared. We did share the heart—Ethan said we were eating it for the strength it would give us.

"For what?" I inquired as I ate from that alternately fibrous, tender organ.

We skinned the deer together, before which we had to hang

it up. Each of us cut off two legs at the first joint and then perforated the tendons of what remained of the hind legs and threaded a rope through the holes we'd made above the hock and together hoisted up the carcass to hang off a lower limb of the big maple. Ethan showed me how to split each leg from the root of the tail to the crest of the joint and open the skin from the inside of the foreleg. Once we had the hindquarters freed, we put down our blooded, fat-flecked knives and stood facing each other across the slightly swaying ravaged body of the deer. Ethan put his hands under the edge of the hide. I did the same on my side of the deer. He said, "Now!" and together we pulled down and watched the skin separate from the flesh, smoothly at first, though soon the deer seemed reluctant to part with its coat so Ethan hit around each snag with his fist and the skin eventually came free. So I did the same. At those moments when both of us were punching at the animal with one hand and yanking at its hide with the other, it bounced in the air and twisted around between us as we hit it and sometimes took up our knives to cut away the skin when our fists failed to liberate it. Though it was a cool night for August, we were both sweating by the time we'd reached the head—together, though I suspected Ethan had slowed down toward the end to allow me to catch up. He then had me hold the skin away from the animal while he sliced first through the neck to the atlas vertebra where the spine meets the head and then around the head until all of a sudden the head and the hide fell from the body and I caught them in my outstretched arms. I took the head in my hands and held it before my face. "What sound does a deer make?" I asked.

"None—when it's dead."

I was unwilling to allow him this lugubrious response. "When it's hungry," I persisted.

" 'Pass the salt,' " Ethan said in the high sweet voice of a living deer, and while I laughed he bent to the blanket and fetched from it a large metal salt shaker.

"Salt the hide." He put the shaker into my hand.

"You weren't kidding?"

"Flesh it first."

He showed me how. We spread the hide out on the ground near the light of the fire like the bottom sheet on a bed. He took a scraped-out split and sharpened antler to a corner of it and stripped away what meat and fat adhered. He took these in his palm and placed them on a piece of cheesecloth. "Some here and some in the skillet," he said.

"Is that when I salt it?" I asked.

Ethan nearly dropped his fat scraper.

"What's so funny?"

He couldn't speak. I waited. I laughed at myself with him. This caused him further amusement. Even while he laughed, he took the salt shaker from my hand and turned it over and vigorously shook out salt and banged out salt all over the part of the hide he'd fleshed. Then he gave me back the shaker and put the heel of his hand down where he'd salted and put his weight onto his hand and ground down.

"Oh, salt the *hide*," I said.

"But save some for our dinner." He was still amused by me.

"So I was *right*!"

"Yes," he said almost solemnly as he doused a cloth with vinegar and walked off to clean the carcass hanging from the tree.

He had it butchered by the time I'd stripped the skin of flesh and fat. The teeth of his hacksaw held tiny chips of bone, while from the blade of a boning knife hung curled ribbons of white cartilage and crimson meat.

Together we wrapped the cuts of shoulder and loin and flank and neck and hindquarters into cheesecloth. The dry-lightning storm had taken summer with it and chilled the air. It was the false New England autumn, a late-summer night when the trees are full and the ground still pliant but the breezes breathe with the clarity of winter yet none of its ache.

"Will it keep?" I asked.

I might have meant this joy forever and not the butchered remnants of a doe that had danced before us in the flaring of the sky.

"If I brine it," Ethan answered.

I looked around. He couldn't do that here. I didn't want to leave.

"Tomorrow," he rescued me. "Are you hungry?"

My hands and arms were covered with specks of deer. My fingernails were crammed with it. Ethan was blooded even more, though in the light from our fire the blood was gilded and his face serene.

"I'd like to wash first."

He led me to a pond nearby. The moon was spare and the stars haughty. I followed him by taking his hand. It seemed the proper excuse, that he was nearly invisible. But I needn't have touched him to track him. Whom I couldn't see I felt; he left an impression in the air and all I needed to do was fill it. But his hand, his hand was real and now gripped mine so hard it was almost a rejection, and it pulled me along as if to lose me.

Just beyond a stand of almost blue ironwood with its bulbous catkin lamps extinguished lay the pond in a dense grove of tall maidenhair trees, which I recognized from the leaves that resembled small fans pushing at the dark night and from the beguilingly gamy odor of the fruit dropped by the females in the winds of the storm.

"Did you plant these?" I asked, because I knew they could not grow wild in our cold climate and hadn't since the dinosaurs had left.

He shook his head. "Someone did."

"How's the water?" I asked.

He reached into it and came out with his hand cupped and brought the hand to the side of my neck, down which the water flowed beneath my blouse, cold, while his hand remained warm on my neck.

"Any snakes?"

"And frogs and turtles," he answered.

I stood by him and removed my clothes. When I had none on, I said, "Look," and slid into the water head first.

The bottom of the pond was thick with grass and plants, but the water was clean and soon warm with its saved-up summer and it held me as a substitute for him, who sat on its bank and watched me as I moved slowly before him and was quite content with the distance between us while at the same time I wanted him to come in too and cleanse himself and me.

"Do you want to know how it is?" I called out.

It seemed some time before he said, "How is it?"

"See for yourself."

He pulled off one black boot and then the other and his socks and I thought for sure he would roll up his pants like a boy and wade in. But I could hear his thick leather belt creak as he pulled it tight to release the tongue of its buckle and then his cord pants fold to the ground as I saw him pull off his shirt over his head without unbuttoning it. For a few moments he stood with his arms outstretched above him and his shirt between them and his legs solidly locked into the ground. He was a tree there on the edge of the pond, worshiping both earth and sky, as still and as beautiful as anything God had ever seen or might have made.

He was as mysterious a lover as Emily's and as unknown to me as hers to us. *I want to see you more, Sir, than all I wish for in this world.* Yet here he was, clothed only in darkness. *Could you come to New England,* she begged him. *Just to look in your face, while you looked in mine—then I could play in the woods till dark, till you take me where sundown cannot find us.*

He slipped into the water and swam to me. I couldn't see him but felt against my skin the movement of the water that he moved. He came to me in little waves that rose upon my skin and fell from it as the next approached. When he was upon me, finally, he grasped my shoulders and turned me about a time or two and then began to scour my back with sand from the bottom of the pond and then with nothing but his hand. He touched and cleaned me everywhere I was or would ever be, the night so dark by now I didn't see the one who saw me with his hands. "You me," he said, by which he meant only that I should wash him too. So we turned each other around and scrubbed each other clean and laughed when it tickled and played upon each other's bodies with the innocence of children. "Beautiful," he said, when I knew he couldn't see me either. We took shape in each other's hands. We were, like all true lovers, our own creation.

We slept that night up in the blind, covered not with the blanket, which was wet from my having used it as a towel to dry him and then myself, but with the skin of the deer. From its hindquarter Ethan had cut and cooked a steak. We'd eaten it, together with sweet, raw cattail root, before we'd climbed up into the big maple. The rest of the meat he hung high off the ground to keep it, he said, from bears. Far above that, we lay down in our clothes, which smelled of us and of the deer. We pressed against each other because the night was cool and the deer had been small.

"I've never done this before," I said.

"Done what?" His breath was warm on my face.

"I could name many things."

"So could I."

"But you've done *this*," I insisted.

"No."

"With Una. She told me what you'd done. She said you took her to a pond and scrubbed her clean with sand."

"Yes," he said.

"And did you sleep up here?"

"Yes."

"So how can you say you haven't done it."

"Nothing is ever the same."

"As what?"

"As it was. As it *is*."

"So even this . . . ?"

"I've never done this before," he said, using my own words both for me and against me.

"Hold me," I said. "I'm cold."

He was asleep. But he held me anyway in my holding him. Our bodies touched through the night. When I awakened at first light, he was gone.

I had never felt so alone. The forest was quiet with the dying of the night. Darkness streaked the sky and lay heavily upon the rising sun. There was no wind, no breeze, only the hush of breath held as the earth waited for morning to be sanctioned. Ethan had vanished into this strife. There was no evidence he'd been here but for the yearning he'd left in me. The hide of the deer was my doing; its dried blood still painted the undersides of my fingernails. I sat up from the stiff board floor of the blind and opened my arms to nothing.

I wondered the same thing I'd wondered in any bed I'd ever awakened in: How did I get here? Why is the world so strange and why is every day a birth into uncertainty? Where is God? Where is love?

Prayer, I realized, was less a supplication than a questioning. I too was knocking everywhere. That's why I'd come to this valley, as doomed by thirst as the world outside seemed doomed by rancor. Ethan was not the answer to a prayer. He was prayer itself. He didn't exist outside my desire to know him. The more I questioned, the less I learned. So with God.

And so did Ethan knock. As the calls of birds rode through the forest on the lifting early light of day, so did the unmistakable sound of an ax sundering wood issue out of the dense curtain of trees that could not preserve the privacy of sacrifice. I climbed down from the blind and followed this steady, throaty pounding until I came upon Ethan standing on a small wooded hill beneath a huge oak, slaughtering it. The tree was in full leaf, its limbs obscured by their own foliage, its shadow darkening the lesser trees before it. His ax went into the tree low upon its thick trunk, in a cut I saw was parallel to the ground. Ethan bent at the knees and waist with each stroke yet straightened up with its recoil to take back his ax as far and as high as he could before its next attack. He gave back the sun to dawn, radiant from his exertion. His slender muscles tore at his clothes. Sweat danced off his hair each time the ax engraved the tree. When he had sliced into the trunk by about a third he altered his stroke and cut down into the wound at such an angle as to create a notch. This he accomplished quickly. He put down his ax and took hold of the tree and pulled out the triangular notch.

"Here," he said, and turned around and held it out to me.

I moved toward him and took it. "How did you know I was here?"

"Look where you're standing."

"But I was behind you."

"It will kill you," he said, which I took less as a prediction than a warning. I was standing where it would fall.

"Let me saw it with you," I said. "We could use a two-man crosscut."

He ignored my reference to the death of Mackswell Ryther and put his fingers into the broad ridges of the dried blood–colored bark on the notch and turned it over. He traced its dense twisty grain with his finger. I noticed how the calluses on his hand were shiny and swollen.

"Red oak bends the saw blade," he said. "Elms too."

"Then how do you split it?" I guessed at the difficulty.

"A trunk this size would be a saw log," he explained. "But the mills are gone."

"So why are you cutting it down?"

He shrugged. "Because you were asleep."

He walked uphill around the tree and raised the ax to it. "You're still on the fall side," he said, and swung.

As much as I wanted to stand where I was so I could see both him and the tree coming toward me, I moved to the side and slightly up the hill. I found my heart beating in rhythm to his exertion and my body shaking with each shuddering of the tree in its magisterial humiliation.

When he had cut almost all the way through to the inner face of the notch, he put down the axe and said, "Now you."

I went to him and bent for the ax. But he leaned over with

me and grasped my wrist and brought my hand up to the tree and placed it so now my fingers filled its bark.

"Apologize," he said.

"I will not!"

"Not to me." He smiled. "To the tree."

"For what?"

"The Nipmuc believed every tree had a spirit. They apologized to it."

"For what?" I said again.

"For this." He put his hand over mine and said, "Push," so I did and the tree began to move away from me and to groan as it did and its limbs to crack the limbs of other trees as it fell, straight over on the hinge he'd left. Faster and faster it fell and then stopped for a moment and the whole forest was silent holding its breath and I held mine as well until I felt his arms around me. He took me by the waist and lifted me away and flung me to the forest floor just as the huge trunk of the red oak swiveled on its stump and swung around and only then did the hinge pop and the tree rose before it fell completely over and its ax-gnawed, splintered butt stabbed me where I'd been before he'd rescued me or at least thought better of killing me.

He stood over me, the narrow ends of tree limbs on his shoulders, dark green leaves and strips of pollen-swollen catkin flowers caught in his lengthening black hair, along with a few errant strips of the flesh-colored inner bark of the dying tree.

We carried home in the deer hide a small load of what Ethan called biscuit wood, thin short logs he'd cut from the top of the oak, meant to fit into the kitchen stove. A year from now, he said, they'd be just seasoned enough to burn. A year from now, I said, and realized it was unimaginable.

On the way he showed me trees his father'd girdled, deeply

grooved along their bottoms so they would die and age on the stump. It was a woodsman's idle summer work, when trees like our great red oak were not meant to be felled because their profusion of leaves obscured judgment of their lean as well as hindering the pruning of their limbs. Trees were meant to be taken down when they were naked, at their safest and plainest and most vulnerably beautiful.

He was teaching me what Emily called her own backwoodsman ways, for which she felt the need to apologize, in a letter to the one she called her Master, and I felt the need to sanctify. Like me she had, she said, a tomahawk in her side, a rending of our female flesh that needn't be literal to be true and grave.

Where my dress was torn, and my flesh torn open, I felt an ache and from the morning air a cleansing.

Once home, and in my room, he had me unbutton my dress and lower it from my shoulders to my waist and lie down on my other side. I watched him watch my hands dance down my back, one after another as I opened up my dress, surprised I'd be so limber as to be able to embrace myself from behind should I so choose.

He painted me with iodine, which stung and made me jump. He didn't bandage me because, I knew, he didn't want to see the bandage on my skin. He said the air would heal me. He left me lying there with my dress down to my waist, bandaged also in my underwear, of which he took no notice but that made me feel more self-conscious than would my nakedness.

"Rest," he said. And while I did I observed him in my dreamy state leave and come back several times, carrying water and ashes, and finally make a solution of these with slaked lime and in it put the hide of the deer we'd killed. He let it soak and tried to sit and watch it but grew impatient. I moved about on my bed so it might be me he would watch, and watch me calmly and for as long as I might lie there under his gaze and still myself. But he couldn't keep from the deer and went at it with an adz and hour after hour scraped at it and husked it and scoured it until most of its hair had come off and Ethan's fingers were red from what lime had inflamed them.

"Just let it soak," I said. "Isn't it supposed to soak?"

"How do you know that?"

"From watching you," I said. "But I don't know what you're doing it for."

"I'm going to tan it."

"Well don't be in such a rush."

"It's for you," he said. "I want to give it to you."

"Don't rush," I said, though I felt my blood do just that. "I'll be here forever."

I knew he was cooking for me. A most wonderful smell captured me when I was halfway down the ladder and drew me to the kitchen. He stood before the stove, one hand lost in a pot over a small flame.

"What's in there? I want some."

"Brains."

He'd saved his portion for me. I put my face over the pot and breathed in the pungent scent. He worked his fingers through the lumps of slick pale meat, smoothing them into what looked like mucilage.

"I don't mind chewing them," I said hungrily.

He shook his head. "Not for eating."

"No!" I screamed in mock horror and plunged my hand next to his in the warm fragrant paste. He took my fingers in his own and lifted them from the pot. I tried to lick them, his or mine, I didn't care which, but he kept my mouth away with his other hand and shook our held hands over the pot so the strange thick fluid plopped back into it from the tips of our fingers.

"Not fair," I said.

"I'll cook something else for you," he said.

"What?"

"Look." He opened the oven. A piece of the deer's loin was browning in a pan.

"Is that what I smelled?" That and the wood that cooked it.

"It's your nose," he answered, and put a finger there, on my nose, which made me feel for a moment as if my whole head might explode from pleasure.

In their little smokehouse at the edge of the woods, he showed me how to brine the rest of the deer's meat. He had me measure eight drams of saltpeter for eight ounces of sugar and thirty-two ounces of salt. We dissolved this mixture into a two-gallon barrel of water and placed the meat in it.

"How long do we have to wait?" I asked.

"Long past hunger," he said, and placated me by unwrapping a cloth and taking from it a long thin slab of cured meat coated in black pepper. I bit into it. It seemed to disappear into my tongue. I took the rest in one piece.

"I thought it would be tough," I said.

Ethan put his hand near my mouth for his share.

"Oh, my God!" I opened my mouth. All gone.

As for the deer's brain, the paste Ethan had made from it he used to oil the deer's hide. He massaged this into the outside of the hide. The inside he coated with tallow rendered from the suet of what he joked was a wild boar he'd killed but soon admitted was a domesticated farm pig whose smoked chops he fed me while he massaged the hide as it was stretched over a sawhorse. Back in the smokehouse he stretched the skin on a scaffolding over a fire of hard green hickory, which produced little heat and no flame but a curling scented smoke that appeared to be absorbed into this darkening mysterious remnant of the animal we'd last seen dancing in the lightning.

While the smoke annealed the hide and sealed its pores, Ethan and I opened the barrel in which the deer's meat soaked and stirred the white mold that had formed on the brine to keep it from hardening.

When the deerskin was finally tanned, he asked me what I wanted made from it. Nothing, I told him. I wanted it as it was, like a piece of paper before it's been cut up to be made into the pages of a book, empty but for its own unwritten history, mine alone.

Ethan rolled us a cigarette as we sat around the kitchen table after dinner. Simeon was alternately talking and then reading aloud, as he'd grown accustomed to do on those occasions when Ethan and I were there to have dinner with him. It was as if Simeon believed that language was a net in which he could capture and keep us, Ethan in particular, who never spoke to him. He would sometimes quote Emerson, "Politeness ruins conversation," to try to get Ethan to laugh, but only I would grace him with amusement. This in turn might inspire Simeon to a further Emersonian absurdity so far as we were concerned: "In every house there is a good deal of false hospitality." "In our house there's no hospitality at all!" he'd bark, forcing me to please him with my instant contradiction. But what he most believed from Emerson—that society everywhere is in conspiracy against the manhood of every one of its members—he could not lampoon because he believed it truly. Manhood for Simeon was not some swagger and did not reside in his trousers; it was a man's past as captured in his blood and embodied in his ancestral home.

Emerson, Simeon told us, wrote his first book, *Nature,* in the house in Concord called the Old Manse and later rented by Nathaniel Hawthorne in the first few years of his marriage to Sophia Amelia Peabody. On an upstairs windowpane in that house there was etched a dialogue between Nathaniel and Sophia: *Nath.' Hawthorne. This is his study; 1843. Inscribed by my husband at Sunset Apr. 3ᵈ 1843. In the gold light S. A. H. Man's accidents are God's purposes. Sophia A. Hawthorne 1843—.*

If Ethan recognized any similarity between this and his carving his own name into the wall between his room and Una's, he gave no sign. He went right on smoking our cigarette and passing it back to me and taking it from me again.

At which point, Simeon went to take out his own cigarette and found his Viceroy package empty. He crushed it in his hand and threw it on the table between us. "The right front bedroom of the Old Manse was known as the Saint's Chamber—for all the misbegotten clergymen who'd slept there and dreamed their degenerate dreams. Hawthorne hung on a wall of the Saint's Chamber a picture of his daughter, whose name was . . . Roll me one of those, will you, boy. Whose name was . . . I need a cigarette. Una." As he said the name, Simeon looked directly into his son's face and held out his hand to him, palm up.

Ethan's only reaction to this confrontation by way of seeming coincidence was to remove a piece of cigarette paper from his leather pouch and to fill it deliberately with tobacco and to hand this to his father, unlicked.

Simeon completed the transaction with his own thick tongue

and with a smile lit the cigarette and began to read from Randall Stewart's new edition of Hawthorne's Italian notebooks a description of his encounter with Penini, the young son of Elizabeth and Robert Browning in their home in Florence, Italy: " 'I never saw such a boy as this before; so slender, fragile, and spritelike, not as if he were actually in ill-health, but as if he had little or nothing to do with human flesh and blood. His face is very pretty and most intelligent, and exceedingly like his mother's. He is nine years old, and seems at once less childlike and less manly than would befit that age. I should not quite like to be the father of such a boy, and should fear to stake so much interest and affection on him as he cannot fail to inspire. I wonder what is to become of him—whether he will ever grow to be a man— whether it is desirable that he should. His parents ought to turn their whole attention to making him gross and earthly, and giving him a thicker scabbard to sheathe his spirit in.' "

"The Brownings!" I exclaimed, to indicate my own interest in them and to shield Ethan from this virtual disowning of himself. "I was named after his sister!" Which wasn't true. I had her name, but I had it by chance. My father had named me from a book that listed baby names. He had chosen it, he told me, because most people wouldn't be able to spell it; I would be proud all my life, he said, to humiliate them with my name alone.

I was too late anyway. "Is that supposed to be me?" Ethan asked.

"Oh, no," I said before I understood he wasn't talking to me.

"You," his father breathed back to him with the word contained in an envelope of smoke. "And the boy," he added.

Ethan was silent again. He had spoken to his father finally and in a way that made it seem it could not have been for that boy's whole age and more since he'd last done so.

"The boy," said Simeon to try to stay his son's attention. "He's yours."

"Mine," said Ethan noncommittally.

Simeon pointed the stub of his cigarette at me. "She told me so herself."

"Impossible," said Ethan.

"It's true," I confessed. "I did."

Ethan smiled at me, less with mirth than with the luxury of truth. "Impossible he's mine," he said, and left no doubt what he meant.

I went to him that night. I found him on his bed, encased in moonlight. His eyes were open. He lay corpselike in his small domain, frozen in his beauty, the truth forever private.

I lay down next to him. I had to push him to the side to fit. He moved as easily as if he were spirit or could anticipate my desire, which amounted, I realized, to the same.

I arranged my nightgown modestly. But it had softened so by now it mimicked every piece of me and was itself the trespasser upon my flesh I wished his eyes would be and then his hands and then the rest.

"You spoke to your father," I said, my voice so soft I might myself have been fracturing a decade of silence.

"I did," he whispered back.

"Did it feel the way it used to?" I wondered.

"I don't remember anything," he answered.

"Until when?"

"You," he said, and with that word embraced me. With that word alone. And still I wished, if only word could be made flesh.

I let myself lean against him. He was hard, but he yielded to me to the extent that he didn't move away. We touched along our sides, from shoulder to ankle. I tried to feel not him, or myself, but the fusing of the two of us.

He was coming back to life, he'd implied. Through me, he'd confessed.

He finally turned and put his arm over me, less a rake than an anchor in that he didn't press me to him but at least kept me by him.

"Una," he said dispassionately, as if referring to Nathaniel Hawthorne's daughter.

"She says you're always there. Is she always here?"

"I couldn't remember," he said. "Especially her. Nothing. That's why I'd go there. To see her."

"What about Jimmy? Why did you lie about him?"

"No," he said.

"That he couldn't be yours."

"He couldn't," he said firmly.

"Why not?"

"She's my sister," he said, and took his arm abruptly off my body.

I responded to my father's letter.

Dear Dad:

You'll be happy to hear I'm not going back to college. I'll pay my own way from here on. I've always paid my own way except for the money. I'm now paying more than ever. Soon there will be nothing left of me. Wouldn't that be a sight you'd like to see.

Guess what. I'm in love. No one you know. No one I know. Maybe that's why I love him. I plan to be with him forever. However long forever lasts. His hair is growing back. This means more to me than it would to you.

This place you call a wasteland I call paradise. That war you mention is done here. By the time it finally comes there, here won't even be here. But it's terrible all the same. I may be withdrawn, as you say. But as I've learned from my lover, the exile is compelled to embrace what the exile has foresaken.

Don't say hello to Mom. Say something else.

Your long lost daughter,
Sariannah

There was no postal service any longer through Postmaster Dickinson in Greenwich. Not only did a man named Tony Lannin no longer deliver mail by car, but the post office itself had been discontinued. I used this as an excuse to visit Una and ask her to drive me to the Enfield post office.

I found her in the kitchen of the parsonage. Once again, she seemed to have been waiting for me. She sat with a cup of coffee at the table. There was no cup put out for me, but she was staring at my empty chair.

I sat down and showed her my letter before I sealed it.

"Lover!" she said before she'd finished reading. "Who?"

"You know who," I said.

"Jeremy!" She leaned over and put her arms about my neck.

I took her by the wrists and looked into her eyes. "Why would that please you?"

"So it *is* Jeremy," she exclaimed.

"Ethan," I said.

She shook loose of me and walked away from the table. "That's why it would please me."

* * *

Una drove, as she did most things, with abandon. She hiked her bias skirt up over her knees and I watched her long bare legs dance on the pedals, the muscles in her left leg tightening each time she depressed the clutch. She wore a sleeveless blouse from which her golden arms descended to the steering wheel and they crossed over each other at each curve because Una would not let go except when she sped up on a straightaway and then took both hands off and sometimes reached over and squeezed my thigh to let her touch tell me how much fun she was having. I told her I didn't think I would ever learn to drive. She said I'd never have to.

After we crossed the old railroad tracks, she kept going west instead of taking the direct route of Monson Turnpike south, so that she might speed south on Clifford Road and slow down only by the western shore of Greenwich Lake, which she said was shaped like a lady's breast and there, she pointed out as she shifted down the car to a growl, was its nipple.

"Where?"

She stopped the car and insisted we get out. As had been true at Quabbin Lake, here were the torn-down remains of summer camps, which had been left standing just long enough for some campers to have held a reunion earlier this summer.

"Here's where the nudists wanted a camp." Una stood on the prettiest section of the shore, which was also its most exposed. "Too bad the commission wouldn't let them. It would have been so much fun."

I wasn't shocked to hear of nudists. Such strange people had been gathering all over the country in ever-greater numbers as the Depression deepened. Only lately, with the threat of war, were they no longer being pictured as often in magazines, whole families photographed in shadows or from the side or back, always smiling, even their backsides smiling in the sun.

"I would have made a good one, wouldn't I?" said Una.

"They're all fat!" I exaggerated, but sometimes it did seem that the only fat people left by the slimming grip of the Depression's deprivations were, or became, nudists.

"Not me!" She started to unbutton her dress, then stopped and said, "You first."

"Don't be silly."

"We can take a swim."

"Do you remember the ice?" I asked.

"What ice?"

"The ice Ethan used to cut from this lake and take home to you on his sled."

"Who told you about that?"

"You did."

"I know!" She grasped my dress at my throat. "It's all true!"

"Don't," I said.

"How else?" she pleaded.

"How else *what*?" I asked and realized in those timeless moments when she didn't answer that it was through me they sought each other, my body they shared.

I mailed the letter to my father from the Enfield post office. It had already begun to be torn down. The postmaster, Ed Howe, sold me my stamp. "Springfield," he said, as he licked the stamp in exchange for his prying. He had lived with his wife and children in six rooms on an upper floor of the post office. Now they were gone from the valley and he lived alone in one room. His father, also Ed Howe, had been postmaster as well, and secretary of the Masonic Lodge down the block and deacon of the Enfield Congregational church that had been sold to the commission and three years ago this very month was burned to the ground, probably, said Ed Howe, by some of Governor Curley's Woodpeckers who had been fired from their jobs for incompetence or, as Ed called it, their slippery ways with axes and peaveys. Across the street from the post office was the Swift River Hotel. It was empty. The town was empty. There had been two farewell parties this past spring, between which the last town meeting had been held and $1,800 appropriated for a memorial in the new Quabbin Park Cemetery, in honor of the soldiers of recorded wars who had come from Enfield, Massachusetts, of which there was nothing living left but a postmaster in his post office.

On our way back to Greenwich Village, Una said, "You shouldn't have mailed that letter."

"Why?"

"Because you hate your father. And your letter will make him love you."

"I don't hate him. And he'll never love me."

"Then why did you tell him there'll be nothing left of you? Are you telling him you're going to die here?"

"He's taking my soul away," I answered.

"Your father?" she asked, but she knew what I was talking about.

"The way Simeon Vear says you took Ethan's."

She smiled and reached over from the gear shift and put her hand on my arm. "Yes, I did, didn't I?"

"But not his body," I said. "Never his body. He told me—Jimmy isn't his. Jimmy can't be his. Ethan is your brother. He never . . . you never . . ."

Una laughed. "My brother! If only that were true. But we did take baths together."

*   *   *

Ethan loved Jimmy not because he was his but because he
was hers. He didn't see himself in Jimmy. He saw Una. And what
I had seen in Jimmy and thought was Ethan—the black eyes,
the pretty and intelligent face of the Browning boy, his also being both childlike and manly—was *Vear*, as passed by Simeon
through Una. It was Una who gave Jimmy what Ethan loved most
about him: the impetuous, insuppressible greed of his desire—life
itself.

When it became early September and time for school to
start and there were no schools to start in, Jimmy came to me
for schooling and to Ethan for learning. He came most every
day. He came for himself and as ambassador from his parents.
They remained behind at the parsonage together in the passion
of their restive marriage and Jeremy alone in the tortured comfort of his abandoned church, where he wrestled not with the
triviality of God but with the enormity of man, while Una sat
alone in the house in exile from what love is lost when the lover
travels. Jimmy came not with their permission but with their
knowledge; he hadn't asked for the former but warranted the
latter by telling them where he was going. "My parents told me
to say hello," he would announce each time, and he would fill
that small *hello* with an actor's dole of disaffection and desire.
I would send no greeting back, which in itself was salutation
enough to keep us all engaged.

Simeon was tickled to have his grandson come around and
no longer disappeared all day to wander his property and take
flowers to the hole wherein his great love had been buried at the
age of twenty in 1912. He said the county would be sending tru-
ant officers after Jimmy to force him to school just as the commission sent its lawyers to force him, Simeon, to sell his house

so it could be dismantled and drowned. It was their little conspiracy, Jimmy and Simeon's, hiding from the law that in Jimmy's case would never come and in Simeon's needn't but would.

Jimmy and I sat at the kitchen table studying the Pilgrims. I taught him about the Puritan Separatists from Scrooby who rebelled against the corruption of the Church of England and the depravity of Oliver Cromwell (because he played cricket!) by seeking asylum in Holland. From among these people came the eighty-eight Pilgrims who sailed on the *Mayflower* in the last month of 1620. My relatives. "Ours too . . . almost," said Simeon, who laughed at my own pretension and then with the utmost seriousness and great attention to detail described for Jimmy the "starving time" that would have killed them all had not the Wampanoag Indians come to their aid.

Ten years later came the thousand of the Massachusetts Bay Colony, led by John Winthrop. Within one short decade Winthrop wrote that it was New England itself that God, not he, had found and given to his people, New England that God had chosen to plant his people in. But first, he promised those with him on the *Arbella* that they would be as a "city on a hill."

"Where have you heard that before?" I asked Jimmy.

He closed his eyes and sought the words. He grabbed my wrist and held me there. "You *bitch*!" he said as he remembered how his father had been preaching from Matthew when I'd left him for Ethan.

Now and then Ethan and the boy went off by themselves. I was no longer jealous. Jealousy now belonged to Jimmy when Ethan and I went off, sometimes for a walk in the woods and sometimes, in the middle of the day, up the ladder, where I could imagine what Jimmy thought we were doing.

I found him once listening at my door, when I'd put my book aside and gotten up from my bed to help Ethan finish the tongue he'd made for a cat I'd taken a liking to. It was one of many animals cruelly left behind in the valley by departing residents, domesticated pets that seemed capable of little but trembling in their loneliness before they were consumed by braver, freer beasts. A gray male moggie, it had the faintest of ghost markings that put me in mind of the little bit of French Canadian ejaculated into my father's otherwise blue blood and thus my own. Ethan had drowned the cat because otherwise we'd have to make a hermit of it, and I knew very well, he said with a sarcasm so charming I took it as further evidence of his healing, that there were no hermits in the Vear house. He had done a remarkable job preserving the cat's vibrissae and combing them out with a tiny brush that left them actually moving in currents of air of which we were otherwise unaware up here at the top of this sealed and solid house. And he'd kept the cat's own eyes, even to the depth of their tapeta, so at night, if I were in my bed and not alone or beside him in his, I might see the cat's eyes glow and know that whatever meager light the distant stars enwrapped me in allowed the cat to see me too. So said Ethan, who made no distinction between life and death, the living and the dead; he was, after all, a young man with his own grave and marker, who brought dead creatures back to what for him was life.

The cat's own tongue had been discolored by its drowning, so Ethan had carved one from balsa wood and had me help to fasten it with papier-mâché between the jaws. He then melted wax and applied it to the tongue with a bristle brush and shaped the tongue with a small potter's rasp. Finally, he handed me a striper brush and tube of cadmium red oil paint. "Make it real," he said. So hard did I concentrate upon doing just that, holding my breath each time I touched the brush to the tongue, that I heard and was disturbed by another's breathing on the other side of the door. I put down the brush and paint and went to the door and flung it open. There was Jimmy, smiling, unrepentant, by me in a flash.

"Holy cow!" he said. "That's the Oehlschlaegers' cat!"

We became a family, the three of us, with Simeon our patriarch. Once we taught Jimmy to smoke, we spent afternoons sitting together out behind the house, enjoying Ethan's hand-rolled cigarettes and pretending at least to educate Jimmy. Jimmy was caught between us Vears and the Treats to whom he returned most nights. Rather than be divided, he was augmented, all the cheerier for serving as the object of desire to so many. He was swollen with his power. This was observable not only in his eyes, which were able to look with simultaneous disdain and worship on those of us who loved him, but also in the hardening and shaping of his body as it shed its boyishness and carved its comely way into the world.

Late one hot afternoon he and I went to find Ethan in his room. As usual, we pretended to race for the ladder, which was wide enough for one. Jimmy always conceded at the last moment and let me rise ahead of him. I knew he looked up my skirts. I didn't so much invite it as permit it. I loved the smile he gave me when he climbed out next to me on the top floor, completely unashamed, sweetly complicit.

We often were forced to look for Ethan in his room. Ethan remained more comfortable alone. Simeon had finally been able to pay Ethan what for the old man was perhaps the ultimate compliment: that he, Ethan, was like the great Nathaniel Hawthorne himself. Hawthorne too liked to hide in his bedroom—on Chestnut Street in Salem, Massachusetts, where from behind the curtain of his window he would watch his neighbors tread back and forth from church, trying to guess in which direction they appeared emptier, and he wrote to his friend the poet Longfellow that some witchcraft had carried him off and he couldn't get back and he'd made a captive of himself and couldn't find the key to let himself out and even if the door were open, he'd be afraid to step out into life. Hawthorne ate his meals alone in his bedroom right until the time he married, said Simeon, winking at me beneath the thick black hedge of an eyebrow, making a match, though this wasn't true of Ethan, who not only ate with us (though sometimes silently, sitting closer to Jimmy than to me, watching Jimmy eat as if he'd somehow carry nourishment back to Una) but cooked our meals after having more often than not killed what we ate.

"You remind me of Emily." So I said to him that day when Jimmy and I found him sitting at the small table in that large, empty room of his, from which not only life but even the material mess of boyhood had been evicted by Una's defection twelve years before. He sat looking off into the very space that hung there looking back emptily at him. Ethan neither inhabited the world nor was inhabited by it. Just as he was visible in darkness, so he was sometimes invisible in light.

"Who's Emily?" he asked quietly.

Jimmy rolled his eyes and indicated with a theatrical gesture that I was about to open my big fat mouth.

I had spared Ethan the infliction of Emily Dickinson with which I had occasionally burdened Jeremy Treat. Unlike us ordinary mortals, Ethan had no need of her art. He was her manifestation in a man, solitary but not isolated, able, as Emer-

son put it, to embrace solitude as a bride—a shadow made of
light.

"You brought me the book of hcr pocms. She lived alone in
her bedroom. There came a time when she rarely left it. If she
had visitors, she would talk to them from behind her door or
from the top of the stairs. Her whole life is a great mystery."

"So is everybody's," said Ethan.

"Especially mine," said Jimmy brightly as he extended his arms
from his sides to invite our scrutiny of his unfathomableness.

"I want to take you there," I said.

"Where?" asked Jimmy eagerly.

"Not you. Ethan."

"I want to go too," said Jimmy.

"Where?" I asked.

"With you," he said to me. "And you," he said to Ethan.

The three of us set off early on a splendid warm September
day, which was fitting, because it must have been the equal of
the day that caused Emily to write one September that her flowers were bold as June—Amherst, she said, had gone to Eden.
We walked out toward Pelham until we found a ride in the back
of a truck that stopped for us on Turnpike Six and would have
taken us all the way to the center of Amherst had I not banged
on the back window and had us dropped in the east village on
Spaulding Street by the old Thurber house so we might walk in
by way of Main Street and the town might open before us like
the daylilies she so loved.

There were autos everywhere, many with their tops down,
whizzing by us east and west, and people on actual stone sidewalks, including the kind of gentlewomen in plush who embarrassed Carlo, the dog Emily had when she was a girl. And

everywhere there were young people, students from the colleges, mostly boys, breathless with learning or the lack of it, loud, quick, vulgar, between my age and Ethan's but seeming of generations or species apart, naive where we were seasoned, worldly where we were innocent. All of us would soon be dead; they from war, we from love. How much better to die like us.

Ethan too sank into himself. This was a new world. The Swift River Valley had been contracting since before he was born. People had been fleeing. Businesses had been failing. He must have thought they were abandoning the whole place to him. Why should he ever leave, if one day it would be his alone? In that, he was, as he'd said, the opposite of a hermit.

Once we crossed a genuine Dickinson Street, so named, we came immediately to what for her was "Eden—the ancient Homestead": the house called the Homestead. It was her father's house and there she'd lived. I shouted, "There's where she lived!" and pointed to the windows at the corner of the second story, two windows to the south, one to the west from which we'd come. Jimmy grabbed my hand: "Let's go in." "We can't," I said. "Why not?" he demanded. "It's not the Dickinsons' house; it belongs to the Parkes family now. They've told me not to visit anymore." I had been in her room. Had I had the skills of Ethan, I would have climbed up the house and into her window. But I'd had to beg my way in, and had, and had put my hand upon the mattress of her narrow sleigh bed and had opened the closet and buried my face in her embroidered white dress with its flat tucks and dropped waist and had locked my eyes into Emily's eyes staring at Elizabeth Barrett Browning on the wall and had sat at the tiny cherry table at which she wrote and from which through her thin curtains she could see the house next door, *a hedge away*, where her brother lived with his wife, Sue. Sue was Emily's best friend and perhaps greatest love. "Where you go, I will go," she told Sue. "We will lie side by side in the kirkyard," though whether she meant among or within the graves—alive or dead or both—is unclear. Whichever, they would have a "union by which two lives are one." It was more than Sue had with Austin—he betrayed her with another man's wife, whom he often met here, right at the Homestead, this Eden that Sue had come to call immoral.

I was welcome at that other house, the Evergreens. We walked to it over the well-worn path down which Austin had walked to his lover, observed from her room by his sister, who never walked in the direction we did now to the house next door.

Emily's niece, Mattie, lived there by herself. She was seventy-two years old—too late to have children though she'd once had a husband. She was the last of the Dickinsons.

"Miss Renway," she said immediately upon answering the door.

Ethan looked at me strangely, puzzlement creasing his dark sad eyes.

"My last name," I explained reluctantly, wishing to retain what little mystery I had for him.

"Come in," she said. "Have you acquired my new edition?"

"Of course," I said, which is what I'd responded each time she'd asked. I couldn't imagine her aunt so repetitively enterprising.

Years before, I had laid my childish hands upon but could not buy the 1890 Roberts Brothers *Poems* printed on calendered paper to thicken it for fools who thought the poems cumulatively thin. I had, however, owned since junior high school the next year's fourth printing of that volume, which I loved all the more for such imperfection as the appearance of the poem "This is my letter to the world" not within the text but within the table of contents, which was rather like finding a flower growing from one's pillow. And this book had served me well until I treated myself, on its very midwinter publication day, Friday, February 26, 1937, to Martha Dickinson Bianchi's—Mattie's—Little, Brown and Company edition of *Poems of Emily Dickinson*, for which, on my detour home from school that day, I paid four whole dollars at Johnson's Book Store on Main Street in Springfield, Massachusetts.

"Shall I sign it for you?" she offered, convinced I carried it everywhere.

"If your aunt will also," I said. She gasped before she laughed.

Since I'd last been here she'd moved the 1840 Bullard painting of the Dickinson children—Emily, Austin, and Lavinia—from the Homestead. It was in need of cleaning and restoration—only Emily shone through—and was hung above a cherry chest of drawers in which Lavinia had found some of her late sister's poems.

The painting I liked most was in the front hall, by an Italian named Azzo Cavazza, *Sarah and Abraham at the Court of Pharaoh*. Cavazza has them pretending to be sister and brother instead of wife and husband; therefore, should the Pharaoh want to make love to Sarah, he would be fooled into thinking Abraham need not be eliminated as a rival. I wondered what Jeremy Treat would make of such imposture; so far as he believed, ties of blood were no impediment to venery.

Sue Dickinson had bought the painting after she'd learned of her husband's affair with Mabel Todd and had hung it against such thick red William Morris wallpaper as seemed to have bled in waves of crimson gore from the sallow molding. Sue later chose the same color in damask for the black horsehair sofa on which her husband and his lover had rendezvoused in the dining room of the Homestead. Once Austin had died and was safely out of Mabel's clutches, Sue had moved this trysting couch to the Evergreens and had it reupholstered in that red damask. I wondered whose side she'd sat on when she'd sat on it, and why she'd sat on it, and why she'd wanted it in her house with her husband dead and his lover alive. Was betrayal so much a part of love that it might be folded into love's best memories? Was love the color of blood and pain its deepest feeling? Sue lived without Austin and with that sofa for eighteen years. Mabel got to write sourly of her rival in 1913, "Poor old Susan died last night"; indeed, Mabel outlived Sue by twenty years and was the chief editor of her lover's sister's poems and letters until Mattie took over. It was Mabel's drawing of the saprophytic Indian pipe that adorned the title page of Emily's first book, never seen by her. To look upon it was to see the unimaginable and at the same time to try to so absorb it that one might become the body off which Emily would feed and know and see what it was impossible for her to know and see—that she was a public poet and her little corner room had opened to the world.

Mattie offered to take us to her study, which I remembered was in the back of the house. "May we see the library first?" I asked. It was one of two rooms closest to the front door. As we entered, Mattie lit a small oil lamp that gave more shadow than light to the books whose spines formed an impenetrable maze upon the walls from floor to ceiling.

Jimmy gazed in wonder. "How many *are* there?"

"Three thousand, seven hundred, forty-nine," Mattie answered immediately.

"Really?" He seemed as shocked by her knowing as by what she knew.

"And to answer your next question—yes, I've read each and every one."

Jimmy hesitated only long enough to look theatrically at each book-stuffed wall. "Baloney!"

Mattie laughed. "And yet you think I've counted them one by one!"

She was as charmed by him as all were.

Ethan, I noticed, stayed close to Jimmy, as one stranger will to another in a new place. But he shared none of Jimmy's awe. Books were of no meaning to Ethan. His father or I might read them, or even read to him from them, but they meant no more to him than a doctor to a dead man.

Suddenly the lamp went out.

"Hey!" said Jimmy.

"Aha!" said Mattie, as if she'd fooled us somehow. Which she had.

The lamp, she explained, as we moved closer to her in the dark, was a courting lamp. It held so little oil that even if it were full, it would soon burn out and thus provide for lovers what darkness they were too demure to summon for themselves.

She squeezed my hand as she spoke—to remind me of the secret she had shared with me (and I suspected with all others who visited and showed the requisite reverence for the poems before the poet, for whom we merely had a few buttons missing): this was the room in which Austin Dickinson was laid out in death and to which Mabel Todd, the woman to whom he had written, "You are my Christ," came in secret to see him one last time before the grave would replace her embrace with its own, this library, this maelstrom of incurable words.

We finally walked to Mattie's study, where the desk was covered with poems and letters. I looked through them, more to touch them than to read them.

"I'm bored," said Jimmy.

"But you're in the death room," I told him.

He thought I was fooling. Then Mattie said, "Please don't call it that."

"Who died?" asked Jimmy avidly.

"My little brother," said Mattie.

"How old was he?"

"Eight."

"How old were you?"

"Seventeen."

Jimmy pointed at me. "She's seventeen."

"Here's Gib's hair." Mattie presented the lock of golden hair to Jimmy on the same piece of white paper with blue lines in which Emily had folded it.

He touched it and I touched it with him.

Ethan showed no interest in these things. But Mattie did in him.

"Who are you?" she asked, though I'd introduced him upon our arrival.

"Ethan Vear," he answered politely, the first time I'd heard him say his name, which for me only deepened his mystery, for I couldn't encompass him in what he was called or in what he called himself.

"I know your name," said Mattie impatiently. "I don't forget things. I'm the last one left. When I'm gone, she's gone. So when I ask who you are, what I mean is, what are you doing here?"

"Seeing the world," said Ethan.

Mattie laughed in a kindly, even conspiratorial way. "That's something she might have said."

"Who?" asked Ethan, a response that brought Mattie Dickinson, after a moment's disbelief, even more amusement. She pushed our hands away from her little brother's hair, folded it away, and said, as if she could now read Ethan's mind, "Come, let's go visit her."

The cemetery had been, at the time of her burial, three fields away to the north, and though it was the same distance now, the fields had been built upon. Even the cemetery was different, not only more crowded but, in the case of Emily's headstone, replaced and revised. It had been Mattie herself who had ordered the stalwart new stone, with Emily's name in peculiarly large and aggressively serifed letters, balanced like a hopeful rainbow upon this message: CALLED BACK.

Mattie held Ethan's arm not only during our walk to the family plot but for the entire time we stood before Emily's grave. As she spoke, she looked into his face, her words for him alone. "I barely recognized her. She'd been embalmed. No one had ever seen such a sight. I was nineteen years old. I'd seen death but not this. She looked my age or not much more. She might have been getting married. There were flowers everywhere. Not around her. With her. There were violets at her throat. A single pink lady's slipper on her breast. She so loved flowers. Aunt Vinnie tried to put two heliotropes into her hand for her dear dead sister to deliver to Judge Otis Lord. In case, I suppose, we meet after death those we loved in life and can carry on with our nonsense. I don't imagine he'd been embalmed. He died at the age I am now. She'd look like a child next to him. As you to me. But her hand was stiff with death or chemicals or both. So Vinnie placed those heliotropes by the side of her hand. They were the color of lavender and blood. Look—there's Vinnie now."

She walked with Ethan a few paces to her left, where Vinnie lay. Jimmy followed and I was there alone with Emily, who lay beneath my feet in what she called her little cottage, her sweet safe house, her glad gay house. She wasn't seven feet from me, plump from the eternalizing venoms, dusted by the dead dropped petals of her flowers, a passionate virgin resistant to the pallid innuendoes of her final supple suitor, death. It wasn't so much the daisies I wanted to interrogate as her. I wanted her to rise up from the grave and comfort me. We knew so much of love, we two, who'd never known it. Our bodies were impenetrable, as our minds were porous with imaginings and such pleasures of the flesh as perish without once having been. Must I give up my mystery? I wondered, or was it better to enter eternity as she had, growing out of death instead of disappearing into it? More people wanted to know her than any person born. More than Joan of Arc. More than Jesus or Mary. She was the greater mystery, for she had left more of herself than perhaps any person ever born and in dying had taken more away. As for me, I was married to a ghost, though he was not a ghost and we weren't married. She'd know what this felt like, this longing after so concrete an illusion that one breaks one's hands in reaching for it. And what did life come down to? Does he love me? Does He love me?

As I had entered the Swift River Valley for the first time seeing it with her own eyes, New Englandly, so I returned to it for what I knew was the last time, from the west on this hot September eve, and I saw what she had seen: the mountains dripped with sunset and the hemlocks were tipped in tinsel by the wizard sun and the fire spread across the grass until the small dusk crawled on the village and blotted out all the ruined houses but his own. She departed from me then, and I was left alone with him, my beloved.

There was no other way to be with him but alone. He inspired solitude. He was wrapped in such loneliness that to touch him, to look at him, was to be cast off and drawn in at once. He was both inescapable and inaccessible. He turned me back upon myself even as he caused me to think of nothing but him. I became him, I who had been so strongly myself that I might incorporate Una for him and suffer no loss.

He returned from Amherst intrigued not by the prospect of life beyond the Swift River Valley, only by the image of Emily Dickinson embalmed, in contrast to the wild animals given life in death by him with his shears and knives and stuffing rods and galvanized wire and batting and tow and glue and linseed oil and glass eyes. He seemed equally in love with life and death and thus, in his strange way, in perfect balance.

"Do you know why they bury them?" he asked but didn't give me a chance to answer before he said, "Because they look *dead*."

"And what's in your grave?"

"I am."

"Show me."

I thought he wouldn't. As much as I wanted to know, I didn't want to see. But he dragged me by the hand out through the back of the house and into the forest, which grew darker as the trees thickened. Their crowns mingled to create a vast shadow, a vague darkness over everything in the middle of the day that was not the same as the darkness at night. It was thicker and warmer and vastly more sad. The ground was dry and empty. There were no shrubs, no berries, no wildflowers waiting to die happily in the snap of a lover's hand. "Nothing for animals to eat," Ethan explained as he helped me over the fence around the cemetery. "They leave us alone here."

The marker on his grave was even more forlorn than when I'd first seen it. The wood was more decayed. The lean more earthward.

"This is where we met," he said, gladdening my heart with the expression of such ordinary sentiment.

"When you rose out of the grave," I kidded him.

"Yes." He disappeared off behind some trees, from which he returned with a shovel.

"I'm the family gravedigger," he explained.

"Including your own?" I asked with as much skepticism as I could summon.

"And you're wondering how I got the dirt back in?"

"Of course!" I exclaimed, though the revelation had been his.

"Here." He handed me the shovel. "It's *your* turn." As I began to dig I wondered what he meant and then remembered him casting aside the stones over the grave of Sarah Rowlandson and weeping over what he found. It was my turn, though my own tears came long before I found what I found, tears of anger and frustration and mostly fear that he would lie there, dead, decaying, and when I looked up to see him next to me, he would not be there and never would have been. Yet I sensed him, watching me, bending his body slightly with mine as I went at the earth with the shovel and rising slightly with mine as I came up and flung the dirt away. I wondered if he saw my tears, which were quiet tears and fell into his grave as if I were burying him and not the opposite.

What little sunlight struggled through the canopy of trees came down in wires from the sky, mixing with the dust I raised so that it met itself on the way back up. When I had dug enough to have stepped off the earth and into it, I thought to grab hold of that retreating light and let it take me up and out and as far away as light could go, anywhere but here in the darkness of the grave.

But then, at the same moment the point of my shovel came against something hard beneath the dirt and shattered it with a cracking sound, a beam of sunlight hit that very spot and flashed back into my eyes, blinding me.

I threw the shovel down and looked up for him where he stood against the darkness of the trees, a soothing darkness that restored my sight and let me see him there and watch him pick up the shovel with one hand and pull me with the other out of the grave even as he straddled it and bent toward it and then kneeled with my hand on his shoulder as he slowly and carefully with his own hands near the blade of the shovel spooned out dirt until he was done and rose to stand next to me and said, "Look."

There he was, lying in the grave just as he stood above it.

It was a mirror.

He had buried the mirror at an angle so that it gave back not the tops of trees and pricks of sun and threads of sky but himself, at the foot of the grave, staring into his own black eyes.

I laughed, with relief and also at the gesture itself, a boy in love who buries the very piece of glass before which he'd stood with the girl who'd left him and had taken him with her in her leaving. He wouldn't have wanted to see himself, because she would no longer be next to him. In burying himself, he'd tried to bury her too. For who could say that a mirror didn't hold inside its silvery skin each image it had seen, each act it had witnessed.

I leaned against him. He was alive. And he was there, by me—real, substantial, not an image of whom I could see in the grave but the very one who cast that image into the grave.

I looked at him down there. He was so beautiful, more beautiful than I'd ever seen him, lying in the grave within its appeasing shadows cast by the distant tops of trees, the hard angles of his face softened, the spartan grip of his body relaxed, his eyes heavy with the slow approach of peace. Where the shovel had cracked the glass there was merely in the middle of his body a shallow fissured web that spread upon him modestly. I reached to touch him there, outside the web, upon the body I could feel upon my own. I did, I touched him, and looked down upon his image to see this first intrusion of my body onto his. But he was, I realized, alone.

"Where am I?" I said. "Where am I?" He was alone in the mirror in the grave. "Where am I, Ethan?"

He turned toward me and turned me toward him and for the first time took me in his arms and held me hard enough to make whatever was between us disappear.

I cut his hair before we went to church. It was his idea to go to church and mine to cut his hair. He seemed unable to believe how much of it there was, as it fell around him onto the floor in the kitchen. When he'd put his hands in it, and clenched it between his fingers, it hadn't seemed so much, though it must have felt strange after so many years of his being shorn and his hair not growing. He watched it fall from the scissors in my fingers down the bedsheet I'd cut a hole in and placed over his head to the golden bruised wood, where it gathered around us like the petals of a moist black flower.

"Don't make it too short," said Simeon, who stood by us in his suit with a clean white shirt for church and held the broom with which he'd sweep up his son's hair. "I like it better long."

"You would," said Ethan.

"I wear my hat to church," said Simeon.

"That's not what I meant," said his son, puzzling Simeon but not me.

"We could use a mirror around here," I said, and Ethan tried to find me to see if I were joking.

I left it long enough, his hair, long enough for him to seem transformed, from a prisoner of death to whatever kind of gods had walked the earth before the earth was taken from them.

"How do I look?" he asked.

I blew some stray unfallen hairs from his neck, and he shivered.

"Like a child," said his father.

We were the only ones attending church. Whatever few might be left in town had better things to do on a Sunday morning than praise a Lord in whom the more they believed the less they trusted. Neither would they find much benefit in a minister who appeared to have given up love of God for scrutiny of man. I'd once read on the marquee of a church in Springfield, in parody of a sign made famous in Depression sweatshops, IF YOU DON'T COME IN SUNDAY, YOU WON'T GET IN JUDGMENT DAY. What did it matter here, where heaven was rescinded?

The Treat family seemed in wait for us, frigid figures in a crèche, Una at the piano, Jimmy in his place before the pews to sing, Jeremy behind the pulpit, tall and strong and rigid with purpose, his coat so black it glowed, his collar so white it vanished.

On the marquee had been an unattributed quote from Emily Dickinson:

I THOUGHT NATURE WAS ENOUGH
TILL HUMAN NATURE CAME

If he'd thought to lure me with her words, he'd failed; it was Ethan I'd come with and come for. What little need I'd had of church was gone; my fellowship was private now.

And if he'd chosen her words upon which to base his sermon, then his sermon would never end.

We took seats in the middle of the church, I between the two Vear men; our pew gave a little sigh as we sat down and then a crack as Simeon, removing his hat, shifted his weight. His long white hair fell down his back silently but for a moment in the middle of its fall caught the sun from the window and sent a small sharp fragment of light darting up a wall and onto the skin of the bell above.

At that moment, as if the bell had rung, Una played a chord on the piano and Jimmy took a deep breath, winked at us, and began to sing:

> No more a child am I this day
> Than Christ upon the day he died,
> No more will I escape the way
> That I have sought but never tried.
> Surrendering my soul to You
> I sacrifice what I have been—
> God counts the false among us true
> Whose innocence becomes our sin.

When he was finished with this most salutarily terrifying Puritan hymn (with its famous Jonathan Edwardsian chorus: "The house of God is where I dwell / One slender thread constrained from Hell. / Partake of grace from where I sit, / Spider above, beneath . . . the Pit!"), Jimmy waited for his mother before he sat down.

Una joined him in that space between the pulpit and the pews. Together, they looked out, slowly, as they would over a packed, appreciative congregation. I saw Una find Ethan, but her clear, kind eyes passed right over him and settled upon me. She drew my gaze back to Ethan and only then did she look at him, with me or through me I couldn't tell, nor whether I saw him with my own eyes or hers. He was immediately at my side, but I perceived him somehow at a distance, locked in his youthful beauty, locked away, never to be possessed. Was his remoteness a property of his own or a manifestation of my fear that I would never possess him for myself and he would never love me as I loved him? Or was it how Una saw him, way at the back of the church at her wedding, or as her brother, always inside her, never entering her? I forced myself to look away from him and back at Una. She wasn't looking at him at all but was staring at me, staring with such intensity that I felt she was not only looking within me but was removing me from myself and with me whatever of Ethan I had managed to hold. I closed my eyes against her intrusion and her taking. Her image remained, along with Ethan's, inside me, as if I were the vessel for their union.

And Jimmy—whose was he? I opened my eyes and there he was, watching me with the droll disdain of a very young man who pretends not to want what he wants for fear of losing it. He was, as Jeremy had told me but as I had come to define him for myself, the perfect boy—a mass of contradictions on his way to brash uncertainty. He didn't let me out of his sight until his mother took him by the hand and led him to the front pew, where they both sat down, their backs to me, their faces now uplifted not to God but to the man before them.

Jeremy himself looked heavenward but preached, as I supposed all good preachers did, of earthly things. He made specific reference to the annual Nazi party rally in Nürnberg's Hall of the Fifty Thousand on what he said was only this past Tuesday; I could picture him sitting alone in front of his radio as the

MBS *Headlines* show dramatized Hitler's announcement of his plan to attack Czechoslovakia and Jeremy having no other god to turn to moved the dial to the Enric Madriguera Orchestra on NBC-Blue and shivered to the beat of the music.

He spoke of the world at large and the terrible damage man would once more, and soon, inflict upon it. Cities would be graveyards. Forests would be battlegrounds. Churches would be brothels. What God left us when He left the world to us, and what we build upon what God left us and within what God left us and under and over what God left us, we desecrate. What do we hate more: God or ourselves? the world as we found it or the world as we made it?

He spoke of the Swift River Valley that would soon be drowned not by the rivers that flowed through it but by the strangulation of those rivers.

He spoke of himself. He said, "I too thought nature was enough, until human nature came. I was content to remain here in the land of my fathers until such time as the hand of my leaders cast me out. Like Jonathan Edwards, I had particular secret places of my own in the woods, and like him I used to retire to them by myself and be much affected, in my case by solitude itself, which I believed was a gift from God, not that we be alone but that we be able to be alone and that time with ourselves might prepare us all the better to love those we worship and worship Him we love. But I might as well have been living in paradise. For the serpent came and it was Eve herself, that very daughter of delights from the Song of Songs, who said what has always been translated, 'Ye shall be as *gods*,' *elohim*, not gods at all but *rulers*, rulers of the earth. There is the temptation. Who would want to be as God when he can be a man? For only a man might praise the prince's daughter, her thighs, her hands, her breasts, her neck, her nose. Her nose? 'Thy nose is like the tower of Lebanon which looketh toward Damascus.' How princely must be the man who can tell a woman her nose is like a tower and still she accompanies him into the field and to lodge in the villages and to get up early to go into the vineyards to see if the grapes do grow and there to make love. God created the world when he made the Garden and destroyed it when he made the Flood. So they plan to flood our little garden. Our dams may hold back the water, but they can't hold back the blood. What happens here, happens everywhere. As for me, since my church is empty, I'll preach and pray here no longer. Let me leave with some words of another poet. There is another poet, you know. Another New England lady. Anne Bradstreet.

> 'Stained from birth with Adam's sinful fact
> Thence I began to sin as soon as act:
> A perverse will, a love to what's forbid,
> A serpent's sting in pleasing face lay hid.' "

He had me ring the bell with him. He put his hands over mine on the rope and raised them high. I was forced to go on my toes each time before we came down together and experienced that slight delay between effort and sound, in which there was a silence combined with the pulse of the previous peal beating in the body of the air outside the little church.

"Is it the behavior of the world that's brought you to original sin?" I asked.

"Sarianna"—he said my name with no small satisfaction as we rang the bell—"you must be the only one here who actually listened to me. Even the only one who would were the place not as empty as heaven on Saturday night." We rang the bell. "But aren't you confusing me with Anne Bradstreet? The way I do you with your Emily Dickinson sometimes?" We rang the bell. "Do you remember when you first arrived and I asked you if you knew Milton? I was referring to his God who formed us free." We rang the bell. " 'They themselves ordained their fall,' He said. They themselves. We ourselves." We rang the bell. "As for Anne Bradstreet, I was more interested in the idea of loving what's *forbid*."

We rang the bell on his emphasis of the word. We rang it again. I was put in mind of when he talked to me of Tukhachevsky executed and Nanking ravaged and the *Panay* sunk and with each disaster touched my tongue with his imaginary poison. Now it was my hands he grasped and with them he haled the sound from the bell, imaginary cracks of cannon over one more peaceful valley doomed to depredation and annulment. We rang the bell again.

"And what might that be?" I finally thought to ask.

He pulled on my hands; the sound of the bell was his answer.

"Then what are we ringing for?" I asked.

"Them." Though he brushed against me from behind as we grasped the bell rope, I could feel his gaze pass by my shoulder toward the back of the church. Jeremy and I were making the music to accompany the reunion of Una and Ethan. There they stood, facing each other, arms at their sides, frozen in the ragged strips of sunlight and lean shadows of the narrow beams that stilled the church against its will to founder.

"How could you!" Jeremy whispered, and let go of my hands.

I turned to face him. "What?"

"Bring him here."

"It was his idea."

"Worse yet. Look at her!"

"She looks fine to me."

"She's not moving." He was right, not in that she wasn't moving, which was apparent, but in recognizing that his cherished wife was always moving, was never still, was defined by her energy and her passion and an animation that contrasted not only with Jeremy's brooding stillness but with the dull slow passage of time itself and with the silent hold of death.

"Neither is he," I said.

"I'm losing my wife," he said with the kind of mournfulness I'd thought he saved for the world at large.

"No," I said, for were that true, I would lose her too and Ethan to her.

"He's taking her."

"Where?" I asked, for they continued not to move.

"Back to the grave," said Jeremy, and by himself now rang the bell and rang it more, rang it with such force as to explode the world with sound.

Ethan came toward us, Jeremy and me, leaving Una at the back of the church, alone, looking first at us and then at Jimmy and Simeon, who sat together on a pew, Simeon talking, Jimmy listening with so much rapt attention that like Una I wanted to hear what it could be that so captured Jimmy and kept him away from me as he was kept from her. I imagined the old man was taking my role as teacher and was surpassing my story of Henry Gale with that of Hawthorne's Matthew Maule, also upon the gallows, pointing at his enemy and saying, "God will give him blood to drink!"—there is nothing quite so comforting to the innocent as an avenging God.

How divided was I, I thought, in my loves, Ethan approaching, Una distant, Jimmy diverted, while Jeremy took my hands again and put them on the rope and rang the bell one last time. Then he kept my hands beneath his and with his own arms wrapped mine around myself, protecting me from Ethan, who walked down the church embraced by light and by light transformed into an image of the boy he'd been when he'd died of love.

"You shouldn't have come back," Jeremy said to him.

"I never went away," Ethan responded. "You know that."

"Back to *her*," said Jeremy.

"I'm not here for her." Ethan looked back at Una, who remained exactly where he'd left her. "I told her so."

"Then who are you here for?" asked Jeremy, but he knew, for he gripped me all the tighter.

"Sarianna," said Ethan, my name from him still so unfamiliar a sound that it startled me, "I need to talk to Reverend Treat. Alone. Please go see to Una."

"I have nothing to say to you," said Jeremy.

"I have something to say to you," Ethan replied, smiling quite charmingly at his adversary.

"Let me go," I said, though I liked the lock of Jeremy's arms around me and did not like being dismissed so men could carry on their business.

Jeremy released me, more, I thought, because he was curious about what Ethan might want than that he would want me to console Una.

"So be it," said Jeremy, in surrender.

I went to Una, not because Ethan had ordered it but to ease my terrible sense of aloneness. Jimmy remained with Simeon, enthralled, unaware of the struggle all around him for his mother's soul and mine. Ethan was off somewhere with Jeremy, most

likely in the meadow out behind the church where he customarily went after his service and where he had touched me with a
fingertip upon my hand and moved it and somehow claimed me
as his own. What could they be speaking of but the unimaginable, for what could they say to each other that could lead to
anything but violence? And I was left uncoupled, for the first
time in my life unhappy by myself, lonely, the church a universe
and I adrift within its boundlessness.

And Una—Una was a fixed star, standing absolutely still at
the back of the church in a beam of sunlight of which she
seemed herself the source. I walked to her and into her light and
the moment I entered it I entered her. I saw Ethan as she had,
young again as she was too, the boy she'd loved, her own half
brother, who would no more yield to her now than he would
then, which only inflamed her. It was a passion I wished upon
myself, damned and unbearably human. How could she endure
it, this thing I now experienced? It was a kind of hunger that
feeds upon itself and knows no satisfaction and as it grows in
pleasure grows in pain.

I opened my arms to her. "You poor thing."

Only now was she aware of me. She smiled with such joy that I
might have been Ethan himself and said, "I love you. You brought
him back. I love you!" and fell laughing into my embrace.

I was surprised when Jeremy returned alone. I looked for
Ethan's blood upon his hands. I searched for Ethan.

"I'm alone," said Jeremy, reading my eyes. He didn't look
at Una, who stood by me, silent, smiling, out of place. "He's
outside."

I started to go to him, but Jeremy put his hand on my arm.
"Stay here with me. I'll tell you what he said."

"Tell *me!*" said Una.

"He wants to tell you himself." Jeremy put his other hand on his wife. "Find him." He moved her gently toward the door of the church.

"Go with your mother," he called over to Jimmy, who was still sitting there listening to Simeon.

Jimmy rose immediately but waited for Simeon to stand before he left the pew. As the two of them approached Una, Jimmy said to her, "I know about your mom."

"Courtesy of none other," said Simeon, lifting his hair and putting on his hat and then reaching into the pocket of his clean white shirt for his Viceroys as he pushed open the church door for his daughter and his grandson.

When the door closed behind them, it sealed us in. The church became dark, the windows buried in clouds that cloaked the sun and the church's visible wounds healed by the gentle lifting of the light. There was a peacefulness I'd not felt before, a presence of God in the way the shadows gathered on the floor and the air was cleansed by darkness and prayer sang silently from the empty pews.

Once again Jeremy and I stood by each other in the little church, but only I kneeled, while he stood beside me, and I said, "Thank you, God, for not forgetting I exist."

Jeremy laughed. "You'd bewitch the devil himself."

"How am I to take that?" I asked.

"As praise, alas," said Jeremy, holding out his hand and taking mine and lifting me toward the front pew, where we sat again as if all else had been rehearsal for this time as life was said by some to be rehearsal for eternity and not the sole performance that it had to be.

"What did he want?" I asked.

"I'll tell you in good time," said Jeremy. "But first . . ."

"Why did you send Una to him out there? Don't you know . . . ?"

"I know everything," said Jeremy. "I know the very things you don't. Jimmy isn't his. The old man came to me and told me he had fathered Una on Millie Ryther and that he worried how they played together and would I talk to her. So I talked to her, which even then meant listening." He stopped to smile, not at me, at her, who wasn't there, at her those years ago when she was fourteen and at her outside the church now, given up by him to Ethan. "She guessed he was her brother or felt it or something, the old man never told her but she knew. She didn't care. But he wouldn't yield to her. He never did. So she took me, not in his place but to have him rescue her from me. But when he appeared at our wedding, it wasn't to take her away but to see her off. She never recovered from that." He shook his head sadly, taking her woe upon himself, grieving for her who caused him his own great grief.

"I knew that," I said. "I knew her pain. I knew that Jimmy isn't Ethan's."

"Nor mine," said Jeremy, cured of sadness through the pleasure of surprising me.

I knew enough of conception if not of its exercise to say, "How can that be?"

He smiled indulgently. "It took her time to welcome me."

"Then whose?" I asked.

He shook his head. "I don't know. Una doesn't know. No one's. Everyone's. God's."

"And that makes Jimmy perfect?"

"That," he said. "And you."

He reached over and put his hand upon me, no more then, his hand upon me, my shoulder, my arm, down my side, halfway between my shoulder and my waist, gathering up my dress in his fingers.

"Do you mean I'm perfect," I asked, "or that I make Jimmy perfect?"

"You're his first love," he answered, leaving it at that, to answer both.

He reached behind me, for my dress was buttoned from behind, and took a button between a thumb and a finger, I couldn't feel which finger, and moved them together so the button slid through its hole. It was quite unlike unbuttoning it myself. It was a strange relief and comfort, and the clean air rushed to my skin.

"You mustn't," I told him.

"I have no choice," he said, and moved his hand upon my back, spread it out between my shoulder blades.

With his other hand he reached behind himself and undid his collar and let it fall to the floor, where its landing shook the church and nearly brought it down.

Jeremy Treat was still upon me when I opened my eyes and saw over his shoulder through the window of the church the face of a woman. It was my own face, as clear as in a mirror. I hadn't seen an image of myself since I'd left the Treat home. Even the mirror in Ethan's grave had failed to hold me. Now I was in another kind of glass, clear glass, that reflected nothing but through which I could see so far into infinity that I encountered my own image around the endless curve of space. But the way I looked was not the way I felt. My face was tranquil, my eyes were filled with joy, not surprise, not tears, and I looked at myself with knowledge of who I was and acquiescence in what had been done to me.

I knew I was imagining it. I was creating some separation of my vision from my body as a way of abiding the loss, not of my innocence but of experience.

I closed my eyes and disappeared.

"What did he say to you?" I asked.

Jeremy and I sat by each other on the pew, staring straight ahead. We might have been a couple in a couple's bed, wider than what I'd ever slept on in my room on Dickinson Street or at Mount Holyoke College or in a boardinghouse in Amherst, Massachusetts, or in my room or Ethan's way up on the second floor of the big stone Vear house. We might have been resting against a headboard with pillows behind our necks staring off across the room that held the echoes of our shame and pleasure. He was fussing with the buttons of his collar. I was moving my legs restlessly against the hem of my skirt.

"He asked me to marry you," he answered.

"But you have a wife!"

He laughed. He laughed easily and without pretense, as if instead of chiding him I'd amused him and this had been my signal that I forgave him.

He turned to me. He looked into my face and explored it in a way that made my eyes burn. I felt he was memorizing me.

"Help me with these buttons, would you, Sarianna." He bent his head before me. He placed it gently on my breast. His hair was, from his efforts, curled more than usual and smelled as much of me as of him.

"You *have* a wife."

"With more graceful fingers than yours," he said as he raised his head and hands and did his own buttons.

I pictured Una's fingers, not merely as I'd first seen them, long around the handle of my valise, but also coming up around my face and reaching down my neck, and I could hear her telling me what now I better understood, that she didn't want to know he was dead and she didn't want to know he was alive. Ethan. She loved not so much the mystery as the emptiness; one she couldn't solve, but the other she could fill. With Jeremy. With Jimmy. With me.

"Yes, I do have a wife," he said. "I thought I'd lost her but I haven't."

"And yet you seem to think you have room for me."

"And you for me," he said, and looked at me in such a way as to leave no doubt what he meant.

"You'd think I decked my bed with the fine linens of Egypt," I said.

He clapped his hands. He enjoyed Bible games; they took him from this world to one more fanciful and fixed if hardly less brutal. "It's your eyelids," he said. He moved a finger upon one, then the other. "I've always been taken with your eyelids. You should paint them for me."

"With what?" I asked.

"You tell me. You're the woman." Now he traced my lips, to feel me speak.

"Galena," I said, "and lapis lazuli. My mouth with cochineal. Do you know what that is?"

"I know who wears it," he said.

"It's made from the dried dead body of a female—"

He removed his finger from my lips.

"—insect," I went on and watched him smile in wonder even as he slid away.

"You don't understand, do you?" he said.

"How could I?" I ached. I was numb and in pain at the same time.

"He wants me to marry you," he repeated. "He wants me to

perform the ceremony. Here." He slammed his hand down on the pew. "In my church. He wants to marry *you*."

There was no one outside the church. The church stood isolated by the slant of a mid-September sun, paint-peeled, kneeling in the dry dirt, only its belfry alive with sunlight glancing off the bell and its tiny crown aquiver with the remnants of the bell's toil. Jeremy stayed behind, as I imagined a man would in his lair, to enjoy his conquest in solitude and by that act of separation to annul the very woman he has taken. And Ethan had fled, for much the same reasons, I expected, except for him separation had long become the means to union.

It didn't occur to me that he still might be with Una until I went into the parsonage through the back door and found her alone at the kitchen table. Hers was a solitude so great that it amounted to abandonment. Rather than find myself pleased that Ethan was no longer with her, I wished he were there, to care for her and console her, at least until now, when I walked up behind her and let my hand graze her shoulders as I moved past her into my customary seat.

"I'm sorry," I said.

Only now did Una look up into my face. I had never seen her so beautiful and so content. Her eyes were half-closed, her mouth half-open. She said, "Me too."

I didn't understand. "For what?"

"I saw you," she said.

"Where?"

"In the church."

"I saw you too." I wondered if she'd been so filled with Ethan that she'd forgotten how I'd gone to her at the back of the church and she'd embraced me because she'd thought I'd brought Ethan back to life.

"I thought so!" She laughed and took my hands as she had so many times and leaned forward. "I couldn't believe how lucky I was. That you'd look up and see me at the window. He was so still—I know exactly what that felt like. Like a dead man! Alive one minute, completely dead the next. And you couldn't move except your eyes, your eyes were so angry and I thought I saw tears churning around in them. You don't know how much I wanted to come to you right then. But I couldn't. It wouldn't have been right. So I came here and waited for you. I knew you'd come to me. Who else could you talk to about this?"

"You saw me?" I could say nothing else. "You *saw* me?"

She nodded. "You poor thing," she said, just as I had said to her in the church. "I saw you. And all I could think was I wished it was me."

I pictured us, all three of us, Jeremy upon me, I beneath Jeremy, Una outside the church at its window. I could make no sense of it. "Which *one* of us?"

"Both of you!" she exclaimed, and was generous in allowing me credit for this revelation.

"What about Ethan?" I asked.

"It's a miracle." She let go of my hands, not to punish me but to draw Ethan in the air as she described him, or to attempt to hold him there because she could see him now. "He looks just the way he did when he left me. He hasn't aged at all. Everything is the same—his clothes, his hair, the soft way he talks to me, like everything's a secret between us." She brought her hands together; I couldn't tell if this meant he'd disappeared or she felt she'd joined him.

I had intended by my question to ask only whether Ethan too had been at the church window, watching me. Is that why he'd fled? I couldn't ask her now. She was too much in love with the phantom boy she saw before her.

"What secrets did he tell you?" I said to enter into her sense of him.

She drew back. "I can't say."

"Why not?"

She couldn't contain herself. "Because he has to tell you himself!"

"I think I know," I said. "Jeremy told me."

"That skunk! He would." She rose from her chair and walked about her kitchen, from one end to the other, back and forth, to the sink, to the stove, to the refrigerator, to the knives on the countertop whose edges she tested first with a fingernail and then with the flesh of that finger. I thought of how women haunt their kitchens, taking sustenance from meals long since cooked and eaten, dishes cleaned and dishcloths folded, voices drifting off and promises of love undone by food and drink and satisfaction until the women are alone, each woman is alone in her kitchen, walking back and forth, explaining.

"Jeremy couldn't resist you, Sarianna. I know I told you he was the irresistible one. It turned out to be you. I know I told you to give him what he wanted. It turned out to be you again. He did want your body. I told him myself how beautiful it is. We love you. We all love you. Jeremy and Jimmy and I love you. And when Ethan came back, we loved you even more. You gave us Ethan. And in return I gave you Jeremy. Jeremy sent me to Ethan so he might have you for himself. Poor Jeremy— everyone he loves loves Ethan. Don't you see?—he's sacrificing me to have you. But he's also sacrificing you to give me Ethan back. I'm sorry for what he did if it wasn't what you wanted. But he had no choice. Here." She handed me some tissues, scraped one after another out of a box on the kitchen counter.

"Do I look like I'm crying?" I said, amused as I was by how desperately she strived for what was mine.

She drew close and smiled at me and took my hand with the tissues and put it beneath my skirt.

"But Ethan wants to marry *me!*" I pushed against her hand until the tissues floated to the floor.

"On the first day of autumn." She danced away as if she were to be the bride. She twirled around the kitchen with some flowers she'd grabbed from a vase, spraying drops of water on my face. "He wants you very much."

"He does?" I asked.

"He told me so himself," she said, and handed me the flowers. "He told me to tell you."

I walked home north by way of Monson Turnpike and went west on Soapstone Road at the old Soapstone Railroad Station, where the narrow platform had been leveled but its wooden planks not yet removed. I stood on them for a few minutes and pretended to be waiting for a train. The train came. I got on. As it left the station, I looked out the window and saw myself there on the crumbled platform, waving good-bye.

I wondered how I'd permitted myself so transparent and fatuous a fantasy. It was enough that I'd seen Una at the window of the church and thought it was myself. If Jeremy Treat had taken my innocence, such as it was, he'd replaced it with knowledge, a fair and just exchange. That he'd forced himself upon me, or thought he had, relieved me of any participation in my own undoing, save pleasure.

It wasn't pleasure of the flesh so much as of the spirit. By taking me, he'd saved me. The same might be said for this valley, drowned before the blood of nations stained it forever with much greater sins of man than those of a country preacher upon the body of a girl who'd coaxed him to his ruin.

As for marriage, I couldn't imagine it with anyone but Ethan and even with him it didn't seem the gift that Jeremy and Una deemed it. My feelings about it were in keeping with Ethan's own, or why would he have had Jeremy Treat deliver what was less a proposal than an appointment. Marriage had nothing to do with earthly vows and everything to do with eternal love. I was enough of a realist and little enough of a romantic to know this. Ethan knew it too. He'd gone to the husband of the girl he'd loved enough to die for and asked this man to marry him to someone else. No wonder Jeremy had ravished me. Una had been right—he'd had no choice. Jeremy knew that for all his life since the moment Una had been brought to him by Simeon, he'd served not God but Ethan.

No wonder Jeremy spoke of having killed Ethan. No wonder he'd memorized the marker on his grave. Because Jeremy had taken Una, Ethan had taken Jeremy. And now, in taking me for his wife, he would bind Una and Jeremy more closely even than in marriage. Like him, they would possess nothing as much as what they'd lost.

Emily called marriage a *soft eclipse*. Mine wouldn't be. Mine would combine the beauty of darkness with the simplicity of sunlight. My husband would be my religion and he the eclipse that I'd address, every morning, as the Dickinsons did the one they called Father, all but Emily, who knew we have no fathers, only husbands.

I continued on Soapstone Road past the unmarked spot at the southern edge of the Vear forest where I'd learned by now I might turn into those woods toward home. Instead, I went into the mostly struck down woods on the opposite side of the road and picked my way southwest over fallen trunks and limbs until I came to the Jason Powers Cemetery. There I thought I'd rest and postpone my arrival perhaps enough to bring Ethan out looking for his untested bride or at least to have him wonder if my delay might be caused by my hesitance, as impossible as that might be to contemplate, to marry him. I also wanted simply to stop, to be by myself, to think the way one can only in a grave-yard, pointedly.

As I neared the small hill in which the few graves had once been set so closely—out of touching concern, no doubt, for winter's deadly chill—I smelled burning. I recognized it almost immediately as tobacco, that earthy, bewitching fragrance that if air were to be perfumed would be perfumed with it. The smoke itself I didn't see until I came upon its source, Jimmy lying side-ways in the very grave I'd dug out for myself the day I'd hooted for him and he'd come at me with the limb of a tree. His hair was longer now and even, at the end of summer, more variously colored: gold, bronze, copper, auburn, and some strands nearly white with hunger for the light. His church pants were too short for him, showing his socks and the tiny golden hairs above his ankles. The cigarette he'd rolled was flat and loose and shred-ding. He pressed it hard between his fingers as he raised it to his lips and took a shallow puff and looked at me through the smoke he slowly let his lips release.

"Want one?"

"Sure." I didn't, but it gave him something to do and a way to show me how he'd learned from Ethan. His long fingers were more like his mother's than Ethan's, to be expected given the mystery of his paternity. But his movements were Ethan's ex-actly, as he sat up and flattened the paper against the top of his thigh and tapped out the tobacco in a way that recalled for me how Ethan had released the sawdust from the vial in his desk drawer before he spelled out Una's name with it. Jimmy even licked the cigarette as Ethan did, with only the tip of his tongue protruding from between his teeth.

He handed me the cigarette and removed a small box of matches from a pocket of his dirty church pants. He struck the match. I bent over with the cigarette to my lips. He held the match just far enough away so I had to lean toward him.

"Sit down." He moved aside to make room for me in the grave.

He saw me wince as I kneeled and again as I placed my hands behind me on one side of the hole so I could lower myself slowly.

"What's the matter?"

"I don't know." The pain had surprised me as much as it had him, though the moment I felt it I realized it had been hiding in my loins.

"Where does it hurt?" he asked as his mother must have so many times when he was small and as reckless with his body as he had become in time with his feelings.

"It doesn't," I said.

"Stop lying." He moved slightly from my side, where we had been squeezed against each other, so he could feel me with his hand. It went right to my hip, as if he knew.

The moment he touched me, I began to cry.

He seemed utterly surprised but as much delighted as he was concerned. He didn't want me to suffer, but when I did suffer he wanted me to show him my suffering.

"Is that where it hurts?" He lifted his hand rather than press it harder against me. It was a mature and fetching gesture, assertive in its very restraint.

I nodded. "Inside."

"It always hurts inside," he said, and tried to smile my pain away and at the same time to excuse his philosophizing.

"What are you doing here, anyway?" I asked him.

"Don't change the subject. Besides, what are *you* doing here?"

"I came here to think."

"I think you came here to cry."

"Maybe you're right." He knew how to summon my tears. Now my cigarette was wet; gratefully, I threw it away.

He put his arm around my shoulder. "I came here to get away," he said.

"From what?"

"Myself," he said, when I'd expected him to say it was all the rest of us.

When I didn't respond except to sniff back my tears and try to dry my eyes with the cloth on the shoulder of my dress, he was compelled to explain. "Sometimes it just gets to be too much. Being somebody. Sometimes you just want to stop. I don't mean to die. Just stop. But the more you want to stop, the more you go. The more you feel like you're racing inside. The more you feel lost. The more you just *feel*. I didn't used to feel anything. Now I feel everything."

"Like what?"

"Everything. You know what I mean. You shouldn't ask me that question." He took his arm off me now. He punished me further with his dark eyes. "It isn't right."

"What isn't?"

He shook his head. He wouldn't say it. Instead he said, "Whoever hurt you."

"Who said it was a person? Maybe I just fell down."

"There's always a person in there somewhere." He took hold of my hand. "Let's just sit here, Sarianna. Want another cigarette?"

"Not at all."

"Me neither."

"You shouldn't smoke," I said.

"What are you, my mother?"

We laughed at that together.

"What am I going to do?" he asked with a peculiarly cheerful forlornness.

"We could always sit here until the waters come," I said.

"What a great idea!" He tightened his grip on me.

Instead we sat there until it was nearly dark. I asked Jimmy what he and Simeon had been discussing so avidly in the church and Jimmy said, "Do you remember that night when we first met Mr. Vear in the cemetery and he was putting flowers in my grandma's hole?" I thought of the old man at the riddled graveyard, trying to find some shadow of his lover in a trough of lethal dirt that once held her body as closely as had he. *Riddled* might have been an Emily word, used for a graveyard: full of holes, full of mystery.

Jimmy didn't wait for me to answer before he told me the tale that Simeon had told him. He told it in such a way that it might have been he, Jimmy, who had been in love with Millie Fitts Ryther, the most beautiful woman in the world, the wife of his best friend, Mackswell Ryther. She was only seventeen when they met, getting married to Mackswell, my supposed grandpa, Jimmy said, who got killed my first day here. Mr. Vear didn't know what to do, because he was married himself to a lady named Elisha Vear and Mackswell was his friend and he was more than twenty years older than Millie, he was, Mr. Vear, because Mackswell was ten years younger than him. But he already drank too much or didn't hold what he drank as well as

Mr. Vear, who sometimes drank with him and drank with him even more after he met Millie for the first time at the wedding and he fell in love with her right there and then. It's a terrible thing to go to a wedding and fall in love with the bride. A lot of men probably do that, but by the end of the wedding day they either come to their senses or they fall out of love with the bride. But he only fell more in love with her the more he saw her and the more he knew her. He was even afraid to dance with her at the wedding, not because his own wife Elisha was there and not because Mackswell Ryther was there and was her husband by the time the dancing started. He was afraid to dance with her because he was afraid he would die before he'd get a chance to dance with her again. That's how you know you're in love— when you're as afraid of love as you are of death, because true love and death always go together. They have to. True love lasts forever. But death is the only thing that lasts longer. He'd go hunting with her husband and think about shooting him. He'd go fishing and think about drowning him. But he didn't because he couldn't bear the thought that he would do anything that would make Millie cry even if it meant he could teach her to laugh all over again. Millie came from Holyoke. That's where Mackswell had found her. He brought her back to the valley and married her right off. He didn't introduce her to anyone because he either didn't know how wonderful she was or he knew just how wonderful she was. The four of them used to go out or visit together all the time. Mr. Vear hardly ever spoke to Millie. He was afraid to do that too. He was afraid to talk to her because he was afraid that everything he would tell her would be a lie and the one thing that would be the truth he couldn't tell her. So the way he started to talk to her was he started to read to her. No one else wanted to hear him read. Mackswell and Elisha would block their ears when Mr. Vear would start to recite the poet Walt Whitman after dinner or some of those other people he likes. But Millie loved it. So he'd read to her. Sometimes when the others were there and they were invited to listen too. And then alone. He read to her all of *Moby-Dick*. Every single word. Have you ever seen that book? It's this big, Jimmy said, and held his hands apart; in the space between them I could see time passing and the lovers become entangled in the net of words. Always read to a girl, Mr. Vear said, whether you have something important to tell her or nothing to tell her at all. He got to look at her while he read to her. He would jump ahead with his eyes and memorize the next few words so he could look up and watch her. In the beginning she would be staring off into space or out the window or at the book. But then he began to notice when he looked up to watch her that she was watching him. That's when he began to suspect he was more important to her than the book he was reading. That's when he said he started to talk to her. But he never got up the courage to tell her he loved her. She told him first. He thought he'd go deaf after that. He thought you only get to hear something like that once and then you go deaf. He did go deaf, he said. He went deaf to everything but her voice. She told him she loved him. She told him she loved only him. She didn't say she didn't love her husband. She could never say that. Only that she loved only him. He didn't go into all the details, Jimmy said, not that he had to, but one day she said she was going to have a baby and the baby was his. Mr. Vear's. How do you know? he asked her. That was the first thing he ever said to her that made her angry. That's the one question, he said, that a man should never ask a woman. You can ask a woman anything but that. Of course Grandpa Ryther never asked her that same question, and look what hap-

pened to him. Maybe he should have. The night she had the
baby Mr. Vear didn't have to ask to be there because Mackswell
Ryther asked him first. They took her to the hospital together.
Grandpa Ryther drove and Mr. Vear sat in the back seat with
Millie. He held her hand the whole time. It was the first time he
felt it was allowed. She squeezed his hand every time the pain
came. He told her she was strong. You can say that again, Mackswell said from up front, and Mr. Vear wanted to kill him then
and there. When they got to the hospital they took Millie away
and Mackswell told Mr. Vear he was really grateful to him for
coming along. He took whiskey in a flask out of his pocket and
started to drink it. Mr. Vear didn't want any. By the time a doctor came out and told them that Millie was dead, all Mackswell
could do was cry and drink more. Mr. Vear didn't cry. He never
cried again for the rest of his life. The doctor said the baby girl
was fine. He asked the husband, who was Mr. Ryther, if they
had decided on a name. Mr. Ryther screamed at the doctor.
Something about *they*, meaning *we*. There is no more *we*, he
screamed. That's when Mr. Vear told the doctor there was a
name and he told him what it was. That's how my mother got
her name.

This was the last time I spoke with Jimmy while he was
alive. I wish I had let him come with me, as he asked to, to the
Vear house that night. This wouldn't have meant he would have
lived longer but only that I would have had that much more
time with him. Had he come, he would have learned sooner
about Ethan and me. I didn't tell him in the cemetery. I couldn't.
I didn't know yet myself how I felt about it. I did know, and was
correct, how Jimmy would feel about it.

As it was, we stayed together till nightfall. The day cooled and darkened without becoming threatening. We lounged in the grave the whole time except when Jimmy excused himself to pee and I covered my ears so I wouldn't hear though he went far away to do it and when I couldn't see where he was I was afraid he'd gone and left me.

When he came back I realized how easily I might have lost him and so that was when I asked, "Did Simeon say how Mr. Ryther died?"

"Not exactly. I mean, he said a tree fell on him. But he didn't say *how* the tree fell on him. He said Grandpa Ryther was drunk, so maybe he fell under the tree instead of vice versa."

"That's not what *vice versa* means," I said.

He took less kindly to criticism now. "Are you still my teacher?"

"Not officially." Jeremy hadn't attempted to pay me since I'd left his home and church.

"Good," said Jimmy, as if it would be wrong for him to take such liberties with a teacher as he did with me, grasping my hand, pressing against me when the sun went behind a cloud and eventually, at sunset, putting both arms around me to keep me warm, himself as well.

Slowly, as the day died and he teased and tempted me with the story of his birth, he told me the rest of what Simeon had told him, a simple story without conclusion. Mackswell Ryther and his daughter moved in with Simeon and his son soon after Elisha Vear had died, so soon, in fact, that they had stood by while Ethan dug his mother's grave in the Vear family plot and as Simeon lowered her in, casketless, had held up the headstone that proclaimed of Simeon what was being made obvious at that very moment, that Simeon's business was with the living, in particular with his daughter, Una. Simeon hated Mackswell for his

drinking and then even more, said Jimmy, for going around saying that the child in Una's belly was his grandchild by the Congregationalist minister. Ethan hated Mackswell for not stopping
his daughter from moving out and for being so drunk and stupid
that he didn't even know she wasn't his daughter. Ethan hated
Mackswell almost as much as he hated Simeon for being Una's
father and because of that for sending Una to my father, Jeremy
Treat. Then I got born, said Jimmy, and that same day Grandpa
Ryther got killed. A tree fell on him. Grandpa Vear said that's
what they told the police. They didn't have anything to hide,
he said. They used a two-man crosscut saw. They couldn't have
planned it, because they didn't talk. Ethan had stopped talking
to Grandpa Vear nine months before. Just as long as it took to
get me made, Grandpa Vear said, said Jimmy.

I found Ethan in his room. I looked nowhere else. On my
way to the ladder, I'd seen Simeon's reading lamp glowing in his
little corner of the big stone house. I imagined the old man
there on his bed, rehearsing *The Marble Faun*; he'd been reading it aloud to us at night. As I'd climbed the ladder, I recalled
how Hawthorne characterized the murder conspired by the two
lovers—*closer than a marriage-bond*. This, I realized now, had
been Simeon's way of telling me how he and Ethan were bound.
I amused myself on my climb to think how tangled we would all
become if I married Ethan. Were we to follow Hawthorne's
plot, he and I would have to murder Una, his half sister, though
she might be saved by having me marry him in her place.

Ethan was sitting at his little table. It was a warm night;
he had no shirt on. The light from the candle absorbed the
years from him. He looked as close in time to Jimmy as he did
to Una, swung between them just like me. He looked a boy as

much as I a girl, though I imparted to him more innocence than I could any longer claim for myself.

He had on the table before him the small glass vial. I went behind him and put a hand on his shoulder and bent over to see what he'd done with the sawdust. It was only my touch that made him aware of my presence. He rose and turned and faced me.

He looked into my eyes. "What's the matter?"

How did he know? It was the first time he'd asked after me. Even when his arrow had gashed my side he'd merely put his fingers to my cut. When he'd seen my arms bloodied by the forest's many pricks and edges, he'd told me only what to wear and shown himself immune to pain.

"Jeremy . . ." I began and realized as I said his name that I was Ethan's revenge upon him. Of the two men I was, like Una, both victim and provocation.

"I'm sorry." Ethan put his hand to the side of my face.

"Why should I marry you?" For I loved him not to marry him; I loved him perhaps not to have to marry him, or anyone else.

"You shouldn't," he answered.

"Then I won't."

"Until I ask you myself."

"Ask me," I said.

He put an arm around my shoulder and turned aside so we were both facing the table. There, in the candlelight, I could see what he'd written. Out of the sawdust that had come from Una's name and his own, carved out of the wall between their rooms, he'd made mine: Sarianna.

The next nine days before our Wednesday wedding on the 1938 autumnal equinox were unlike any in my life. Ethan no longer disappeared at night except to take me with him. And then we only walked, my hand in his, because I could no longer see him or sense him in the dark. This was a relief. He became more tangible as he became less spectral, quite the opposite of gods, who are legitimized by otherworldliness. We didn't hunt but merely emptied his traps for food. He showed me how to set the traps and how to drown small game in order to preserve as much of their meat as possible and to keep it tender. He said this was a thoughtful death, as much for the animals as for the hunter—the gradual slowdown of the blood through their bodies left their flesh unshocked and supple. Drowning was a good death, slow, painless, and in its final moments as serene as it was frenzied in its first. As we walked through the woods at night, we saw flying squirrels leap across the moon, heard bats squeaking as they tied the clouds in charcoal lines and consumed what bugs had bothered us, felt the wind from the wings of golden eagles, and watched a wildcat fight a porcupine and end up blinded, crashing into trees in its retreat. Anything Ethan trapped that needed to be hung he hung, but he always cooked the same thing, long-hung, for me and for Simeon, or what was freshly killed that needn't hang. His father read to us, the rest of *The Marble Faun*, the *Pierre* of Melville, written at the request of Sophia Hawthorne to balance the savagery of *Moby-Dick*. Ethan sat after dinner in his bare feet listening to his father, whose reading he preferred to his talking, because it made their reconciliation simpler. (The old man said why marry when marriage fostered grief and we had found such gladness, yet he kept congratulating us and saying he was keeping his fingers crossed, this most unsuperstitious of men.) When the rains came four days before our wedding Ethan built a fire and for four nights running we sat before it and I watched how the flames rose and fell upon the bottoms of his feet and their light was cast between his long thin toes and I tried to catch it on my lower lip where he sometimes put a finger before he kissed me, lightly. He also used the fire to heat water for the giant galvanized tub I'd had to fill in privacy and to bathe in in even greater isolation, for I'd sensed its memories of the young bodies of Ethan and Una, as happy as they'd ever been. Now he kneeled by me and put soap on me with a harsh cloth that softened as he rubbed my back. I was wet and naked before him in the candlelight but he bathed me as he might shine brass and left me rosy and unbreached. At night we slept in my bed or in his, or he slept on the floor beside my bed, so as not to be apart but not to couple either. We seemed to take turns sleeping, I watching him, he me. One of us was awake when the other awakened. At daylight before the rains came we might climb down the stones on the outside of the house and he would pick from the summer's last huckle-berries and feed them to me with his fingertips turning black from the juice left from my lips. One morning in a downpour we came upon what Ethan said was an olive-backed thrush feed-ing off a shrub it crowned, a lone bird that must have drifted northwest with the rain-charged winds from where it bred way off in what Ethan sometimes referred to as the world.

The rain died down the morning of our wedding but picked up as the hour approached and the winds shifted somewhat to the southeast. We didn't care. Simeon had hired an old lum-berman and his horse and buggy; we rode to the church that early afternoon with a roof over our heads and a couple of horse blankets for curtains, while the old man up front talked non-stop to his horse as the rain peppered the slickers worn by both of them.

Simeon said we were by custom not to see each other before we wed, so he sat between us and told us to look only at him. But we saw, as the saying went, right through him, which is to say, we not only caught his humor but retained what Emily Dickinson called, in what turned out to be a most apt poem for the day of our wedding, *the privilege of one another's eyes.*

I wore the dress that Amelia Fitts had worn the day she married Mackswell Ryther. It had been brought to the Vear house with the other effects of Mackswell and Una in 1920, eight years after the day of Una's birth and Millie's death, ten years after Millie married Mackswell when she was my age, seventeen, and Simeon had fallen in love with her as he saw her for the first time and she was in this same dress. He hoped, he'd said, to dance with me in this dress if I would wear it for my wedding to his son; he'd danced with it empty too often in his empty, silent house, his lover dead, his wife dead, his son a ghost. It was less a bridal gown than a princesse dress, not as white as it had once been, seamless at the waist, fitted perfectly to her and me, a simple dress that worn became, as every good dress should, complex.

Ethan wore what he always did, brown cord pants, faded blue shirt, black boots, but at my insistence, not his. He had offered to dress in black, in white, in whatever someone dressed in to get married, he'd said. But I'd told him he must look as I'd first seen him clearly, small against the Winsor dam yet grand within my mind, to which he answered that it must have been within my mind, because he'd never been to the Winsor dam. I laughed at how he confounded himself in attempting to do the same to me and told him he should wear a tie, which now he did, as did Simeon, short wide triangular blades of thick rough silk that barely reached the top button of their trousers.

Simeon wore his usual black hat with his long hair tucked

in under it. Ethan wore no hat at all and his hair was quickly growing long again, almost over his ears, one lobe of which I pictured with an earring like the ones I wore, left behind in the old stone house by Una when she'd fled in her attempt to cause Ethan not only to stop her but to possess her, tiny stones of lapis lazuli, the azure of the sky that hid behind the clouds that as we approached the church grew as black as Ethan's eyes.

Upon the church marquee there appeared the following, unattributed:

FROM HIM THAT HATH NOT,
SHALL BE TAKEN EVEN THAT HE HATH

Jeremy had discovered, and must have assumed I knew, that these were the words that more than any other in the Bible frightened Emily Dickinson. He was mistaken if he thought they would affect me similarly. To me they were perfect for a wedding, which was its own paradox, as much a robbery as a bestowal. Two might become one; one might become none.

Una stood just inside the church door, out of the rain, which the wind blew across her in waves like a curtain on a stage. She had a Brownie camera in her hand and brought it to her eye. "Just the two of you," she said, and motioned Simeon to the side, where he went, completely out from under the huge black umbrella he held over us.

Awaiting us inside were dozens of people. There were families I'd thought or known had gone, gone from their homes, gone from the church, gone from the valley. Some I knew by sight and name and some by sight alone and some I didn't know at all— the Snows were there and some Doubledays and the Uraciuses, the Woods, the Olneys and the Goodspeeds, the Sabins and the

Ouellettes, the Cottons, the Hinds, and all the others sitting so quietly. They filled every pew, every inch of every pew, leaving no room for us even had we planned to sit and watch ourselves be married. Most of them were wet, even those with umbrellas hooked half-open drying on the forward pew. And no wonder—there'd been no cars, no trucks, no carriages or horses outside by which they might have been transported here. All had walked, or flown so far as I knew. I wondered if they'd come to see me married to a ghost or see me married by the man who'd outraged them a dozen years ago by marrying a child who they were sure carried his, the man who on the floor of this church had taken me. Could they tell? Did our shadows lie upon that floor or just the hollows left by his knees in the soft degraded pine?

Jeremy, the moment he saw us from the pulpit, nodded toward Una, who was at the piano. She immediately began to play, simple, sad chords broken into arpeggios. With the first note, Jimmy rose from the front pew and took his usual place before the congregation. He was dressed in a new black suit and a shirt so white it purified the very gloom brought in through the church windows by the darkening storm. He looked like a clean, young version of his grandfather Vear in his suit and his fanatic independence. Jimmy's hair was brushed back severely off his forehead and his temples, and I saw for the first time the nobility of his forehead and the utter beauty of his perfect face. The dark eyes, straight nose, white teeth for a moment clenched between almost snarling full lips, strong jaw, the still-delicate eyebrows that nonetheless had darkened and flourished with promise of compelling manhood. Yet his voice, as it rose through the church, was again the angel's voice I'd heard when I'd first heard him sing. And now he sang the saddest, most beautiful song I'd ever heard:

When my lover comes
to see his mournful love
the sun-drenched shore will be covered
with beautiful flowers.
But I don't see him—
alas, my lover isn't coming.
While he tells the wind
of his passion and his grieving,
gentle birds, he will teach you
a sweeter song.
But I don't hear him. Has anyone heard him?
My love has fallen silent.
You, mournful, wearied echo
of my grief,
return to him and he will softly
ask for his bride.
Hush, he is calling me, hush, alas!
No, he isn't calling me. O God, he isn't there.

It was my voice in which Jimmy was singing, not an angel's, mine, a woman's, lamenting her loss of love and lover. I looked for Ethan beside me, and he too was gone. I grasped Simeon's sleeve. "Where is he?"

Simeon smiled and buried my hand in his and pointed both our hands down the center aisle. There was Ethan walking away from me, into the last echoing notes of the mournful, enravishing song. Jimmy stepped aside to make room for him. Ethan stopped before the pulpit. Una left the piano and joined Jimmy before the two of them sat down; on her way past Ethan her hand touched his at the same moment her other hand took Jimmy's and she smiled, not at either one of them, not at Jeremy, not at me; she smiled into the air before her, as if it were peopled with understanding.

Jeremy waited until his wife and son were seated and then, from behind the pulpit, he raised his hand toward Simeon and me at the back of the church and motioned for us to come forward. Simeon moved my hand to the inside of his arm and started to walk me down the aisle. Had Una stayed at the piano, she would no doubt have played the wedding march. But there was no music now except the wind's, which in the strange, anticipatory quiet of the church both enclosed it and filled it with its throaty drone. The whole church trembled, but the creaking of the old pine timber was almost wholly lost in the generous gusts of the unceasing wind.

Nearly everyone in the church turned their heads to look at Simeon escort the bride down the aisle. Jeremy didn't have to, for he was facing us, and Ethan stayed facing Jeremy, and Jimmy gave me only his profile as he seemed to be trying to see out one of the windows, just like a boy, more interested in the storm outside than the ceremony within.

As soon as Simeon and I reached Ethan, Jeremy, without so much as a glance at us, looking out over our heads at the congregation, began to talk. This was not going to be, he said, a sermon—he wasn't going to preach. This was a wedding. This was an occasion less for admonition and advice than for celebration and reflection, though perhaps in reverse order. "The first governor of our state," he said, "John Winthrop, wrote to his beloved wife, Margaret, when they were apart, 'I kisse my sweet wife and rest thy faithfull husband.' This is the same wise man who knew, as he said, that the life most exercised with trials and temptations is the sweetest. Here in our simple church in our simple town in our simple valley we honor the ambiguity of such thought over the more celebrated and simplistic dogma of St. Jerome, that renowned sage of matrimony, who said it was as disgraceful to love another man's wife at all as one's own too much. John Winthrop knew that it was as easy to love another man's wife as one's own too well. The only marriage I know of is my own, and as all of you know I have been accused of loving my wife at all, let alone too well. Which I do—I love her too well. As for loving another man's wife, I don't as yet but soon will. John Winthrop said that children—he called them the best wits and fairest hopes, and has there ever been a better characterization of children than that—he said that children are perverted, corrupted, and utterly overthrown by a multitude of evil examples and by licentious government. He was referring to the seminaries, but he might as well have been talking about us. St. Jerome's proposal was 'with the ax of virginity to cut down the wood of marriage.' What an apt metaphor for this time and this place, where today we gather in our own quickly depleting woods to marry this virgin and this child. Should any here have reason to oppose this union, speak now."

If Jeremy had expected Una to rise in protest, he gave no indication. He waited barely long enough for anyone to breathe, let alone protest. Only the wind howled in the brief silence left by Jeremy's fine voice, with which it had been in losing battle during what had been more a confession of his own than a benediction for us. But when Jeremy spoke again, the wind had gained in confidence from its short solo and now drowned him out as he said in what might as well have been a whisper so much as it could be heard by any but us, "Ethan Vear, what have you for your bride?"

Ethan held out his hand to Simeon, who reached into his coat and produced not the ring that Jeremy no doubt expected but the burial doll that Ethan and I had found in the grave of Sarah Rowlandson. Ethan took it from his father and handed it to me. I held it to me as if it were a living child, one of John Winthrop's best wits and fairest hopes, and remembered as Ethan took my hand in his, and as he surely meant for me by this gift and this gesture to remember, that it had been by Sarah Rowlandson's grave that he took my hand for the first time. In that moment he had taken possession of me from myself while at the same time he had given me to myself. That, I realized now, as I prepared to give myself to him forever, was love's great paradox. Love stole more than it left but gave more than it stole. Love was both thief and benefactor. Love left nothing behind but the emptiness it filled. Love was nothing without pain and nothing without pleasure.

"Sarianna Chase Renway," Jeremy cried my name into the crying of the wind, "what have you for your husband?"

I took from beneath my dress at its breast a flower, fresh and bloodred. It was a mayflower, belied by its own name since it died by April. Yet I had found this one living in September, alone in the forest, immortal, it would seem, for even now and even picked and even crushed between my breasts, it lived. It was, like Ethan, if Ethan was like it, imperishable.

Jeremy reached out toward the flower as I moved it toward Ethan and Ethan moved to take it from me. For a few moments the three of us touched the flower and, around its stem, one another.

"This is the lily of the field," said Jeremy. "Christ's flower."

"Yes," I acknowledged, and understood why he might have thought I would mean it for him and not for Ethan. "But it's also known as the daughter of the wind."

As it was, for the Greeks had believed this flower opened and closed in rhythm to the wind's caprice; in fact it was darkness that shut it and sunlight to which it exposed its nest of wet dark stamens.

"How apt," said Jeremy as for the first time the wind breached the church, blowing out a window and riding in with streaks of rain within its snarled skirts.

"Pronounce them!" cried Simeon above the uproar of the wind.

Jeremy stepped between Ethan and me. He took each of us by the hand and turned us to face the congregation and raised our hands aloft with his. "Man and wife," he called into the storm.

Only Jimmy rose. The rest sat where they were, fixed by wind and fear. Only Jimmy rose as if only Jimmy might share the pleasure of the embrace to which Ethan and I gave ourselves in our escape from the preacher's grasp and from our separate pasts. Only Jimmy rose to seal our kiss not with his witness but with his flight, up the aisle of the church and out the doors that before they could close behind him burst from their hinges and flew off toward the subversive hills.

It was the Great New England Hurricane of 1938, *maelstrom in the sky*. It was the worst hurricane ever to fall here, worse than those of 1815, 1788, 1635, and what was thought by those who can read the history of a forest in the writing left by the flooring of its trees to be the year 1400, when only such natives lived here whose blood would flow through the ages into the veins of my dear young husband.

It was the war come here early, God's war, which was not with man and not even with nature but with time. While the storm destroyed twenty-five million feet of timber above the Quabbin watershed flow line, it also took twenty million more that would have been cut anyway for the waters to collect. Not since the Western New England Hurricane of August 19, 1788, had the forests come under such attack.

Our storm approached from the south, where it devastated Rhode Island and proceeded up the Connecticut River Valley, ripping out all those younger white pines without sufficient root systems and leaving them downed in some places with only the outer edge of the grove standing, those trees that had been forced over time to learn the lesser winds and now were left alone like parents of the dead.

So too were most of the houses taken that had not already fallen victim to the plans—and the plans' prime mover, the bulldozer—of man. The parsonage was gone, all of it, reduced to rubble, the kitchen, the piano in the parlor, my room and shredded graveyard quilt and Ethan's candle blown to hell. The church, however, was left with its walls, though not its roof or belfry. Jeremy and Una slept there that night, slept beneath a pew apiece, once the winds died down at ten-thirty.

Before that, in the late afternoon and early evening, the wind had blown at more than a hundred miles an hour for almost three hours. Some six hundred people died in New England, though only one in our valley so far as we knew. Those strangers who'd attended our wedding had only happened upon our nuptials; they were in the church as shelter from the storm or because they knew somehow that the church would not survive beyond this day and felt the need to witness such an act of nature upon a holy place as would soon be done around the world by man. They remained until the roof blew off and then themselves disappeared into the storm by whatever means they had arrived.

As for us, we paid the storm no heed. And what it paid to us we took as wedding gift, not the revolt of Nature against us but its wild celebration for us.

The old lumberman, Mr. Giguere, refused out of fear to cart us back and gave up his horse and rig only when Simeon grabbed the reins from him and climbed up to the driver's seat. "Just married!" he screamed into the wind, which blew the cigarette from his mouth. "Get the hell in!" he ordered us and we barely were before he whipped the horse and off we rode just as the first boards of the church's roof flew off and some of them paddled the parsonage as we rode by it toward home.

Any doubts we might have had that the storm wanted us to bear witness to it as much as it to our wedding were removed when it ripped the roof and side curtains from the buggy and sent them spinning off like skirts at a barn dance. Now, as the rain came at us sideways and melted us together in our seat and wrapped us up in ropes of warm dark water, we could see such great and cleansing destruction as could only have been both purposeful and senseless. What houses had remained in place were blown apart, the stronger of them gradually and the weaker in a single breath, an explosion of walls and beams and furniture, and shingles that were pages of a book strewn wide to tell a story by its fragments. Younger trees were uprooted entirely and some of them stood on their heads so their root balls themselves became their heads, hair wild in the wind, balls of mud for eyes that followed us as we rode untouched among them even as some were flung across our path or over us, parallel to the ground, arrows with their limbs and leaves as feathers. Older trees held their ground but were snapped off in pieces in the air, crackling like fire as they disintegrated. This was no *undeserved Blast* that *felled the Cedar straight*; it was a warning missed by all who ducked their heads to dodge the storm but not by us, who rode right through it and heard in the salvos of the wind and saw in the smearing of the rain the guns and blood that waited just behind the clouds. These were not purifying waters and winds; they were the tears and lamentations of God.

But our tears and our cries were of rain and joy, as we maneuvered to the edge of the razed Vear forest and saw the stone house standing, bouncing in the waves of rain, lit up in the darkness through its scouring. The winds as they hit it became visible, returned into themselves or forced to veer around the house and carrying with them water and leaves and moss and dirt and stone and human parts.

The winds had shifted to the northeast. They had carved up the Vear family cemetery and done to much of it what the commission had accomplished in every other. Holes were left and most had been spooned clean of their inhabitants. Silvery bones and jewels of rain-washed flesh and banderols of graveyard finery were strewn beneath the sudden clearing, open to the sky and finally, when it would come, as it must, to the light. Headstones had been flung off and broken and their messages and names and dates interchanged. Some Vears now lived three hundred years. Sin had been severed from its unpardonableness. Ethan Vear was now, on his wedding day, "by His own." As for his hand, it was in mine. And everywhere were fragments of a mirror, too small to reflect anything but each drop of rain that pelted them. Perhaps the entire earth was the same, a mirror, saying to God, "Look! This is what *You* are."

Embedded in the great scarred wooden door of the house were many tiny stones and several thin branches that must have reminded the door of Indian attacks and a single small sharp bone that Simeon said was someone's finger, blown out of its grave and pointing its own way, and ours, home.

The wind and rain followed us in. We all three had to push the huge door closed. The moment we succeeded, the great roar of the day, to which we had become oblivious, ceased. We were bombarded by a silence so intimate we didn't speak and couldn't even move within it. We simply stood there and stared at one another, happily, gratefully, a strange little family that was at once both reconciled and conceived.

It was Simeon who spoke first. He said, "My hat!" and touched his head to find his hair uncovered. So white it was almost golden, it lay long upon his black coat like a girl's upon her back when she emerged from her bath at Mount Holyoke. And thus did he merge into my past in this peculiar way, my new father, who by his very contradictions was made sound. "Where's my hat!" He laughed. It was storm-borne still. It was flying off to ride upon the highest of the thunderheads.

The rest of our clothes, however, clung to us. Their wetness chilled us. My dress became me. We each went to our own part of the huge house to strip and dry and dress again, in house-clothes. We couldn't bear to be apart and met together by the fireplace. Ethan shoveled ashes out while Simeon laid the bark and kindling. Ethan struck a match and lit the bark and as it flared leaned logs against the fingers of the fire, which held them up until they were ignited and then encircled them and pulled them down into the heart of the flames, deep and wet with heat.

We moved the table closer to the fire and there we ate the food Ethan cooked and drank the wine Simeon opened; in fact, he and I drank most of what proved to be only the first bottle while sitting together before the fire waiting for Ethan to finish roasting the little quails he'd been keeping and the squabs Simeon told me not to call pigeons and the one plump partridge he cut up for the three of us, not equally, for he took meat off the bones for me and thus gave his bride more than his father or himself and made sure I knew it. Each bird was seasoned differently— with garlic and lemongrass and rosemary and black pepper and salt and juniper and sweet basil and other little twigs and leaves he wouldn't name that tasted of licorice and green apple and autumn itself. He roasted small potatoes with the birds; different potatoes absorbed different flavors and were themselves like game, their skins crusted, their flesh rich and almost oily. It was an unexpected feast, not that I was surprised by Ethan's accomplished cooking but that there was so much food and it was almost unnervingly complex in its nuances and that we ate so slowly and drank so much wine and smoked as if the meal were over only to have it begin again and yet each cigarette Ethan rolled tasted better than the one before, which was not the normal way with cigarettes, as I had learned. We talked among us of the food, of course, and of the storm, which we could feel diminishing even as we could hear it now, rain against the windows, the scratch of passing leaves and twigs and branches and sand and stones against the windows, the coming and going of the wind when before there had been the unrelenting wind that had swallowed its own sound. We talked among ourselves of many things so simple and observable that they became part of the meal itself, served, devoured, enjoyed, forgotten, lost. It was a happy table, a family table, at which the three of us—as our voices wove in upon themselves, interrupting, disagreeing, praising, yielding—wed.

They wouldn't let me clear the table but did so themselves. Whether they were affected by the wine or by their growing sense of fellowship or merely by a playful desire to amuse and enchant me (which they did), they kept glancing off each other and laughing and nearly dropping the plates and silver. When they finally had them all stacked by the sink, I said to leave them and I would wash them later. This caused them both to turn around together and stare at me and look at each other and stare at me again and then to say, as one, "Okay," and to laugh in such a way I couldn't tell if they were joking or jubilant.

Simeon came back to talk with me and smoke with me while Ethan stayed in the kitchen, busy, but not with washing dishes, for I didn't hear the alternate keening and sighing of the water pump. After a time, he walked toward us with a tray in his outstretched hands and three small round bowls upon it. He placed one before each of us. In it was homemade vanilla ice cream covered with small dark berries, some of which had burst their skin and bled their black blood into the cream that was melting fast because the ice box clearly could not keep ice cream hard.

"Go ahead," said Ethan eagerly.

Simeon was faster with a spoon than I but still I found I longed for something sweet and rushed a spoonful to my mouth and was overwhelmed by just how sweet the berries were and almost hot from having been heated on the stove.

"Cherries?" I asked, and remembered then how Una had described the black cherries he grew for her and warmed before he put them on vanilla ice cream and fed them to her. It was a lover's ritual, then, and I was offended only by my lack of even one to share with him. I envied his life before me. I suffered no jealousy of Una; I merely wanted to have been her. I wanted him to have fed the cherries to me.

"No," he answered. "But I told you that's what they'd taste like come now."

"Hagberries!" I remembered and was happy enough to weep. To whom else would this be the finest of all wedding presents, a sour fruit turned sweet upon the same schedule as love was born and thus expressed. The greatest gifts were those that came wrapped in small forgotten moments.

"Let me," he said. I thought he meant to wipe my eyes until I saw him put his spoon into my bowl and raise it to my lips.

Then we danced. Simeon asked me first. He held out his large rough hands to me with their tobacco-goldened fingertips. He said, "Maybe if I dance at this wedding, I'll not keep dancing at the other."

"I won't be used to kill a memory," I said.

"Too late for that," he answered.

"But there's no music," I protested.

"Aha!" he said and from the high, deep, heat-darkened mantel of the fireplace produced a music box. He gave it to Ethan and held open his arms to me.

Ethan turned the handle slowly, and from that little box were pinched tiny bell-like tones that played a sad and simple familiar folk melody. Simeon put one hand upon the small of my back and in the other took my own hand. He moved gracefully and carried me with him, slowly, turning to the right, humming the melody very softly and on a beat slightly ahead of its emergence from the music box. Though he held me at a half-arms' length, I could feel our melting together, not our bodies but their presence, not here but where he'd first seen Amelia Fitts Ryther at her wedding and been afraid to dance with her. There had been, I realized, no memory to kill. He'd never danced with her until now.

The house was filled with ghosts, all those ancient Vears who gathered here to watch an old man weep and laugh at once, carry a girl in his arms around the room they too had lived and died in, mourn her passing even as he found her. And here were all the women gone, Millie Ryther and Elisha Vear and his daughter, Una Treat, whom Ethan saw dancing in his father's arms.

I don't remember how I passed from one to the other, father to son, old man to young. Ethan danced with me in what was not a dance but a holding on to each other as his father turned the handle of the music box and sang in his crusty old voice the traditional song it played—"Don't leave me love until the leaves have left the tree / And summer dies as I shall surely die when you leave me." He also caressed the box with the hand that wasn't playing it and claimed it had once belonged to Henry Thoreau, who had left it behind at the Old Manse in Concord. There Hawthorne would sit with Emerson and Margaret Fuller and Franklin Pierce and Annie Fields and James Russell Lowell and even Thoreau himself, who had forgotten the music box had been his, and listen to this very music when they weren't telling ghost stories.

Ethan danced with me even when the music stopped and Simeon stopped talking and took a glass of wine to bed. We could see the glow of his lamp from that far end of the house, where he lay in bed with the pictures of Millie and Elisha held up on his stomach like a book, reading aloud to them from themselves.

Before we went up the ladder to the top of the house, Ethan and I stepped outside. The storm had passed. The sky was clear; in it the moon shivered from the risen winds. More stars than ever filled the void with their waylaid promises. Beyond the old clearing around the house was the new, greater clearing all the way to the horizon. The Vear forest had been leveled by the hurricane. Now the land lay curved and open like a sleeping woman from whom the covers have been lifted. We suffered the illusion we could see all the way to the dams, when what we really saw was our own reflection off the dark wall of night.

Back inside, we did the dishes together. I washed, because I loved how the ashes changed from feathery as I took them dry out of the bucket into a wet spongy pith. Ethan removed each clean wet pan or dish from my hands and folded it first into the dishcloth before he clenched it dry against his chest or stomach. Each of us was Una for the other, but I inhabited her more than he, because he'd not stood with her at the parsonage sink, and now I stood where she had by his side, at this very spot, cold rinse water running down her arms beneath her sleeves and finally down her sides.

I was still wet when we climbed the ladder and pulled it up behind us. This pleased me, because it allowed me to ask of him something familiar, that he knew how to do and had done before, if not to me.

"Dry me," I said as I followed him into his room, whether he wanted me to or not. I lit the candle on the table, raised my dress to my waist, sat down on the edge of his narrow bed, and then took the dress off over my head without unbuttoning it.

He didn't know with what. I pulled his thin summer blanket up to my side and brought his hand to me and put the blanket in it. He pressed it against me. Soon I was dry, and soon warm.

When Emily wrote to a friend and said there was no account of Eve's death in the Bible and thus that Eve might be alive still, she concluded that Eve was herself: *I am Eve, alias Mrs. Adam. . . . I the same.* The world is new and a woman feels the first and only woman when love strikes deep and floods her. *Was bridal e'er like this?* But she wrote of what she called *fleshless lovers,* because she wrote of herself, and we were that no longer.

Yet the flesh, once satisfied, resigns. What is left is light or sight or spirit, call it what you will. What is left is a leaving of the body. He was in my arms, and I in his, but we might as well have been apart. There was nothing between us, and everything. I didn't know who I was, or he. We were indeed like ghosts, waiting for what we'd never known before was the privilege of desire.

In its place came sleep, or what I thought was sleep. I couldn't tell its darkness from my own, or darkness's illusions from my dreams'. Inside the room the candle had gone out and left us visible only in what light came through the window from the stars and moon. It was in that little window, lit from behind by the stars and moon, that I saw Jimmy Treat, staring at us, how long he'd been there I didn't know, his face seemed to float in the last calm waves of wind before the storm would die and withdraw from the air its energy and life. "Jimmy!" I called. Ethan awakened. "Look," I said. Jimmy was gone. "You're seeing things," said Ethan.

Because I was seeing things didn't mean they were unreal. Ethan rose quickly from the bed. His nakedness startled me. Beauty without touch is painful, humiliating.

I wouldn't let him leave without me. I knew he would again some night, but not this one. I jumped out of bed. We watched each other dress. In so covering our bodies, we exchanged them and finally were, back where we started, married.

We had sheltered Mr. Giguere's horse in a brick potting shed, emptied by Simeon when Elisha Vear had died. Ethan hitched the horse to the buggy and had me sit beside him on the high, narrow driver's seat.

The hurricane had littered all the paths and trails and roads. Trees were down and so were deer and birds and chimney stones and articles of clothing, some of which resembled pieces of a person. Ethan was forced to steer around whole plains of storm-tossed rummage and thus to deviate from the path that Jimmy would have taken in the past to the big stone house. I called to him nonetheless—"Jimmy . . . Jimmy"—into the exhausted night. Each time when I was done, Ethan would say, "He's not here." But he always waited until I had run out of Jimmy's name, the way we let a person finish praying though we know from the first words its futility.

It was dawn by the time we reached Quabbin Lake. The winds had thrown trees into the water and, with the rains, had rearranged the shoreline. But Jimmy wasn't hard to find. He was floating on his back, not far from shore, his shirt still gleaming white in the gash of morning sun, his black suit buttoned up so he resembled now his father, the preacher, more than his grandfather. I remembered a vocabulary-building phrase we'd been taught in high school Latin—*mulier submersa inveniatur supina, vir autem pronus*—that the other girls had found a cause for indelicate laughter because they assumed that what went unspoken were the reasons for the drowned woman to be supine and the drowned man prone: the weight of her backside, the weight of his genitals. But Jimmy floated as he did because, like the wolf on the bookcase, he made death beautiful and God could not bear not to take one more look upon His work.

We rode the body the short ride back to the church. Its roof was gone. Jeremy lay beneath one pew, Una beneath another. They might have been dead themselves.

I awakened Una. She looked at me and smiled grievously. There was enough of him upon me so she didn't go to see her young boy dead in the buggy in his wedding best.

Jeremy did. He stared down at Jimmy. He shook his head in renouncement yet went back into the wreckage of the church and found the disembodied bell. He sat down in the dirt and put the bell between his legs and smashed against it with a shard of broken pew, three times for the death of a child, three times, over and over, pausing only to allow the utter silence of the valley to interrupt the muted pealing of his grief.

I knelt beside Una. Ethan came and stood beside me. He looked down at us both. Out of each of his dark eyes came a single tear.

He left us as we were, together. With Jimmy laid out behind him in the buggy, Ethan moved off into the ruined landscape. Mr. Giguere's horse picked his way hoof by hoof through the downed trees and the fallen stars of window glass that apprehended the morning sun.

That day passed without our moving from the church except when I went for water and a bit of food from the remains of their kitchen. The three of us were there alone, a family again, I in Jimmy's role as child and savior. The early-autumn sun was swallowed by the roofless church and in its turn illuminated it in such a way that all its prayers melted into one and all its hymns broke forth in Jimmy's angel's voice. There were no birds to sing. Those that had escaped the winds had not returned and never would until the waters closed over such land as they had nested in and watched us humans stuck here on the ground. The singing all was his, his voice unheard except by those who by his death had been reduced to spirit.

It was near dark when Ethan returned. He had beside him on the bench, positioned so his head was on his lap and his gaze was on the sun and moon that shared the twilight sky, Jimmy.

He carried him toward us as he might a newborn child, so lightly was he burdened, so eager was his step. He went to Una and handed her her son. She giggled at how light he was, and real. She was as strangely gay as she'd been all day, which I'd taken to be an indication not of happiness but of severance from everything but memory. Then she put out her hand to Ethan, who took it, and with Jimmy held between them now they walked off in the direction of the old stone house.

EPILOGUE

The flooding of the Swift River Valley commenced August 14 of the following summer, 1939, and continued until June 22, 1946, when for the first time water flowed over the spillway east of the Winsor Dam. This slow accretion coincided closely with the measure of the Second World War. On September 1, 1939, Germany invaded Poland. Two days later the United States ambassador to Great Britain, Joseph Kennedy, told President Roosevelt, "It's the end of the world, the end of everything." The valley went slowly blind to the drowning of the rest of the world in its own blood. All the world's tears gathered here until they reached the very tops of the mountains.

Months before the war began, the people still living in the valley were to have been removed. All roads into the valley had been barricaded, and those barricades were manned by guards.

But I had left before the order came to leave.

It is not for me to say whether I made a mark upon such a place before it disappeared from human sight and understanding. I did not look back upon what could no longer be seen.

I had left to bury Ethan, never to return.

Jeremy and I found ourselves alone in the shell of the church. I'd never seen a man so troubled. It had been one thing for him to have lost his faith in man and thereby in God; worse to have had his only son taken by the storm. I went to him as Una hadn't and let him hold me. How different was his embrace in grief than it had been in lust and fury. He gave more of himself and took more of me. I yielded to his sorrow. I felt a strange, incorporeal arousal in the contradictory passion of his diffidence. His grief absorbed him wholly, his being melted into mine.

We took a walk we'd never taken in my early valley days when we walked most everywhere. We walked together toward the big stone house. On the way, we passed Mount Zion. He spoke to me then for the first time that day.

"Would you still like to climb it?"

Once again I had cause to ask him, "Have you memorized me?"

"How could I?" he said. "I don't even know who you are."

I had felt the same from Ethan. When a man enters a woman and in so doing takes her body, he doesn't so much open her as close her, or close himself to her. Open her body, and her soul flies out.

"If I climb it," I said, "I'll do it alone."

We continued on. The Vear house, I found, was now visible from what seemed miles away. With the trees down, its stones rose in a glittering gray heap at the horizon, gripping the earth like a huge beast that even the hand of God can't lift onto the Ark.

I prepared him. "Una's here."

"And you're here." He grasped my wrist and took me hostage.

He pushed against the great wooden door in which were still embedded the projectiles from the storm.

The moment we stepped inside I missed my husband. He was, I realized, embodied in the very material of the place he lived, in the stones of the hearth and walls and the boards of the floor and even the feathery ashes in the bucket by the sink.

To the extent he was real, and alive, he was alive in these and these were his reality. So too I must be to him, in my summer dresses and the burial doll that was my wedding band and the hide of the doe he'd tanned for me and the shavings of the wood from the wall between our rooms from which he made my name. We're too hard to grasp in ourselves. We become, for others, the things they give us and the things we touch, even with the breezes our bodies make as we pass by. This is what was lost in the flooding of our valley—every life that was ever lived beneath the waters. Gone.

So was he. I could feel it in the house. He was there and not there, as had always been the case, but everything shrank from me. The wolf no longer jumped out at me. The handle of the water pump shrieked and the water would not come, not because the well was dry but because it had been flooded by the storm when the wellhouse blew apart. His father lay upon his bed with Jimmy next to him. The old man had his arm around his grandson and a closed book in his lap and an unlit cigarette between his lips. Jimmy, I now saw, had a spike in the bottom of each foot. He was dressed, again, but for his shoes, in his wedding suit, but Simeon had draped his thin red blanket over the boy's shoulders because the house was chill with autumn and with death. Jeremy now let go of my wrist and said, "It's more than I can bear." That's when Simeon, with his black Vear eyes, invited him to sit on the bed with them, perhaps to share the boy they loved and perhaps to look at the photograph of Una's mother, so like her daughter as to be her.

I climbed the ladder for the last time and went to Ethan's room and was surprised to find him alone. He lay on his back on his bed in much the same attitude as Jimmy lay downstairs, but Ethan was more alive, if such might be said of the dead, if not more beautiful. My first time here I'd wanted to discover the difference between life and death. For Ethan there was none; he had brought Jimmy back to life, to the extent he had made him perpetual in his beauty. For me, the difference lay before me.

Una was in the next room. Her room. My room. She too lay on her back on her little bed. But I could see the breathing in her breast. I could discern the progress of her smile. I could see my reflection in each of her open eyes.

Like the doe we'd killed together, Ethan had died with his eyes open. That they had been closed was the only evidence against Una and spoke only of her presence, though on his pale, still lips I could see the outline of her own, her mouth over his, drawing the life right out of him.

His death was declared accidental. And I declared myself his wife, though of course I was not officially. We'd had no blood tests. We'd obtained no license. Simeon would never have pointed us in the direction of such officers of the state who would hold such powers as he would never grant them. I was indeed the alias Mrs. Adam, though I was still his wife and as such demanded he be buried outside the reservoir flow line, in the Quabbin Park Cemetery.

Simeon and I were there alone, Jeremy having insisted he'd seen Ethan buried before to no good effect and Una merrily insisting Ethan wasn't dead. Even the gravediggers had withdrawn for now, though their efforts had been so recent that the small lines of dirt they'd dug were dripping back into the hole. They were at work nearby on another grave, awaiting my signal for the lowering of the casket.

I had chosen the box for Ethan and had watched him be placed in it. Before it was closed, I put into his hand the triangular notch of red oak he'd cut out for me in the forest from the tree with which he'd nearly killed me. Then I took the hammer from the hand of the undertaker from Belchertown and nailed the casket shut and with it all the love I'd ever have for any man but those who carried my own blood.

When the box was lowered to the bottom of the hole, I threw in ceremonially the first heap of dirt and then, partaking of my own sacrament, all the rest, while Simeon smoked and moved his arms along with mine as his phantom shovel helped his only son to disappear from everywhere but where Simeon would thereafter be.

He and I lifted the tombstone together. He had carved it. I had composed it. While the gravediggers set the stone, I said good-bye to Simeon. I never set foot in the valley again. And Simeon, according to legend, never set foot out of it again. With the Vears' trees blown down and the cemetery outrooted by the winds, the commission felt vindicated by nature herself and decided it would be too much trouble for human beings to take down the big stone house. Thus, on August 14, 1939, when the diversion tunnel was sealed and flooding began behind Winsor Dam, the waters moved slowly to surround the house. And so they continued to do until the house was covered up completely one winter day, when smoke could be seen coming from the huge pilastered chimney and then briefly from between the thin scales of ice that floated in the cold water drifting toward the staggering dams. Old man Vear was froze within, they said, reading aloud to his grandson who lay next to him, as still as those waters that *are so for that most fatal cause in Nature, that they are full.*

I was by then on the other side of the country, as far as I could get from where my love was buried and where, I thought, my past was with it. I wrote to my father one last time:

Dear Dad—

Today's my eighteenth birthday. I've moved as you can see—from the postmark—and have no plans to return in my lifetime. Have much to tell you, need little space— hence the postcard.

I was married—my husband died—my son was born this morning—name Edward—don't know who his father is.

The boy who would have sung for our birthdays lost his voice.

Tell Mom Everything.

Your faraway daughter,

Sariannah

P. S. Back at college. My treat.

The world war felt to me, as the Civil War had to Emily Dickinson, an "oblique place." My war had been laid away in the Swift River Valley. Nonetheless, I worked as a seamstress in the war industry in San Francisco in order to live and educate myself on the income. I found the academic atmosphere suitable for a profligacy of mind and a chastity of body and became a scholar, private tutor (I could not abide agitating more than one mind at a time), and, under the name Sariannah Renway Vear, the author of two controversial books about Emily Dickinson: *Alias Mrs. Adam: The Reflowering of a New England Mystery* and *Beautiful Tempters: Emily Dickinson and Susan Gilbert Dickinson.*

The title for the second came from a letter not to Sue but that same letter to Jane Humphrey in which Emily wrote of the "lamps eternal" by the light of which she might see so deeply into Jane that she would encounter herself, as if in that realm of you in which two lives are one. I would have preferred to call the book *Darker Spirit*, from a most revealing letter to Sue herself, but the publisher, as publishers will, felt my favored title too negative and my less favored the more enticing. (They were wrong.)

My son, whom I raised alone, came over time to accuse me good-naturedly of having devoted my life to a dead poet. It was true, I admitted, that I hid behind Emily Dickinson. But at the same time I hid Emily Dickinson within me. The more she's explained, the more mysterious she becomes. To write about her is always an autobiographical act. Everyone who reads her, looks for herself; everyone who reads her deeply, finds herself.

Wedlock being "shyer than death," I loved no one but my son until he met the girl he married. She became the first person I'd loved since I'd loved Ethan and Una and Jimmy. But I remained as chaste with her as I had with the rest of humanity since my wedding night; I had tended my flowers since then only for my own bright absentee, my Ethan. Hanna died with Edward when their car left the road on their way back to me and their infant son from a dinner on Mount Tamalpais. From that day on I have taken care of James. Not long after the death of his parents, still bereaved, we moved to a "new peninsula" up the coast. Cleone, that rare treasure on the sea-girt peninsula that quite matched Hawthorne's Salem. It was there I received one day in the mail a note written in a hand I recognized immediately. It was postmarked New Salem, Massachussetts, January 2, 2000. All it said was this:

Dear Sarianna,
    Smile!
    Love, Una

I turned it over and there was the picture she'd taken at our wedding. Ethan was wet and young and handsome and happy.

The rain was a thin jeweled veil. Where I'd stood next to Ethan there was no one. I could sense my presence in the empty space, even in the way Ethan's left arm was held to accommodate my hand. But I was an unseen presence and vastly more interesting than I would have been had my face appeared with my hand held up before it or even as it was on that last day of my youth.

My receipt of that photograph and Una's note was one reason I decided to bring Ethan's body to Cleone. If Una were alive, and as nearby as New Salem, I wanted to take Ethan away—not so much from her as from what pain I imagined she suffered at visiting his grave, which I had no doubt she would. My other reason was my own approaching death, from a disease that used to be unmentionable, brought on, said my doctor, by my habit of smoking cigarettes, unfiltered, no less, hand-rolled. I bought a double plot on a west-, Pacific-facing hill. I had even ordered the headstone and before leaving for Bradley Field had the inscription chiseled:

ETHAN VEAR

HER HUSBAND

SARIANNA VEAR

HIS WIFE

"THE GRAVE OUR LITTLE COTTAGE IS"

Thus did I travel east with my grandson, James, to retrieve my husband. And there, on the first spring day of this new century, in the Quabbin Park Cemetery, right where I'd left him, did I find him.

I had not, of course, expected to find Jeremy Treat. Nor his own sons, young enough to be his great-great-grandsons. It was Jeremy, it seemed, who, of all of us that long ago, war-shadowed summer in the Swift River Valley, was the most likely to be called immortal. I found him impressive still, by virtue less of survival than of stature. He had not been destroyed by the war whose approach he'd felt so keenly and whose savagery he'd assumed. His trust in God had been betrayed and his faith in man forsaken. But he'd found strength, clearly, in cynicism and arrogance and such lust as would have him marry in his old age a girl of seventeen and produce such boys as these. How, I wondered, could he allow them to take the place of the boy he'd lost? Jimmy had been perfect. Jimmy had been, as Jeremy had tried to tell me when first we spoke, a *deus puerilis*. These boys were merely strong and comely and obedient. When he said, "Open it!" they did. Jimmy wouldn't have. He wouldn't want to have seen Ethan like this.

Ethan was Jimmy's age. He was completely without evidence of decomposition. But his beauty wasn't of the kind he fashioned out of creatures he mourned and mounted. He was alive in death, supple, warm. He didn't move, yet neither was he still. He gave off quiet light, like a star's that when we see it may no longer be.

Next to him lay Una, just as young. She wore the same pink dress that Ethan had taken from her closet. Unlike Ethan's, her eyes were open. She'd had to find her way to him, after all. She stared up out of the grave. Though her eyes didn't move, neither did they leave the stricken face of Jeremy, even when he buried it between the shoulders of his two strong sons.

Ethan and Una's hands were clasped where their bodies were pressed together in the narrow confines of their home. In their other hands, across their bodies, they held between them the notch of oak I'd left for Ethan alone. I took it from them, surprised to feel their fingers weren't fixed upon it. My own fingers felt the words it held before I saw them. Carved into the wood were the same words I'd had Ethan's father put on the head-stone: LOVE IS LIKE LIFE—MERELY LONGER.

It was then I noticed the wood dust from the carving, sprinkled across his faded blue shirt and the top of her dress where it touched her thin, pale chest. It formed letters, a name, I was sure, but before I could read it the wind came up from the south where spring was born and carried that dust, that name, that life, off toward the dark deep waters.

ACKNOWLEDGMENTS

For various facts and impressions concerning the Swift River Valley, I am indebted to the works of J. R. Greene, including his edition of Walter E. Clark's *Quabbin Reservoir*, to Thomas Conuel's *Quabbin: The Accidental Wilderness*, and to publications and maps of the Metropolitan Parks System and Friends of Quabbin.

For insights into the life and work of Emily Dickinson, I have been aided by the writings of Richard B. Sewall, Cynthia Griffin Wolff, Polly Longworth, Helen McNeil, Adrienne Rich, Genevieve Taggard, George Frisbie Whicher, and Joel Myerson.

It was in Perry Miller and Thomas H. Johnson's *The Puritans* (volume 2) that I happened upon a line of Edward Taylor that became a favorite of Jeremy Treat, though for reasons of chronology it goes unquoted in this novel: "Who in this Bowling Alley bowld the Sun?" Miller and Johnson also introduced me to John Williams's *The Redeemed Captive Returning to Zion*, wherein its author was in 1704 "made to take my last fare-well of my dear Wife, *the desire of my Eyes,* and companion in many Mercies and Afflictions"; emphasis his.

Eric B. Schultz and Michael J. Tougias's *King Philip's War* provided useful information about the Indian wars as well as Mary Rowlandson's quotation about giving up smoking. In this province, Chandler Whipple's *The Indian and the White Man in New England* was also helpful.

*   *   *

As for friends, confidants, correspondents, cicerones, and ge-
niuses, my profound thanks to Henry Dunow, Jennifer Carlson,
Leslie Gardner, Dan Smetanka, Abby Durden, Joan Menden-
hall, Kathleen Fridella, Leslie Meredith, Stephen Rubin, Elisa
Petrini, Lisa Queen, Gail Hochman, Larry Ashmead, Nicholas
Delbanco, Elena Delbanco, George Garrett, Elizabeth Crook,
Robert Pirsig, Wendy Pirsig, Nell Pirsig, Peter Manso, Anna
Avellar, Nicholas Bakalar, Daniel Goldstine, Hilary Goldstine,
Dan Chartrand, Stephen Shapiro, Michael Palmer, Michael
Posnick, Andrea Leers, William Tillar, Diana Tillar, Debra
Tillar, Rob Ciandella, Nicole Ciandella, Daniele Ciandella, Jef-
frey Tillar, Mary Tillar, Max Tillar, Colin Tillar, Rebecca Straus,
my children, Sara, Jacob, and Benjamin, Luke Farrer, my aunt
Ellen, who sent the tape, and my aunt Mary, who went to sum-
mer camp on Quabbin Lake not long before Sarianna Chase
Renway first set foot in the Swift River Valley.